Destruction of Obsession

Catherine Miller

DEDICATION

For Beth, who simply wanted something to read. And for my Mum, without whom none of this would have been possible.

CONTENTS

ACKNOWLEDGMENTS

Credit must be given to Gaston Leroux for the original *Phantom of the Opera* which has inspired so many adaptations. Now I must humbly submit my own.

I

She had done it. The Scorpion felt warm between her hands even as the cool underground air chilled her to the bone. Erik's seemingly disinterested manner did nothing to quell the horrified realisation of her choice.

What had she done?

He had said she had a choice, that if she truly wished to remain unattached to a monster she had simply turn the Grasshopper and she would be free. In her childish selfishness she wanted nothing more than to be free of all choice and decision. All those people, blown to bits because this angel, this man, this *monster* wanted his living wife. She had cried out for guidance, for any sign to guide her to the right path which would grant hope for her future. A mere wisp of a voice echoed in her ear as the final moments of the clock ran out, signally the end of Erik's dreadful ultimatum.

Such a good girl, Christine.

So she had made her choice, had turned the Scorpion until the sounds of water could be heard above her shuddering sobs. When her name frantically being called met her ears her sobs turned into pleadings for the life of her beloved Raoul and the foolish man who had tried to help her. If only they could understand she was beyond saving. This fallen angel had claimed her for his own, and no power available to their mortal hands could stay his long, dead fingers from ensnaring her once again.

Even her own feeble madness had been nothing compared to his. Left to her own devices, she had attempted to create a third choice, one which would allow the innocents to go free, while she, with her tainted soul and rendered heart, would be the only victim.

But he had denied her that also, filling her head with that unbearable voice as he told her over and over of her naughtiness for behaving thusly. Finally he had bound her to a chair, securing her so surely the tips of her delicate fingers had begun to go numb within minutes. *Choices.* These were not choices. These were the decisions made based upon the evaluation of consequences, ones she had weighed and enacted.

His eyes were on her as she knelt, grasping at his finely crafted trousers, begging for the life of the two men about to drown. "Why should his Christine need her lover when she has such a loving husband?"

Was he? Was he her husband? Did the simple touch of a metal figurine truly bind her to this... man, forever? But if it would arouse his compassion enough to turn the spigot of the water away from the demise of the man she loved, she could sacrifice the last vestige of her freedom.

"Erik, Erik *please*. Don't you trust your wife? I chose the Scorpion! I chose *you*!"

He abruptly pulled away from her clutching hands and stalked around the room muttering obscenities before again coming before her defeated form. "Erik's wife has given him no reason to trust her! Even now, when she should be giving him some means of affection to commemorate their happy union—convince him that she could be a happy little wife—all she does is look at him with *tears* for her lover!"

Christine did not think her sobs could become any more wretched, but as this man who had meant so much to her thundered out his anger and frustrations, she felt the loss of sanity creep over her once more. She was naught but sixteen. He wanted a wife, and all she knew was to be his student, nothing more. There were few marriages in the Opera house, most simply illicit gropings in darkened corners. Her mother had died so very long ago and she had no memories of how she behaved to her father.

And so she did nothing, and cried like the child she was until his polished leather shoes came to rest under her gaze.

"Erik's poor little wife must be tired after her wedding, and it is her husband's duty to ensure her health." Christine could not tell from whence it came, but a vial was pushed to her lips and she did not care to struggle. She had tried to die once this night, a second time would make no great difference.

She could not tell the effect of the drugs at first, she felt entirely herself aside from her still leaking eyes and head which pounded from both abuse and tears. But one moment she was lucid and the next she could only vaguely see Erik's shadow as she was enveloped by his darkness and taken to where she could only surmise was her bedroom. Were they to consummate their marriage now? She was too tired to care. Better he do it now while she was floating outside herself then when she could feel every bone and cold ounce of flesh pressed against her pallid skin.

Oh God, what have I done?

Just as soon as her body reclined on the bed coverings he had provided her, he rose and departed, leaving her to the emptiness of her darkened room and befuddled thoughts.

-X-

She could not tell how long she had slept. Her head still hurt and her eyes had a continual squint as she tried to assess the shadowed room around her. When she had stayed with Erik before, she had asked him with full expectation of his refusal if he would be kind enough to open her door a crack as to let in light from the exterior rooms. She had never been fond of the dark. The darkened state of her room spoke volumes of his continued displeasure.

Fumbling about her night table, she located the small matchbook and lit a candle with trembling fingers. Her room had remained untouched. A small smattering of blood decorated one wall, and other disturbances were evidence of her madness of yesterday. The other side of the bed was cold and the bedclothes smooth, so her... *husband* had not slept with her.

She was a coward. It was obvious she would have to leave her room at some point, but Erik had always promised this would be her sanctuary, a place for her to do as she wished.

Except die.

Such morbid thoughts were not Christian, she knew, and her father would have been horrified if he knew.

Oh Papa.

Whenever possible, her father had taken her to Sunday Mass, both for the service and also for the music. When the pipe organ filled the stone walls of whatever church, cathedral, or chapel they happened upon, her soul had risen to meet the notes as they echoed in the hallowed halls.

Erik could not possibly be her husband. There had been no vows, no sacraments, and most certainly no priest. He claimed to love her, to desire her, and yet when faced with her own wishes and desire he continually spurned her in fits of rage. That was not love. Love was the simple touches and conversations with her Raoul, whose smile set butterflies aflutter within her, and promises to love and cherish her were obvious to behold.

As such, she would preserve her modesty. In his mind she was his wife, but they were not married by the church and therefore she could not possibly allow any untoward attentions. If only she fully understood what such attentions were. There was desperation in Erik as he clutched at her, which could not possibly be how love was intended. Though love him she did not, she did not hate him. *Could* not hate him.

When he was not in one of his rages—was her Maestro and companion—she could lose herself to whatever magical art he bestowed upon her. His sadness was the worst of all. How could one be cruel enough to hate that which lies at ones feet, begging and pleading for affection and forgiveness?

She did not know which Erik she would face when she left her bedroom, nor could she immediately tell as she looked upon his seated

5

form, seemingly calm, as he read a book. As soon as his piercing yellow eyes rose to meet her arrival she wanted to retreat back to her room.

"Ah, she awakens! Is Erik's little wife hungry?" Erik's continued use of his detached mode of speech was enough to warn her of the dangerous ground she was treading. She had wanted to inform him of her continued status as *mademoiselle*, but at the cautionary glare she received at her lack of response, her timidity overcame her.

"I would very much like breakfast... Erik." The humourless laugh which burst from his malformed lips startled her into retreating slightly away from him, which earned her yet another glare.

"If you had cared for breakfast, my dear, Erik suggests you awaken much earlier than this. Dinner time is a more apt description." For a moment as he continued to stare at her from his motionless pose, she was afraid he would starve her in his anger. With one more calculating perusal of her from head to toe, he practically glided from the room into the small area which served as a kitchen.

Christine cautiously followed him, partially for she was afraid to upset him further by retreating to her room, but more pressing was the morose voice in her mind reminding her of his inhibitions in drugging her the night before. Nothing suggested he would be more reticent in the future.

Before she had even made it into kitchen, Erik was already pouring a deep Merlot into the glass by a place setting full of bread and cheeses. He poured himself a glass as well before sitting down in the chair across from the one she sank into. Suddenly ravenous from lack of nourishment the past days, Christine devoured most of her sustenance before slowing when she met Erik's look.

"I... thank you for the food." Christine was rather proud that her voice only slightly wavered at the beginning, not nearly as uncertain and afraid as she felt.

"Did Erik's wife truly believe he would deny her proper nourishment?" Though Erik had replaced his mask at some point while she slept, Christine could clearly see the horror and disgust shining in his eyes. "I will always care for you, my Christine."

Slightly ashamed of her presumption, Christine began fiddling with the remaining morsels which littered her plate. Refusing to meet his eye, hoping to never have to bear witness to such conflicting emotions again, she wondered how long she was expected to remain at the table before she could escape to her room where she could wallow in peace. How could he make her feel so guilty? He had bound her, the testament being the bruises which encircled her wrists, and to Raoul he had...

Horror. Hot, angry tears blurred her vision as self reproach consumed her. She had taken food from this... *monster* and had not even dared consider what had befallen her beloved...

"Christine."

She could not bear the sound of her name in such a questioning manner, not when Raoul could have perished on the other side of the stone wall, already fading into similar disintegrating flesh as her father.

She gasped as Erik slid her chair so that he knelt before her. She had not heard his approach, nor was she prepared for the slender fingers to slowly advance to her cheek. Her name was no louder than a breeze as he breathed each syllable with such reverence it left her frightened.

"So beautiful..." He stiffened slightly and withdrew his hand. "Are you no longer hungry?"

"I... I am afraid I have lost my appetite." She could not look at him as she warred within herself. Did she dare ask him of the happenings of last night?

Erik rose so swiftly she cringed into the mahogany dining chair, wishing it could swallow her whole so she would not have to face whatever new emotion he chose to throw at her.

"Is it because Erik touched you? Does he repulse you so? Or is this some new way for Christine to leave Erik, she will *starve* herself. Well Erik will not allow it! He will provide for his Christine, his *wife,* and she shall never, *never* leave him!"

Where the sudden burst of courage originated, Christine could not imagine, but she found herself standing a scant few inches away from Erik's heaving chest as she met his gaze with a furious one of her own.

"It is because I cannot bear the thought of consuming food prepared by the hands that murdered Raoul!"

Erik was quiet. Too quiet. When her ill advised outburst ended, the realisation of just how far she had erred left her reeling back.

Erik hissed. Erik grabbed. Her already tender wrists protested his touch even more so than her conscience dictated. What were once tears begotten by anger, they now flowed freely from fear—fear of his ire, and fear that he would hurt her further.

"You shall *never* mention that boy's name again." This sentiment was punctuated by him shaking her by her oh so painful wrists—not enough to jar her irrevocably, but enough for her tears to escalate to helpless sobs.

"It would appear I have not given you sufficient evidence of our marriage. Is that what you want? A wedding, a priest to ordain our vows before *God?*" He practically sneered the words. "Christine would not treat her husband this way. So perhaps she does not *think* of him as her husband. For Christine would be a *good wife!*"

And she would. If it meant he would release her, stop hurting her, stop scaring her. She did need a wedding. She needed the concrete evidence of her hopelessness, that a priest himself had given her to this man, for she would not, *could not,* believe that her choices last night constituted a marriage.

Seemingly unsatisfied with Christine's lack of response, Erik tightened his grip to unbearable measures.

"Please Erik, *please,* I will be a good wife, just *please* stop hurting me!"

Though there was little force behind the motion, when he released her she still fell to the floor, clutching her freshly throbbing wrists protectively.

"Erik would never hurt his Christine," he informed her rather petulantly. "Christine must be mistaken." He looked thoughtful for a moment, and she worried what new accusation he would throw at her. "Erik understands this must be a confusing time for you." His expression smoothed slightly as he took in her crumpled position on the floor. "I forgive your insinuation."

Her continued sobs were obviously not the apology he was expecting from her. When he crouched down in front of her she recoiled, earning her another quelling look, and then he was reaching for her again and she cried out and…

But his grasp was gentle as he cradled her abused wrist in his palm, slowly lifting her sleeve so he could study the flesh itself. She had never heard such a lament. A mix between a sob and a wail, he brought her sensitive skin to his dead lips and kissed it. How she hated it—hated that the cool lips eased some of the persistent pain and made her wish he would hold them longer.

All too soon—or was it not soon enough?—Erik's cries became nothing more than the slight shuddering of his shoulders, and she found herself being lifted. Memories of dark, looming tunnels pervaded her mind, and she was half prepared to be lifted onto Caesar. But no, Erik had taken her back into her little room, with the rumpled bedclothes she had not smoothed before departing, and was placing her carefully against the pillows.

She thought he was leaving her there, but as quickly as he had left, he returned with a small bowl filled with what appeared to be water and a soft white cloth. Ever so tenderly, he rolled up her lace sleeves until they reached her elbow, and began laving her reddened and bruised flesh with more apology than he could voice.

Christine did not know what to think. Although he had been the one to hurt her, hurt *Raoul,* there was a gentle side to him. That was the side she had grown to love throughout her childhood, and what she dearly missed even now. But he had scared her too much, lied to her too many times for her to trust him now. He had proven that her will did not matter, nor did the will of others stronger than her. It was *his* will that mattered.

"My dearest Christine. Such a good girl." Erik had apparently washed her skin sufficiently as he placed them on her night table but took up her hands once again before she had time to move away. She wanted to pull away, honestly she did. But he looked at her so beseechingly, so piteously she remained frozen.

"Erik he did not…. *I* did not intend to hurt you." Oh his eyes, how they burned her very soul! "I will give you a wedding Christine. We shall be bound by a priest, and you shall wear your pretty white dress, and Erik swears—*I* swear, this shall never happen again. Not to my good little wife."

She could not say no. Though she knew nothing of Raoul's fate, nothing of her own, when he was being to gentle, and his eyes pled so, and his apology was so sincere…

Her head bowed, and with tears in her eyes, she could only nod as Erik kissed her hands so very fervently, and with tears glimmering in his nearly colourless eyes, he all but ran from her room with only a quick word of resting her blessed head while he made his preparations. And then he was gone. Alone with naught but freshly bathed wrists, and the quiet of Erik's home pressing around her like a vice, she was left with only one errant thought…

What had she done?

II

She supposed there were still lingering effects of the drug Erik had administered the night before which would account for her ability to fall asleep so quickly. Or perhaps she had not slept as long as she thought she had. There was no timepiece in her bedroom, and the passing of time was now subservient to Erik's whims as much as the rest of her existence. She no longer felt tired, and when she awoke, the customary light was seeping into her room signalling her return to Erik's good graces.

What exactly that meant for her she did not know. He had promised her a wedding—a wedding she had not asked for, nor did she want. At least, she did not think she did. She did not wish to live with a man in sin, but to marry Erik in such a fashion would be giving her consent, both in a holy union, and for the subsequent consummation. Is that why he wished for a legal binding? To bed her? And what exactly did being bedded entail?

Mme. Giry was a private person, and even when Christine had become involved with Raoul she had never deemed it necessary to reveal the secrets of the marital bed. Being a good Christian girl she knew the removal of clothing with one to whom you are not married would be of the greatest transgressions, but that did not answer the fundamental question of what it meant to consummate a marriage. Raoul had kissed her, and skimmed her shoulders with his hands, but that was the extent of their relations.

She wished Erik would talk to her. Not in the disassociated manner she was so used to when he was angry with her, but simply address his expectations so that she might not be forced to shy away from his every move, in fear of his underlying intent. Christine was not a girl conditioned to solitude. Firstly when travelling with her father, he was constantly doting on her with love and affection instead of material possessions. At the opera, the regular influx of performers and stage hands never left much time to be alone, and she had grown accustomed to constant thrum of life surrounding her, though she might remain aloof. But here, removed from all human contact save the man she could not be sure possessed all of his sanity, the silence threatened to consume her.

Unsure of his return, and desperately feeling the effects of her prolonged state of dress, Christine retired to her small connecting bath to scrub herself of the horrors of the previous days. As she stripped out of her dress and prepared to step into the awaiting water, she considered how she was about to wash the last of Raoul's touches from her skin. While it satisfied her that she would also be removing Erik's icy fingertips, the notion that Raoul would never again caress her cheek or smooth her hair was almost too much to bear.

But still she continued, laving the foaming soaps into her tresses, and glaring at the marks upon her wrists. They had not been this abused in appearance yesterday. While Erik's attentions had been well meaning, the abrasions from her bindings as well as the prolonged disturbance of her circulation from Erik's grasp had left them chaffed and discoloured.

Unable to think of anything else to wash, and as the water was rapidly cooling in the already frigid air, Christine rose from the bath to comb her hair and dress. The mirror above the basin was the only one in Erik's home, and certainly for good reason. For all the tragedy of the last few days, she looked relatively normal. There we no dark circles shadowing her eyes, nor was there evidence of last night's tears. She looked sad, she supposed, but she still looked like… her. She wondered what she would look like after her wedding.

Ensuring she was sufficiently dry, she returned to her bedroom to find something appropriate to wear. To what she did not know. She had not heard from Erik yet, and perhaps he had forgotten about his ill conceived notions of a wedding. With that last foolish hope, she removed a garment of pale blue, with sleeves that came to only her elbows. She was being spiteful, she knew, but she hoped if Erik could see evidence of his temper he would remember to treat her with gentleness.

Unlike the day before, she went about tidying the room, delaying the inevitable encounter as long as possible. Before long the room was as pristine as she could make it, although she was unsure of how to fully remove the blood stains from the wall.

When she walked into the main living space, Erik was nowhere to be seen. What that meant for her she was not certain. Not wishing to be startled, she cautiously entered the dining room, and finally the kitchen. There stood Erik, looking quite domestic as he boiled water and removed pastries from a brown bag and arranged them strategically on a delicate china plate.

"How naughty of you Christine, wakening before Erik is fully prepared!

He only required a few more moments."

Christine stood dumbfounded. He was teasing her. She did not know how to react to this *new* Erik. She had difficulty enough with the ones she had already encountered! First her Angel, then Maestro, then Madman... was this pastry wielding man to be her husband?

Her thoughts were interrupted as Erik had apparently finished his breakfast preparations and was expertly manoeuvring a tray of tea things and the plate of buttery confections, all the while waiting for her to pass through the doorway before him. Still wary of this change in attitude, she slipped passed him as quickly as she could, taking her usual seat at the table.

Erik deposited the tray and set about serving her. A teacup filled, a dash of cream, two sugars. Her favourite. When she had been forced to stay with him before, he had not allowed for her preferred amount of sugar, claiming the additional sweetness would be a determent to her voice. Either he had no immediate plans for performance, or he was attempting to please her.

She hoped for the latter.

He placed the entire plate of delicacies in front of her, only preparing a cup of tea for himself—black, with a splash of lemon. Their tastes could not be more different. When she was fully prepared to dive into the sumptuous feast before her, she was startled when Erik rose abruptly and once again was on his knees before her.

Out of nowhere she could detect, Erik produced the loveliest white rose she had ever seen. Gently grasping her hand, he kissed her knuckles once before looking into her eyes. She was reminded of a small boy, anxiously holding out a dandelion freshly plucked from the earth, bestowing his latest gift with a watery grin.

But Erik's face was hidden behind a mask, and she could only see the apprehension and rather obvious fear of her rejection. Christine was not cruel. His posture was one that if she blatantly refused him, it would be similar to kicking a small puppy when it asked for a pat on the head.

So she took the rose with a quiet thank you, and looked away from the answering beam which shone from his eyes. Suddenly finding her steaming tea fascinating, Christine avoided anymore gestures of apology by delving into a decadent Danish.

"You do not ask why I give you a white rose, Christine. Your curiosity usually exceeds the limitations of my patience. Has your inquisitive nature slipped into your tea?"

Apparently Erik was not going to allow her the opportunity to remain a good girl through silence. She was curious, as most of his gifts consisted of red roses, but she had far more pressing matters on her mind at the moment than to understand the nuances of floral colorations.

"I... had not..."

He continued on as if she hadn't spoken. "It is white, Christine, because

I would not have you question my trust in you. White is for innocence and worthiness. Erik wishes his wife to know she is worthy."

Christine kept her gaze downcast. Worthy of what, exactly? Being a murderer's wife? Certainly that did not require great amounts of accomplishment. She had not considered how her worthiness as a wife was to be measured before. She and Raoul through their pretend betrothal had always been on equal footing; every thought and feeling shared in careful consideration for the other. But Erik was another breed of man altogether, and she found herself questioning her own worthiness just as Erik tried to confirm it. If she ignored his obvious disregard for human life, there was no doubting the mental prowess at his disposal. How could she be worthy of a man so austere and ingenious?

"Thank you, Erik," was all she could manage without breaking her voice. He continued on as if she had not spoken.

"Erik knows his poor Christine has been unhappy. He has no wish to keep her from the nice things she likes to eat. Please, do not stop for Erik's sake."

How could she eat when her spirit felt so down trodden? Erik had seemed quite content this morning; perhaps she should risk asking a few of the questions which pressed so cruelly upon her mind...

Clasping her hands tightly in her lap, she steadied herself to face Erik's potential wrath.

"Erik."

Erik quickly set down his teacup and looked at her intently, obviously slightly surprised at her directness.

"I was wondering if I might... ask about your plans for today."

A wife may ask such a question of her husband, could she not? But Christine had never witnessed a proper marriage, and she was quite frightened of asking anything of Erik at all, let alone plans which included *her*.

"You mean *our* plans for today, Christine. I certainly cannot get married by myself!" He chuckled rather forcefully.

No, he could not marry without her being there. And her last vestige of hope, however misguided, was that he had forgotten the entire incident of last night. A fool's hope.

"I have found you a priest to perform the ceremony. The chapel is just outside the city, so we shall be leaving just after you finish your meal." His eyes glittered for a moment. "And after you put on your wedding gown."

"Now eat, Christine. Erik's bride must not faint at the altar!"

-X-

She was not sure how, but when she returned to her bedroom upon Erik's insistence, upon her bed lay the most delicate white gossamer gown she had ever seen. The skirt was ruffled into a magnificent array of shapely femininity, while the bodice was of a slim design to offset the fullness of the skirt. If she could admit it to herself, it was exactly the type of gown she would wish to be married in.

To *Raoul*.

She was so tired of this. Whenever she was graced with some new trinket, bauble, even the simplest of treats of a neighbouring bakery, the joyous smile which threatened to erupt was squelched by the overshadowing reality that these gifts should come from the man she loved.

Her hair was still damp from her bath earlier, so she moved to her lone mirror to try and convince her curls to behave in a somewhat becoming manner. Even though she was not attempting to instil any sort of feelings within Erik, this was still her wedding day and she wanted to look the part. She also felt she looked far too childlike with her hair down. All big eyes and curls, she had anxiously awaited the day when it would be deemed appropriate outside roles for her hair to be moulded into the elegant twists of sophisticated women.

Satisfied with her hair, she returned to the bedroom to strip out of her blue gown. Taking care not to wrinkle it as she returned it to the wardrobe, she also replaced her current everyday corset with one more befitting the finery of her bridal gown. Lace trimmed on the outside, with the softest of flannels on the inside, it was truly of remarkable craftsmanship. Lastly the flowing gown was placed over her head, only to discover the tiny pearl buttons which adorned the back were impossible to clasp by herself.

Dismayed, she contemplated replacing the gown with one she could fasten herself, but Erik had been in a remarkably good mood this morning, and she did not wish to anger him by insulting his selection.

Nearly in tears from mortification, she emerged from her bedroom half expecting Erik to mock her for her incompetence.

Instead of the "foolish girl" she had expected, there was a choked gasp as Erik beheld his bride for the first time, and quickly closed the distance between them. Nervous of whatever thoughts he could be about to express, she quickly filled the silence with her scrambling excuses for her attire.

"I could not reach the buttons on my own, and there is no one here to help me, and I thought of putting on something else but I did not wish to make you angry and..."

Midstream, Erik gently grasped her shoulders, ungloved fingers touching bared skin, and pivoted Christine so her back was facing him. His breath, his touch, his very essence sent shivers down her spine as each button slowly was looped and her exposed corset was finally hidden.

"Perfect," Erik murmured, and Christine questioned whether she was meant to hear it. He finally brought her around to face him. Timidly, he raised one hand to tuck a stray hair behind her ear, and then grasped her hand in his. "Come along my Christine, I think the wedding bells are ringing."

Christine heard no such thing, but she followed obediently as Erik moved to the door. Suddenly he stopped, grasped her hand a little firmer, and with such a horrified expression shining through his eyes…

"Christine cannot possibly go through the tunnels without a wrap, she shall surely catch cold!" He fled to her bedroom and returned with a winter white cape which he carefully clasped around her shoulders.

"There now! Come along Christine, we would not want to keep the priest waiting!"

And with the practiced working of his fingers that she could never hope to duplicate without his instruction, he opened the door and resumed the gentle pull on her arm, propelling them to the outdoors.

How she longed for the biting cold of a winter breeze on her face. The tunnels were certainly chilling, and for a moment she was grateful Erik had the presence of mind to retrieve such a warm garment. There was no lantern, so by the time they reached the entrance of the Rue Scribe Christine was practically clinging to Erik's arm for fear of becoming lost or falling.

She wondered if he had neglected a lantern for just such a reason.

When they emerged from the darkened corridor, Christine was startled. She had eaten breakfast just minutes ago, yet the stars twinkled cheerily above her head. In her surprise she had released Erik's arm, but now he was once again tugging her to follow. Happy to simply be out of doors she ignored where he was leading her, and enjoyed the fresh air.

She supposed it was quite late as there were few people about, but before long they stopped by a covered carriage which Erik hoisted her into, then promptly followed. Giving a quick rap to the ceiling signalling the unknown driver, there was a lurch, then the steady movement of wheels turning against cobblestone.

Erik had drawn the curtain on the little window to the outside world, and she nibbled her lip trying to determine the consequences of asking him if she could look out. He could say no and leave it at that. He could say yes, and she could absorb all of the delectable sights she could before returning to her prison. Or he could fly into a rage at her audacity to question the action he had just performed.

She felt irrational. This was the same man who had buttoned her dress with no more touching than necessary, who had brought her fresh pastries in the middle of the night, and had retrieved a cloak when she was foolish enough to leave without one.

"Erik, might I look outside?"

From his seat across from her, his eyes had not moved from her since he sat down. It was almost as if he feared she would jump through the door if he was not careful. He sighed. A long suffering sigh a mother would give a child who pestered for yet another treat.

"If Christine must."

Oh. Well that was far easier than she had anticipated. A wave of remorse hit her for expecting the worst of him. He had promised to never hurt her again... perhaps he meant it.

She slid to the edge of her seat and as a courtesy to Erik kept the blind partially closed. There were not many street lamps lit in this part of Paris, but the fresh air did wonders for her spirit, and she contented herself with watching the darkened trees pass by.

After about an hour Erik drew her away from the window. "This will not be the last night you spend out of doors." He promptly shut the blind from allowing any more night air into the confined space, and resumed his relaxed posture.

Christine sat quietly for another quarter of an hour before the carriage drifted to a stop. Erik exited first, holding out a gloved hand to assist her descent. Rather hesitantly Christine accepted it, suddenly more than grateful as her foot caught in her voluminous skirt and she tumbled toward the ground. She remained undamaged as Erik quickly caught her round the waist and kept her tucked into his side as he instructed the cabby to wait.

Befitting her status as the blushing bride, Christine awkwardly remained close to Erik, as he began walking to the small stone chapel wherein they would be forever joined.

The chapel was indeed small. She was not sure of their exact location, but obviously the parish was not more than fifty people, judging from the limited amount of pews. An elderly man hobbled to the couple in the doorway, a warm smile on his face.

"You must be the happy couple! I must say, it is quite unusual to request a wedding at such an hour, but I understand the eccentricities of young love."

As he came closer, Christine noticed the glazed blue eyes and the vacant look they held. He was most assuredly blind.

"Sir, we would like to proceed as quickly as possible. There is a long journey ahead of us and I would not wish to exhaust my bride prematurely."

The priest chuckled. "No, I would suppose not." Christine's blush darkened, though she was not entirely sure why. "Alright then, if you will accompany me to the altar for the exchange of vows."

As Erik walked her up the aisle she felt a pang of sadness that her father was not the one on her arm. This was it. In these four walls she would forever sign away any hope of escape and marriage to her beloved Raoul. Marriage was sacred, she had agreed to this. God would wish her to be a good wife to Erik, would he not?

The priest began his commencement reminding them of the gravity of the vows they were about to take, that this union should not be made because of lusts of the flesh, nor of misplaced obligation. He could not see the tears that welled in Christine's eyes, nor the nearly panicked look Erik was giving her as he beseeched her not to flee, until finally it came time for the vocal recognition of their vows.

"I, Erik," she nearly whimpered—he could not even give her a last name! "Take thee, Christine Daaé, to *my wedded Wife*," she wanted to beg him to stop there, not to make her go through with this, but he continued. "To have and to hold from this day forward, for better for worse, for richer for poorer, in sickness and in health, to love and to cherish," but she did not love him! "Till *death us do part*, according to God's holy ordinance;" there he barely disguised his sneer, "and thereto I plight thee my troth."

And then the priest was directing her to repeat her vows, but her throat felt closed, and Erik's grip on her hands were too tight and...

"I, Christine Daaé, take thee, Erik, to my wedded Husband," the tears flowed freely down her cheeks. "To have and to hold from this day forward, for better for worse, for richer for poorer, in sickness and in health, to love, cherish, and to obey," she choked on her words, but at his pressing look continued. "Till death us do part, according to God's holy ordinance;" a sob escaped her, "and thereto I give thee my troth."

Then Erik was slipping a ring on her finger, but she could not see it as he had captured her within his steady gaze, "With this Ring I thee wed, with my body I thee worship," he was going to touch her? "And with all my worldly goods I thee endow," she would give him all the worldly goods she possessed if he would release her! "In the name of the Father," oh God, "and of the Son," please do not allow it, "and of the Holy Ghost. Amen."

"What God hath joined together, let no man put asunder." He cheerily clapped Erik on the back. "I now pronounce you man and wife. You may kiss your bride."

Erik ignored the ill advised touch the priest had placed upon him, and instead leaned in so close she could feel his breath on her waiting lips. So softly, so gently, he pressed his dead lips to hers.

And then it was over.

III

When they parted, Erik was crying. Not the heaving sobs she expected of him, but the silent tears that broke her heart as she witnessed them puddle at the seams of his mask. His long, slender hands cradled her head between them, and he eyed her with such concern, so much love, it made her own tears flow faster.

And then she remembered.

He had asked for a *living wife*, one who would not recoil at his touch— one that would not die if he kissed her. And even though she had not wanted this, had not wanted *him,* she would not faint, and she could not pull away. Not when he looked like he would die himself if anything should happen to her.

With a shock of horror, he realised it was impossible for anything *not* to happen to her. Not when Death's lips had been impressed upon hers. He had killed his Christine! She would die just when she believed herself at last his wife, and all because he had selfishly tried to possess what was too pure and sweet for him to hold. He should have known he was not meant to love—to *be* loved. It was written in every twisted line of his disfigurement. Erik was a monster. Erik did not deserve this beauty trembling within his hands; trembling, no doubt because of the life being stolen from her body due to his wretched kiss.

It was not Erik's fault! Erik would never hurt his precious wife! This was the priest's doing! He had sanctioned—no, *charged* him to kiss her. Erik did not reject God, and he feared judgment too much to rebel against the direct instructions of His messenger. He had not forsaken the church, the church had forsaken him. From his birth he had sought the promised comfort of the beckoning pipe organ, but even the clergy had denied him. His mother had made it quite clear if they ever saw the gruesome features that conjoined into a face, an exorcism would be ordered to eliminate the demon within. How he longed for God's forgiveness, but for some sin he could not identify. He knew the ungodliness of murder, but what had been his crime that this corpse-like exterior was to be his penance? Was his soul tainted from birth? And now Christine was breathing her last breaths against his misshapen face, and it was entirely the priest's doing.

After a long moment, her heart remained beating, and in gratitude to divine mercy he placed his forehead against hers with as much contentment as she had ever seen from him. Only the questioning from the priest as to their lingering caused Erik to pull away. He ushered Christine toward the church registry which would signify the legality of their marriage. Erik signed his name in the illegible scrawl known so intimately at the Opera House, and beckoned her to do the same. Not knowing what else to do, she retained her maiden signature, and hardly protested the action. She was married now, and had promised to obey.

With final well wishes from the priest, Christine found herself back in the waiting carriage, unsure of what this new chapter meant for her. Her husband—what a notion!—had not spoken since their vows, and she was loath to begin the conversation. This time he was not staring at her, but the dark wall over her left shoulder. For what seemed like ages she waited, but Erik made no movement, and she worried what twisted turn his thoughts would take.

She moved to the seat next to him, gently putting her arm on his sleeve to gain his attention.

"Erik?"

His head jerked in response, as though he had not caught her change in position. "Was there something you needed, Christine?"

She felt rather guilty that he would think the only reason she wished to speak to him would be to ask for something.

"No, I just thought we should… talk."

He looked genuinely confused. "Talk. Why would Christine wish to talk to *me?*"

And she thought she felt guilty *before*. "Erik, you are my," she took a bracing breath, "my husband now. I would like to ask… what that means to you."

He turned to her so quickly she could not help but shrink from him. Her fears were confirmed when she saw the anger in his eyes. "And why would it mean anything different to me than it did your young man? I had the right to kiss you! Even your priest told me to do it!" His voice, his beautiful voice, which had been raised to such high levels, softened and he grasped a handful of her skirt tightly in his palm. "Christine did not mind did she? She is such a good little wife, letting her husband kiss her pretty pink lips."

He was frightening her. His expression was frantic as he implored her not to turn from him, to give reassurance that she did not hate him for his kiss. The grip he had on her clothing did not relent, and it was impossible to back farther away from him given the confines of the carriage. She did not know how she could live like this for the rest of her life—constantly in fear of asking the wrong questions. Why could he not simply explain his expectations? Dear, sweet Raoul had never demanded anything of her, but surely Erik had something in mind for how his wife was to behave.

Oh she was not a good wife! Not when she remained silent when he so desperately needed her comfort. She could see his anger rapidly returning at her continued inaction. "Is it such a sin that I should desire my *wife?* I gave you the wedding you required! You did not die when the kiss of Death was upon you, yet still you recoil from Erik!" He had gotten so close to her she could feel his cool breath wafting on her face. She cringed away, fearing his temper would consume the man who had sworn never to hurt her again.

"Please Erik, I am so very sorry!" He released a noise of disbelief while his hands gripped her shoulders.

"If you were so very sorry, then why would you not apologise with a kiss like so many other wives do?" His grip tightened, and those dreadful tears returned unbidden to her eyes.

"You swore you would not hurt me again!"

He released her immediately, yet the anger did not quiet. "So I did. And you swore your faithfulness to me not an hour ago. Perhaps you should consider what that means to your *God.*"

He rapped quickly at the ceiling of the carriage, and leaping into the night before the horses even had time to fully stopped, slamming the door behind him. Suddenly left alone, without even the movement of the carriage to comfort her, Christine curled up in the corner of the darkened enclosure and wept.

She had never truly considered the meaning of marital vows. The words were clear, but Erik had caught the underlying implication she had failed to acknowledge. Faithfulness. She had been so overwhelmed by the words of obedience and love she had forgotten the final words. *I plight thee my troth.* As a whole the vow was her pledge to remain faithful to her husband no matter the circumstance, and by asking him his expectations, he assumed she was comparing him to Raoul—a previous suitor. Could she do nothing right?

Still an hour outside Paris, walking was out of the question. Especially since back was… where? To find Raoul? The Opera House? She had no home. She was now legally wed to Erik, and she could only enter his home at his whim. By his leaving her here, it was obvious she was meant to *stay* there until he returned. She had not seen which direction he had gone, or even if he had left the area entirely.

After a quarter of an hour had passed, the door to the carriage swung open. Burrowing her head in her arms so as not to require looking at the man who was continually scaring her with his anger, she was not surprised when the door closed and the blind shut. The figure did not approach her at first, and when there was no familiar rap at the ceiling to signal the driver, Christine's tear stained face rose to enquire.

The man staring at her was not her husband. Though the darkness outside was just beginning to twinge with the rising sun, the blind being closed only enabled the slightest illumination inside the cabin. Christine thought she knew fear. When Erik raged at her there was a quickening of her pulse, her eyes would widen, and the urge to escape him was undeniable. But buried subconsciously was the underlying truth that he would never do her permanent harm simply to do so. But she knew no such thing about this man. Desperate for a different outcome for herself, she grasped at the last shreds of possibility.

"Sir," her voice only wavered slightly. "I'm afraid this carriage is occupied, please find another."

The answering chuckle was not encouraging. Sliding a bit closer, the man brushed her curls in a mockery of tenderness. "Oh yes, I'm quite aware it's occupied, dearie." He grabbed her. What was once a flick of a curl became an entire handful yanking her away from her protective position and slamming her further down on the carriage seat. The rest of his body soon followed.

"You look so beautiful in your pretty, white dress." His tongue ceased his wagging long enough to take a swipe at her cheek, leaving a shuddering Christine in its wake. "When I saw you go in the chapel, I knew I had to have a taste." His eyes glittered in the dark light of the carriage. "That masked freak of a husband of yours won't want you after this." Christine whimpered. "He'll get your marriage annulled once he's seen how soiled you are. I'll be sure to visit you when you're working at the nearest whore house."

His mouth went to her neck, biting cruelly into the juncture of her shoulder, causing Christine to cry out. Where was Erik? Did he leave her here with this man to punish her? All thoughts were driven from her mind as this strange man began pulling at her bodice, ripping the delicate fabric to shreds. His breath smelled of decay and smoke, and it threatened to choke her as much as the hand that clasped firmly around her throat. His hands followed, nails perforating her flesh as they squeezed under her corset. "So soft," he whispered in her ear. "I wonder if you're as soft everywhere."

Christine was crying in earnest. To think she had worried over possible consummation with her husband, but she realised now the true dismay of conjugation with a stranger only intent on using her body for his own carnal appetites. Erik might have been over zealous in his passions, but he *loved* her! He would never tear her flesh as he scrambled to unite with her!

The man's lower body was pressed into her own, a foreign object protruding into her thigh quite painfully. She feared it was a knife. Would he maim her as well? His teeth found purchase in swell of her breast, and she felt the blood trickle into the pure white remains of her wedding gown.

"I wonder if I'm the first *man* to have you." His grip tightened and his voice took on a disgusted note. "Would you really let that monster touch you? "

Christine could not stop the angry retort, half masked by the sobs being wrenched from her throat. "*You* are the monster! Let me *go!*" She attempted to wriggle out from under him, but this action only seemed to excite him more.

His breathing was coming in pants as his hands groped further down her body, cupping her most intimate place, and then pressing hard. His lower body soon replaced his hand. Though separated by clothing, the object was now being forced repeatedly into her sensitive places, pounding pain into her entire being. With every thrust he left another mark, until his hands left her hips and fumbled with the front of his trousers. Shoving her skirts to her waist and tearing her pantaloons from her thighs, he was about to press into her again when she let out a wail for Erik to come and then—

He was gone. The carriage door had been flung open and the man swiftly torn off her. She slid to the floor and curled up in a ball, desperately covering her legs with her tatted skirt. Through the open doorway she could see the man, who she now could identify as the very carriage driver employed by the Opera house, on the ground gasping for breath, a cat gut giving his neck a final embrace. Erik was looming over him, seemingly speaking, but Christine could not make out the words over the terrible sobs coming from her throat and the pulsing blood in her veins.

She hurt so very much. Her breasts were bleeding freely and her womanly place felt terribly bruised. The slight discolouring of Erik's handprints on her wrists seemed a gentle pat in comparison. She had never known such violence until today. Though it was wrong for Erik to have treated her thusly, she finally understood what true malice entailed, and she had been the unsuspecting victim.

When a presence blocked the door once again, she cringed, pushing herself into the wall of the cabin, wishing it could swallow her whole. Erik had given her a white rose—the rose for purity. What was pure about her now? She had been touched, defiled, and how could she possibly be worthy of being *any* man's wife? His parting words had been that of questioning her faithfulness. She *knew* he would annul their marriage now that she had proven beyond a doubt of her wantonness!

"Christine?" When she maintained her cowering posture, the voice broke. "Oh Christine, *please,* he cannot hurt you anymore. It pains Erik so to see you weep!"

Her head raised ever so slightly so as to confirm the figure was in fact Erik. When her eyes settled on him and she caught sight of his outstretched palm, she leapt for him. Clutching hysterically at his cloak, she buried her head in his bony chest. "Oh Erik, I did not mean to! You have to believe me, I am so very sorry!" Her mouth found his in a desperate version of a kiss. "See? I can apologise like a good wife!"

He jerked away from her, causing her to cry out all the more. "Christine will be *silent!*" He took a further step back, much to her dismay. "You dare sit there, weeping and bleeding and *apologise* to your husband? Is it your desire to make him feel even more guilt?"

Christine could not understand. Why should he feel guilty? She was the one who had betrayed him within the first day of their marriage. It was her bosom that was peppered with the attentions of another. Why should her willingness matter?

"Because I was unfaithful... you said so yourself!"

Erik laughed. She wondered if she would hear it after something joyous, not the sardonic resonance to which she had become accustomed. "Oh you foolish girl." What could have been an endearing phrase was biting in the venom he infused in it. "You consider this monstrous attack to be more of an offense than your dalliance with your young man. Your naivety astounds me." He was no longer moving away from her, but was standing a respectful distance, keeping cautionary eyes trained on her as if he feared another assault upon his person... his *lips.*

Christine felt dizzy. She did not wish to fight with him. At most she wished he would come closer, promise her no one would touch her that way ever again, and then clean her wounds as he had done her wrists. But he just stood there staring, while the body of her assailant lay a scant yard away.

Oh God.

A wave of nausea swept over her as she saw the unbuttoned trousers, the pasty pallor, and the bulging eyes staring into nothingness. The rope had been removed from round his neck, but a grotesque ring was still visible where it had strangled him. She was a good, Christian girl. She did not believe in murder! But as she looked at this corpse she felt only relief that he was forever unable to harm her, and she felt sickened by her extreme gratitude for Erik's merciless penchant for the blood of those who wronged him. Now that they were man and wife, did that include those who hurt her as well?

She was steadily becoming weaker as her wounds continued to bleed and her thoughts were doing nothing to help her condition. Erik moved closer as her seated form wavered. "Forgive your Erik, Christine, you are injured! Now is not the time to discuss such unpleasantness."

And finally, *finally* he was embracing her, unclasping her own bloodied cloak from her neck and wrapping her in his own.

He picked her up, cradling her in his deceptively strong arms, and climbed to the driver's seat. The air was still chilled, but the sky was just beginning to lighten, and Christine was grateful for not being replaced in the carriage. She was not certain she could ever be comfortable inside once again. Erik was being exceedingly gentle with her, but released her as soon as she was settled. Perhaps irrationally, Christine despised the lack of contact. When Erik was not touching her, other hands were capable of doing so, and their intentions could not possibly be fathomed. Now that the adrenaline and fear had ebbed, she was exceedingly weak. There was a great possibility of her sliding out of the seat if she collapsed, and she found herself entwining her arm with his, not fretting over the consequences. Her head found his shoulder, and his fine evening wear that had looked quite befitting of the solemnity of the occasion, dried her silent tears.

Erik made no move to dispose of the body in any way, but seemed intent on leaving the dreadful place behind. "Sleep, my Christine." His voice took on a lulling quality as he grasped the reigns and urged the horses on. "Your Erik shall take you home and then he will tend to your wounds. All shall be well."

And she believed him.

Before she had quite succumbed to the lovely call of sleep, she heard his whispered words not meant for her conscious mind to heed. "Erik is *so* sorry Christine. He only left to keep his temper. He never, *ever* would have allowed you to be touched in such a manner if he had known!" The tears were evident in his voice. His beautiful, heavenly voice! "And now I am to take you back to Erik's home where he shall have to see ever bruise, every cut," he could not continue for a moment and she heard him gasp back the sob threatening to escape. "I do not wish for the first time I see you undressed to be as your nursemaid. I am not even certain of how far he went in his violation of Erik's poor Christine."

Erik had been gradually pulling her closer, until finally her head was in his lap and he was crying over her curls. "But Erik *swears*. If Christine… if his good little wife were to ever allow his touch, it would be different. So very different! He would be so very gentle with his precious Christine!" His tone turned slightly bitter. "But that brute has ensured that Erik's first touches upon his wife will cause her pain as he tries to heal her!" Erik's dreadful laugh, though hushed, echoed around her. "He is dead now! As will be any other man who touches Erik's living wife!"

And Christine slept in the lap of her husband.

IV

She awoke to Erik whispering in her ear. "Christine must wake up now, Erik has to attend the horses, and he does not wish to move her head." Realisation of exactly where her head was positioned had the still bleary Christine attempting to right herself. In her sleep befuddled state she did not remember her injuries, and when she moved her arm to reposition the cloak more tightly around her shoulders, she was made to cry out in pain as the torn flesh above her once pure bosom stretched at the movement.

Erik came immediately to console her. "Oh Christine, I will work very quickly and then you shall be bandaged properly. Please attempt not to move." Christine nodded as Erik rapidly unbridled the horses and led them to their stalls.

When he returned to her, he gently picked her up, and she leaned her head into his chest, breathing his scent which no longer smelled so much of Death, but instead crisp night air with a hint of horse flesh. She shifted to place her arms around his neck, and she felt his soft breath against her ear. "Hush Christine, be still. We shall be home soon."

Erik's gait was soothing as he passed through the Rue Scribe, and she was quite glad of not having to traverse the darkened tunnels trailing behind him. Unlike before their wedding, he was holding her close, and she could simply float above the ground waiting for her warm bed and possibly a cup of tea. Because of the pleasantness of the journey, she was surprised how quickly Erik was opening the door in that impossible way, and walking into the living room.

"Would Christine like to be tended to on the couch or in her bed?"

Feeling supremely childish, Christine nuzzled further into Erik's arm while mumbling "my bed please" into his chest. Erik complied, taking care not to bump his burden against any furniture, and carefully set her down on the waiting bed.

This was becoming a routine for them—Erik leaving her to bring back bandages and cleansing materials. Christine sighed. This was a pattern she would very much like to see changed. Most brides on their wedding nights await their husbands for the consummation of their marriage, but Christine was waiting for Erik to wipe away the touch and residue of one who was most certainly *not* her husband.

Before such thoughts could overwhelm her, Erik returned with arms laden with supplies for her care. He meticulously lined them up along the side of the bed, ending with a vial and syringe. Christine's eyes widened at the last of the provisions. "Erik, I do not... I do not wish to be drugged!"

"You may change your mind after I begin. Erik simply wishes to be prepared." He reached forward to move the cloak off her shoulders, revealing the scraps of bloodied bodice and bruised flesh. Christine grasped his wrist before he came into contact with her skin.

"Is it going to hurt?" Her eyes beseeched him to answer in the negative, but Erik only sighed and grasped her hands between his own.

"Erik promises to be as gentle as he can, but his Christine will most likely feel some discomfort," he shuddered. "Possibly even *pain.*"

Christine nodded, though she could already feel the tear prickling behind her eyes. Erik's hand returned to her chest, but he quickly hissed and pulled away. "*Oh Christine.*"

She was suddenly ashamed of herself. Whether it was the numerous marks left by another man yet again reminding him of her unfaithfulness, or because her injuries were so revolting he could not bear to look upon her, Christine reached for the cloak to cover herself from his assessing gaze.

"That's alright Erik; if you'll just tell me what to do I'm sure I can take care of myself." She blindly reached for the ointment with tears once again making their decent.

Erik pushed her hands away roughly. "Is the idea of your husband caring for you so repulsive you feel the need to *hurt* yourself?"

Christine blinked at him. "You... you pulled away, I just thought..."

He let out an angry huff. "You think Erik *wants* to see you hurt? You think he *wants* for the first time he touches your lovely breasts to be to bandage them?"

The last thing she desired was an argument. "Erik, please, my body hurts and... please *help* me." Her hand clutched at Erik; suddenly afraid he would leave her—leave his poor tainted wife who now only wished for the comfort of her husband. She was so very sore, and the longer she was awake, the more she was beginning to remember of the attack and what precipitated her aches.

Erik released a sigh that seemed to Christine's traumatised mind almost a whimper, before he was soothing her back into her pillows and releasing her hands from their frantic grasping. "Hush now, do not cry. Erik shall *always* help his Christine." Those hands which mere days ago would have set her trembling should they brush her person were now rubbing calming circles into her palm, and she relished the contact.

She was reclined, and Erik's body was perhaps unnecessarily close as he leaned over her, ever so lightly pressing the damp cloth to her wounds. "Such loveliness should never be tainted with such marks." Her answer cry was muffled by the ghost of his lips against hers. "Christine really must stop her tears. Angels should not weep." Those deathly hands whispered across her face as they swept her stream of tears into his enveloping chill.

Though he meant the words as a comfort, Christine's sobs increased. She *was* tainted, and she could not possibly be considered angelic now. Erik had spent too much time underground, too much time *alone* to fully understand the magnitude of her fall from grace.

Yet he continued to cleanse her skin testing the fabric every so often to see if it would release without pulling the newly formed scabs. At first it caused her to moan, but eventually it softened, allowing for the removal of her wedding gown. She eyed the discarded gown wistfully. What was once the embodiment of her childhood fantasies was now a tangible article showcasing her contamination.

Erik's breath grew heavy as he completed the visible skin and implored Christine to understand as he tenderly turned her on her side and undid the heavy lacing of her corset. Before it fell away, he returned her to her back and laid the cloak across the swell of her breast, but leaving the full extent of her injuries uncovered. The slash marks of the man's fingernails cut deeply into her skin, nearly to the rosy tip, and Erik took every care to disinfect and purify the area before applying the ointment.

"Erik loves his Christine," he stopped for a moment as he waited for her to look at him. "She knows this, does she not?" Did he? *Could* he? He must have seen the doubt in her eyes for he abandoned all pretence of healing and seemed intent on her understanding his feelings.

He did not touch her. Though his fingers—his lips—remained floating above her face, her neck, her breasts, his breath caressed them all as it skimmed and curled around her. His scent had not returned to its deathly aroma even after his return to the underground, and she found the crisp night air to be quite soothing as it embraced her.

Her chest which once heaved with sobs now trembled beneath his non-touch, though from fear or some other nameless emotion, she did not know. "Erik loves his Christine so *very* much. His touch is different than that monster's, is it not?" He was whispering in her ear, words spoken in such lulling tones she felt she was drifting on every cadence, helpless to do anything but believe them to be true.

"When the time comes, Erik shall be so sweet to his wife, she will not be able to help the love she feels for him." The tip of one icy finger skimmed the lines of her throat. "She will not remember this pain, nor this fear, for Erik shall be so *very* gentle." His finger drew higher, tracing the outline of one closed eyelid as Christine remained under the spell of his alluring voice.

"But now, I need to know where else you were *violated.*" And the spell was broken. Christine's eyes flew open, staring at him with trepidation. Erik was tense, though he did not seem angry.

"What... do you mean?" Erik touched her hair, tucking stray tendrils behind her ear. She shuddered as she remembered the last time she endured such a gesture.

His voice was quiet again as he whispered his intent. "You must tell me where else his body touched yours." His fingers held her chin, captivating her eyes in his. "Erik *must* know Christine."

How could she answer such a question? She was becoming frustrated at her own innocence as she could not even tell her husband if she had *lost* her innocence. She certainly felt as if she had...

"*Christine...*" Erik had begun stroking her cheek in an attempt to provoke an answer.

"Erik I don't..."

His fingers caressed her lips as tears of anguish resumed their decent. "Just tell your Erik what happened, Christine. He shall love you no less no matter what words you speak."

So staring into the translucent eyes she had come to equate with protection, she told. She told him of her naïve hope for his mistaken entrance into the carriage, of how tightly he had gripped her hair, how she felt stifled and unable to breathe as his weight pressed against her, and then finally how that foreign object had left her feeling bruised and so utterly confused.

Erik never left his position next to her, but his small touches had ceased as his hands clenched into fists at her recounting. By the end, she timidly slid up against the pillows and shyly asked, "Erik... would you... hold me?"

He remained still for a moment, looking unsure himself, until finally his arms opened slightly. "Christine may have whatever she wishes."

She clambered onto his lap as she had her papa when she was small. Erik was stiff at first, obviously unsure of such actions, but as she sobbed her sorrows into his cravat, his arms wound around her back and he held her close. The softest lullaby hummed in her ear, comforting her mind as she released the stress and torment of the past hours.

Christine sniffled wretchedly. "Erik, what did he want of me?" He stiffened beneath her. "Why was he unbuttoning his trousers?" Erik sighed. His hand had found a comfortable home nestled in her hair and he stroked her scalp as he pressed her head onto his shoulder.

"Oh my sweet little wife." She thought she felt a kiss upon her head, but she was not certain. "That...*man*, was attempting to take what was not his. What you felt was his means of enacting his brutish desires on my poor innocent Christine." He held her tighter. She did not mind.

"Is that what you will do when we must," she looked at him with wide frightened eyes. "It hurt me, Erik."

His hands cupped her face as he stared into her eyes, *willing* her to believe him. "When Erik lies with his wife, she shall be a *living* wife, not a girl begging to be released." His tone turned softer. "I know he hurt you. But Christine must understand she shall never be hurt that way again."

Christine huddled further into her husband, finding it difficult to believe him, yet wishing to all the same. "I heard from Jammes it always hurt girls the first time." She paused. "Erik, was that my first time?"

He muttered a curse before shifting her awkwardly on his lap. "No."

"But how can you be sure?" A gasp of horror tore from her throat. "Could I be *with child?*"

"*No!* Christine, from what you have spoken—and for Christine's sake, she had better have told Erik the entirety of the encounter—that man never fulfilled the act. You cannot be carrying another man's child."

If that did not count as the losing of her virtue, was she truly as corrupted as she thought? She could not be with child if Erik was to be believed, and she hoped with time all remnants of her attack would be expunged from her flesh. Perhaps... perhaps she was still simply Christine. Erik's Christine. He had heard, he knew of what had transpired, yet he did not withdraw from her, but instead tended to her care while explaining matters as a husband should.

After another moment of silence, Erik laid her back down on her bed, shifting the cloak to retain her modesty as he reached for the gauze he had prepared. "I shall have to change this once a day. I do not trust your knowledge of inseting infection for you to do it yourself." Christine nodded. Erik was proving quite trustworthy in medicine, and he so far was respecting her desire not to be stuck by the invasive needle still lying innocuously on the bed.

Her eyes began to droop as he wrapped her wounds, but Erik tapped her cheek before they were fully closed. "No sleeping Christine. You need nourishment to heal, and I am afraid a pastry some hours ago is not going to be sufficient." He eyed her sceptically. Not convinced by the steadily closing eyelids, he reached for her again, pulling her from her welcoming bed and carrying her to the kitchen. Christine wished to cry out in protest, but Erik seemed to know how best to handle these things, so she rather begrudgingly allowed his absconding.

She expected to be deposited at the dining room table, but Erik seemed unable to leave her out of sight, so he promptly placed her on one of the small counters which made up his kitchen. She sat obediently as he set the kettle on to boil as well as a bit of broth. While waiting for both to heat, he prepared the tea pot, and found a slice of baguette to accompany her soup.

If she were being honest, the hard counter was difficult to sit on with her bruised intimate places, but as Erik was continually sending her covert glances ensuring her continued presence, she could not complain. While her thoughts were filled with infidelity and pollution, she forgot that his must have centred on the possibility of her loss. So she remained still until he was satisfied with the meal and had left her for only a moment while he took the tray into—she supposed—the dining room.

But when he returned and once again held her in his arms, he passed the table and slid her into the pulled down sheets and placed the tray of tea and consommé in her lap. Looking at the single serving, she glanced up at him as he stood staring at her from the far end of the bed.

"Are you not eating?"

"You are the one who requires sustenance, not I." He took a step toward the door.

Christine took a sip of tea, but when Erik took another move to leave she halted. "Please don't leave me! Won't you just," her eyes landed on a small chair in the corner of the room. "Will you please stay with me?"

Erik relaxed at her request, and Christine was struck at his willingness to go if that was her wish, even when it was obviously not his desire. He brought the chair to her bedside, though not *too* close, and watched her eat the broth and savour the sweetness of her tea. He was still intent on pleasing her it seemed, as two sugars were most decidedly dissolved within the steaming liquid.

The room was silent except for her quiet swallows and the sound of her rather congested breathing. She half wondered if his insistence on warm liquids was in fact for her continued health or rather the preservation of her voice. Resentment was not her intention, but as she drank the last drop of sweetened tea she could not help but wonder if that would be her last. If he did not intend to demand the rights of a husband then surely he would enact his rights as her Maestro.

Her meal entirely consumed, Christine placed her teacup back on the tray just as Erik rose to retrieve it. He avoided contact with her as his fingers brushed the blankets surrounding her, and he just as quickly removed them. "Does Christine require anything else?"

She shook her head slowly. He was always so formal with her. Given his current shift in attitude, she was not certain she would feel comfortable making a request even if she had a need. Erik began to exit the room with a nod, confirming his withdrawal from any scrap of bond they had established when she remembered her most fervent desire.

"Erik, wait!" He paused just inside the doorway. "Might I... have a bath?" Erik stiffened. "I still feel... dirty and would like to wash."

"No." She looked at him in surprise at his curt response to her plea. "Erik does not wish," he released a longsuffering sigh. "Erik does not wish to be like *him.*"

Her confusion must have been evident by her expression for Erik pressed on. "Christine could not possibly keep her bandages above the water by herself, so Erik would be forced to help her." He was becoming agitated, and stepped back into the room only to begin pacing around her bed. "Must Erik be denied everything? That he be forced to touched his wife's naked skin for the first time only to place her back in bed and leave her there to sleep?"

His pacing stopped. "So no. Christine will have to wait until she can bathe on her own, and not suffer her poor Erik to more torment." She was not given time to counter his argument before he was striding from the room, tea tray in hand.

She could not hear his departing footsteps, nor any other sound indicating his location. Left alone, her thoughts were left to swirl and convulse in unpleasant ways. Though he had left the kerosene lamp he had used to light the room while tending to her wounds, she felt lost. With Erik near, she was distracted from the harsh realities of her supposed wedding night, but now the shadows cast in the corners of the room seemed to flicker with malicious intent.

In an effort to dispel such fears, she lowered the light until the darkness swallowed her. Memories of pushing, pulling, hurting hands immediately invaded her senses, disallowing any hope of recourse. Her thoughts had dragged her so far back into the memory she could not even hope to fumble with the lamp in hopes of casting away the darkness that so frightened her. In a last desperate attempt to quell the madness, a piercing cry for her husband escaped her. *"Erik!"*

His response was immediate. The door was thrust open, and the tall silhouette moved rapidly to her night table and relit the extinguished flame. All formality and anger was gone as his frantic eyes roamed over her for signs of her distress. When his eyes landed on her tear stained face, they held only concern. "What troubles my poor wife? I left you the lamp if the dark frightens you so." She sniffled piteously, hoping he would offer to stay until she at least fell asleep.

He did not.

When no answer was forthcoming as to the cause of her tears, he let out a sigh and turned to leave her yet again. "No, Erik please do not leave me here alone!" She made to rise from the bed, fully prepared to follow him to whichever room was his destination of choice.

"Stay where you are, you foolish girl." He scowled at her, but it lacked his customary anger. She settled back onto her pillow, content that he at least had not departed.

"Will you stay with me?" She looked at him with wide, innocent eyes, not at all acknowledging the baser instincts she inspired within him. He sighed again, the weight of the world seemingly placed on his bony shoulders at her request. He moved to resume his position in the chair when her timid voice stopped him cold. "Would you... lie with me?"

She had never seen him speechless before. His mouth opened and closed, and his eyes beheld an almost... frightened quality. "Erik does not trust himself to be in Christine's bed."

But she did. He had covered her naked breast instead of abusing his power. He had refused her a bath because he was afraid of his inability to control himself faced with her nudity. And she wanted to feel safe tonight, and the only way for that to be a possibility was to have his strength granted to her unconscious mind.

Seeing her resolve, Erik crossed to her wardrobe. Pulling out a long sleeve flannel nightdress, he returned to her side and helped her thread it onto her arms without putting undo strain on her injuries. Satisfied by her covered state, Erik lowered the lamplight till it cast only the faintest glow, and made his way to the other side of the bed. Not daring to pull down the covers, he shyly stretched out across the still made bedclothes.

Christine curled on her side facing Erik. He did not look the least bit comfortable, but with his stoic expression and eyes set resolutely away from her, she felt safe. With the most timid of movements, she reached a hand to the sleeve of his elegant evening coat and clutched a pinch of material between her forefinger and thumb.

And so, with tangible evidence of Erik's continued presence easing her mind, she fell asleep.

V

She awoke screaming. Though the vivid images had faded into the abyss of her subconscious, the terror gripping her soul remained fast. When would she be able to spend a day without tears as her constant companion? Her hands searched the opposite side of the bed, desperately seeking Erik's bony frame to steady her, but the bedding was as cold as the surrounding air. The door was firmly shut and the lamp had run out of oil, leaving the room far too dark for her comfort.

As she tried to extract herself from the cocoon of sheets and blankets, whimpering and crying all the way, the door was thrust open and a strange man entered. Far shorter than her husband, this man lacked the grace and fluidity Erik possessed, yet he was barrelling towards her as if it was his right to see her so undressed in her own bed chamber.

"Erik!" Her panicked cry filled the room, echoing around the stone walls and reverberating in her mind.

Just as the unknown man had gotten close enough to touch her, Erik's presence appeared. With a gasp of relief, Christine stumbled from the bed, nearly falling in the process but was caught by two unfamiliar arms. "Do not touch me!" She clawed for release, desperation for the safety of Erik nearly choking her, and finally, *finally*, she was freed and allowed to stagger into her husband's chest where he clutched her fiercely.

She was not given enough time to quiet her sobs before the strange man was trying to extract her from Erik's grip, until at last her husband seemed to have enough of her being pawed at and thrust her behind him. "Daroga, if you value the continued use of your fingers, I would highly suggest you keep them *off* my wife."

When Christine peeked out from behind Erik, she did indeed recognise the Persian. Had he learned nothing from their last encounter? He had nearly lost his life to Erik's madness, and had foolishly taken Raoul with him! Through his actions she had lost her last possible vestige for escape, and yet here he was, standing in her bedroom as if he could possibly help her *now*.

"Erik, I am not leaving until I have seen the girl. She has been in your care for three days and she awakens screaming. That is not entirely comforting."

"Perhaps this conversation should be continued *outside* so my wife can dress." The Persian made to leave the room, but paused when he saw Erik make no move to follow.

"Oh I see. I step out and you threaten the poor girl into twisting her tale into one that will satisfy me." Erik took a menacing step forward. "Come now Erik, this can end amicably. Let me just talk to the girl."

Erik sighed. A mixture between anger and resignation, he turned to gently pull Christine from the room behind the already leaving Daroga. Though the matter seemed settled between Erik and his companion, Christine felt no such requirement to see the man's curiosity assuaged.

"Please don't make me go out there; I don't want him looking at me." Erik's tugging on her arm ceased as he turned to look at her.

"The last thing I would allow is for a man to *look* at my wife, Christine." She sniffled, but remained unconvinced.

"Why is he here? He... scared me, Erik." She looked at him with overwhelming sadness. "Why did you leave me alone?"

Erik moaned. "Does Christine know how much it hurts her poor Erik when she looks at him that way?" Christine shook her head. "You must trust your Erik. The Daroga is going to inform the gendarme if he is not satisfied of Christine's condition." He brushed a curl softly with his fingertip. "I would not wish my wife to become a fugitive."

That frightened her all the more. "But... why would he do such a thing?"

Erik laughed humourlessly. "Perhaps you have forgotten the rather unconventional means by which I secured your hand. Some might take that to mean you were not here by choice." His tone took on a hardened edge. "But Christine, I would remind you of your vows as we talk to this man. No matter how it came to be, we *are* wed."

He led her from the room and her steps were only slightly reluctant. Her body still hurt considerably, and there was a dull throb between her legs when she moved. She blushed at the thought of asking Erik to see if she had suffered permanent damage to her most intimate place.

The Persian was seated in Erik's usual seat, and glared at the hand Erik had on her wrist. Instead of dropping her arm, he brought her closer to his side. "As you can see, she is just fine."

"Erik, I see no such thing, she's half hidden behind you." When Christine took a further shuffle behind Erik, he brought her out completely.

The Daroga rose swiftly to get a closer look at his comrade's new wife.

"She is injured!" The glare he cast Erik made her shiver. "What have you been doing to her?" In the scuffle with her bedding, Christine's nightgown had shifted to reveal slightly bloodied bandages, and in one place, the edges of a bite mark were clearly visible.

Christine clutched feebly at her night dress and was about to defend Erik's behaviour when he left her side entirely. Instead of injuring the man as she expected, he crossed to the other side of the room and folded his arms. Left entirely alone, Christine felt small and helpless. She looked to Erik for reassurance, but he was casting hateful glances at their visitor.

She reached a hand for Erik to take, but he shook his head and remained where he was. Perhaps he was trying to show he lacked any true control over her, or maybe he feared being any closer to the Persian would lead to his immediate disposal. Nonetheless, feeling horribly abandoned, she felt the tears beginning to prickle. "Erik did not do this." Her vague gesture at her breast was met with a disbelieving look.

How dare he?

Though she was grateful for his attempt at intervention all those days ago, the distinct feeling that he was partially to blame for her predicament welled within her.

"You are under no obligation to him—yours is not a true marriage." The disbelief had given way to pity as he eyed her distress.

"If you *must* know, I was attacked on the way back from the chapel." She suppressed the shudder that ran through her at the thought. "Though I fail to see why this is any business of yours."

If possible, the Persian's look became even more filled with appalling amounts of misplaced compassion. "You must be confused, my dear, Erik would never set foot in a church!" He laughed, clearly amused by the prospect.

She wanted to demand he move back—that he was standing too close and Erik too far—but when he laughed at her, making her seem like a confused child instead of Erik's wife, she lost control of her temper. Though she was not generally one for such outbursts, this man had insulted her husband, and questioned her virtue by proclaiming them to be unwed. The insinuation that Erik had somehow maimed her in the consummation of his lusty passions was not to be born.

"We *were* married in a church, Monsieur, in a simple ceremony of me, my husband, and a priest. But I can assure you, God was also there that night, and heard my vow to this man." Her voice quivered as she tried to contain her angry tears. "You come into our home and accuse Erik of doing," she could not bear to utter the words, "unspeakable things to me, and then what? Expect me to come away with you?"

The smile slowly slid off of his face as he watched the trembling woman in front of him try to put up the pretence of strength. "I would have you come back to your fiancé."

The room became deathly silent. With wide eyes, Christine tore her gaze away from the Daroga to settle on Erik's still form. Why was he so quiet? Surely he would intervene, stop her from leaving, *anything*. But all he did was stare resolutely at the floor as this man before her spoke cunning words of treachery and attempted to lure her away from her rightful place.

But oh… is that not what she wished? That somehow she and Raoul could be reunited, free from all entanglements of the Opera and its dangers. If only he had come sooner—before their wedding, or before she saw the horrors of true violence. But now—now she understood. Erik had told her of the foolish notions of her mind, that she should consider the actions of that dreadful carriage driver to be more of a betrayal of her vows than her persistent clinging to the memory of her past love.

All that was required of her was to slip the ring off of her finger, and tell this man that she was indeed mistaken. He would take her by the hand, lead her into the world above, and no one would ever know what transpired between her and Erik. Raoul would embrace her, possibly weep over her wounds, but they would soon be forgotten by his sweet assurances of love and protection. They would go to a different priest, one who could *see* her as the blushing bride, and she would once again sign a church registry, only this time, as Christine de Chagny.

She gasped at her wickedness. To enact such a deceit would be to lie before God! And no matter how much her heart fluttered as she thought of the wedding she dreamed of, with *Raoul,* she knew such fantasies could never come to pass. With new resolution in her heart she stepped toward Erik. How she wished he would look at her! The Persian seemed to misunderstand her movement as one to say goodbye. "You are doing the right thing."

Christine ignored his comment as she stood before her husband. Though her words were directed at the intruder, she did not turn to him, but faced Erik decidedly. "I think you have said quite enough, Monsieur, and if you do not mind, I would like to be alone with my husband."

"I am not sure that is wise, Christine. He is likely to try to beguile you into remaining." Though he made no move to take her away from Erik's presence, he also showed no intention of departing as requested.

"That would not be necessary, for I am staying." Erik looked at her then, shock written blatantly in his eyes. "Please leave us be." Their eyes remained locked, his desperately seeking confirmation of her words.

"Erik what have you—?" And finally Erik took action. Moving swiftly to the Persian's side, he grasped him firmly by the arm and began pulling him from the room.

"I believe my *wife,*" his voice had the faintest of quivers as it caressed the word, but quickly hardened as he continued ushering his guest from the room, "has requested your absence, Daroga. You could at least be so courteous as to comply." Before he had fully removed him from their dwelling, the Persian made one last plea to Christine for her return to sanity.

"Is this truly what you wish? If I leave here tonight, I shall not return, nor shall I assist your fiancé in his pursuit of you." Her heart clenched at the mention of Raoul, but her decision had been made days ago, and now it was time to stand by it.

"It is. Thank you for your concern, but you may tell Raoul," she cast a fearful glance at Erik for her unthinking use of his name but found him more concerned with glaring at the Persian. "You may tell him that Little Lotte is with her Angel of Music, and it is not for mortals to interfere."

With that, Erik pulled him the rest of the way out, shutting the door harshly behind him.

Suddenly feeling quite weary and sore now that anger no longer lent her its strength, she sank into the sofa with a sigh. She could hear quiet rumblings of raised voices outside, but found she had made too many choices this morning to try and intercede. If Erik wished to kill him, that could rest on his conscience. She simply wished he would hurry and decide so he could see to her breakfast.

She laughed with a touch of hysteria at her morbid thoughts. Feeling utterly dejected, she pulled her legs up to her chest, resting her chin on them as she stared at the space where a door once appeared. Her breasts ached and she could feel additional warmth seeping through the bandages, leaving a tepid residue on her nightgown. She felt oddly detached as she confirmed her theory, and supposed her tumble with the bed clothes had once again torn the freshly sealed wounds, though at this moment she did not care.

It felt like ages before the front door was again opened and Erik slipped into the room. Relief swept through her that the Persian was not behind him, and she was comforted that he made sure the door was properly latched before turning towards her. The morbid laugh bubbled forth again. What was once a torment in its ability to cage her, she now loathed its ability to open to the outside world.

Erik took measured steps in her direction. Why was he not overwhelmed with gratitude? She had agreed to stay! Is that not what he had begged her for? She did not feel like herself. Her face felt hot, yet her hands felt terribly cold. They felt like her husband's hands. If she were to touch him now, would he understand how his feel like Death's icy grip, trying to pull her down to the fiery depths?

He did not speak, but left to bring in the same articles he used last night to change the soiled bandages, only this time there was no water basin, only a small jar of paste and swabs. The syringe also sat threateningly upon the table. She did not wish to sleep again! It was her nightmare induced screams that made the Persian enter to begin with! Her arms still clutched her knees, and she eyed Erik warily as he sat down next to her on the settee. He tried to pry her clasped hands apart, but it was not until he let out a dreadful sigh that she relented. Satisfied at her cooperation, he undid the lacing at her collarbones allowing for full access to her injuries.

She was numb. Perhaps if she did not feel so very lost she would have noticed the way his fingers trembled as he removed the old gauze, or how he fumbled with the jar of paste, nearly dropping it in the process. But while her eyes had followed his movements, her mind had not processed the actions, and she was startled as his finger, encased in the substance, smoothed over her scabbed flesh.

She flinched as his shaking hands hit a particularly deep laceration, and his entire body recoiled. And then he was on his knees, kissing her hem as he sobbed into her feet, wails obliterating the words into meaningless exaltations. It felt so very wrong. Though this had been his posture before, usually as a lament to some form of her betrayal, she was utterly confused as to what was now her transgression. She did not mean to move away from him!

His cries died down to a more manageable level, but his fingers remained pressed into the skin of her bare ankles. "Why would Christine *choose* to stay with her poor Erik?"

She could not bear his position, as it showed the paradox of their marriage—their very relationship over the past months. Either he was the towering figure which reduced her to tears, or the cowering child begging for the affections of his only hope of love. Futilely she tried to make him rise, but his grip on her ankles only tightened in response as he refused to look at her. Silently, she sank down to the floor beside him.

At her movement, he rose to cast a disbelieving look at her diminutive posture. "Christine should not be on the floor."

A sad smile crossed her face. "Nor should you." One of her hands reached out for his, and she stared at him as they both knelt on the floor. She remembered mass some years ago, when Papa had been asked to play the recessional for a young bride and her groom. They had knelt before the altar and swore their everlasting faithfulness to one another. "You are my husband, Erik. I stayed because I am your wife."

She felt the tremors which coursed through his frame as she held one of his hands between her own. His other hand rose and skimmed the slope of her throat as he gazed at her intently. "You could have left. Christine's young man would have been more than happy to forget any promises she made to her Erik." He said the words as though they felt foreign on his tongue. "Yet you stayed. With me."

Breath ceased to be taken as she prayed he would not ask if she loved him. It would be wrong to lie! She stayed for that was her duty, not because she had an outpouring of love for this man. Her husband. How those words confused her! Though she had said them over and over to herself in hopes of comprehension, it did not seem possible to attribute such an intrinsic word to such a man as Erik.

The fatal question did not come, though she wondered if perhaps indeed that was the question she should have feared after all, when next Erik raised his hand to skim the plump pink softness of her lips. The way he looked at her, with such undisguised yearning made her tremble. She had not kissed him since her outburst in the carriage, so desperate was she for his continued acceptance. Could she kiss him again? He had only kissed her once—inside the church—and it had not been so very dreadful. He begged for affection. Was that also not part of her wifely duty? If not to love, then to at least give some semblance of warmth? She could not imagine living out her days in a stagnant world devoid of touch.

Though he did not speak the words, his desire was clear, and though she quivered, though her mind dizzied at the thought, she slowly nodded her head in consent.

His mouth did not reach her lips, nor did they skim the apples of her cheeks. Instead, they left only the faintest trace across her brow, and she felt more his breath than the feel of his skin. Perhaps it was wretched of her, but the dreadful flush that came over her as her anger at the Persian's presumption fled at Erik's icy touch, and just for a moment, she revelled in the contact.

He pulled away abruptly, his breathing quick and short. His fingers still trembled as they withdrew from her person with only the most brief final caress, and then he stood, holding out his hand to assist her removal from the floor. His fingers stayed firmly around hers as he looked upon them thoughtfully, before deliberately making slight circles with his thumb. "Such a good girl, Christine, letting your husband kiss your pretty head."

His eyes held such a haunted quality when they rose to meet hers, it made her stomach roil. Teaching Erik the most basic of human affections should not have been her responsibility. He was born of two parents, two individuals who were given the charge of this helpless child, yet instead of raising him to the best of their abilities, shielding him from the scorn of the unforgiving realities of the world, they eviscerated his humanity almost beyond recognition.

Leaving him alone.

He had never spoken of his past, and perhaps it was pure conjecture on her part, but someone must have birthed him, and unless she died in the endeavour, there was no excuse for his abandonment. And as she looked at the expressionless mask which did nothing to hide the torment in his eyes it became all the more clear the importance of her affections to her poor, unhappy Erik. Unless she could heal him of past wrongs, there was little hope for their future.

So when she smiled slightly at him, she could not be sure if it was for his reassurance, or her own.

VI

Erik gave a shuddering sigh as he stood and gently pushed Christine back onto the settee. His hands no longer trembled as he once more coated his finger with the unknown substance, but paused before pressing it onto her flesh. "Would Christine be so kind as to move her hair?"

Her hair had fallen over her shoulders, and the curls were blocking the worst of the injuries. She was rather surprised he did not wish to do it himself, but obliged by pulling it behind her as she leaned back against the cushions.

"Good girl, Christine," he murmured as he ever so gently smoothed the paste into the seeping wounds. She tried not to show how it stung, but the bite at her collarbone was so very deep, and Erik had to slip under an overhanging piece of flesh as it pitifully tried to mend itself. She whimpered.

"Erik is very sorry, Christine, but he cannot allow you to risk infection." He continued his attentions, and she was sure he was trying to be gentle, but every twitch caused her to wish she could fling his hand away and ask him why he insisted on continuing her torment.

Suddenly, a sickened thought floated through her mind. Was this truly for her benefit or simply so he would have an excuse to touch her? He apologised for her discomfort, but perhaps that was just a ruse to—*no*. She would not entertain such thoughts. This was the man who had allowed her to sleep unmolested for two weeks in his home, and he was not currently preventing infection for the sake of doing so.

"Erik?" He had seemed mesmerised by the movement of his finger across her skin, but looked at her enquiringly when she spoke.

She did not know what she had intended to say. The silence was grating as he worked, and all she wished was for him to speak to distract her from his efforts. She remembered the haunting melodies he would sing as she cried as a child, and she desperately wished to be lulled in such a manner once more. She closed her eyes so she would not have to view the hardening of his expression as he prepared his refusal, but her desire to hear his voice overwrought any trepidation. "Would you sing to me?"

He blinked at her, finger poised over her bosom as he pondered her request. "Why?"

She sighed and shook her head. "You do not have to Erik; it was only a passing thought." He continued to look at her, almost as if he thought if he continued long enough the reasoning behind her request would become apparent.

He had sung to her before of course, as that had been the foundation of their relationship so many years ago. But in those days his voice had been used for a purpose. Yes, she found comfort in its cadence, but selfishly he had ensnared her into his world through his vocalisations until she was left as nothing more than a revelling nymph bound eternally in his world of darkness. When he had lulled her to sleep on that cursed carriage ride it had been to prevent her further injury, as well as to give him time to think, not necessarily for her peace of mind. So why did she request it now?

When Erik continued to do nothing but stare, Christine fidgeted nervously in her lap, half wishing to bolt into the kitchen to scavenge for breakfast, not only to assuage her hunger but also to get away from his penetrating gaze. Just as she was about to do just that, uncovered wounds or not, Erik shifted and began to hum.

She did not recognise it, not when he began, and not when she was pressed against the cushions as he continued to care for her. His voice rose and fell, and never once could she tell the direction of the melody before it would crest and tumble into a further lilting wave. So distracted was she, Erik's pronouncement of her sufficient bandaging came as a pleasant surprise. He had even gone so far as to draw the neckline of her nightgown into a delicate bow so as to once again cover her modestly.

Erik remained pensively on the settee, looking once more on the plush carpet instead of his wife sitting beside him. For all his regaling that any of her desires would be fulfilled should she but ask, he certainly seemed to question such requests once voiced. But now, all she wished was a simple breakfast and a cup of tea—with sugar.

She knew she would sing again. In truth, she missed it terribly. But then, she found she missed it long before this daily reprieve. Had it been two days? Three? She did not know. But this longing to return to the soul satiating nature of her art transcended her marriage, and in fact dated to before Erik had been revealed as nothing more than a man. When she had faced the betrayal by her Angel, a piece of her soul had perished as well, leaving a terrible ache in its stead.

Wary of the consequence of startling him, Christine reached out a hand to tug slightly on his sleeve. He must have been expecting it, for he only swung his head slightly to look at her, though he lacked the normal exuberance of contact with her. "Erik, I'm quite hungry and I…" she recalled his biting words in regards to her bathing last night. She looked at him with imploring eyes. "I would very much like to bathe."

Erik sighed and plucked at his shirt sleeves, seeming to contemplate how best to respond. "Christine may not submerge in a bath. If she *swears* to her Erik she will not get one *drop* of liquid on her bandages, she may wash." She felt utterly ridiculous having to make a promise to her husband regarding her bathing rituals, but she was grateful he was at last allowing her to remove the final remnants of her encounter.

She nodded her head in assent, but that was apparently not enough to assuage his misgivings of the entire endeavour. "Say the words, Christine."

Biting her lip seemed to be the only way to keep from snapping back that he was being utterly ridiculous, but eventually she managed to choke out a promise. Erik rose from the settee and pulled her with him, stepping quite close as he did so. "I am just trying to protect my wife; you know this, do you not?" Her irritation seeped away as she saw the genuine concern in his eyes. "Erik does not wish to hurt you, and if your wounds keep reopening, he shall continue to do so."

Christine felt rather wretched. Even when he tried to protect her from further pain, she doubted his motivation enough to be annoyed at his concern. "I understand, and I shall be very careful. I promise." Erik stared at her for a long moment, seeming to judge her sincerity, and when he found it to be satisfactory, he pulled away.

"While you wash, I shall prepare your breakfast. Do not be too long or Erik shall be forced to fetch you." His tone suggested that would not bode well for her, so she nodded once again and retired to her room.

It felt slightly foreign when she entered, as if some presence had tainted its sanctity. The sheets and blankets lay in a tangled mess on the floor, and she wondered how this day would have begun had the Persian not interfered. Would Erik have been in bed with her when she woke? Or perhaps he would have brought her breakfast in bed while they discussed how best to spend the day. Foolish notions, perhaps, but she found herself longing for the normalcy of a happy marriage. And maybe—just maybe—she and Erik might have that after all.

She had promised Erik her bandages would remain unperturbed, so she merely filled the basin with warm water and found a soft cloth in which to wipe her soiled skin. Stepping out of her slightly bloodied nightgown, she was once again faced with her reflection.

When she left this room before, it was arrayed in her bridal endowments. Now, as she stood naked before the mirror, she felt older. She had expected to feel different when she returned from the church, but never in her wildest imaginings did she expect to feel like this. Her throat bore the purple markings of fingerprints, and she hated to think how her chest would appear when exposed. She dipped the cloth into the water, carefully wringing out any excess before bringing it to her arms. Bruises shadowed on her wrists and elbows, while there were fine slices on her forearms from that—*man's*—fingernails.

She felt infinitely better when the abused flesh had been cleansed, and she eagerly moved to attend the rest of her body. There were bruises on her hips, as well as shallow cuts, and she wondered again what exactly had been used to harm her. And yet—perhaps it was better she did not know. Perhaps there was a blessing in her ignorance. That she could emerge from this room and pretend she was how she had always been. Bruises were no stranger to her at the Opera, and she could pretend that when Erik cared for her, he was just like the minder of the corps de ballet who bandaged all the young girls who were hurt in rehearsals. And she and Raoul could—

Oh God.

She had not been mindful of what the Persian's presence and words had truly meant. The events of the morning had happened so very quickly, and while she had thought Erik had *killed* them, there he stood, whole and alive. And he had wished to take her back to Raoul. She was a stupid, stupid girl, for ignoring what his words truly meant for her *now*.

Erik had not killed him.

The future she had dreamed of had still been possible, had still been within reach. And yet—it was not. For even though her mind had not allowed her to realise the implication, the fact remained that while Erik had killed—he had not killed her beloved. And she had promised.

With her new outlook firmly in place, she dried the remaining water from her skin, and quite proudly noted the complete lack of moisture to her bandages. What a devastating fall from the stage she had! She giggled at the thought.

Instead of wishing to showcase her bruises like yesterday—was it only yesterday?—she carefully choose a high collared pink day dress which she found to be quite becoming when settled over her proper undergarments. She especially liked the tiny buttons on the front of the gown which allowed her to dress unassisted. She was not an invalid after all, and certainly could dress without Erik.

Heeding his previous warning, she took little time to arrange her hair, but simply pulled it back in a plait tied with a matching ribbon. She wondered at Erik's preference for her hair. He was becoming more forward in touching it, and his fingers seemed to find any curl a welcome comfort as it twisted around the tip. Yet she knew some men still preferred it up to showcase a woman's collarbones. Was he such a man?

It was rather odd considering Erik's tastes. Now that she considered it, she knew very little of her husband. There were the basic preferences she could glean from his home, but as to the why... she had no notion. He slept in a coffin, yet provided her the Louise-Philippe room. He wanted a true marriage, yet he had seemed so reluctant to spend the night in her bed. Perhaps when they were *truly* married he would be different, but until then, it bothered her he would continue to sleep in that horrible tomb. She may not love him—*did* not love him, but he was a man, and he was her husband, and he deserved to sleep in a bed. In—dare she think it?—in *her* bed.

She had tarried too long in her thoughts as she could hear Erik's footsteps outside her door. Before he could knock and question her delay she hurried and opened it to reveal a very placid husband. "Ah, so you are capable of bathing without damaging yourself. I had my doubts."

Well, that certainly was not complementary. She was about to storm back into her room and lock the door, but before she moved she caught a slight twitch in his eye that belayed amusement. This teasing side of Erik was so very foreign she doubted she would ever become fully comfortable with it, especially not when such behaviour was initiated by some comment about her competence. She already felt enough of a child without his provocation.

She stood a little straighter as she looked at him rather imperiously. "I am capable of following instruction, Monsieur. Something I would think *you* of all people should know." Erik simply shook his head at her antics.

"Forgive me. You were indisposed for quite some time and I grew concerned." The crinkle of his eye had disappeared only to be replaced with one of longing. "You look so very beautiful, Christine."

She blushed and looked down at his immaculate shoes. How was she to respond to such a thing? She certainly could not return the compliment, though when she slowly swept her eyes over him, she was impressed by the fine quality and cut of his suit. He was terribly thin, *too* thin to be considered a handsome figure. But he was tall, and his eyes were so very captivating and well—he was hers. She had not considered that before. He had made reference to it before, stating that she was his, and he was hers, but she had never thought of how it was to *own* someone. Mere days ago such an idea would have repulsed her, and left her trembling that he would ever believe her to be his possession, but now...

Now she wanted him to protect her in the same voracious manner he protected his possessions.

He held out his arm to escort her to the dining room, where a spread of omelettes and toast awaited her. Once again, a simple cup of black tea sat before Erik's seat and she frowned at the sight. She wished to protest his nutritional deficiencies, but he was waiting to seat her before her own breakfast and she quickly remembered her ravenous state.

The eggs were light and cooked to perfection, and the smattering of gruyere melted quickly on her tongue. She nearly moaned at the taste, and had to remind herself to retain her dignity by not consuming it as rapidly as would be her preference. Erik looked on at her from his seat, quietly sipping his tea.

"Erik." He eyed her warily. So far conversations she had initiated had not been received well, but she wanted to continue the progress their relationship had made the past days. She was growing more comfortable around him, and he had certainly shown he was capable of tenderness. She had yet to sing again, and supposed it would be a few days yet until her throat would be capable of producing such sound without damage. But now she wished to express her gratitude for his kindness—perhaps to promote furtherance in future, or maybe simply to... thank him.

"I want you to know how grateful I am for how you have cared for me. And for..." she looked at her buttered toast suddenly wondering if Erik went to market like a normal man, or if he had someone in his employ to do such mundane tasks.

"Yes? What is Christine trying to say?" She looked at him trying to impart how much it had truly meant to her.

"Thank you for saving me." He blinked at her for a moment before turning his gaze to his tea.

"Of course I saved you. How could I *not* save you? Did you truly think I would not?" His voice had sharpened at the end and she could see this was swiftly dissolving into one of their many misunderstandings.

"No, Erik! That is not what I meant." She scrambled in her mind to find some way she could relate her feelings to something he could possibly understand. "As my husband, is it not your duty to protect me?"

He gave her a look that so clearly said "of course, you incredibly foolish girl."

"And as your wife, I am trying to... thank you for doing such an... admirable job." As soon as the words escaped she felt idiotic. Why would it matter to him if she said thank you? He had already told her it was his duty to protect her, therefore the gesture was unnecessary. Most likely it was even unappreciated as it made him think she was surprised by such actions.

But the longer she looked at him, the more vulnerable he seemed to become. Instead of the posturing, teasing, or incredulous looks she had seen so far from him this meal, his eyes were swimming as he stared at her. "Really?" It was a desperate plea, someone clinging to the words they could not bear to believe without confirmation. "Christine should not lie to her Erik." Before when he had asked such things of her, she had remained silent. Not now. Not after what had transpired.

"No Erik, I would not lie to you. You are a very good husband, and I am..." dare she say it? "I am fortunate to have one as caring as you." She did not love him, but even at his worst—when he was screaming at her after she had ripped his mask away from his horrific face—had kept her his prisoner for weeks, she *could not* hate him. And it was no different now. There were women whose husbands beat them, mocked them, and reaped all kinds of abuses on their wives. He had saved her from such brutal treatment, and perhaps this was simply the posturing of a girl over her rescuer, but he did not seem so very terrifying anymore. *Oh Raoul, please forgive me.*

Erik cleared his throat, an odd sound coming from him. She had never heard such a human sound emitted from his blessed vocal chords. "Christine is a good girl. Erik is—*I*—am fortunate to have such a lovely wife." He eyed her half eaten plate. "Now finish your breakfast."

She smiled at his change in topic and did just that. Instead of tea he had supplied hot chocolate. It was a rare treat that was warm and thick and *delicious,* and Christine drank it all greedily.

Erik seemed quite contemplative the rest of the meal and she hoped he would not lash out at her as he had before. She knew it was his thoughts that tormented him so very much. They seemed to twist her words into a mockery of her intent, never allowing for the possibility of her genuine speech.

She found that the longer she sat at the dining room table, the longer she wished for the complacent domesticity of married life. When she was betrothed to Raoul, they would sit and imagine their lives in the future— small children tottering around the fire as they sat embracing on the sofa. A blissful family. When she was young she pictured her Angel as a constant companion. Earthly men were mere impediments to the otherworldly beauty bestowed on her through the ethereal nature of *him.* She supposed they would continue to make such music, but no longer would she be aspiring as the prima donna. No, he would keep her in his home, forever to sing at his whim. But perhaps…

Perhaps if she was no longer his pupil, there could be a possible blending of her two dreams. She could sing for him, but not as a personal doll to be required to sing by her master. There were wives who sang for their husbands—songs of love and devotion. Poetry in the liquid form of song. If she could show Erik how wives could treat their husbands, perhaps he would grant her the home above ground, the sofa before a blazing winter fire, and maybe—children.

She had never considered not having a small child of her own. Even when thoughts of marriage seemed a far distant enigma, whenever she would see tiny dimpled fingers peeking out from a cocoon of blanket she felt the warm calling of motherhood. But working in the Opera it would have been a scandalous dream and impossibility to have allowed for such a thing. And of course not before marriage. So when her Angel—*Erik*—had demanded her continued faithfulness she had agreed, not fully understanding the depth of her sacrifice. But now, as she sat nibbling on the last crust of toast and staring at her husband, she wondered if she might resurrect old desires after all.

She was being ridiculous. Erik would never want a child, nor was she ready to endure the method by which children were procured. But she could begin to be a wife to him, if only in such duties as cooking and tidying the house. Now that they were married, she did not suppose they would be leaving the underground for very long periods of time, and such responsibilities might distract her mind from the tedious silence which pervaded the murky rooms.

But first, Erik would have to agree. He had already seemed to withdraw from the conversation, and in fact had not looked upon her since he had told her to finish eating. But she was determined now, and he could bluster at her all he wished and she would prove to him that she was not a child.

And she could be his living wife.

VII

Her difficulty was finding a way to ask him without provoking his ire. He rose as soon as she had finished the last bit of toast and swept her dishes into his arms and left the room. Determined, she followed behind to see him pour slightly bubbling water into a basin to begin the washing. He must not have expected her to follow, for he turned abruptly and cast her a sardonic look as she stood awkwardly in the doorway.

"Did you require anything else, Christine?" She felt like letting out a petulant huff at his constant assumption that she was in need, but refrained in hopes of keeping him in an obliging mood.

"No, I..." she wondered if perhaps showing him would be more effective than asking. With that in mind, she unbuttoned the tiny buttons of her cuff and rolled her sleeves to the elbows. Her bruises were decidedly ignored. Walking swiftly to the basin, she poured in a small amount of cool water from the nearby pitcher, making the water a more manageable temperature. Grasping the wash rag in her hand, she lathered a good amount of soap into it before she began the tedious process of scrubbing. She was rather fond of this frying pan now, as it had cooked her omelette to perfection, and if she were being honest with herself, she had quite a fondness for all things delicious. But perhaps it was Erik who deserved to be congratulated for the success and not this pan...

She glanced at Erik to gauge his reaction, and was none too pleased with the horrified look he was giving her. "What are you *doing?*"

Suddenly unsure, she looked down at the pan to find nothing damaged. Though she had led a relatively sheltered life in the Opera house, with meals provided in communal dining halls instead of personally prepared rooms, she had helped do the tidying at whatever inn had been kind enough to house Papa and her. It was not cast iron, so it should be perfectly allowed to submerge in the soap riddled liquid.

Then his question was based on her action in general. She stood a little straighter as she looked at him primly. "I am washing my breakfast dishes." His answering glare did little to intimidate, so she rushed to finish his explanation before he forcibly removed her from the kitchen. "Erik, you cooked for me, and I just wanted to do something to..." his glare slowly devolved into one of incredulous perversity. "Contribute."

He sighed. She wanted to go back to her scrubbing so she would not have to decipher the myriad of emotions he could possibly be feeling, but that would grant her none of the privileges she was attempting to achieve, so she stood resolute before him.

He approached her quietly, gently taking away her rag and grasping one of her wrists in his hand. She supposed she should be frightened, but his manner was calm, so she allowed him to manipulate her as he wished. His other hand rose to unroll her delicate sleeve before he buttoned her cuff then showed the other arm the same attention. "Erik shows you love in this way for he cannot show it to you the way he would desire. Perhaps someday you will allow him to, but for now, I must be content with this."

In what way did he desire? He must have noticed her confused expression for he let out another sigh—more exasperated than the one before. "Christine is so very innocent, and it pains her Erik when he wishes to taint her with his love."

That she could not allow. He confused her, angered her, entrapped her, but she did not feel tainted by him. She refused to think on what matters made her feel the sickening filth that clung to her skin, but she could not abide such nonsense!

"I would not be so innocent if you were to explain what you mean!" He was startled by her outburst but she would not back down as she finally was able to express the frustration that had brewed within her for days. "I want to be able to *talk* to you, Erik! You are my husband, and while it is your duty to protect me, it is also your duty to explain what confuses me so!"

"Hush Christine, you are getting upset." She jerked away from his soothing hands because she did not wish to be placated! She wanted to have a normal marriage! And until he could learn not to pamper her like a child, but could treat her like the living wife he asked for, she would continue to be nothing more than a prisoner in a gilded cage.

"No! Erik, *please*. I do not want to live like this! Do you not wish for me to love you?" Now it was his turn to recoil from her, and the anger which had previously dissipated returned in a vengeance.

"And what would Christine wish to know that is so important she would withhold her love?" His breathing was harsh as her words were forever twisted into the mangled remains of her intent, almost to the point beyond recognition as Erik's mind had their way with them.

"Not specific things, just to know that I may ask them without you becoming angry!" Angry tears were beginning to prickle her eyes as she tried desperately to think of how best to handle him. He was not a man whose actions could be predicted. It was base instinct one had to rely on, and one could only pray that what meagre understanding had been obtained from brief observances were enough to protect from harm. She doubted her own abilities.

And she doubted his ability to take her words as they were stated. She knew she could prove them through action, if given sufficient time. If only he would give her the opportunity. Bracing herself for his continued anger, she chose a different course.

When she moved toward him, he reflexively retreated. Undeterred, she continued until she stood a scant breath away. He eyed her warily, his temper no longer seeming to be the most dominant of expressions. His face was pulled away, almost as if he were afraid she would touch it, and she stared directly into his eyes as she sank to his feet.

He staggered away from her, his eyes darting nervously at this unexpected position. Before he moved too far, she grabbed the leg of his trouser to keep him still. "Erik, please just listen to me." He did not seem to want to do so, as his hands fidgeted haplessly, obviously aching to pull her up from the hard stone floor.

"I want to be a wife, Erik. I want to cook meals, and tidy the house, and sing in the afternoons. Like—" she hesitated a moment but pressed on, not wishing to go through this ordeal twice. "Like a normal couple." He was motionless as he stared down at her, and she could not tell if her words had been well received. Her tongue seemed to have loosed itself for she was saying far more than her mind knew to be wise.

"I want to sit and have you read to me in the evenings. You know so very many things, and I want to be able to talk to you of what you know." Her voice caught in her throat as she tried to find the courage to continue. "I do not want to be afraid of you anymore."

Erik could stand it no longer. He sank to his knees as well, clutching fervently at her hands as he implored her. "Never, *never* fear your Erik! He loves and adores you so!" She smiled at him sadly.

"I know you do." And she did. She had always doubted his love, that somehow if she refused to believe it to be real it could be ignored. But that was a childish notion, and she was a wife now, and she had duties of her own. "You must give me time to love you as well, but I cannot be a prisoner and your wife, Erik."

And she had proven her willingness to stay had she not? The Persian had given her opportunity to leave, yet she had refused to be a deceitful charlatan. So she remained. But it was imperative that Erik know it as well, otherwise the constant mistrust of her every action and motive would be the ruin of them both. She was his obsession, and it was up to her to convince him there could be more. There could be a marriage.

"I would much prefer to be..." his eyes glistened as she spoke, "your wife."

He said nothing. There were no tears, no praise of her faithfulness. He simply stared at her so intently, she feared her soul would be torn asunder.

Just when she was about to give into despair, turn from him in acceptance that he was incapable of trust, or *true* love, he let out a breath, and his hands rose to whisper through her hair.

"I cannot let you go Christine. Please do not ask it of your poor Erik." She had not seen his face since that fateful night, nor did she intend on viewing it now, but she knew—in some future day—they would have to face the physical manifestation of his twisted soul. Before she thought expressions could only be judged from the face as a whole. But not Erik. His eyes. Oh his eyes! They held such pain and depths of pleading her heart nearly broke in sympathy. Her tears once born of anger began to swell in the answering compassion that threatened to burst forth.

"I would not ask as your wife, Erik. Allow me to *be* your wife." He looked at her a moment longer before the shutters of his being were firmly closed.

"Christine does not know of what she speaks. There are responsibilities she could not *possibly* fathom. That I only hope to *shield* you from!" That was true. She could fully acknowledge the idea of Erik lying atop her as he completed their marital union to fill her with revulsion. But he *had* to understand there were things she was willing to do! Until... until she *was* ready.

"I know that! And you... you are not wrong for wanting such things from me, Erik. The Bible is very clear that it is a husband's right to expect such things from his wife." Now it was her turn to plead. "I just ask that you give me time! Allow me to heal—allow me to *learn*."

"Why do you want to wash dishes like a scullery maid?" He looked at her sceptically, seeming to cling to her action instead of have to face the truth of her words.

She sighed. "I would like to care for you the way I can. I would hope you could be satisfied with that." At his look of outrage and protestation, she quickly added, "For now!"

He did not seem convinced. They were still kneeling before each other on the floor, and her knees began to protest the prolonged posture. Erik sensed her discomfort and gently clasped her elbow and helped her rise, though he did not release her. "You would wish... to... *care* for your husband?"

She reached her hand up to his face, skimming the seam of his mask, but not daring to harm him by its removal. "Yes."

He nodded absently, and she doubted he was able to fully absorb the magnitude of her words at this moment. "Christine said she wishes to learn." Suddenly he looked at her, and unease overtook her as he began to pull her from the room, the basin of water and dishes forgotten. They passed through the dining room, and for one terrifying moment, she feared he was taking her to the bedroom.

She had not meant marital congress! When she had spoken, it was of books, of philosophy, of music she had thought! He had not agreed to her desire for time, and she felt the crushing weight of facing the same horror of yesterday, only this time by Erik's own hand.

But he did not enter her room, but instead lowered her to sit once more on the settee. He did not sit beside her, but remained standing—a looming presence in her betraying mind. Why was she not a better actress? Such irrational fears should never pass through her mind, let alone threaten to overwhelm her!

"Can you read?"

She nearly sobbed in relief, and was thoroughly disgusted with herself. It took a moment for his question to seep through the pounding of her blood as it rushed through her veins, but when she did, she wished she could be more insulted, but there was a rather mortifying layer of reason to his enquiry. She had no formal education, it was true, but her father had painstakingly read to her from every book he could keep on his person. Most days it was the Bible, though she had been exposed to works of literature as well.

But she would listen, not reading herself. Her fondest memories involved her curled up in her father's lap as he deftly turned pages one handed, as the other was occupied petting her buoyant curls. She had picked up quite a bit from peeking at the words, and he had pointed out letters and formed the sounds, but the words were difficult. When she had moved to the Opera house, learning to read music was more important than actual words. Erik had taught her the pronunciation of libretto, but that was to be expected as most were in their native tongues.

"Your silence would seem to give answer enough, am I correct?"

Her cheeks burned. Was he just now realising how stupid a wife he had acquired? She would have thought her actions over the past months would have been portrayal enough, yet here he was, furthering her embarrassment by making her give voice to her inadequacies.

"I can read... a little." And it was true. Mamma Valérius had tried valiantly to get her to sit and learn her letters, but Christine was a flighty child, and was much more inclined to scamper out of doors than to mind her elderly guardian in matters of schooling.

She was looking steadily at the floor when he moved away before coming to sit beside her. He was a learned man, she knew, and how could she possibly hope to converse with him when anything which passed her lips would seem naïve?

His finger ghosted over her cheek, and his breath soon followed. "It is nothing to be ashamed of, Christine. You said it yourself. It is my duty as your husband to teach you." And just then, she felt the first swelling of love within her breast for this man. Her husband. Her Erik.

He seemed to know of her childhood memories, as even without the firm pressure relaying his intent, he coaxed her to sit nearer to him and of her own accord she cuddled even closer. Though he had instigated the contact, he still stiffened at the final closure of space between them, but seemed to calm as her head nestled against his shoulder.

In his hand was a book, with a worn leather cover and pages which seemed to nearly fall from the binding even as they lay placidly on his lap. There were words embossed into the cover, but it had obviously been so well loved the she could not even begin to make out the letters. Even now Erik's hand smoothed gently over the faint etching, and he breathed the title in reverence. *"La Belle et la Bête."*

A fairy tale? She had expected him to choose a book more serious in nature, but there was an obvious fondness as he gazed upon his beloved treasure, and she was more than happy to sit and listen to his melodic voice lull her into whatever fantasy he pleased. "Will you read it to me?"

He *tsked* at her reproachfully. "Christine, the purpose of this exercise is to teach *you* to read." He gave the cover one last caress before opening to the first page. She knew the story of course; she was not quite so lacking an education. Her Papa had told her the story many times, and she was hoping such knowledge would aid her in this endeavour.

It did not. Though she recognised some of the words, it was the structure of the written word which frustrated her. Erik was patient, only prompting her when her huffs of annoyance made her jab the page petulantly as she asked after a word. More than once he had pulled her finger away before rubbing the paper gently—almost in apology.

After only a page of halted words and stumbling pronunciations, she had enough. "Erik, why is this necessary? Why can *you* not just read it to me?" His indulgent look did nothing to quell her irritation.

"Christine should not feel as though I must do everything for her. If I am to allow you to..." he closed his eyes and breathed deeply, almost bracingly as before continuing. "If I allow you to be a *wife* as you have requested, that means as your husband I grant you independence."

She was silent as she absorbed his words. Had he heard her, then? Was he truly considering allowing her the freedom a true marriage would allow?

His eyes swivelled to hers, and they were narrowed almost into a glare. "And Erik may wish to be alone sometimes as he cannot possibly entertain his wife *all* of the time. I have many things to tend to of my own, you know."

Well that certainly was not insulting. *He* was the one who kidnapped *her* and forced this marriage to begin with! Instead of snapping at him, she chose to take her frustrations and—if she admitted to herself—hurt feelings to be nursed privately in her room. Rising swiftly from the settee she moved to do just that, when she felt a sudden tug on her skirt which sent her sprawling back into Erik's lap.

"Erik, how *dare* you! I am simply removing myself from your company as you apparently have such other *important* matters that require your attentions."

"You are a foolish girl." And he tucked her neatly back into his side, with an arm wrapped firmly around her waist. He had used that term once before, only with the biting sting of anger, and she thought that someday he might use it again as an endearment. She was correct. He had laced it with such a tone of fondness she could not possibly think he was offended by her flight. But it did not cause her indignation of his impolite gesture any less prominent.

Instead of making her continue the troublesome reading lesson, he turned to page two and continued the story himself, even going so far as to meld his voice into that of the characters. Soon she was lost in the world he created, and she never wished to read anything herself again—not when Erik's rendition was so beautiful and moving.

When Papa had told the story, he had simplified it into something appropriate for little ears, but Erik did no such things. The sisters were evil, malevolent creatures and when Erik spoke their words there was a cruelty to his tone which made her shiver. The beast was the most terrifying. Deep, rumbling words drowned out almost entirely by growls and hisses.

As she listened, the more she saw why this book was so important to him—why at every turn of the page he would smooth it down most tenderly. At the final climax when the Beast was embraced by his lady love, if she had not been listening so intently she could have missed it, Erik seemed to struggle with the words. This was his story—of what he dreamed could be for him. Only there was no magic spell she could break with the simplest of kisses, no protestations of love.

She cried. She had not meant to, and she was once more berating her childish emotions. But she could not help it, not when the story so very well captured the loneliness of two souls who only had to overcome the horrors of a curse beyond their love. The beast had his failings, had treated her horribly in the beginning, had frightened her beyond what many could endure, yet she still learned to love him. Through *time*.

Erik offered no soothing words, but his touch became a little more firm, a little more reassuring, and she welcomed it.

No matter what she thought, no matter what past mistakes they *both* had made, they were all they had now. She would have to learn to look beyond his dreadful ugliness, beyond his penchant for murder and bloodshed, and he would have to learn to trust her, be gentle with her, and to give her time to love him.

But *together*—maybe—just maybe—they could learn to be happy.

VIII

Erik knew nothing of love. His childhood had been devoid of any such manifestations which could possibly be confused as affections, and his adult life had proved similar. Until now.

Christine was currently pressed against him in such a delicious torture he knew no equivalent. No earthly pleasure he had tested could ever be sufficient now that he had felt the warmth of her skin radiate into his cold sinews.

He read to her. That had not been his intent as he led her into the sitting room, but as he heard her stumble over each unfamiliar word, he knew she would soon lose patience. And he was loath to allow her to move from his side as he could not possibly anticipate when she would be so willing in the future.

But she had made him stay with her the night before—on their wedding night. When such passions should have been awoken for the both of them, they were cruelly denied by the same world which so despised him. Was that God's way of mocking him for his treachery of ensnaring such an angel?

She had let him kiss her precious head. Perhaps she was expecting him to brush her lovely lips with his, but as he stared at such innocence, he could not risk their contamination with his sin once more. And yet—she had not died when he kissed her at the altar. She had not recoiled, and her tears had not increased. Though they certainly had been present.

Oh how they tormented him! She was always crying. And somehow, he was always the cause. He was a fool to think he could do anything but cause her pain. She was such a good girl. He had watched her grow, and he knew better than anyone how malleable she could be. That *boy* had taken advantage of her naïve innocence, almost to his very demise.

She had told him they were only pretending at their engagement, but he knew the truth. Such pretty lies she could weave! But no more. These thoughts always consumed him, no matter how much he might try to control their vicious stings.

She had stayed. She wanted to be his *wife*. He rolled the words around his mind but no matter how he tried, they would not take hold. He wanted to believe her—he would *die* to believe her—yet it seemed such an impossibility.

Her hair tickled his throat. Even though she tried to contain it with her delicate twists, he could still feel the silken strands caress his skin. He wanted to touch it. Each time he allowed himself that one small delight, the tremors he felt lasted long after he had released her.

When she had tried to storm to her room in that childish display of petulance, he had not thought, merely reacted. She was walking away. He grasped the first thing his fingers could, and he pulled. When she landed on his lap, he had to stop breathing. He had carried her—on multiple occasions—but it had not felt like this. She was warm and pliable, and every delicate curve and slope begged to be skimmed. Just to—*feel*.

He had not felt anything for such a very long time. It was better that way—safer. When his emotions swirled, clouding the already turbulent current of his thoughts, his actions could not be predicted. He knew what a dangerous force he could be. Years of finely honed skill were a terrible thing to unleash.

He missed her smile. The radiance that shone forth from her rosebud mouth as her sparkling eyes bestowed the receiver with such warmth. While they had never been directed at *him* he had benefitted from witnessing them in the stolen moments of her instruction.

And she was his *wife*. She should smile when he gave her pretty things, or when he touched her hair, or when he made her breakfast. He had yet to make her proper meals as their married life had not as of yet been conducive to his full culinary capabilities. He had learned for *her*. He had no true interest in the art, visible by his painfully thin body—the body of a corpse. Good wine was what he appreciated, something to be savoured as he lost himself in the seductive powers of his music, not lavish meals to be eaten alone.

But now—she said she wished to cook for him. Like a *real* wife. She would sit at the table with him, sipping her wine that stained her lips that most perfect shade of red, while he dutifully ate whatever she deemed to put on his plate. Like a good husband should.

If her reading skills were an indication of her ability to follow a recipe, he would be choking down some rueful meals to be sure, but he would do it gladly as his Christine was the one to care enough to put forth the effort.

Oh how he loved her! Her breath blew small puffs of warm air onto his evening jacket, reminding him of her very real, very living presence. But he wondered how long she would be content to sit here in the silence, and he did not know if he could bear to see her walk away.

Such had been his motives the last few days. Whenever she would enact some small kindness, even just to look at him without hatred or malice that he knew her to be capable of, he felt like weeping. His own poor mother had never been able to do so, and here this sweet child made him feel like he could be more than he had ever been before. But it would have to come to an end. If he allowed it, she would turn back into the trembling weeping child who had stayed with him before, and he could not bear to see her cry.

So he lashed out at her—both in fear and in genuine feeling. Oh but how he truly loved her! He *did!* Even when his blood boiled that she could continue to think of the *boy* even after their marriage, how her eyes would cloud and he knew her thoughts to stray to the life she could not have. Whenever she was particularly kind she would have a stricken look of remorse that nearly obliterated the rapture of her sweetness.

He had spoken of how he wished to lie with her—of how cherished she would be if ever they consummated their union. But how could he possibly consider such a thing? Could ever really hurt her in such a way? He was no fool. He knew she would feel pain, whether from the act itself or from the mere fact that it was *him* upon her—within her.

But he longed for her. Not even full contact. Even if she would allow him to hold her—touch her. He would not think of the absolute bliss he would feel if ever *she* were to touch *him.* That was far more than he deserved. His body was tainted, both by the physical scars that he had born since birth and cruelty of others not fit for this world. She had not seen his face since their marriage, and he fully intended for it to remain hidden. Perhaps she could forget, could grow used to seeing only a mask and never the true flesh of her husband. Then maybe she could love him.

He sighed. Those were the dreams of a man possessed. Whatever rational thought persisted in the recesses of his mind laughed at such notions. She now knew he had not killed her precious boy, the *Daroga* had seen to that. He thought if he could keep her in ignorance she would continue to stay out of sheer necessity, but still she had stayed.

For now.

She stirred against his side, and made to pull away. What vulnerability that could possibly have escaped from his musings was quickly sequestered beneath the practiced blankness of his visage.

"Thank you."

Ah yes, she was thanking him for entertaining her with pretty words and tones. What fascinated him more than her platitudes was the small smile that tugged at her lips. Though not nearly as vibrant as ones he had witnessed from some hidden alcove, it was for *him* and thus worth cherishing.

"Are we agreed?" She looked at him expectantly, and he suddenly wondered if he had missed some word or gesture that would have belayed her meaning. When he simply continued to look at her, she saw her plump lip turn slightly downward, and he longed to tug it back into a more flatting expression.

"Are we agreed that I am a helpless case?" When he remained staring uncomprehendingly, she pressed on. "Besides, you reading to me is so very nice." It was true; she had a long way to go before she could easily settle in with one of his many books and happily waste the day away, but he was by no means giving up on her. He had been able to teach himself to read, and quite proudly, with little difficulty.

What Christine lacked in mental aptitude, she made up for in beauty.

Perhaps that was shallow of him, perhaps it was some sort of compensation for his own physical inadequacies, but he would not change her for the world. And he would gladly trade his genius for the blessed curse of normalcy.

She had a stubborn curl that blatantly refused any sort of coaxing on her part to remain in whatever tangle she wished for it to be kept, and its constant presence tormented him. He knew the silken texture it held, only outmatched by the satin of her skin. Both of which could be felt if he allowed himself the pleasure of tucking it behind her ear.

And he did.

Each gesture was a test on his part—of her fortitude and his own. The more he did, the more he longed for such contact again, and the more she endured, the more he believed she *could* endure without perishing under the weight of his affections.

Their reading lesson had squandered many hours, and though he thought little of food for himself, he knew she would be wanting for a midday meal. Not that it was midday. He had found down here in the bitter cold and darkness, days stretched far longer than a normal man's. If he was not careful, it was easy to be swept into months and years without any knowledge of the rising of the sun and moon. He kept one gold pocket watch, one that held no history or meaning. It was a bauble he had purchased on a whim after… well, after he had found Christine.

Time was not important as he ghosted through the halls of the Opera House. The interior was vast, and little sunlight entered the garish interworkings of his home. For that matter, he rarely left the intricate labyrinth of his own construction. But when he had found his Angel, the matter of time began to matter.

A creature of light, she rose with the sun and slept with the moon. Scheduled meetings had to be kept, and it was imperative he be able to time her schedules to their fullest extent. But every plan had its flaws. Though he tried to remember her needs, too often he would be in such a state of ecstasy from the pure joy produced by her voice he would keep her well beyond any reasonable hour. Her body would begin to quiver, her eyes would droop, yet she never begged to be released.

Oh no. Such beseeching only occurred when he had physically taken her to his home. And even though she had revealed through the removal of his mask precisely what kind of monster adored her, he could not regret it. Not when it led to his ring on her finger, and her acknowledgement of their marriage. But now his wife needed to be fed, and he had to be sensitive to her needs. Such was the nature of marriage after all.

Christine stared at him with wide eyes as he rose, and he sighed. Every movement must be carefully judged so as not to frighten his skittish bride. Was he truly that unpredictable? He thought her to be the one whose actions could not be foreseen.

"Must you look at your poor Erik that way?" His words turned rather petulant. "Perhaps you would prefer me to remain seated all day while I allow you to starve?"

She laughed. *Laughed.* Not the hysterical sound he had heard come from her glorious throat when stress had become too much for her, but a whimsical sound that reminded him of flowers and sunshine—both unfamiliar objects.

"I am sorry Erik, I do not mean to laugh. You just..." Another giggle escaped her lips and he thought perhaps he misjudged her—hysteria was common enough in young women...

"I believe you!" She believed what? This girl confounded him. Her every action held such infinite possibility as to intent he could not possibly be expected to understand, yet she apparently *did* expect such a thing.

He sighed again, frustration creeping in at her ability to make *him* feel like the moronic child. "You believe what, Christine?"

She must have sensed his change in mood for she quickly sobered. "I believe you will take care of me." Her eyes fell to her hands as she twiddled each delicate finger. His frustration ebbed as he wished to slide his hand between hers and see if she would be willing to play with *his* fingers. "I know I said it before, but for the first time... when you said that... I realised how it had never occurred to me that you would *not* care for me."

He nearly rolled his eyes at her nonsense. Had he not been telling her those very words for months, if not years? What had now changed to make her finally believe them? When she rose to follow him to the dining room there was obviously the slightest twinge of pain as she moved her hip.

And he felt angry—so *very* angry.

Angry at himself for not being able to control his anger enough to keep from hurting her. He was angry at that bastard for touching what was his. *Hurting* what was his. But he was also angry at her. And that made him nearly fall on the floor to beg for absolution. He was angry she could only come to believe him after he had saved her. Now any future feelings she blessedly may come to feel would not have to be subject to scrutiny as he determined whether they were from gratitude or genuine affection.

And he hated it.

He killed a man yesterday. On his wedding day. How fitting that his marriage should be christened with blood. Not the smattering of blood of a virgin bride as her husband opened her upon their marriage bed, but the cooling blood of one he had murdered. He had not thought about it since he had left the corpse behind, but as he reflected, it mattered little. At most the Opera would have to find a new driver to employ, and he certainly felt no remorse.

More curtly than she seemed to expect judging from the slight flinch, he told her to follow. He would allow her free reign of his kitchen soon, but not until she had a proper meal in her stomach while she explored the cupboards and familiarised herself with its workings. Until such a time, he would continue to provide her sustenance.

The kitchen was a small room with only a few shelves and cupboards as well as the stove. Truthfully it was the warmest room in the house as his sitting room's fireplace had been damaged with the turning of the Scorpion. When they entered he saw Christine shuffle toward the range slightly, drawn in by its warmth. He had become more adept in its upkeep since she arrived, as her meals required its maintenance far more than his needs demanded, but the constant wood burning was tedious, and already his mind was making plans for renovations. Perhaps a form of kerosene could provide a flame for heat...

Christine cleared her throat and he grimaced at the sound. He had been indulging her lately, though for good reason, he knew. Like many youths, Christine had a fondness for sweets and for years she had obeyed him resolutely when he demanded she consume no more than absolutely necessary so as to preserve the tonal quality of her voice.

"Are you going to eat with me this time?" She looked at him with such resignation, as though she already knew his answer but still held the slight hope that by enquiring she could change his response.

"Do you wish for me to eat?" Her eyes lit up all the more by his question, and she visibly stood a little straighter.

"Oh yes! I am not used to eating by myself." Her tone turned rather sheepish. "And it feels rather odd to have you watch me." He chuckled at her naivety. He *always* watched her, long before she ever graced his home with her presence, and whether or not he also had a plate of food before him would do little to change such a habit.

"Do you have a preference?" He began taking stock of the remaining food stores. She peered curiously over his shoulder, intrigued at seeing what was available for the first time. Though this was the second time she had been with him while he cooked, it was the first she was in possession of all her faculties.

She pointed to the cured ham and baguette and he promptly set about putting together the very commonplace meal. However, when he only prepared one and began to gather a drink for his wife, she gave him a glare before going to the fixings herself. And prepared him a sandwich.

Christine had said she wished to make him meals, but actually witnessing such an event was staggering.

She *cared.*

Whether it was duty, or from genuine feelings of affection and—dare he think it—*love,* he was no longer sure it mattered. There were many marriages that began from some sort of contractual arrangement, not the humble stirrings of young adoration.

And she was such a very good girl; he could not imagine her instigating any sort of affections. Could he risk it? He would be putting his very soul into her delicate white hands as he asked to hold her—*kiss* her—and he was not sure he could survive the rejection.

But if she did—if she were to spurn his attentions in a horrific display of fear and disgust, he would rather die than continue in such a world. She was still wounded, and he knew there was no possibility of true union until she was free from such physical torment, but her lips were unmarred from the savage ravishment she had endured.

And he had the seductive prowess and music and age that she could not possibly hope to overcome. All that was required was the sacrifice of his morality—something he had lost long ago. And had he embraced the dark so very long ago? Perhaps his wife, with her quintessential *goodness,* perhaps she could survive being tainted with his presence. Perhaps through *her* he could receive his salvation.

Was it not through her companionship he was finally admitted into the very cloister that had shunned him for the whole of his life? Her purity might cleanse his soul from the egregious sin that held him in such a state of revulsion with Christine's *God.*

And he knew then it was up to him—with all his madness, rage, and genius—he would be the one to purify himself through the sanctification of their union. So when she looked at him with sheer innocence and barely concealed nervousness as she held *his* sandwich, he knew it was right. For she was his wife.

And his wife wished to eat with him. She wished for him to read to her, to *sing* to her, and if last night were to be believed, wished to *sleep* beside him. And perhaps, someday, she would wish to love him. Perhaps, if he could show her how supremely gentle he could be while she continued her convalescence, she would come to wish for his touch as well. She had asked to be a wife instead of his prisoner, and if that were to be born, he would have to learn to be a husband instead of her keeper.

He had been her Angel, her Maestro, but now—with a sudden burst of clarity that outshone the dreadful cloud of madness which was a constant vice upon his mind—now he wished to be her *husband*.

So he gathered *two* goblets of water, *two* napkins, and placed them before *two* dining chairs. And then, when both plates were set before each unsure spouse, he finally looked back at her, with hope for the rest of their future meals—for *both* of them.

"Yes, perhaps I shall dine with you."

And she *smiled*.

IX

Christine had no idea that making such an item could fill her with such a feeling of warmth. Of course it was not really the meal that was important, but that Erik seemed to be—*trying*. He had not said if he was willing to make this into a real marriage, but his simple act of sitting with her while his long, deft fingers wrapped around the sandwich *she* had made for him made her feel proud, and she could not help the smile that emerged, nor did she suppress it as she had felt prone to do in Erik's presence before now.

It was a simple meal, and truthfully she had not been very hungry to begin with, but she ate because Erik wished for her to do so, and now, as she happily munched on the crusty bread and meat she was infinitely glad of his suggestion. It was such an insignificant thing, she knew, and it was foolish for her to value his acquiescence so highly. For all she knew, he might regularly eat at this time therefore nullifying the gesture.

But the way he watched her as he deliberately took each bite, not to see if she ate, but to see that she saw *him* eating made such a routine seem unlikely. He did not speak again, but that might have been due to his small bites and careful chews. She had not considered it before, but the mask would act as an encumbrance for the normal range of motion so quickly taken for granted to others as they chewed freely. She suddenly felt guilty.

It was due to her comfort he remained covered, and she had not allowed him but a few moments alone since her—*move*—to his home. At first that was due to no fault of her own, seeing as it was his whim which determined where she was kept in relation to his person. But recently it had been *her* who begged for his continued presence, disallowing him to see to any personal needs he might have required. And she knew he would never reveal himself to her if there was breath left in his too thin body. Satisfied by his eating and how comfortable this silence seemed to be as opposed to the oppressive weight she was sadly growing used to, she made no attempt at conversation.

Soon their morsels were naught but crumbs, and she rose to clear the dishes before he could do the same. Determined this time to successfully complete the dishes, she hurried to place the dirty plates in the water from breakfast, only to find that what once had been a steaming vat of liquid had given way to the chilly temperatures of the underground climate.

With a sigh she placed their luncheon dishes on an empty counter and tried to locate how Erik had heated the water to begin with. On the stove was a large cast iron pot which upon consideration she could not possibly lift without aid. And having to ask Erik for such menial assistance was precisely what she was trying to avoid.

Seeing no other course, Christine made to lift the water filled basin in hopes of pouring the contents successfully into the awaiting vessel for heating. But as she situated her hands around the wide rim, she was suddenly pulled away by a firm and insistent tug.

"What are you *doing?*" Erik was looming above her, but instead of anger there was a sort of disbelief about him, as though he could not understand her very action.

She huffed in response as she stepped away from him. "I believe you have asked that very question before." He continued to stare at her, obviously not satisfied with her explanation. "I am going to heat the dish water."

"You are going to fall and douse yourself with water, you foolish girl." He made the statement so factually for a moment she forgot to be offended and nearly believed him.

In her outrage she moved to prove him wrong but he quickly stepped in her path and poured the basin into the awaiting pot and stoked the fire to encourage a faster boil. When convinced of the range's cooperation, he turned back to her. "Have you so quickly forgotten your injuries?" His eyes narrowed slightly. "Or perhaps you enjoy me changing your bandages?"

She flushed at the thought. Of course she had not forgotten, but she was certainly doing everything in her power to push such memories from the forefront of her mind. And *she* did not believe herself to be so incompetent as to be unable to walk over a—relatively—smooth surface without saturation.

Erik sighed as he took in her slightly protruding lower lip which had settled into an obvious display of pouting, and began opening cupboards. Curious by his action as he could not possibly be about to make her yet another meal, she was surprised when he began listing off available foods, as well as the location for utensils, plates, goblets, tea things and the like. There were not many of each, and rarely more than two. She wondered if he had obtained additional place settings because of her or simply because it made for less imperative washings. The thought left her feeling bereft either way.

By the time he was showing her the few cookbooks which lined one small shelf to the left of the range, the water was simmering pleasantly, and using a nearby towel as a barrier from the heated metal, returned the steaming water into the basin. He did not remove himself from his position, and the thoughts returned that luncheon had not meant what her silly mind had twisted it into, and she sadly watched him fill the basin with both the breakfast and lunch plates and goblets.

And then he removed his coat. It was such a startling act she stood wide eyed and simply stared, but when he placed it unworriedly upon the counter and began to unbutton his cuffs she was truly astounded. She had lived with this man for weeks and never once had she seen him in less than formal attire, yet he was now standing before her, rolling up the sleeves of his crisp white dress shirt preparing to wash *their* dishes.

She had never seen so much of his skin before. Of course there was the withered skin which comprised his face, as well as the slender, skeletal hands which she had become so familiar, but perhaps she had thought his wrists and forearms would be—different. They were not. Terribly thin, yet deceptively strong, she knew, and they were covered by the same papery skin as what other flesh to which she had been exposed. The only difference she could see were the tiny white lines which marred the delicate skin.

Scars.

She blinked stupidly at him for a moment more, only to be removed from his revelry when his voice broke the silence. He was not meeting her eye, in fact he seemed to be resolutely staring at the proffered item—a towel. "You may dry."

Oh. He meant for them to work *together*. Still shocked by this new development, she rather stiffly took the towel in hand and dutifully dried every dish handed to her. She was able to put her kitchen tour to good use as she remembered most everywhere they belonged, and only on two occasions did she have to ask, to which Erik would give a patient direction.

Soon, they were finished and the kitchen was returned to a proper place of order, and she felt rather bonded to Erik now that they had completed such a menial task together. As she placed the last utensil in its proper drawer, Erik came very close to her side and waited for her to turn towards him.

"Come."

The last time she had followed such a command led to her rather humiliating reading lesson, but she knew better than to disobey him when he made such forceful requests. He bypassed the settee where they had spent so much of their recent hours, and instead took them beyond to the immense organ which towered menacingly above them both. She knew what sweet melodies he could extract from the ivory keys, but far too often she had born the soul numbing sounds of his anger and rage poured exactingly from the silver pipes.

Warily she sat, not at all sure of his mood as he gave little away as he stood for a moment longer watching her. She certainly had no knowledge of how to play the instrument, and was curious as to why he had set her here while he remained motionless. His lack of conversation was tiring, for whenever he was silent she always assumed there was some important detail she was missing that would have alleviated her doubts quite quickly, but as she groped in her mind for any such hint, she could only assume he wished to have a music lesson with her.

Though the notion of him singing filled her with delight, now that she considered her own state of health she found her throat to be rather sore. It did not hurt to swallow, but there was a residual ache as if she had wrenched her neck rather painfully, and she doubted she would be able to manage any form of voice to his stringent standards.

All thoughts of her sweetened tea were slowly melting away and she mourned the loss acutely. It was ridiculous to have become so attached after such a short time, but ones preferences in regards to tea was highly personal, and his demanding her acquiesce to *his* desire for her steaming cup of liquid delight was quite infuriating.

The longer she sat, the more troubled she became. Why was he just standing there? But she dared not question him, for while they were in the world of his music, *he* was the Maestro, and she but his humble protégée.

He did not bid her rise only to replace himself on the bench, nor did he bark at her to begin her scales. He moved to the far corner of the room, where an unobtrusive black case leaned quietly against the wall. As he brought it nearer, she could make out the sumptuous lines which could only house the familiar object of a violin.

He had once told her of the nature of his music. Don Juan Triumphant would burn her very soul, while Mozart would only make her weep. As he placed the violin tenderly beneath his chin, she wondered what emotions he would wish to draw from her—for he could play *her* just as well as any instrument in his possession. And it frightened her.

She closed her eyes as she helplessly allowed him to communicate without the words he failed to express, nor the words she could not bear to hear. If Don Juan had been a terrible sob, the beginning of this refrain would have been the accompanying wail. Such sorrow and loneliness were so blatantly clear it took her only a moment to feel the welling of tears as they accompanied her emotions which so rapidly mirrored his own.

Wanting to confirm the forlorn feeling, she struggled to open her eyes to see if Erik felt the same melancholy which had come upon her. But before such action could be taken, the air shifted. No longer the oppressive weight of longing and despair, the melody began spreading dulcet tones of sweetness. Gentle notes covered her in the softest of caresses as they put forth visions of warmth and happiness, and she remembered the days in her girlhood as she ran along sandy beaches while the waves lapped teasingly at her feet. But still there was an undercurrent of something—more.

And the undercurrent suddenly overtook what once was sweet and soft and so very lovely, melting into something powerful and strange—and this time her eyes did fly open as they sought her husband. His eyes were not closed, but they watched her carefully, and his eyes blazed with a passion she did not recognise. They did not burn with the anger she had seen so very often, but instead there was the longing of the first, mixed with the love of the second, only to be outshone by a hitherto which required—something.

She did not know why, but she felt like she needed to go to him—to beg his fingers to stop their torturous fury upon the strings even as he continued to play. Her breath came in pants as she was hit by wave after wave of soul absconding song, and her tears resumed, even as quickly as they had been diminished due to the charming comfort of the second movement.

When she felt she could bear no more, Erik again twisted the refrain once more, into the most joyous rapture she had ever endured. All hints of longing and sorrow had dissipated until no more than a haunting memory remained. Jubilantly his fingers moved, but she could no longer bear to look as her tears remained as her turbulent emotions could not accept any more transformations.

The music trailed off with an expert flourish that only Erik could hope to perform, and they were both left winded and drained. She remembered how she had longed to go to him, but her body refused to move, and Erik seemed just as frozen as she.

Her tears did not quiet, and he stared at them for a long moment before coming forward and kneeling before her. Must he always do such a thing?

"Forgive your Erik, Christine, perhaps you were not ready." He had grasped her hands between his, and as she looked at them she could see the indentations where the strings had pressed unmercifully into the pads of his fingers.

She shook her head, not at all certain of what he spoke, but desperately needing to hear an explanation for such discordant sounds. "Erik, what was that?"

He moaned into her hands and he grasped them, not truly mindful of how sharp his bones were against her own fingers, but she did little to try to loosen them. "You asked to be able to talk to your poor Erik, but he does not know the words. So he tries to *show* you." He looked at her then, eyes wide and imploring as he poured out the utmost of his soul, just as his music had done while she listened.

"Erik was so very alone, even when you were with him, for poor Christine was always thinking of her *boy* and never of how she hurt her Erik." She remembered the despair and supreme loneliness he had made her feel while he played, and the guilt threatened to crush her under its weight. She had not meant to hurt him! He just seemed to never understand the magnitude of his action—how they hurt *her*. So she lashed out in her thoughtless manner which did nothing more than anger him, but now she realised, he was not angry. It was the desperate lashing of a wounded panther as the thoughtless girl continued to poke it with a sharpened spear. She felt so very sorry, but remained silent so as not to discourage him from continuing his explanation.

"But then you agreed to be my wife." One of his hands released hers and she flexed them slightly to restore what circulation had been lost while his stroked her cheek ever so slightly. She did not pull away, nor did she lean into his touch, but he did not seem to mind her inaction. "And Erik is so very happy to be with you. And you let him kiss your pretty lips when we were married, and Erik *tries* to tell himself he needs no more, but..." his words trailed off as his fingers found their favourite curl and twisted it into a covering of silk for his dead digit.

And that was the sweetness. If his refrain should be believed, and judging from her own feelings as he played, he drew comfort from her presence, as well as a peaceful serenity which calmed the spirit. But still, there was a persistent ache which lingered and niggled at the recesses of the mind—a never departing presence.

He moaned again, an even more remorseful sound than the last, but he did not remove his gaze from hers, or his fingers from her curls. "Addiction is a strange thing, Christine. The more Erik touches you," the hand which had been grasping hers trailed tantalisingly on her skin, and it made her shiver. "The more Erik *loves* you, the more Erik *wants* you." His fingers whispered over her lips and finally his eyes diverted to set their desirous gaze onto the plump morsels which tormented him no matter her expression.

She should pull away—*push* him away. That would be the sane gesture performed of the rest of humanity if this being knelt before them, confessing his innermost desires which included such carnal appetites. But with each touch and word she remembered the stirrings of whatever emotion had claimed them both as he played the seductive tones which called her to him. And though she was frightened and did not fully understand the implication, she remained still, simply allowing him to do as he wished. For was that not his right as her husband?

But it truly did not feel that way. She was not submitting to his caresses simply because he bore the title of husband, but from remembered tremors which had beseeched her body for his touch. And she was horribly confused.

His face neared hers and she continued to tremble from the onslaught of emotions and reactions, and her hand clutched fervently at his wrist where she could feel his heart drumming mercilessly in his chest. Christine remained frozen, unable to move or even blink. As Erik leaned even further, gauging her reaction with each minute advance, a scream rose up in her throat—whether from terror or exultation, she could not answer—but she did not release it. For as soon as it threatened to escape, as soft as a feather against her hand, Erik allowed his lips to touch hers.

He pulled away, and his eyes were intently searching her face for any sort of reaction. But there was none to be found as she had not yet absorbed the pleasant numbness that had seeped into her skin at his touch, and she had not settled on the entire lack of—*revulsion* that she should have felt.

But Erik could not read her thoughts, and as she sat upon the bench entirely unmoving as her thoughts swarmed within her own pretty head, he could not bear it and stood. Surely she was entirely disgusted by him, and she probably was about their kiss upon the altar that he held most dear to his heart.

"Christine should leave her Erik now."

Christine did not know what thoughts troubled Erik, but when she looked at his shuttered eyes, and the stiffness of his posture has he stood and moved away from her, she knew it was best not to pry. Feeling utterly rejected by his obvious displeasure from their kiss, she moved to her room feeling oddly hollow.

It stung more that what kisses *she* might find pleasant would be so repulsive to *him* and her hopes for their future marital harmony. She sat on her bed twisting the sleeves of her dress as she did so, wondering what Erik must be feeling. For him to send her away would mean he was either in a temper or about to enter into one if provoked. But had she not determined that his anger was a result of hidden pain?

And it was the duty of a wife to comfort her husband. She would not enquire, nor pester him with questions as to the source of his pain. But she would not leave him alone.

Steeling her courage, she cautiously entered the room awaiting harsh words of displeasure at her disobedience. But when she saw his crumpled form as he sat upon the organ bench, his poor masked head in his equally dead fingers, she was consumed with the deepest of sorrows. Even if he chose to rage at her, she would stand her ground. Because he had reassured her when her Papa had passed, and though she did not know the source of his misery, she would be his comfort as well.

As quietly as she could so as not to startle him before she could perform her intent, she sank to the floor below him. He looked at her, and she saw the beginnings of anger overtake the desolation of his eyes, but before he could speak, she took his head in her hands, and pressed *her* lips to his.

This kiss was not the frantic pandering of her frightened self after her attack, but it was the kiss a wife would give to her husband when words could not possibly offer enough to soothe. It was not simply a brush of warmth against cold, but a pressing of her will that he *feel* her compassion, and when his lips moved ever so slightly against hers in return, she knew he had relented. His fingers found purchase in her hair, and she felt the fine silk strands of his own.

They were both breathing harshly when at last they parted, and she stroked his masked cheek tenderly. "What did the fourth movement mean?"

His own fingers mimicked hers as they brushed against her cheek in the same reverence one would caress the finest of china. "We can be happy, Christine. Erik *swears* it. When we are one, when we both are *whole*, together we will have the most joyous of marriages."

And she believed him.

X

"Do not scratch, Christine."

She sent him a hateful glare as she tried desperately not to give in to the terrible urge to treat her tender new skin with the relentless scratching it so demanded. This was *his* fault.

Not the bites themselves of course. She was not so uncomfortable as to blame him for those, but he was deliberately withholding the soothing balm which quieted the dreadful compulsion. He said that if applied too often it would not allow the scabs to breathe; therefore there would be a greater likelihood of scars. And apparently it would "not do to have her pretty white skin so permanently evidenced of her mistreatment."

She had huffed, even kissed him lightly but he merely offered to play her something sweet and soft to distract her, but feeling put out that even her *kiss* should do nothing to move him, she took the book of fairy tales he had been reading with her and shut herself in her room to properly sulk.

But when she plopped on her bed she suddenly felt lonesome. Though she supposed it was still considered *her* room, it had not been used strictly by her since their wedding. Every night Erik would come in to say goodnight after giving her time to change into her nightdress as well as any ablutions necessary before sleep. But he would always linger in the doorway, not so subtly eying the empty side of the bed even as she lay in her own. She would wonder if tonight was the night he would insist he partake of his husbandly rights, but each night she concluded that perhaps it was worth risking such matters so long as she would not have to be alone.

So each night she would ask him to stay, and she could not determine if his sigh was from exasperation at the inconvenience or relief that she would ask it of him. And he would settle a top the bedclothes beside her, never beneath, and he never touched her. She would try to keep her eyes from succumbing to sleep for she was terribly curious to know if he slept—and the morbid part which she tried desperately to ignore wished to know if he ever removed his mask. The more she thought of the dreadfully necessary object, the more she wished to test her fortitude in regards to her Erik's face. For how could they have a proper marriage when she could not bear to look at the face of her husband?

Ever since their kiss before the organ, he had been more attentive than before. Though his touch had always been gentle when he tended to her wounds, now he was being exceptionally tender. Never once did he add more pressure than absolutely necessary, and he would even hum a soothing melody if she should ever feel discomfort.

She would catch him staring at her lips throughout the day, especially when they read together. The second time they had breakfasted—upon much pleading on her part that he should eat— she looked at him expectantly, wondering what she should do next. When all that was given was the same questioning stare, she rather timidly asked him to read to her. They had retired to the sitting room and Erik and chosen the Hans Christian Anderson before he simply—stood.

She had sat on the settee and watched his eyes flicker from the place at her side to the leather reading chair situated near it. He was waiting for her to *choose*. So staring into his eyes, she slid her hand to the seat next to her and patted it gently as an invitation. And he came with a muttered, "Such a needy wife I have." But when he sat so very close and petted her hair affectionately, it made her feel like it was a very pleasant thing indeed to be a needy wife, and settled in for a lovely morning with her husband.

But now she was sitting in her bedroom utterly alone. It was a rare thing these days for any sort of solitude, and though admittedly she was the one to have instigated it, being away from his ever watchful eye was reminding her that such was the healing process and it was not his fault.

And she truly did not want any reminders of that incident, so instead of storming from him like a child she should be grateful for his efforts. Perhaps a song would distract her from the horrible burning itch that only succeeded in turning her skin a vibrant shade of pink. Erik had said that though it matched her blush quite becomingly, it was not worth the lasting effect.

When she had determined to return to Erik to ask forgiveness and plead for the proffered diversion, there was a soft knock upon the door. She did not doubt who it was, though she did startle slightly at the sound and its potential meaning. He had not once raised his voice to her in the days since their kiss. Was it a week? Ten days? She had no way of knowing. She had asked him once for a calendar and he had looked at her as though she had suddenly begun to speak in a foreign tongue, and she had let the subject drop for fear he would think she was discontent in the secluded world that was his home.

She rose from the bed and cautiously opened the door. As presumed, Erik's tall frame shadowed the doorway, and he seemed to find the carpets to be very interesting specimens which required thorough attention. Christine stepped back and returned to her position on the bed, allowing him to speak in his own time instead of press him for his reasoning behind his entrance as was her wont.

He stepped into the room slowly, and his eyes appraised her for a moment before shifting back to the floor with a sigh. "Erik is very sorry, Christine."

She wished he would look at her so she might better judge his frame of mind. "What have you done to be sorry for?" His fingers twitched, and though she could not tell how, she *knew* he was wishing to be closer to her. "Would you like to sit?" She made a gesture to the bed, and he sighed once more, though this time she knew it was in relief.

The fingers which had been so unsettled seemed pleased at their closer contact as he settled beside her, and they even went so far as to fiddle with the a bit of trim which adorned her skirt. "I am sorry I cannot give my wife what she asks. I am sorry I made Christine angry." He peered at her rather accusingly though his words did not reflect the emotion. "Erik is sorry you left him."

She felt wretched. If she felt the bitter pangs of loneliness from the few minutes she spent away from his company, she could not imagine how he must have felt not knowing if the pleasant days they had spent together had at last come to an end. Her eyes became misty at the thought, but she blinked determinedly against them in hopes of quelling such emotions before they would overwhelm her.

One of her delicate hands found the chilly palm of Erik's own, and she held it while she leaned forward and closed the short distance between them. Though she only brushed his covered cheek with her lips, he still gave a tiny moan of bliss at her gesture, and his hand tightened considerably around hers.

"I am not angry, Erik, and I am sorry I upset you." She shifted again as her mind drifted back to the reason behind her frustration. "I have just been terribly uncomfortable today and I took it out on you, and that was wrong of me. Do you forgive me?"

Erik gave a sound of complete derision, which from any other man would have greatly resembled a snort. His fingers skimmed her cheek and he looked at her with such sadness and love it made her heart flutter. "Angels should not apologise to their captors."

She closed her eyes to stop the horrible feeling of despair that washed over her at his words. She *refused* for him to think such thoughts. She would rather he catch her as she fell from the pedestal he placed her on then live her life alone in the clouds. "Erik, you are my *husband,* not my captor, and you must accept that I shall make mistakes as well." She fiddled with the button at his collar as she thought of which words could possibly express to him the imperative nature that he understand her fallibility.

"You think that I am perfect, but I fear that love has blinded you. You cannot bear my faults as well as your own." She did not think he believed her as his expression did not falter, nor did his hand release her. But perhaps with time he would come to understand they could only be truly happy when they were equal. As for now, she would be content with whatever agreeable mood he would give her. "You offered to play for me… would you still?"

He looked thoughtful for a moment before he leaned toward her, and pressed his lips to her temple. "I suppose if I must." She was glad he complied so easily, and he did not begrudge her the momentary lapse in good wifery, no matter how he huffed and his words portrayed it as an inconvenience.

Erik held her hand as he brought her back into the sitting room, but he deposited her on the settee before going to the immense organ and seating himself. His fingers caressed the keys for a moment, almost as if he were contemplating which song was begging to be released from the confines of the pipes and ivory.

He had lied to her. Mozart could not only make her weep, in Erik's capable hands it had the ability to liven her spirit from the daily drudge of gloom and confusion which threatened to become her natural state of being. There was clarity in the music not to be found in her constant struggles to understand Erik's whims. The music was quietly cheerful and did more to heal her emotional conflict than the cream had done for her wounds. Erik could show her through his music what his words and actions failed to, and at the moment the light, airy sounds caressing her ears told her that Erik was happy.

But his happiness, she learned, was not to be contained in domestic evening concerts for her sake. His exuberance and unfettered joy erupted into boundless creativity, which resulted in him refusing to leave the organ for more than a few moments at a time. Oh yes, he had played for her, but to her sorrow it had lent him to spend days on end preoccupied with new compositions. Most times he would not even play, but would simply remain hunched over the organ frantically scrawling out harmonies and arrangements without pause. The first day she tried to coax him away with sweet words or promised touches, but he silenced her with a "desist, woman!" and turn back to his music.

He no longer slept with her, and she woke up multiple times with nightmares plaguing her vision. On such occasions, he would shift his playing to a soothing lullaby, but the ache would never fully leave her chest as she drifted back to sleep. She *missed* him.

After the third restless night she determined her day would be spent differently. Her reading was steadily improving, much as her voice lessons had done when she truly began to practice and apply herself to the task. She would tidy up the rooms, though she earned a rather dreadful glare when Erik caught her straightening his papers.

But not today.

While exploring the kitchen—a necessity when Erik was no longer responsible for her meals—she had discovered a rather simple cookbook which housed many different recipes that seemed quite simple to follow. But more importantly, she could recognise most of the ingredients without having to beg Erik for translations.

The mastery of baking was an art she had yet to even attempt, let alone prove competent. She had the cookbook open to a very simple recipe for sweet biscuits, but the flour proved quite uncooperative, even going so far as to explode quite unhelpfully when she attempted to lift it. She knew it was wrong, but she found the kitchen to be quite fairy like when covered with a fine dusting of white powder, though she knew Erik would have a fit when he saw it. Obviously her cleaning skills were to be tested as well.

The sugar fared much better, and she only spilled a few granules on the side of the bowl which she promptly pressed onto her finger then adeptly moved into her mouth. She found baking to be quite enjoyable. The directions were more difficult to follow than understanding the ingredients required, and she could not comprehend what it was asking her to do with the butter. Instead of asking Erik for assistance, she decided that guessing was an excellent alternative to risking her husband's temper, so she simply added it into her large bowl as well as the proper allotment of eggs. The recipe demanded salt, and it seemed quite an odd thing to add to sugary confections, but once more she found she could not understand the amount. Taking the small teaspoon she had found, she filled it to the brim before adding it to her congealing bowl of powders and eggs.

She took a large wooden spoon and mixed until the sticky dough looked thoroughly combined, and with unpractised hands she spooned them onto a large metal pan she had found by the oven. She had seen such biscuits in tiny bakery shops of course, and they always came out looking perfectly round and very delicious. And she was sure Erik would be impressed if she could manage such a feat herself, so she took a knife and tried to manipulate each one until she was satisfied with her first attempt.

While they baked she set about preparing Erik's favourite tea. She had watched him prepare it and it certainly seemed simple enough. She would feel like an imposter of a wife if she proved unable to remember something as commonplace yet utterly crucial as her husband's tea preferences. That is what this was after all. Boredom was undoubtedly part of her sudden divergence into the realm of the kitchen, but selfishly she was hoping to lure Erik back into *acting* as her husband if he could see her efforts in acting like a proper *wife*.

When her labours appeared a golden brown—though not *nearly* as perfectly shaped as those in the shops—she carefully removed them from the encasing warmth of the oven, being sure to keep her skin far away from anything able to scorch or maim. When she had eaten these herself they had always been cool, but she felt rather anxious to be in Erik's company once more, so she prepared a plate with a few as well as poured a steaming cup of tea. Though it felt foreign not to add her customary dash of cream, she respected her husband's wishes and simply added a slice of lemon and placed everything on a pretty tray she had found in the bottom corner of a cupboard.

She told herself she was being ridiculous when a flood of nerves unleashed upon her. Though he had been ornery for days, she had to believe he would return to his attentive self at *some* point, and this was certainly the only way she could think to ensure such a happening took place sooner rather than later.

He was still at the organ, but his body was limp and slightly bent and he was—sleeping. She had never seen him in such state of unconsciousness, and while she felt hurt and annoyed that he would go so long ignoring her, seeing him in such an endearing state that none other than *her* would ever see made her feel warm. She was loath to wake him, but the small girl who resided within her demanded he praise her for her tea service, therefore waking him was a necessary evil.

Touching him did not seem wise, as a startled Erik could easily lead to physical damage for her, and anger or weeping on his. And this was meant to be a kind gesture. So instead, she rather noisily placed the tea service on the table next to the organ, while she kept a safe distance away from her slumbering husband.

At the clatter of china plates, he started awake, and turned to look bewilderedly at Christine. She looked at him placidly as his initial reaction was to glare, but as he took in the assortment of items before her he softened. "What is all this for?"

For such a brilliant man he could be quite obtuse. "It is for my *husband* of course, as he has been working very hard and has been refusing to eat." She did not add that he was also refusing to speak to her in a civilised manner, nor spend any of their lovely afternoons on the settee. "I made you sweet biscuits."

His eyes drifted to the plate of sugary confections. "So I see." He looked up at her then, and she tried to communicate how very important it was that he come and sit with her—*anything* but this eternal solitude. He must have understood for he rose stiffly from the bench, and carried the tea tray to the side table. She tried to hide how unhappy it made her that he chose the leather reading chair instead of sitting with her on the settee.

Their settee.

She had never seen Erik so unkempt, for he had hardly been devoting his time to the refined modes of hygiene while possessed by this voracious compulsion to compose. Though she supposed she should not judge as when she looked down at herself she noted that the explosion of flour had not left her unscathed—which certainly explained the odd looks Erik was giving her as well.

"Will you not try one?" She looked at her biscuits fondly. Though they were far from perfect, they were infused with good intention which she hoped he would be able to taste.

Erik settled his teacup on one knee while he reached for a morsel with his other hand. He stared at her while he raised it to his lips, and bit off a small corner which sent crumbles cascading down his rumpled evening suit. There was the slightest downward turn of his mouth as he chewed, and he quickly sipped his tea afterward. Did he not like her baking?

"It was very kind of Christine to bake for her husband." She looked at him expectantly, and he took yet another bite, then another, until at last he had consumed the entire thing. She had heard that men were more pliable when they had evidence of their wife's labours in their stomachs, so she thought now would be the proper time to voice her question.

"Why have you been ignoring me, Erik? I have been quite lonely without your company." He sighed, and deliberately flicked crumbs off his suit so as not to look at her.

"I do not think Christine could understand." She sat a little straighter in indignation.

"You think I *cannot* understand? How could I possibly when you do not try to explain?" Her voice grew slightly quieter. "I thought we were making progress."

He moaned as his hands clenched in his lap. "Christine, you expect too much of your Erik! How can he possibly tell you when he does not wish to admit it to himself?"

There were things, she knew, that were beyond her understanding. But if ever they were to be honest with one another, their relationship would have to be born of communication—which Erik was sorely lacking. However, arguing with him would prove nothing, except to provoke a response based on the rants of a man so pushed beyond the brink of emotional control he lashed out at his willing victim.

So she let the subject go, and simply prayed he would tell her at his own time and would return to the loving husband of which she had become so fond. Yet that did not make her feel particularly warm towards him, so she took the rest of her biscuits and made to go back to her fairy land kitchen. As a means of comfort, she absently picked up one of her biscuits and for the first time tasted it herself.

She nearly gagged at the taste.

Turning quickly on her heel, she looked at Erik with the remaining revulsion of her concoction. "How could you *eat* this?"

Erik had seemed to crumple before she left—his head in his hands as he stared at the Persian rug beneath his feet— but at her outburst he looked up. "Erik's wife made it for him. So he ate."

She wanted to cry. The morsel was revolting—obviously her teaspoon which lumped sugar so delectably into her tea was not meant to heap salt into her sweet biscuits. But more than that, she felt the warm rush of affection that Erik would be willing to choke down a vile wafer simply because she had provided it.

She sniffled in hopes of keeping her tears at bay, and took a step back toward her husband. "I… I seem to have made quite a mess of the kitchen. Would you…" he was looking at her hopefully, and it made her heart clench. "Would you help me?"

Erik rose quickly, taking the tea tray in hand while also removing the horrid biscuits from hers as well. She followed warily behind him, not sure how he would react to the wonderland of the kitchen.

He gasped at the sight, and turned to her with wide eyes. "I must say I am impressed Christine. Never had I imagined you would make such a formidable figure in the kitchen." She smiled ruefully at his comment, though if she were honest with herself, eternally grateful he was not angry.

They worked long and hard scrubbing the kitchen from top to bottom to remove all evidence of Christine's afternoon happenings. Erik was near tears as he watched Christine put the rest of her biscuits in the fire, and he only allowed it when she had promised she would make something for him again, only this time per his translation and guidance.

She was dreadfully tired when they finished, and resolved to go straight to bed. Erik was not hovering as she had hoped, but was steadily inching closer to his organ. But she was so very weary of being in her cold room alone, and even though Erik did little to add additional warmth to the room, she never felt quite as chilled when he was near. So after she had changed from her soiled dress, she stood with bated breath as she asked him to stay with her. He had frozen at her request, and she almost felt the bitter sting of his rejection, but slowly he nodded and she smiled.

Tucked in bed, with Erik in his *rightful* place on his side, he began to hum her lullaby. But just before her eyes succumbed to the seductive call of sleep, they paused at the sound of Erik's voice whispering through the darkness when he was sure to have thought her already in blessed unconsciousness.

"Erik is trying so very hard to wait for you to heal, Christine. But he has tasted your lovely lips, and it drives him nearly mad to be so close to you."

His sigh seemed to seep into her skin. "But he must wait for you to heal, and so he tries to distract himself with music, but every note seems so dull in comparison to my wife's sweetness."

His voice took on a nearly desperate edge. "But Erik cannot wait much longer, my Christine. And you have asked for your husband to return to you, and return he must!"

His breath tickled her ear as he breathed his final words. "And Erik's living wife shall know the love of her husband, just as your Adam knew his Eve."

XI

She had thought he was making a confession into the darkness, but obviously she was foolish to have thought he would not know she had yet to succumb to sleep. But from his words, she began to understand why he was so cold to her those last few days—he was trying to save her from *himself.*

Of course eventually he would have to consummate their marriage, but she had not considered that he would be tempted to do so in their pleasant routine they had established for those few blessed days. With shuddering clarity she realised she would be willing to submit to him if it meant he would resume his attentions throughout the day.

Her stomach clenched at the thought, utterly terrified at the notion, but she tried to suppress it lest Erik notice her change in demeanour. She must have been unsuccessful for he sighed once more, before putting one of his long dead hands in her hair and petting her gently as he hummed.

He *could* be gentle. In truth, he had *sworn* he would be, and she would have to believe him. For she did not think she could live knowing she had a brute for a husband with whom it was her wifely duty to surrender. But she would not know how Erik could perform unless she allowed him to *try.*

Though her stomach did not settle, his hand felt very nice against her hair, and the song did indeed make her wish for the encompassing darkness of sleep.

So she did.

And when she awoke, Erik was gone, and the bed showed no signs that he had ever been with her at all. For an indefinable reason, such a thought troubled her greatly. Had she imagined he was speaking to her once more? Would she once again have to rummage through cupboards for breakfast materials, only to find she had no appetite once she faced the lonely dining room?

She was being a coward, but if Erik was continuing with his compositions this morning, there really was no reason to rise. Petulance rose within her as she considered he would not notice if she *never* got up. She would wither away beneath her comforting shroud until she resembled his corpse-like frame—a fine couple they would make.

She snorted quite unbecomingly as she flung back the blankets and made to ready for the day. Such thoughts of morbidity would get her nowhere, especially not after her carefully drawn conclusions as to Erik's motives. She was a *wife* now, and she would certainly act accordingly, even if that meant expressly telling her husband of her willingness to participate in fully sanctioned acts of union. Her cheeks flamed at the thought.

When she emerged from her room, fully washed and dressed in a soft lilac day dress, she had prepared herself to draw Erik away from his organ once again—though without vile biscuits as her companion. But instead, she saw him drawing on his long black cloak while nimble fingers expertly fastened it around his neck. The previous day's dishevelled appearance had disappeared and made way for the immaculate dressing of which was his custom. But he was *leaving*. And Christine found such a notion to be quite unacceptable.

"Where are you going?" She wanted to beg him not to go, but a part of her also wished to voice her desire to leave the confines of his home.

"We are running low on supplies; I am simply going above to rectify the situation." He spoke quite curtly, but as he saw her widened eyes and fidgeting hands belaying her anxiety at being left alone, he softened. "You shall be fine, Christine. I would not leave you if it were not perfectly safe."

You did before.

She gasped in horror at her thoughts. And though she had not spoken the words aloud—that she had at least a small remainder of will to preserve her wretched life she had not let such thoughts slip from her lips—Erik seemed to have known to where they had turned in any case.

His eyes held so much sorrow, and guilt overwhelmed her for blaming him. It was not his fault, she *knew*, yet sometimes as the scabs had pulled away from her newly healed flesh leaving shiny pink skin in their wake, she had blamed him. Blamed him for his inability to control his temper, blamed him for marrying her, and blamed him for— everything. But it was never her intent to have him know of her unfaithful thoughts.

She made to apologise, but he shook his head slightly and held his gloved hand out for her to take. She did gladly. "Perhaps you would like to accompany me?"

It was irrational. She was safest here in his home, where stone walls and impenetrable doors were her haven, and the outside world was where *true* darkness prevailed. But as she held his hand, she realised she would be gripped by the same terror being alone in his underground kingdom as she would if he tossed her into one of her favourite parks in the above. For he would not be there.

And where her husband was, there was her safety.

So in a small voice, she looked at him with thankful eyes that yet again he was considering what *she* desired, and put her comfort before his own. And how could a man who time and again had demonstrated his devotion prove to be a torment in his husbandly rights?

"Yes, please."

His lips twitched in a sad version of a smile, and just like on their wedding day, he left her at the door to retrieve a cloak for the forgetful wife he had chosen. She refused to reflect on the fate of her last beautiful cape, and instead determined to make Erik *feel* her compliance throughout their outing, for she did not know if she possessed the courage to make her decision known regarding their consummation.

He returned promptly, and instead of the shimmering winter white which had once graced her shoulders, a far more practical navy blue wool was fastened around her neck by an intricate silver brooch. Her fingers longed to touch it, but instead they chose to seek out Erik's before she was lost in the dark tunnels they were about to traverse. Erik still took no light, but she did not doubt his capability as he led them expertly through each turn and doorway.

She was still startled to not see the cheerful beginnings of morning as she would have expected having woken up only an hour ago, but instead darkness was descending on the world. Shadows were long, and the blue of the sky was giving way to the velvet covering of night.

Erik took them through unfamiliar streets and alleys, and though there were still people milling about as they finished their daily business, they were rarely seen. However, when they came upon the familiar line of shops and bakeries, she smiled. They obviously would have only a few moments before they were closed for the night, and she supposed it was possible they had sold out of their wares earlier that day, but seeing the very stores she had frequented with... Raoul. He had brought her here when he wished to dote on her with some sweet or candy.

But as Erik led her to the finest bakery on the street, she found she did not mind the change in company.

She was right of course, the selection was scant, but as Christine took in the sights and smells of a world she had grossly taken for granted, she did not mind. Erik would stand in the shadowed doorways and hand her gold pieces to buy what she wished, but each time she exited he would take her purchases and carry them like the dutiful husband he was proving to be.

Eventually they had entered each shop that was still open, and even a few that were not. But Erik seemed to possess a great talent for opening closed doors when he caught Christine looking wistfully in a store window.

They even passed a jewellery store, but it was not the sparkling gems which twinkled at her happily as her eyes passed over them; it was the plain gold wedding bands. She twisted her own as she perused them, suddenly feeling a sense of inadequacy.

Though there was a physical representation of her married state displayed upon the third finger of her left hand, there was no such claim upon Erik. And it troubled her greatly. Of course it was common among the lower classes for only the women to have such seals, as allowed by the more traditional vows that Erik himself had spoken to her. And certainly he would buy one for her if she wished for him to have one, but it did not feel the same.

She had stared at them too long for Erik tugged gently at her arm as indicated their need to move along. She obeyed rather pensively, still harbouring the lingering dread in the pit of her stomach that told her she had committed some egregious error.

As they turned back the alley which had led them to the lovely street of shops, she could not help but ask Erik a question which had plagued her since the beginning of their outing. "Is this normally how you retrieve supplies?"

He did not answer at first, merely kept her hand tucked in the crook of his arm as they strolled the now fully darkened streets of Paris. She was about to ask again thinking he had not heard her when he spoke.

"It is not."

Getting Erik to expound on his dealings was proving to be much more work than she had anticipated. But she had promised herself he would not find reason to be cross with her, so she simply stopped walking and looked at him expectantly so there was no possible way he could think she was satisfied with his answer, but without the pleading he found so troublesome.

He sighed as he turned to face her, obviously understanding her lack of movement. "I had thought my wife would enjoy an excursion as she had not left our home in many days. Was I incorrect?"

She *had* enjoyed it immensely, and with Erik protecting each entrance she felt quite safe to peruse each shelf and item to her heart's content without fear of any recourse. He had seemed as though he was planning on leaving her this morning, and perhaps she had imagined it, but his shoulders ever so slightly relaxed at her enquiry that she accompany him. He *had* wanted her to come. He had wanted to make her *happy*.

And quite suddenly it became of great import to her that *he* be happy as well. It was not so important that she learn his secrets of grocery acquisition at this particular moment. She shook her head, "No, you are not incorrect. I have enjoyed it very much."

She was quiet the rest of the walk back to Erik's home. *Their* home. He

85

had said so himself, but she found it quite difficult to reconcile his underground home with something that could be considered hers. Their outing in the crisp night air had not been overly trying. From what she could see, no one gave Erik a second look as he clung to the shadows, but perhaps she had been too busy taking in the site of the lovely trinkets and baked goods to notice.

Perhaps someday, when they had a *real* marriage, she could ask him for a home above ground where she could grow pretty flowers and sit in the warmth of the sunlight. He could stay in his music room during the day, and they could read in the evenings.

But she could only ask once she had done her wifely duty, and unlike their wedding, she wished for this night to be chosen by *her*. Even though she had resolved so in her mind, she was still frightened and nervous, and so very terrified of the actual act that she did not fully understand. She prayed for Erik to be as gentle as he promised.

So perhaps they could enjoy each other's company before marital congress was established while she attempted to gather her courage to initiate such contact.

Such an opportunity presented itself when she followed Erik into the kitchen and visions of her disastrous first attempt at culinary excellence flooded her mind. Yet even though she had made such grievous mistakes, Erik still dutifully ate what she had given, simply because she had cared enough to provide it. And suddenly she wished for nothing more than to be able to shower him with confections that were to his liking.

But she could not do so without first asking for his help.

Erik was a tall man, and it was certainly evidenced by the height of his shelves. He also had quite a penchant for placing vital items on the upper most ledges, and this was proving problematic in her quest for molasses. While Erik was still placing items in their proper place, she had pulled out the still dusty cookbook she had used last time, and found another recipe. Only this time she knew for a fact one of the ingredients was located on the uppermost shelf and quite beyond her reach.

She eyed Erik as he methodically emptied pockets and put away spices and salts, and found she did not wish to trouble him. It was one thing to bring over a book and ask for him to read the instruction; it was another to interrupt his task for assistance in one of her own. The doorway to the kitchen was narrow, and she doubted she could fit one of the elegant dining chairs through it in order to stand upon it.

She remembered as a child in Mamma Valérius' home when she was feeling particularly naughty she would climb upon the countertop in reach of whatever treat was hidden away too far from her greedy hands. She was always scolded for it of course, usually with cautions of slipping and danger, but she was much older now and certain she would not fall. Surely her balance had improved over the years.

So gathering up her skirts, she pulled herself onto a standing position on the counter and quite happily clutched the molasses in her hands. Her happiness did not last long as she was thoroughly startled when two arms fastened around her middle and she was clutched quite fiercely and pulled from her perch.

"Is Christine *trying* to kill herself?" He gave her one final squeeze—more for his own reassurance of her presence in his arms than to cause her discomfort—before twisting her around to face him.

He looked annoyed, but mostly frightened, and then, inexorably sad. "I thought we were beyond such demonstrations from my Christine." His hand caressed the side of her head where she had so unmercifully touched it to the wall of her bedroom.

She gasped at his insinuation. "Of course not!" She held up the small jar of brown syrup as evidence of her sanity. "I did not want to trouble you."

His expression quickly changed to that of one incensed. "You think it is better not to *trouble* me than for you to fall to your death and leave your Erik all alone?"

She would not cry. She would hold her ground and make him understand that she wished to do something kind for him, and her tears would only cause him pain—he had told her so many times. So she sniffled, and looked up at him with pleading eyes which begged for him to see past his anger and *listen*.

"Erik, you have been so very kind today, and I just wanted to return the gesture."

He sniffed indignantly, still with the simmering anger blanketed by disbelief. "By attempting to bring about your demise?"

She huffed in annoyance. Half of her wished to turn her back to him, letting him continue to think she was so miserable in their marriage she would resort to the appalling act of suicide, but her more rational being determined he was simply frightened. She knew she was the first companion he had ever known, and without her she had no doubt his death would be swift to follow. And she could not allow that.

Putting aside her own irritation at his determination to think poorly of her, she took his cold fingers in hers and pulled him to the cookbook which rested on the same counter which had permitted her ill-fated adventure.

"Will you help me make these?" She tightened her grip on his hand for a moment, willing him to understand that her request transcended the desire for warm morsels and tea.

Erik turned his gaze from the page to stare at her, and at last the anger left his eyes, and was replaced with the softness she was accustomed to seeing when he was able to perform a menial task simply for the sake of doing it for his wife.

That did not keep him from suppressing his longsuffering sigh. "Must your Erik do *everything?*"

She practically beamed at him and quite impulsively, Christine went on her tip toes to bestow his lips with a kiss. "Yes. For you are my husband."

When she tried to pull away to gather the rest of her ingredients, she found that Erik was not quite ready to release her, nor allow her lips to fully depart from him. Neither were fully versed in the prowess of kisses, but it was sweet, and it made Christine tingle in ways she could not begin to fathom.

But it did make her plans for later that evening not seem so very terrifying.

When Erik released her lips from his intimate embrace, he kept her face cupped between his hands so he was assured the truthfulness of her eyes. "Is Christine happy?"

Perhaps if she thought of it, there were things which would make her unhappy. The darkness from the never ending night, the cold which pervaded her skin and made shivers a common occurrence. But most of all, she was unhappy when Erik had punished her with his absence. She knew that was not his intent, but it sincerely felt like the cruellest form of torture.

However, as she looked him, having spent the last few hours contentedly in his company, she did not seem to mind. And if she remained pliant, if she released him from the bounds of civility which kept him in such torment from her lack of affection, such outings could become regular occurrences.

"Yes, I think I am." He did not seem entirely convinced, but nodded his acceptance regardless. Perhaps that was just one of the many things he would need to be shown through time and action, and simply her word would not be sufficient. And baking together, for *him* would certainly be a start.

And so they did. Erik would only involve himself when she asked it of him, and while she thought eventually he might catch on that she enjoyed his participation throughout the entire process, he would resolutely stand by and watch until she would touch his hand to ask for the meaning of a word, or how to tell how high a temperature the fire needed to reach. That might have been the issue, as Erik was becoming quite covetous of every touch and brush of her lips, and she wondered if perhaps he would begin to never do anything for her unless she specifically enticed him.

But was it not that way with most marriages? She had heard such stories from lamenting wives and gossiping girls, so perhaps it was not so unreasonable for Erik to behave in such a way. And truly, she did not mind. Not now when they were seated on the settee with steaming cups of tea and molasses biscuits melting on their tongues. He was always the second to sit, never wanting to presume she would desire his company—and perhaps she should not. But the less she thought, and the more she gave in to her natural instincts and impulse, the more she desired his presence and affections.

With her head resting lightly on his shoulder—only cushioned by the fine quality of his suit, but certainly not the protruding bone underneath—she asked him to read to her. He was not willing to move, so he merely picked up the nearest book off of the side table, and began to read. She had expected to be swept into foreign lands through tales of the heroism and delight, but instead found Erik to be speaking *in* a foreign tongue. And though she did not understand the words, she was caught up in the inflection and tone of his voice, and found she understood the heartache and final climax quite well.

Erik only paused now and then to nibble at *their* sweet biscuits, or occasionally take sips of his unsweetened tea, and Christine delighted at the soft sighs he would emit at each suspension, and it became quite clear to her what was missing in their secluded lives in this underworld of Erik's creation.

That it was her wifely duty to seduce her husband.

XII

But simple acknowledgement of her decision was not enough. When preparing for her role in *Don Juan Triumphant*, her main difficulty was not in the vocals—though most assuredly it was of the most technical operas she had ever attempted. Her challenge was the subtle seductive powers of Erik's chosen prima donna. Sheer innocence, yet deceptive sensuality left her confused and befuddled, but by the final rehearsal she had been praised for her abilities. Perhaps Erik would be pleased as well.

She could not imagine attempting such arts outside of her bedroom, so all that truly mattered was Erik's agreement to remain with her. Beyond that, she was not sure. She would not equate this with her assault on her wedding day. That man was a brute and a scoundrel, with only lust in his heart. So very unlike her Erik. His treatment of her seemed entirely contingent her treatment of *him*.

When she was giving in her touches—in her smiles—he seemed to want to dote upon her as much as humanly possible. Or *inhumanly* possible as it so often seemed. If she were quiet and sulky, he would ignore her until he grew so terribly sad he would beg for her happiness. He rarely asked for her to love him, perhaps finally accepting it was more pleasant to make his own assumptions in response to her action instead of hearing the dreadful silence she would give for lack of answer.

Was it terribly wrong to be intimate with one's husband when she did not love him? It was not her intent to make him believe so; she simply desired to move their marriage into a state of validity. And if his kiss in the kitchen were any indication, perhaps the event would not wholly be unpleasant. And would it not be better to consummate their union before he became more dissatisfied?

A small part of her feared that he would become bitter and callous toward her if she continued to withhold such vital affection and she wished for this to be an expression of love. At least on his part if it could not be one of her own.

When Erik had finished his foreign story, she had stayed with her head pressed into his side, enjoying the cashmere softness of his suit against her cheek. Without her asking, he pulled her into his lap and rose to carry her to the organ where he placed her gently on the bench. She wondered if this would be another expression of his mood, or simply something to please her. She did not know if she could handle another journey into his mind and soul—not when her thoughts were in such turmoil.

But it was not. He took up his violin and quite sweetly played the lullaby he so often used to lull her to sleep. She was so familiar with its lilts and cadence which inspired such drowsy feelings, she felt her eyelids begin to droop involuntarily.

She shook herself reproachfully, suddenly wondering why Erik wished for her to sleep. Was he bored of her? He could not possibly know of her plans, but here he was, deliberately making her wish for nothing more than her bed and his calming presence beside her.

She gasped in realisation. Was *he* seducing *her*? It was not the passion inducing melody of his third movement, but it was clear he was entreating her to go to her bedroom. And she could only presume he desired her to request his continued presence. And much to her surprise, the notion did not offend her. She had felt guilty for keeping him from his work, but now she realised how hurt he would have been if she shut the door upon him each night, and was glad for her incessant neediness.

When Erik finished, he simply stood looking at her, but she could not quite determine the foundation of his expression. Feeling oddly childish and clingy, she held out her arms. "Would you carry me?"

Erik seemed to relax at her request, and did not even ask where she wished to go. She felt small and insignificant as he cradled her, yet so utterly safe she wished he would not let her go. As he moved from the sitting room to her—*their*—bedroom, he let out an affectionate "such a needy wife I have."

And she burrowed closer still, and even kissed over his heart though she knew he could not feel it. "Yes, and I will not apologise for it, you spoil me so." He held her all the more firmly, and sighed when he stood before the bed and it was time to release her.

Already their routine had shifted. She was still in her day dress, her face unwashed from their morning excursion, and yet Erik hovered as he waited for her to speak. Her heart pounded in her chest as she said her final words before indicating her consent to her husband. But she wanted him to be happy, and she so dearly wished to be a good wife.

"Will you stay with me?"

His eyes blazed with a passion she had never seen before. He moved to her bedside, still with the stiff posture of formality that was so very *Erik,* and he seemed in no great rush. He lowered the lamp so only the slightest of flames survived, barely enough to see the outline of his frame. But his eyes—oh his eyes!—they seemed specifically created for such an atmosphere, and they continued to stare at her with their full intensity despite the darkened room.

He settled at in his usual position next to her, and made no move to touch her. Had she been mistaken? Had he merely thought her tired after a long day's excursion? But it did not truly matter. For regardless of *his* intention, she had her own. She turned over to face him, and with trembling lips and hands, sought his mouth and throat. Perhaps he had expected her kiss, but when her hand fumbled with the top button of his shirt, his hand caught hers in a firm but painless grip.

"What is going through Christine's pretty head to make her behave thusly?" She would have thought he was chastising her but for the quiver in his voice, almost as though he were nervous as well. Could Erik possibly feel as she did?

She kissed the hand which held hers captive, feeling endeared to him at the possibility of his own trepidation of their union. He was not the aggressor—not in this. "I want to be a good wife to you, Erik. A—" her eyes sought his even in the near blackness of the room. "A proper wife."

His hand had loosened at her kiss, and she returned them both to his throat. Much like the fluttering of her own heart, she felt his pulse beat rapidly beneath her fingers, and for the first time she noticed how soft his papery skin was. It was not the fine satin of her own, but it had its own unique texture that was not wholly unappealing.

It was a curious thing. When she had imagined their joining, Erik had always been the one ravishing her—she the passive participant who performed her duty admirably. But perhaps Erik knew that she needed to test this, test *him,* and test— herself. She cautiously unbuttoned another of his buttons, still only looking into the glowing embers of his eyes, while fingers teased the dead skin of his chest.

Her husband was a man of few words, so his sighs were a true testament into his mind. The one he emitted at her exploration was a marriage of a whimper and a sigh, but there was neither sadness nor pain as she looked at him. His entire body was tense, and she felt the pull of the bedclothes as he gripped them. He was restraining himself. From her.

And she knew how he dearly loved to touch her hair, her lips, her skin, and it did not seem fair that he felt such an action would be unaccepted. "Erik, you may touch me…. If you would like." She blushed as she said it, feeling utterly bold and unladylike.

She pressed herself back against the pillows, awaiting whatever touch he wished to bestow upon her, and then it was Erik's turn to lean over her—a foreboding presence to be sure, but she did not feel afraid. Her pulse was quick, her breath short, but there was a certain anticipation in the not knowing how Erik would be with her.

He was not looking at her body, but just as she had done, he kissed her lips and brought his nimble fingers to her collar, and unbuttoned *her* top button. She shivered where his cold touch caressed, and such sensations were only magnified as his hand crept down to the *second* button, teasing the flesh in its wake.

His fingers were trembling, and his kiss became more fervent as his hands whispered over the exposed flesh of her throat. For weeks he had been tormented by the ever present need to touch the expanse of her décolleté, but for the preservation of her modesty and the tenuous trust she had placed in him, he had only allowed himself medical necessity of fingertips. But now, what his fingers had enjoyed, now palms could also savour.

She wondered if she would have to undo more of his clothing for him to further the process, but as his breathing—which ghosted over her skin and bathed her in his essence—began to quicken, so did his hands on her person. The buttons which took her such a very long time to fasten each morning were released in mere moments, yet Erik seemed to delight in slowly pulling back the bodice to his view. No longer were his eyes fixed on hers, but they roamed freely over her state of undress, and he moaned.

"My Christine is so very beautiful, and she is such a good wife to let her husband touch her." He withdrew his hand, and he looked at her with such longing she knew it was not of his desire he should stop, but for concern of *her.*

And she knew it would have taken all of his courage to risk her rejection, so it would be her responsibility to make it known her desire to please him. "Erik, please." She grasped his wrist and brought it to her cheek.

His eyes flew to hers, seemingly startled by her plea. "I spoke truly before." And now *her* hand was pressed upon his masked cheek, and his eyes turned frightened as she brushed over the seam. "A husband should not hide from his wife." But instead of cruelly unmasking him as would have been her action so many months ago; she turned quickly on her side and blew out the remaining flicker of flame.

She returned quickly to his side, not wishing him to think she abandoned him. He had barely moved, and she shifted against him until she was satisfactorily close. His eyes were only the barest of flickers in the utter darkness. But unlike when she had been alone these past weeks, she felt completely at peace. She could have laughed at her overwhelming euphoria that the paralysing fear of the darkness had not come, and it was all due to the man pressed against her side.

She kissed him lightly, and her hands found the seams of his mask once more. But still she did not remove it, not only for the hands which found grasp upon her wrists in a halting manner, but because she had yet to speak the words which she hoped would offer him the comfort they needed before the proceeded any further in this venture. "Erik," she breathed against his lips. "We are equals in the dark. We do not even have to be Erik and Christine if you wish." She kissed the seam of his mask, brushing any of his skin she could with the velvet softness of her lips.

"We can simply be man and wife."

He let out a shuddering sob as he placed his head upon her shoulder. "Just like everybody else."

She supposed that most women, when attempting to seduce their husbands, were taking steps to stir their passions until they were the pliable sources of husbandly good will. But Erik needed more than that. He needed her permission to *feel* his passions, and though still wholly inexperienced in such things, she felt she was beginning to understand the abuses her poor unhappy husband had suffered.

The evils of the world had wished to strip him of his humanity and—for a time—they had succeeded.

And that thought brought her to tears. Perhaps she did not love him, but no longer did she believe she *could* not, and she only did not love him *yet*. But she did feel the overwhelming compassion that she could only feel for her Erik. Her husband.

Erik pulled away from her, and there was a slight thump as something fell to the floor. And though she thought it might have been an article of clothing, she could still feel Erik's coat beneath her fingers as she reached to plead with him not to go, and then he was back, brushing his mask-less face against her skin. She could feel the wetness of his tears mingled with her own as he kissed her.

There was no horror—no evidence that he was unlike anybody else as he kissed her and they cried. His fingers were undoing her buttons, and inexperienced fingers were trying to divest her of the rest of her bodice. In an effort to be of use, she aided him, and soon her dress was gone, and he was growling at the ties of her corset.

She was very grateful he did not ask why she cried, for she doubted her ability to voice the range of emotions she felt as at last he removed all of her clothing, and was pressing up against her. It felt wrong—so very wrong to have him fully clothed. While she had thought his coat supple against her cheek, it felt harsh and rough against the tender flesh of her thighs and breasts.

She would have thought as little corpse-like skin touching her would be a blessing, but she found in the pitch blackness, it was quite unbearable. It was too like her experience before—though she would *not* think of it—and she desperately wanted him unclothed as well. So her hands were pushing at his shoulders, and for a moment his sobs became full of sorrow, until she returned her mouth to his as she plucked at his shirt and coat.

He seemed to understand her distress, as he whispered "My poor Christine" into her skin before rising slightly to undo his suit. Of course she could not see him, but there was a slight rustling of material as it was stripped away from his form, and then he was back upon her, bare skin touching her own. He was so very cold, and she could not tell if her shivers and trembles were from the icy radiance of his natural coolness or from the whispering strokes of his fingers as they explored her pale white skin.

Though she had heard talk of some women pretending their husbands were someone else—shut their eyes and picture old lovers and beaus from years past—Christine had no wish to do so. She did not picture her previous fiancé as Erik's withered lips touched her breast, nor did she picture the revulsion of Erik's deformity. Here, in this darkness, she was being loved by her husband. The very Angel she had loved so dearly in her youth was the one who was making her limbs tingle in such unexpected and unfelt ways; she could not help the whimper which escaped her lips.

His hands had drifted to the swell of her hips while his mouth continued to consecrate her breasts with affections. Though she did not know how much Erik could truly see in the blackness, she hoped he was unable to see the definition of still faintly yellow bruises on her skin. She wanted to be perfect for him—for even a man such as he deserved a spotless bride.

His lips kissed each of the marks which were now such tender new flesh she arched against him. She had been afraid having any man near her bosom would overwhelm her with fear of new abuses, but Erik was soft and his hands gentle. And those very hands were now creeping to the inside of her slender white thighs. His touch did not press, merely coaxed her to move at their slightest brush—and so she did.

Erik's sobs had quieted, though his breathing was still ragged wafts of air that cooled her heated skin. He settled between her legs, and she felt entirely enveloped by his tall frame. There was not a place on her body she could not feel him, and then—oh and then!—his voice was breathing in her ear as he hummed his third melody. And she did not know why—*could* not know why—until he was ever so slowly pushing into her, and she finally understood.

She tried to quiet her sobs for it would not do to make Erik feel as though he were mistreating her, and she knew it hurt the first time—but oh how it burned!—but Erik knew. He did not withdraw, but paused whenever her breath caught, and his voice seemed to fill her mind in such a delicious agony she forgot the pain until he moved deeper still. And when she thought he could not possibly join them more fully, she felt the brush of his hip against her thigh, and heard his shuddering sigh as he kissed her neck.

"Oh how Erik loves his Christine."

And she cried, though not from the pain. She wanted to say it back—*needed* to say it back—for it seemed like such a sin to be united so entirely yet be unable to utter such magnificent words, but Erik did not seem to want an answer as he covered her pretty pink mouth with his own, and shifted his hips ever so slightly.

She did not think to ask him to stop, did not *want* him to stop, for as he moved within her she finally felt as if this powerful man she could not possibly understand was simply that—a man. And he was her husband, and she could love him—someday *would* love him— and she did not once regret giving her consent.

That did not make his intrusion any less foreign, nor did it quell her curiosity as to what exactly was plundering the secret depths of her womanhood. There was still a burning as he moved, but the low moans and exaltations which were emitted from his beautiful throat filled her with contentment. She did not resent his use of her body, for it was natural, and it was right, and she *felt* the love he tried so very hard to show her.

His body suddenly stiffened and he gasped, and finally she felt the first warmth emit from him. He remained still for a moment, catching his breath from the excursion of his love, and clutched her to him fiercely. While he had been supreme gentleness in his love making, he seemed to be gripped with a sudden desperate need to cleave her to himself.

"Erik?" Her throat felt constricted, and the sound was a terrible mix of a rasp and a croak. "Are you alright?" His answer was not prompt as he drew breath after breath even as his head was buried in her curls.

"Did Christine not perish?" His voice was filled with disbelief, and she wondered if he honestly believed such an act would have killed her. She felt the sobs well within her as she desperately tried to stifle them.

"I am alright, Erik." And she found that she was. Her intimate place had a dull ache akin to emptiness, but she did not feel particularly sore. There were no bites, no bruises, and she felt—satisfied. A weight had been lifted from her shoulders now that their union was fully sanctified, and there was a comfort she drew knowing that she truly belonged to Erik now. Because Erik cared for his own, and she found she was becoming quite fond of his protective and doting nature.

Erik released her with a sigh, and left her bed. *Their* bed. She was suddenly gripped with a sudden terror which drowned her previous feelings of accomplishment. Was he leaving her? Whatever tears she had tried to hide suddenly poured forth as she frantically clutched for him, only to swipe at the stifling air.

"Erik, please do not leave me!"

And when all she heard was the open and close of a door, she dissolved into hapless sobs.

XIII

For the first time she felt the cruel sting of *Erik's* betrayal. She was the one who had hurt—had finally felt as though there might be some semblance of affection she felt for him, yet he fled from her the moment he had used her. And she no longer felt like a wife, but more a common harlot in a brothel.

She screamed when she felt Erik's icy touch on her shoulder, a piece of soft cotton in his hand.

A nightgown. From her wardrobe.

She flung her arms around his neck as she tried to quiet her sobs even as he muttered soothing words and petted her hair. "Hush, Christine. I would *never* leave you." But she still felt hurt even as he slipped the airy material over her head and threaded her arms through the sleeves. Her tears refused to stop, and she oh so desperately wished to see his face. Not the withered and sunken cheeks, but to see if he truly loved her, that he still cared for her as her husband should. He had always thought her an angel—an untouched beauty sent to this earth for his redemption. But she was untouched no longer, and his absence—even for a moment—had frightened her.

He tried to keep her from the lamp, holding onto her shoulders and arms, but she pushed him away quite forcefully as she relit the only potential source of light in the room. She was surprised at herself, as when Erik moved to frantically reach for his mask and his clothing, with strength she did not know she possessed, she pulled him back onto the bed and pulled his face into her hands.

She stared at him, but never once did her eyes waver from his eyes as his darted to and fro trying not to see the revulsion which surely she felt for this monster who had bedded her. "Erik, look at me." And he did. "Am I still your Christine?" Her voice was small, and she felt as though her throat had closed of its own accord making the production of sound a truly difficult endeavour.

He looked at her with such horror; it was akin to when she had first ripped his mask away, but without the raging anger that had so quickly followed. "You shall *always* be my Christine." And the horror was fleeing, soon to be replaced by the softness that was only present when he looked at her.

She nodded, feeling only slightly foolish that she had worried that his love for her would only last through the foregoing of her innocence. Now that her frantic need for reassurance had been assuaged, she realised how close they were and Erik's state of undress. And that his mask was still settled upon the floor. She almost pulled away, *looked* away, but when she remembered how tender he had been, and the rush of contentment when he had finished, she found she had no such wish.

"Am I not a handsome fellow?" He must have caught her gaze travelling over the planes of his face, but she was not ashamed. The feelings of wretchedness only came when she had thought him truly ugly, and most certainly he still was. But now, as she lay so very close to him, she found that it had been his actions which had frightened and repulsed her so terribly. And perhaps it was how he had endeared himself to her that he did not seem so very corpse-like. She had felt the very living essence of which he was capable, and it was difficult to still conjure the dead motif that hung around him in such an abject mantle.

She looked down at his chest, and saw his ribs were quite prominent beneath his yellowed skin. The scars she had seen earlier upon his arms were nothing compared to the crisscross of fine lines that made up the texture of his skin. She traced them delicately with her forefinger, wondering at the feel. Erik's eyes watched her as she studied him, apparently waiting for the shudders of vicious horror to overtake her. Yet they never came.

She kissed once above his heart, liking the slightly warmer patch of flesh which resided there. Further evidence of his humanity, for as long as his heart remained beating within his emaciated chest, there would be warmth within him. And as long as *she* lived, there would be warmth to surround him. She dared not glance lower, though perhaps someday she would have the courage to look.

He was uncomfortable, she knew. His body trembled as she touched him, but she did not think they were the pleasure driven responses of a man enraptured. He had given her a nightgown to wear for which she was grateful, and she wondered if he would like nightclothes of his own. Whenever he had stayed with her before he had remained fully clothed, yet now that felt terribly wrong.

"Erik?" She had reached to the bedside and lowered the light until it was a dim ambiance and her husband was more or less bathed in shadows. He had relaxed immediately.

"Yes, my Christine?" He was petting her curls lightly as her head had settled on the warm patch over his heart.

"Will this be your room now?" His hand paused for a moment before he sighed.

"Many wives have their own rooms, Christine. You need not think you must submit to me again." He sounded pained even as he said the words, and the notion that he was resigning himself to a life without her love seemed intolerable.

"I cannot bear the thought of you still thinking that horrid coffin is your bed." He gripped her a little tighter as she spoke, and she knew her words had pleased him.

"Is Erik wrong in thinking you care for him?" He had not said love. Perhaps he knew she could not admit such a thing to even herself let alone her husband, and she was grateful for his replacement. She did care for him—she always had. Even when he frightened her, even when he had threatened her dearest friend, she had cared.

"No, you are not wrong."

His chest heaved with emotion, and if her head had not been resting against it she would not have known, for he made not a sound. And she knew, someday, she would tell this man—her husband—that she loved him.

They lay there for a few moments as Erik calmed himself, but as the distraction of his attentions waned, Christine became once more aware of the biting chill of her—*their*—bedroom, and she moved to climb beneath the bedclothes. And unlike every other night, she wished Erik would join her.

"Will you sleep with me tonight?" Her request was different as well. It was not an invitation to stay as her dark protector—it was the enquiry of a wife who wished for her husband to give into the peaceful slumbering of unconsciousness together.

He sat up as she slid beneath the blankets, and he looked away from her. "I would like to dress." She eyed his face warily, afraid he would not return, or would shut himself away behind formal suits and his mask. But if he was uncomfortable it was her duty to soothe him, so she nodded her consent.

He kept to the outer edges of the room which were entirely encased in shadows that seemed to welcome him. When she heard the opening of the bedroom door she felt foolish for ever thinking the wardrobe was the heavy wood of the outer door.

She shimmied further into the comfort of her bed yet found it oddly bereft when it lacked Erik's presence beside her. Now that she was alone she began to inventory the true state of her person. Perhaps she would hurt more in the morning, but if Erik were true to his word, soon he would return and she would fall asleep in his comforting embrace and would dream of pleasant things.

She wanted him to take her shopping again. He had not said how he normally acquired his groceries and home items, and it suddenly bothered her that she did not know. As the lady of the house, was it not her responsibility to tend to the wellbeing of the home? He had said it was common for married women to have their own bedrooms, which would also suggest men had their own chambers. But she wanted his room scourged from their presence. A shrine to his solitude and misery, she wished to take the remaining kerosene from her lamp and pour it upon the coffin and quite happily light the match and watch it burn.

She smiled at the thought.

"Why does my wife smile?" Erik was standing in the doorway in the most casual attire she had seen. Still in his customary black, he was in what appeared to be his sleep clothes, and the contrast to his stiff formality was startling. But she found it wonderful.

"I do not want to have the coffin in the house any longer." He had yet to replace his mask, and she was grateful, for she was able to see the sardonic raise of his straggling eyebrow.

"We must all accept our inevitable deaths, Christine." She rolled her eyes in response, and patted the bed next to her, not liking the space between them. How curious it was how she adjusted to his touch so quickly!

"But would it not be more pleasant to dwell upon the future?" She looked up at him beneath her lashes as he settled *beneath* the blankets. "*Our* future?"

He froze for a moment, and breathed heavily for reaching to press her into his side. His hand found his favourite curl and he twisted it around his finger thoughtfully. "Perhaps we might find a better use for the room." He tugged at her curl affectionately. "Such a demanding wife I have."

She snuggled against him, finding it quite odd that she found his bony frame pleasant to rest upon, and smiled. "Will you read to me tomorrow?"

He sighed again, and she knew he was being intentionally obstinate. "I suppose if my wife wishes it."

She giggled. "And will you help me make biscuits?" He snorted—a very odd sound coming from him, but she felt warm knowing she was the only one he would be comfortable enough to allow hearing it.

"I think for the time being any such attempts would be best under my guidance, wife." She wondered if he used the word to convince himself she was truly of such a standing as she did with *husband.*

"And will you—" he groaned before she could finish her request.

"Sleep Christine, before you plan Erik's entire day!" She huffed at his insinuation that she was little more than a secretary, but was secretly pleased he was being so accommodating. So far she was enjoying proper marital relations quite nicely—aside from her panic at Erik's abandonment of course.

Afraid that he would leave as soon as she succumbed to sleep, she made her final entreaty. "Promise you will not leave."

She felt him press a kiss against her curls, before whispering in her hair. "Goodnight, my wife." And she supposed that was promise enough.

And so they slept.

-X-

For the first time since she was brought to Erik's home, Christine was not alone when she awoke. Erik was not sleeping, but had not resumed his caresses upon her curls. Instead he was staring at her thoughtfully. She blinked sleepily at him, surprised that he had not replaced his mask during the night. In fact, he did not appear to have moved from his position before she had fallen asleep, yet she had moved from her place against him to her own side of the bed.

She was reminded of their first few nights together—him resolutely staying away from her. Wariness overcame her as she wondered if Erik had used the precious nighttime hours for tormented ponderings instead of the blessing of sleep.

"How does Christine feel?" The question surprised her, and for a moment she could not think why he was asking. But when she stretched and she felt the aching pains and residue from last night's conjugation she blushed and looked away from him.

"I am fine." And she hoped she was not lying. She had expected the soreness and doubted he would notice if she moved with more trepidation for the remainder of the day. At least she hoped. But he had noticed how she favoured the soft cushions of the settee after her assault and doubted he would remain ignorant to her discomfort.

"You are a dreadful liar, Christine." His expression was pained as he observed her, and she did not approve his stiff posture. He seemed shuttered from her, and she had so enjoyed the easy manner of last night that she wished she knew how to improve his demeanour.

"Erik, you *promised.*" She looked at him imploringly—begging that he would see how important it was to her that he not withdraw—that he remain her *husband.*

"If Christine cannot be truthful with her husband, he shall have to forfeit his honesty for her sake." He looked offended at her reminder. "And Erik did *not* move. *As he promised.*"

She sighed and timidly touched his sleeping shirt, finding it softer than even his cashmere evening suits. "I want us to be happy Erik. I want *you* to be happy." She peeked into his eyes. "Do you regret last night?"

If he was offended before he was affronted now. "Of course Erik does

101

not regret being with his wife. *As is his right.*" He softened even as he huffed at her. "But I am sorry if Christine is hurt."

She drew small circles onto his chest as she considered her response. She longed for a warm soak in her bath, but she did not wish for him to think she wished to wash *him* off her skin as she had in the beginning. "I am not *hurt,*" he was about to interrupt her again so she quickly pressed on. "But I *am* tender. Perhaps I might take a bath?"

He seemed to accept this and gently removed her from his person though he seemed almost regretful in doing so. He rose and entered her powder room—seemingly to prepare her bath for her. He had not specifically told her to stay, but so long as Erik was not angry, she did not mind continuing to lie in her bed until he returned.

And soon he did.

She made rise to follow him, but he quickly crossed to her side and scooped her into his arms. "You should not move if you are *tender,* Christine." And though he said the words reproachfully, she wondered if he simply wished to hold her and found this the only way she would allow it— which now that she considered it, was a ridiculous notion.

It was not she who was unused to contact with another, it was him. He was the one who now stiffened at her first touch. He was the one who trembled as she kissed him, and he was the one who broke away first. And as long as she had breath, he would learn that not all touch was meant as a punishment.

She did not think it possible that the scars which covered so much of his papery skin were self inflicted—she *prayed* they were not—and that would mean that someone had deliberately exacted such treatment upon him. And if Erik's skill with the lasso was a skill learned in adulthood, that would mean he was nothing more than a *child.* And the thought made her feel quite sick.

And she did not know how to offer him comfort when he could not possibly know what thoughts fluttered in her mind, so she simply pressed more fully into his arms and pressed a kiss over his heart as he carried her to her bath. He shuddered at the gesture, and she smiled at her ability to affect him—her poor unhappy Erik.

He placed her carefully on her feet before the tub; obviously loath to deposit her on the hard rim of the claw foot structure when she had complained of discomfort in such delicate an area. She felt suddenly awkward as she did not know how to proceed. Should she ask for him to stay? She did not necessarily wish to bathe under his ever watchful gaze, but she did not relish how his moods could be poisoned when he was left alone.

Erik thankfully seemed to sense her discomfort—and from the subtle steps he was taking toward the door she suspected he felt much the same—

he offered to make breakfast while she refreshed herself. "I have added special salts to the water to help your *tenderness.*" He seemed to mock her choice of word, almost as if he was determined to find fault in his ability to care for her, so she not so subtly glared at him for his disbelieving nature.

But he fled before she could scold him.

And she very nearly called after him with a teasing "coward!" though perhaps that was for the best she managed to hold her childish tongue.

She stripped out of her nightgown and stepped into the heated water with a delighted sigh. Erik might have been correct in his assumption that she downplayed her *tenderness* for his benefit. She did hurt quite a bit, but she lacked the bitter resentment of one who was *hurt* from the action.

But she was startled by the dried blood she found upon her thighs before the water began the lovely process of cleansing her skin. Perhaps it was morbid of her, but she was rather glad she bled. It seemed tangible evidence of her purity—that she had *not* been tainted by her ill fated wedding night with that man who was not her husband. Mamma Valérius would read to her from the Old Testament in the evenings, telling her it was important she understand the original Scriptures as well as the new. There were stories of Priests who had consecrated the ordinary objects into their holy reverence through the sprinkling of blood—and perhaps they had now done the same.

Whatever Erik had added to her bath water made it smell slightly sweet, yet it permeated her nostrils the same way his balm would to her previous wounds. She felt languid and lazy in the almost too hot water, and she hoped what Erik had planned for breakfast would take a good long time. She was not particularly hungry, and the idea of staying in this water until it turned cold was thoroughly tempting.

But she knew Erik was prone to debilitating thoughts, and she hoped her presence would remind him of what was now good in his life—and if she were honest, she enjoyed his company as well. Far more than she had ever thought possible. So after she had gently washed the entirety of her skin, she rose from the water and dried herself thoroughly.

And for the first time when she looked at her reflection, she wanted to make herself look pretty. Not for a part she had to play as dutiful housewife or bride, but because she wished for him to think her beautiful. He had told her once that if she only loved him he would be as gentle as a lamb. And though she could not tell if she loved him yet, the more she acted as if she did, the gentler he became. And she adored his kindness.

She pinched her cheeks lightly in order to regain some of the natural lustre which had been lost upon spending her days underground, and she bit her lip hoping to draw out the pinkness. She thought putting her hair up would make her look more sophisticated—more like a *wife*—but if she considered *Erik,* she doubted he would feel the same. And so she left it down, fully accepting it as an invitation for him to run his fingers through her tendrils, and she found she did not mind the notion as much as she should.

Returning to her—*their*—bedroom, she went to the wardrobe to pick out her dress for the day. She ran her fingers over the red silk gown and wondered if it would be horribly cliché to wear such a brazen colour the day after she had truly entered womanhood. She considered it thoughtfully. It was more formal than her usual attire for a simple day spent at home, though it would still be considered a day dress without too tight a corset or bustle. But she had a *real* husband now, and would he not find her very pretty? The neckline was lower than she had been wearing the past few weeks, though it still covered her adequately. Well, adequately to wear in front of one's *husband*.

And so attired, she went to join her husband for breakfast.

XIV

Erik did not disappoint. Not with the fine meal he had prepared, and most certainly not with his reaction to her appearance. He had been removing delectably warm muffins from the oven—with considerably less mess than she would have managed—when she entered and upon depositing them on the counter, he simply stared. Not the stares of the past which left her feeling exposed and uncomfortable, but instead one that made her feel adored.

That did not keep her from blushing, but her shy smile was from pleasure, not embarrassment. Erik came toward her slowly, and as she had suspected, his hand found her free flowing curls. "You are so very beautiful." He touched her in reverence, and for a moment he pulled away—almost as though he did not feel worthy enough to touch her. But she knew that was nonsense. He was just like any other man!

So she placed her hand over his and pressed it upon her cheek, but not before brushing it softly against her lips. He shuddered at her action, and she had to smile at what little gesture could please him so. She felt rather wretched doing so, but she could not help comparing him to Raoul. Always sweet and loving, yet he would not have reacted quite as her Erik did. More vibrant displays of favour would have been required to emote such pleasantness, and she found herself feeling quite pleased at how enamoured her husband was by her very presence. Though she did feel slightly saddened that simple kiss should be such a novelty. That surely would change.

Erik had obviously worked quickly as she luxuriated in her bath. He was once more in his immaculate suiting, and his mask was firmly in place. She had not thought he would so easily relinquish such an article, and she wondered if he wore it not for her comfort but for his own. She would not be so cruel as to deny him his feeling of security if he so wished, but she would not abide performing marital relations with the emotionless mask instead of her *husband*. But perhaps that did not need to be discussed quite yet.

She kissed his covered cheek and he seemed to relax when she made no mention of his mask. "I have made you breakfast."

He was going to make her a terribly plump thing soon with all his spoiling. He did not allow her to assist in carrying the muffins and tea into the dining room and even had scolded her for pouting. "Christine must learn to indulge her Erik," and he whisked away to pull out her chair. When she sank into it rather gingerly, Erik was kind enough to pretend he did not notice her slight grimace at the rather hard structure upon her delicate parts.

The muffins were comprised of swirled cinnamon and sugar with airy crumbles to hold them together, and when she slathered them in butter she could not help the delighted moan which escaped her lips. Erik watched her intently as she did so causing her blush to return more rapidly than she would have liked. He was good enough to not make her beg for him to partake as well, and though he watched her, he had his own luscious breakfast upon a plate before him which he nibbled at occasionally between sips of tea.

She watched his fingers as he pinched bits of muffins and when she looked down at her own hand she was once again struck by the gold band circling her finger. Yet his was naked. And the weight of knowing that there was yet another thing robbed of Erik because he was not like everybody else was crushing. And she did not know how, or when, but he would have a wedding band someday and not simply because she pleaded for him to go out and purchase one.

No, she would go into a little jewellery store and pick out one that seemed to best match her own. She would then make him a lovely dinner where he would sit in his chair and happily eat the plate she prepared for him—and of course not have to choke it down—and she would give him his wedding ring. And he would say how he loved her and she would smile at how happy she could make him, and then he would play something pretty for her.

She must have been lost too long in her thoughts as Erik looked concerned but seemed content enough when she resumed her breakfasting and smiled at him. His eyes always crinkled when she did that, and she wondered if her smiles meant more to him than she would have supposed. It was such a common expression, yet he seemed genuinely awed whenever she did so toward him.

When her muffin was little more than a lovely memory and her tea had deliciously been consumed, she looked to Erik to see if he would remember what he had promised her for a late morning activity. He sighed rather begrudgingly at her expectant look, though she could tell by the slightest twitch of his mouth that he was secretly pleased.

He would not allow her to assist him in cleaning the dishes, citing her continued state of discomfort though she tried to tell him it was not so very bad. He scowled at her. "*Any* sort of discomfort felt by my wife is unacceptable." And she had sighed and kissed his cheek and chose to ignore the way he stiffened at the contact before settling herself on the counter to watch him wash the dishes. Obviously he had expected her to await him in the sitting room, but she tilted her head and with an impish look challenged him to ask her to depart. The counter was even harder than the slightly cushioned dining chair, but she bore the tenderness quite happily as Erik handed her a dish towel and finally allowed her to help him by drying—though he would not permit her movement to put the freshly washed dishes away.

Soon the kitchen was once again the spotless room of Erik's preference, and before she could hop back down to the floor Erik wrapped her in his arms and with his long strides soon had them settled lazily in the sitting room. She would have thought he would place them on the settee, but instead he took them to his oversized leather chair and settled her comfortably betwixt the arm and his body.

She had been afraid he would spurn her after their copulation, but he was pleasantly surprising her with his affections. Perhaps in past she would have found them stifling and caging, but as she nestled further into the smooth lines of the chair yet still pressed enticingly against the bony frame of her husband, she found herself to be quite content.

Erik had taken to leaving a variety of books upon the side tables for just such instances as he seemed loath to leave her for any period of time, no matter if it was simply to go to the bookcase at the far end of the room in search of reading material.

It was a pleasant way to spend their morning, and Erik was kind in only asking her to read small segments at a time—never enough to tax or frustrate but enough to leave her feeling accomplished as she did not stumble or have to ask for assistance.

He had chosen a different sort of tale. No longer the fairy tales that played to her childhood fantasies, this story was one of human suffering and the perils of mankind. She blushed as there was talk of *prostitutes* in such plain speech. By no means did they finish the tragic novel, but Erik closed it all the same, seeming content to simply hold her close and twist her curls around his finger. *Les Misérables* he had called it. Why would he choose such a loathsome story on a day such as this?

It was a more mature narrative to be sure. And perhaps—perhaps it was as simple as that. Erik had always considered her with the childlike purity of one who must be sheltered and tended with the watchful eye of a guardian. And perhaps this was his way of showing her that he accepted her as the *woman* she now was—a *wife*.

"You grow so quiet, Christine, it makes me wonder what thoughts go through your pretty head." He tugged slightly at her hair, drawing her attention away from the analysis of his every action.

Her first impulse was to divert his attention from her thoughts. He would certainly not appreciate her doubting his choice in reading material and she could not fathom what good thing could possibly come of it. But then, such would have been her choice *before* she was a proper wife, and perhaps such fancies were not to be trusted.

"I was thinking how it is such a sad story, and I was curious why you would pick it today." She fiddled with a button on his waistcoat. "Are you unhappy, Erik?" She thought she might cry if he was. She was trying so very hard to be a good wife, and for him to tell her of his continued sadness might cast her into despair.

Erik pulled her from his side onto his lap so he could look into her eyes and see her tumultuous emotions swirl tantalisingly as her thoughts flickered from possibility to reality. "How could Erik be unhappy when he has a wife who is so very good to him?" His hand was gripping her chin, though not harshly even as his fingers pressed ever so slightly into her flesh. "Why should he only ask that she *love* him as well?"

Why must he ask it of her? For as long as she had known Erik the *man*, he had demanded, begged, *pled* for her love yet she *could not* offer it. And when he was content with her action, her words, her *body* they were both happy—or so she had believed. But now as she saw the torment of his expression she knew the selfishness of her behaviour.

She could play house with her doting husband yet never offer the very thing he craved—her *love*.

And she prayed he would not be angry, but her thoughts were beginning to muddle and her throat began to clog with the sobs of her wretchedness, but she could not speak the words he so desperately wished to hear. Love could not be forced, nor demanded—and though she wished now more than ever that such passions were forthcoming upon her agreement to be his true wife, she found herself still unable to do so.

She had expected him to rage at her as he always did when she refused him, or perhaps another soul ripping display of wails and sobs, but neither appeared. She did not feel the tears begin to flow until Erik's cold fingers were brushing them away with the same gentleness she had come to expect from him. And that notion alone made them flow all the more. "Hush now Christine, I am not angry with you."

She sniffled pathetically as she tried to find her voice buried within the pressure welled within her breast. "Oh how you must hate me Erik! I am so very wicked."

He *laughed* at her. Not the mocking sound she had heard so very often, but one filled with utter disbelief and incredulity. "How could Erik ever hate his Christine?" He sobered quickly when her distress did not lessen.

"You have given Erik far more than he has ever deserved. I could *never* hate you."

But he was wrong—so very wrong. She was beginning to glimpse the innocent soul which resided in the tortured carcass of past wrongs and sins, and it was for that reason he deserved all the kindness and compassion she could bestow upon him.

"I shall love you one day, husband. I swear to you."

And then his eyes misted with tears, and she wondered if he did not feel pain by her words. His breath became the shuddering intake of oxygen instead of the smooth cascading breeze that wafted over her skin so smoothly. But he did not cry. Instead he pressed his masked cheek to hers and breathed deeply, intoxicating himself with her closeness, and she prayed that he would infuse his very soul with her earnestness.

He returned her to her place at his side, still unwilling to allow her movement as he reassured himself with her continued presence. And as his hands petted her hair, her eyes strayed to the mantle for the first time in weeks.

She had avoided it in her cowardly temper. The root of her very predicament, the mantle which loomed over the cold chasm of stone did not hold the same horror as it had before. The two ebony boxes remained in their resolute stances upon the wood, and she wondered how if her actions had been different—whether on that particular night or before—if she would feel quite as content as she did at this moment.

When she had stayed with Erik for those two terrifying weeks, he had at least made an attempt to keep his home at a more liveable temperature by lighting the cheerful embers of fire, and she would sit beside it and look as the flames tickled and engulfed the disintegrating pieces of wood. But then she had felt eternally cold, and no matter how bright the fire as Erik laboured over it, she would shiver and draw away from him without concern for the pain it caused him.

But something seemed disfigured about it now, and as her eyes peered into the blackness of the stonework she noticed that what once housed lovely logs and wood pieces burned for her enjoyment was now partially filled with the same stones which made the encasement.

"Erik, what happened to the hearth?" His eyes had been closed as he held her, and only the tiniest slits graced the object of her question with his attention.

"Ah yes, our marriage was not the only outcome of that night, Christine." Surely he had not damaged it so...

He must have felt her stiffen as he chuckled. "No, I did not bring about the destruction of your fireside. Christine did so when she turned the Scorpion!"

How she wished he would not speak of it! Was she so distraught that she could have missed the caving in of such thickly cut stones? She was not herself that night, and perhaps it was possible. But she had no knowledge of how such genius works of engineering could have been formed, so it was entirely possible that the touch of her finger upon the small figure had indeed caused some structural uncertainty to befall the poor enclosure. So she would have destroyed the fire as well as the lives of two men.

"How unobservant my wife is." He clutched her a little closer as he spoke, as he often did when he made comments as to the attribute of his beloved. She wondered if he did so for the reassurance that such a person was truly in existence. "Does that sadden you, Christine?"

It did. Not simply for the lack of warmth it had provided, though she had not thought Erik's home to be any less warm since their wedding. She was rather surprised at herself for not noticing before, but then she had been keeping her distance purposefully these past weeks.

"I would very much like to have a fire." She thought once more of her dream of children quietly playing before the roaring flames as she and her husband looking on approvingly at their games. Even without manifestations of normalcy such as offspring, a fireside was not too dreadful a wish was it? She certainly would not complain at no longer having to keep her shawl at the ready to offset the chilly temperatures. Perhaps then she would not feel so inclined to spend so very much of her day in the warmth of the kitchen.

His eyes opened fully at her statement, and no longer did he seem as relaxed as before. She worried that he had upset him with her request, but as she looked at him he seemed—calculating. So often she saw evidence of his musical genius, but rarely had she been exposed to his abilities in areas of mathematics and construction. Any normal couple would call upon a mason to excavate the loosened stones, but surely Erik would never allow for such commonplace individuals to enter his home.

And most certainly he could not manage to do it himself! She would simply content herself with the pleasant warmth exuded from her stove as well as the numerous blankets and shawls scattered around the sitting room should the chill overcome her.

She told him as much, and he looked at her incredulously. "You think that I would allow my wife to freeze?" She nearly rolled her eyes and retorted that he had seemed quite comfortable doing so for some time now, but she thankfully managed to bite her tongue before such nonsense could be released.

Though he tried to anticipate her needs, Erik did not seem to require the normal comforts allotted by the average human body, and it was quite probable that he simply—forgot. He had not eaten with her until she had asked it of him, nor did he seem to call for the proper amount of sleep. But then, here in his home she had no idea how *her* body was functioning. Day seemed to be night, and her meals were based upon hunger—no longer fashioned around societal civilities or around rehearsals. For that matter, she had no knowledge of even the date.

What a troublesome thought. Though perhaps it was not a necessary awareness, *not* knowing precisely how long they had been man and wife irked her. Erik was no longer studying the hearth and instead was looking intently at the line which creased her forehead. One long digit suddenly rose and pressed it, and he seemed dissatisfied until it had successfully been smoothed.

"What troubles my Christine?" Perhaps it was silly of her, but ever since their conjugation she found Erik was expressing himself through actual vocalisations far more than he had in past. However, it meant she was required to produce answers that would not upset him—and such was her fear for many years. They did well in silence. It was their conversation which could so easily be twisted into misunderstanding.

"Erik, what day is it?" And now it was his turn to frown, and suddenly his expression descended into a look of suspicion. No! She could not allow him to think ill of her when such progress had been made between them. Though his mask made the smoothing of *his* lines to be impossible, she still brushed her thumbs under his eyes and mouth, and brushed her lips across his.

When he responded again, it was far more pliant and resolved to her incessant questions than accusing. "Why would Christine need to know the date?"

She quickly thought of a response that would seem more gracious than simply stating her curiosity as reason enough. "Most people celebrate anniversaries, and I was wondering," she looked at him then, suddenly fully aware that this truly was her reason for finding it necessary to know the date. "When was our wedding?"

He blinked at her, obviously not expecting such a question, though he no longer seemed to be looking for a hidden motivation behind her question. She was afraid he did not know, and suddenly it gripped her that their marriage could fade into the obscurity of time without the proper recognition it deserved. And it felt perfectly natural to desire to celebrate one's anniversary, regardless of the unwillingness on her part at the time. It was of significance, and she would like to look at that day with fondness in years to come.

"We were married on the twelfth day of February, should you like to consider the day the *priest* bound us." His insinuation was of course that they were married before that—upon her agreement to be his living wife. But to her, that day was simply the precursor to the actual event, and forevermore the twelfth of February would be engraved in her mind.

He did not seem forthcoming with today's date, but she supposed that was alright. From her own feeble calculations it was either the last days of February or early March—with spring a tantalising few weeks away. She hoped he would take her on walks in the sunshine come spring. He had said he had constructed a mask that would make him look like any other man—that he would take her for rides on Sundays just as any other man. But she did not care about his mask. She only wished they could do so. *Together.*

"I think that is a nice day for an anniversary."

She felt him press his cold lips to her forehead, and he resumed his brushing of his fingers against her back as he continued to hold her.

"I find I must agree with you."

XV

The rest of the day was spent in front of Erik's organ. He had told her that he wished she would consider singing once more, but the way he said it—it was almost as if he feared that would no longer be her desire. It seemed odd to her—that had been the basis of their relationship for so long, yet now she felt almost wary of reinstating her lessons. She was beginning to accept Erik as a *man* and it seemed almost too late to go back to her Maestro.

But that was his wish, and it seemed so terribly wasteful to refuse to nurture the gift he had bestowed upon her. He did not force her to perform anything too complex. Simple scales mostly, as her voice had not done well with its slight sabbatical from use. Erik would cringe faintly now and again when she hit a particularly sour note, and she felt twinges of embarrassment whenever he would do so.

There was something to be said for being tutored by an angel. He would shout at her certainly—to the point of causing her to cry, but she would also not have to witness the minute facial expressions of his displeasure.

When Erik had thoroughly tested the range of her voice, he had pulled her to sit beside him on the bench where he had played for her. It was not overpowering, but instead was simply a song a lover would play for his beloved because he wished to make her smile. So she kissed him when he had finished, but not before he had brushed her smile with the pad of his thumb.

Dinner was a quiet affair, as neither party seemed to feel obliged toward conversation. She still made sure Erik ate, though she caught him multiple times slipping bits of food into his napkin. He had prepared it with her, so she was sure it was from genuine lack of hunger rather than inedibility. But it still caused her heart to swell that it was so very important to him that she

113

be pleased with him.

And so now she was slipping on her nightgown even as Erik had gone to his own wardrobe to don his sleeping attire. She wondered if he would move his clothing into her room as he had promised his dreadful bed—*coffin*—would be disposed and the room converted. Her hand drifted to her torso without conscious thought. Would it be a nursery soon?

She shook her head determinedly. Of course she would not have conceived so soon! Many couples waited years before having a child, and surely there was some special means by which they would ensure conception. Perhaps Erik would know...

Christine went to her side of the bed and paused. This would not have been the first time she had crawled beneath unmade covers, but as she peered down at the rumpled blanket, there were distinct brown droplets marring the otherwise unspoiled bedclothes.

She was *not* ashamed of her virgin blood being spilled and causing a mess. Or at least she was determined to try not to be. But when she heard Erik's nearly silent footsteps in the doorway she hurriedly pulled the blankets and sheets into her arms so he would not see.

He was eyeing her speculatively, clad once more in his black informalities. It suddenly occurred to her that perhaps he did not possess additional linens for her bed, but it seemed so—*wrong*—to consciously sleep on them now.

"Did the bedding offend you, Christine?" She blushed and refused to look into his eyes, afraid he would see something in them to inform him of her reasoning.

"I... *we*... have slept on these for some time now and I thought it might be... *refreshing*... to have a new set." She looked at him expectantly; praying that somewhere in one of his hidden storage places there was another set of pristine sheets that were just as soft as the ones in her arms.

She chanced a look at him and found him not staring at her but at the bundle in her arms. He shifted slightly, almost as if *he* was uncomfortable, and that notion alone brought her comfort. In all probability he knew precisely why she had a sudden urge to perform a bit of laundering, and hopefully he would feel no great need to question her.

But suddenly she stood a little straighter. They were *married*, and such things were a natural part of sharing a bed. Most likely this episode would be repeated at her menses, and it should not matter so very much that Erik was instrumental in the causing of the bloodstain.

"Is that alright?"

Erik snapped his eyes to hers at her question. "Of course." He left the room rather quickly, and she was left to wonder what she should do with her burden. She never knew how Erik had taken care of such matters of cleansing before. The towels she used for her baths mysteriously disappeared only to be replaced with fresh ones the next morning, and her clothing met a similar fate.

Unable to make a decision, she simply placed them in the far corner of the room—bloodstain carefully positioned on the bottom of the pile. Even if they *were* married, that was still no reason to flaunt such delicate issues.

Her husband soon returned, crisp white linens in hand as well as a pale blue coverlet. She did not recognise the blanket as one of the many throws strewn throughout the sitting room, nor had she seen it any of the cupboards in the kitchen. Would he ever show her his domain in its entirety?

She was always pleased when she and Erik proved capable of performing quite aptly as some mundane task of domesticity. She had seen many couples bicker as they shopped—nagging wives begging to be allowed to patron one final store while haggard husbands berated them for their nonsense. Erik would roll his eyes of course, or give one of his maddening sighs, but she could tell by the slight crinkle of his eyes or the smallest twitch of his mouth that he adored their interaction.

Such was proving the same with their bed making. It was a fairly large bed—certainly larger than any bed she had slept in at the Opera house, and she was grateful for his presence on the opposite side for tightening corners and smoothing creases without extra effort on her part.

They finished quickly, but Erik refused to enter the bed until he had disposed of the soiled sheets—much to her dismay. Not only for the possibility of his noticing—or dare she think *touching*—the stain, but also because she very much wished to know how he had things laundered. There were still so many curious things about Erik that she did not understand, and he made no attempts to enlighten her.

But he disappeared so rapidly only to reappear before she could shimmy out from beneath the blankets that she could not help the huff that escaped her as he made use of his side of the bed. He seemed to mistake her irritation as one being directed at his action, and he hesitated as he began pulling down the blanket. "You do not wish for Erik to sleep with you?"

He looked so very sad! Any ire she felt at his lack of consideration for impeding on her ability to perform wifely duties melted as she patted the cold sheets beside her. "Do not be ridiculous."

He did not seem to believe her for a moment, but finally after staring at her a moment longer, his desire to be near her won out over any suspicion so he slid between the sheets with far more grace than she could ever manage. Perhaps it was the silk of his nightclothes that made him so slippery. She wondered what it would be like to sleep in such a pair...

She blushed thoroughly at the thought. Living so removed from society was surely distorting her sensibilities! And as she lay beside her husband in such similar positions to the ones they were in last night, she wondered if

115

he wished to enact his husbandly rights once more.

Though she felt wretched for doing so, she hoped he would not. Of course it was not for the reason she had once supposed she would. But she was still terribly tender, and she almost thought it would hurt more that it had the night before if he attempted such intimacies. But she would so hate to reject his advances, and she doubted he would recover from such a blatant refusal on her part. At least until he was more secure in her affections, for of course at some point in their marriage she would be too tired for such relations and would decline his desires.

He was so very good at reading her. Or perhaps she was more transparent than she would like to believe. But nonetheless he sighed into the still lit bedroom and turned away from her. "You need not fear your Erik, he will not touch you tonight."

She realised then that she had been biting her lip as she eyed him, and he must have taken such musings to be trepidation. Must he always prepare for the sting of her refusal? She touched his back gently, and he shuddered—though not from pleasure as far as she could tell. It was more a combination of recoil and surprise—and it troubled her greatly.

"Forgive me, Erik." She moved slightly closer until she could rest her arm upon his shoulder and hopefully pull him to face her. He must have anticipated her action as he moved more of his own accord than to any prodding on her part. "I am not afraid of you," she looked away for a moment, not sure how much of her thoughts he would amiable to hearing. "But I would ask that we... wait... a few days before... joining again."

His eyes widened as he peered at her, and she suddenly felt as though he greatly resembled a great black owl she had once seen. His mask was still in place, and she wished for its disappearance so she could better interpret his expressions. He was... surprised?

"You are willing to do it again?" When he spoke there was no doubting his shock at her consent for future conjugation, and she wondered how she had acted that would have given him cause for doubting her commitment to the future of their marriage.

"Of course, Erik, you are my husband. That is what husbands do." But when his words sank in, she abruptly began to wonder if they did not. Erik had been her guide as to the ways of the marital bed. Had they done something so wholly unnatural? But it had not felt so! And though she had no knowledge as to the frequency by which husbands desired their wives, she had certainly thought he might consider it a nightly venture—thus her request for leniency.

"Is it not?"

Her voice had grown timid, and Erik seemed pleased by it. Perhaps it was not her shyness that appealed to him, but it was the way her eyes darted to his as she looked to him for instruction as to the way of men. Such questions only further belaying her innocence and purity.

She was partially lying upon his chest as she looked at him, and his hand tickled her cheek as he stroked it tenderly. "It is. But I am not so thoughtless as to partake of my Christine too much before she is ready." He eyed her mischievously. "After all, she was quite *tender* this morning."

Christine nearly felt inclined to scowl and roll away to her the safety of her side of the bed to escape his *teasing,* but she felt the twitch of her lips as they betrayed her by smiling. "I do believe you like repeating that simply to remind yourself of *why* I might be sore."

Had she truly spoken such words aloud? She had not intended to! And by the sharp intake of breath below her, Erik had not expected it either. But when his eyes crinkled, and the corners of his mouth twisted the tiniest bit, she knew that he knew she had been teasing *him.*

And it felt delightful.

He brought himself up slightly so as to kiss her temple before wrapping one arm around her waist and curling around her from behind. "Be a good girl and turn down the light."

Erik had never slept so close to her before. The night before she had slept abusing his poor chest as if it were a pillow made for her own personal slumber, but this night *he* had initiated her participation in his sleep.

So she reached to lower the light, and just as so many times before, she felt no fear as the flame flickered out and left the room fill with the inky blackness only possible in Erik's underground home.

But she had not expected for Erik to shift his arm, nor did she expect to hear the sliding of material and the light thump as if something was placed on the bedside table. And when his face buried in her curls, she did not feel the cool seams of his mask pressing against her scalp—instead she felt the dry, papery skin of her husband.

And she found it a most pleasant way to be lulled to sleep.

-X-

When she awoke the next morning, the comforting presence of her husband no longer surrounded her, and she shifted slightly to see if he had simply moved away during the night. But as her hand skimmed the icy blankets it was evident that he had abandoned her some time ago, and she could not help feeling slightly despondent at his absence.

Keenly aware how pressing the dark seemed without Erik's steadying frame protecting her from unseen dangers, she quickly reached to light the lamp and frighten the demons away with its cheery flame. A quick perusal was all that was needed to ascertain the he was not hiding in some corner, nor was he sitting in the chair nearest the bed as he had been known to do.

There was a curious banging sound coming from beyond the firmly shut door of the bedroom, and it made her feel slightly nervous—though she could not tell if it was a rational fear or the wanderings of her imagination.

If Erik required something to occupy his time, surely he would choose something such as making her breakfast or tending to his music. That could only mean that someone was attempting to infiltrate his home through the grotesque means of the tools of mortal man.

Suddenly the terrible grip of unease had her in its icy clutches, and all she longed for was the reassuring arms of her husband as he promised nothing would harm her. What if it was a terrible mob come to take him away? How would she live without Erik's guidance?

Wasting no time in search of a dressing gown, she wrapped herself in one of the throws which had been draped over the chair Erik used to frequent, and ran to the heavy door of her bedroom. Why was he not coming to fetch her?

Her hand trembled as it turned the weighty knob, and it took a moment for her to realise that even though she applied the proper pressure and force, the door remained firmly closed.

It was... locked?

The banging sound increased in volume and intensity, and she felt hot tears begin to fall down her cheeks as she continued to pull at the door—frantically hoping it would apologise for its error in immediately opening at her will.

But it remained steadfast, and the dread blossomed into the all inspiring fear of one about to be torn from the beginnings of what happy life had been established these past weeks and—*where was her husband?*

She was sobbing as she wretchedly fell against the door, curling up against the base as she began to pound on the unforgiving wood. *"Erik!"*

And then the pounding ceased and she was sure the lovely sitting room where she had spent so many pleasant days was being trampled by the heavy footed mob as they tore across the plush Persian rug that felt so delightful against her toes, and surely they would find Erik and he would be killed and...

And the door opened.

She scrambled back slightly so as not to be hit by the figure's entrance, but instead of a stranger bent on the demise of her husband, it was Erik who was blinking at her uncomprehendingly as he saw the crumpled form of his sobbing wife. "Why is Christine on the floor?"

He nearly stumbled as she clung to his legs, feeling the relief of his presence so acutely it overwhelmed her. Erik did not seem pleased by her action, as he quickly stooped to pry her away, and he nearly had to use the full force of his strength to remove her clutching hands from his pant legs. "Christine, allow me to put you back in your lovely bed!"

She relented then and so allowed him to pull her into his arms as he carried her back into the bed she had so recently exited. Her arms were wrapped tightly around his neck as she tried to silence her tears, but they had melted from fear into gratitude of his presence, and it had not yet abated.

He slipped her beneath the covers and attempted to disentangle her arms from round his neck, much to her dismay. "Are we being attacked?" She pulled back slightly to look into his eyes only to find them looking back at her with a mixture of concern and confusion.

"Why would Erik and Christine be attacked?" He was petting her hair again in that hypnotic manner he did when trying to soothe either himself or her. "Did you have a troubling dream, Christine?"

She huffed in annoyance, not possibly understanding how he could not be alarmed at the pounding noises outside their home. Unless…

"That was you?" He still looked at her as though she had grown a second, equally foolish head, and suddenly she wondered if it would not be less humiliating to confess to it *having* been a dream. But she could not lie to her husband—especially not when he could possibly think that such dreams plagued her even after he slept with her.

"What was that noise, Erik?" He had least had the decency to look sheepish, and the hand not occupied with her curls settled upon making circles on her palm—which he seemed to find fascinating to look upon.

"I am afraid I cannot tell you." When he looked at her again, he truly did look remorseful. "I did not mean to make you cry."

She sniffled piteously, feeling thoroughly unsatisfied without an explanation as to what had been making such terrifying sounds. "Why can you not tell me? I thought the *gendarmes* were coming to arrest you!"

He looked rather indignant as any soothing motions ceased upon her person. "And you think such bumbling fools could enter Erik's home without my permission?"

She plucked at his sleeve, swiftly missing the contact of his hands. "I was frightened."

His eyes seemed to soften as they beheld her still watery eyes, and he appeared to understand how she truly had been afraid for the disturbance of their underground home. "I cannot tell you, Christine, for it is a surprise for Erik's little wife. Husbands are allowed to surprise their wives, are they not?"

Of all the possible reasons he could have provided her as to the interlude of strident banging, gifting her with a surprise was certainly not one she would have considered. But he looked nervous as he skimmed his finger along the blanket still wrapped around her in her haste of discovery, and she wondered what he possibly could be doing outside her room.

His head rose quickly as he wagged a finger at her sternly. "You did not see anything when Erik opened the door, did you?" She felt as though she would receive a severe scolding if she admitted any such thing, and she found herself quite grateful for the blurry world her tears had created.

"No, I did not. Though will I not see when I go out for meals?" His irked expression was back tenfold.

"Christine shall have to remain in her room until her husband has finished. We would not want to spoil the surprise now would we?" She could not help it. Perhaps she was still a child at heart, and though many people she had known disliked surprises immensely, she found them to be quite enjoyable.

There was a delicious anticipation involved as to what delight was about to be bestowed, and Raoul have provided such diversions frequently. She had not considered Erik as the type to give surprises, especially if it entailed depriving himself her company, but this seemed to cause him a great deal of excitement and she was willing to oblige him as she had Raoul.

But why did it trouble her so to compare the two men?

"Will you be a good girl and remain in your room?" He was still looking at her as if she would bolt from the room to spoil whatever secret he was keeping.

"Yes."

He peered at her a moment longer, obviously judging her resolve, but finally he nodded. "Good. Now I shall bring you breakfast and some things for entertainment while I work. It could take a few days."

Her mouth fell open of its own accord. *Days?*

What precisely had she agreed to?

XVI

She was so very bored, though granted, not nearly as much as she had been expecting had Erik made true on his previous promises to lock her away from the outside world. She missed his presence and the delightful normalcy they had begun to establish, but for once there was not the terrible dread that she had somehow wronged him or was behaving in a way she should not.

No, as she sat propped against a mound of pillows on the very bed that had seen so many monuments to her maturity, she was exactly where Erik wished her. She thought one of the reasons for Erik's extreme thinness was due to his inability to *remember* to procure proper nourishment, and she had worried slightly that he would do the same to her.

But ever proving the doting husband, every few hours he would enter with some new culinary delight or simply a new book to strike her interest. However, if she asked him to remain, he would *tsk* at her and accuse her of being quite naughty for tempting her husband so.

And with that he would slip from the room, leaving her once more to her treats and books. Her reading truly had improved through Erik's guidance. One of the many volumes he had given her was a primer which helped her greatly in understanding forms and structure. She was now even able to understand most of the more complicated literature he had given— though she was certain they were still children's novels.

She was touched by his thoughtfulness. Though he had proven time and again the scope of his genius, never did he make her feel like less of a wife or *woman* for her lack of skill. Well, certainly not for her literacy, though he did seem to scold her for other such things.

She doubted she would ever come close to his intelligence, though she did feel a tremendous sense of accomplishment when she was able to read through an entire fairy tale by herself. But as she closed the book, she found herself missing Erik's rendition as he breathed life into the characters as opposed to her own fumbling renditions.

And he had not wholly abandoned her. He had been working for the past two days, and last night she had been fearful that he would insist she sleep alone. But as she was preparing to morosely feign sleep for the allotted time, he entered once more in his nightclothes and settled beside her. He had been gone when she awoke.

And now it was mid afternoon, and no manner of book or sweet could tempt her into remaining in the bedroom. The pounding had quieted, though there was a peculiar scraping every now and then, though she could not place what it could mean—much to Erik's amusement she was certain.

He had promised to leave the door unlocked, and she was glad it had taken very little pleading on her part to obtain such a vow. She had not tried the door, and she had no true desire to see her surprise before Erik was ready—both for the possibility of seeing it before it was complete or for the risk of disappointing her husband.

She knocked timidly at the doorframe, hoping he would check on her before she was forced to try the knob. She was not sure if she could handle if he had lied to her and she was in fact prisoner in her room. Such things should be in their past, as their marriage had no room for such nonsense now.

Her hand rose to knock a second time, but she recoiled slightly as Erik slipped into the room at quite inhuman speed. "Erik, you startled me!"

He practically scowled at her as he firmly shut the door behind him. "How else am I to enter when Christine is so near the door? Where she could *see?*"

She huffed in annoyance. At least she had tried to gain his attention instead of barging into his work room! "Are you nearly finished?"

Erik sighed as he began to unroll the crisp sleeves of his white shirt. The buttons at his throat were undone, and Christine blushed as she realised she had not seen him look so dishevelled since their belated wedding night.

"I am not finished, but you have been very patient and deserve a treat. Wait here a moment." Where else was she going to go? She managed to contain her childish retort, and watched despondently as Erik glided once more from the room.

She did not want another biscuit! She wanted her *surprise!*

When the urge to stomp her foot overcame her, she gasped slightly at her foolishness. She was *not* a child! And she would certainly remember that she was a woman now and could learn *patience*. Erik had said so!

She returned to her place amongst the pillows awaiting Erik's reemergence. When he did return, it was not in the same untidy suit he had been wearing previously, but was once more clad in all his finery. But there was something—different about him as well. The suit was made of the same quality and cut as was his usual attire, but somehow it seemed more relaxed than the stiff waistcoats that he frequented.

She had been so focused on his suit, her breath caught as she looked at his face.

Instead of the harsh contrast of yellowed skin and emotionless mask there was—well—a *face!* Not necessarily a handsome one, but neither was it particularly ugly. It was simply—normal.

Her legs moved her forward without her consent. It was such a startling realisation that Erik could appear like everybody else the flood of possibilities swept over her. The little house aboveground with sunlit gardens as she picnicked with her husband—children toddling around them, exploring the great big world of God's making...

"Erik told you he had made such a mask." When he spoke her eyes flickered to his, and she remembered. It was not the mask that made Erik the reclusive genius who inhabited the underground, it was Erik himself—who needed *her* to show him how to *be* like everybody else.

Before she could touch his face to find the seams of such a magnificent structure, he was turning her round—not violently as he had wont to do when he supposed her intent on unmasking him, but gently until her back was to him and his hands were resting on her shoulders.

They remained there a moment until she saw a piece of dark silk rise over her eyes and obscure her vision. He made sure to keep each hair from the potentially fatal knot as he tied the fabric covering her eyes in a delicate bow. He had yet to release her, and instead moved to breathe into her ear. "Christine may not see her surprise just yet, but perhaps she would care to join her husband on a stroll."

She shivered as his breath caressed her, and she was entirely grateful for his thoughtfulness. He was not neglecting her, nor abusing her, and though he had not yet finished his project, he was putting her needs before his desire to complete his task and treat her to an afternoon out. She turned her head to his hand upon her shoulder and brushed it softly with her lips.

"I would be most happy to accompany you." She felt him reciprocate her kiss with one of his own into the welcoming curls he so adored, and his presence left only long enough to drape a cloak over her shoulders. She was very grateful she had dressed for the day, even though thoughts of lingering in her night attire had passed through her head as she thought she was remaining in her bedroom for the entirety of the day.

It was one of her plainer gowns, but the green cashmere was entirely suitable for keeping her from succumbing to the cool temperatures of an underground winter. She also could not help but adore its softness, and she could not resist skimming her fingers over the skirt now and then—and perhaps if she were honest with herself she could admit that it reminded her slightly of how it felt to be pressed next to Erik's own cashmere evening coats.

He was leading her then, though this time he was not intent on making her choose to seek his guidance by clutching fervently at his arm, but instead had carefully placed her hand in the crook of his arm and proceeded to take her from the room.

She half expected to stumble over some piece of furniture or rubble judging from all the pounding he had done yesterday, but he was guiding her expertly and she found herself trusting her footing slightly more as they carried on.

It was obvious when they reached the lake as the water produced such a muggy quality in the air. She did not feel it necessary to request Erik remove the blindfold as it would be quite impossible to see in the utter darkness surrounding the path to the Rue Scribe regardless of the silk impediment.

But when she felt the crisp air of the *true* outdoors, she bit her tongue to keep from asking Erik to please release her from the confines of her optical prison. She could feel the delicious breeze against her cheeks, and even felt the slight warmth of—sunlight?

She barely felt his fingers as they undid the knot and was quite grateful for the care he used in tying it as it could have been quite painful had the fine hairs been victim to its grasp.

But that mattered little as she absorbed the sight before her. Their last venture had been during the setting sun—long shadows giving the streets a dismal appearance, though she had certainly been delighted by it all the same. But now—now it was *morning*. She judged it to be quite early still as the streets had the quality of those not yet fully awake.

She hugged him. Even though there were a few individuals milling about as they began the day's preparations, and even though he stiffened at her unexpected display of public affections, she held him with a gratitude she had not known she possessed. "You are very good to me, Erik."

Perhaps it was silly. Many wives would not congratulate their husbands on something as simple as letting them enjoy a morning outside the home, but as the sun steadily rose in the sky, all remaining shadows were beginning to diminish—leaving Erik entirely exposed. And she knew theirs would never be a marriage that could be deemed uncomplicated, but she felt the encompassing warmth of his sacrifice as he gave her the gift of a clear morning outside.

He patted her head rather awkwardly before prying her slightly away and replaced her hand onto his elbow. "Just like everybody else," he murmured almost to himself.

She squeezed his arm encouragingly as he led her through the allies and streets they had traversed before, until finally they were once more staring at the delightful row of shops and bakeries, and *life*, that Christine could not help the exuberant giggle that escaped her lips.

Erik looked at her as though she had suddenly been possessed by an unknown demon. And she smiled all the more and stood on her tip toes to bestow his smooth cheek with a kiss. But as she pulled away she could not help but think that she much preferred the feel of his withered cheek to that of this façade.

But she would not think of such things, not when she had been blessed with such a special outing. She did not know when such a time would come again, and she knew specifically what she wished to accomplish. Erik would have his wedding band.

Even if she had to request the *francs* from him, would he find the sentiment any less prominent? She nibbled her lip thoughtfully, but determined it a necessary risk. But she did not wish for it to totally be unsurprising, so perhaps he would allow her to enter the store alone as he remained waiting outside—for she would certainly not consider being alone without him. Nor did she wish for *him* to be alone in the strange world of early morning patrons either.

Their first stop was at the bakery. Though Erik had been filling her with all manner of luxuries since she awoke that morning, when the breeze sent the wafting smell of freshly made bread in her direction, all past morsels were forgotten.

Erik dutifully proffered the money required to obtain her demanded delight, and Christine wasted no time in tearing off bits of steaming baguette as soon as the item was given to her. Her husband rolled his eyes at her enthusiasm, but there was a distinct twinkle in his now colourless eyes that belied his pleasure at her enjoyment.

It amazed her how his eyes could seem so expressive in the darkness of their bedroom, yet in the day they were nearly transparent. She had stared at him too long it seemed as his good humour faded, and she quickly made haste to distract him.

Pulling off a section of crust, she raised it to his lips as a humble offering of thanks. He was startled for a moment, but recovered quickly as he eyed her carefully before enveloping her gift between his too thin lips. Though she had no idea of the mask's construction, there was no denying that Erik's lips were his own—and she was rather grateful for them.

Those lips had known her so very intimately, and she did not think she could bear to share this day with a different man than her true husband. She giggled as his lips nipped slightly at her fingers, and she pulled away with a blush—much to Erik's amusement as there was an undeniable twitch to his mouth.

But when the little bell above the bakery door tinkled pleasantly, all humour was gone as Erik seemed to contemplate the danger of the new comer. Well that would not do. While she was grateful for his protection, if they stayed more than an hour the street would certainly begin teaming with people, and she would very much like to be able to enjoy her shopping with the man who teased her fingers instead of the one who was currently glaring at the scullery maid who was procuring the daily rations for her household.

She tugged at his hand, and he followed obediently behind her, but he seemed to be perplexed by her direction to the slightly darkened alley beside the bakery. "Is something wrong, Christine?"

She sighed. She would *not* hurt his feelings. The concept of being able to blend into the crowd of customers would not have ever occurred to him, and even with his mask there were still certain qualities he had yet to hide. His height gave him a naturally intimidating ability to loom over one, and matched with the glare he seemed to give every stranger was not going to help them go unnoticed.

"Erik," she paused, thinking how best to begin. He always seemed more receptive when she was touching him, but stroking his face did not seem a wise proposition at the moment so she settled on circling the skin of his wrist with her thumb. "I want you to enjoy yourself with me." There. She had said it. But judging from the confused look he was giving her, she had not been particularly articulate.

"I always enjoy spending time with my wife." Of course he did, and she was glad of it. But she very much wished he could enjoy being with her in front of *people*—at least for short amounts of time. She would not push him, and she would accept however much time he would allow, but she did not want him to simply humour her, but would hope that he drew some pleasure from their outings aside from basking in her presence.

"I know you do, but—" she stopped suddenly, overcome with a feeling that she was about to make a terrible mistake. The distrust Erik had for strangers was one built upon years of experience, and by her making him feel as though he were doing *wrong* for doubting their motivations she would surely make him feel self conscious. And when Erik was uncomfortable, his natural inclination seemed to be avoiding the source at all costs. The only way he would learn that humanity could treat him with something other than malice was by time and experience.

So eternally thankful she had not spoken her thoughts too rapidly, she shook her head at his questioning gaze and rose to her tip toes to bestow his lips with a kiss. "Good, I am glad."

He still seemed baffled by her impromptu stop, and his eyes narrowed at her quick change in subject, but when she was once more tugging at his hand he followed behind before securing her hand into his elbow so they could walk at a slower pace.

But Christine had something specific in mind, and she felt an overwhelming urge for Erik to share in her excitement. She did not see the pretty dresses in the windows they passed, nor the bookstores which promised hours of entertainment in Erik's lovely sitting room. Her gaze was focused on the jewellery store which came ever closer the faster they walked.

She was worried for a moment that it would be closed, and she paused at the door suddenly feeling rather shameful for not simply telling Erik her desire for his wedding band. Surely he must think her a foolish girl who wishes her husband to buy her pretty jewels. But he was not looking at her that way, he simply took her pause to mean she was waiting for him to open the door like the gentleman he was, and so she entered, Erik close behind her.

Christine did not bother looking at what other options there were to behold, she merely made her way purposefully to the window display where she had first seen the plain gold band that she knew should someday be Erik's.

Erik was not looking at the glimmering objects, but was looking at her with a curious expression. They both turned however when the shop attendant entered from the back room.

"Ah, my first customers of the day!" The elderly man looked Erik over appraisingly, and then looked to Christine. "Are you here to purchase a trinket for your lovely wife? Is it her birthday? Anniversary?" Erik simply raised his eyebrows in response, as he had no way of knowing why exactly she had dragged him to this particular shop.

"No, Monsieur, we are here to procure a wedding band for my husband." She was not looking at Erik as she rather cowardly did not wish to know if he disapproved her desire for tangible evidence of *his* being married to *her*. So she instead looked to the shopkeeper, who nodded pleasantly in her direction.

"That happens quite often I am afraid. The groom remembers to purchase an engagement ring, but in the rush to the altar sometimes his own ring is overlooked." He clapped his agreeably. "But no matter! Did you have one in mind?"

She was not sure of proper protocol when handling such expensive items, but it seemed rather ridiculous to make him come over to collect the ring from its perch in the window. "Yes, I would like this one." With careful hands she cradled the ring in her palm before walking to deposit the cool object on the counter separating her and the jeweller.

"A fine choice, my dear. And you sir, are you in agreement?" She braced herself for his rejection, fearing that he would find such a claim wholly a ruse on her part to bind him further into a ritual he did not fully embrace.

"I am sure whatever my wife has picked will be quite suitable." He had not moved from his position toward the door of the shop, but she did not mind so long as he was amiable to the acquisition of his ring.

She still did not look at him, not when she doubted the continued state of living of the jeweller when he requested the sizing of Erik's finger, nor when Erik did *not* strangle the man for actually taking the measurement. She did not look as Erik placed the *francs* in the man's hand, nor when Erik handed *her* the little bag and box which held his ring—as per the store's tradition she was told. Perhaps most couples had a simple ceremony at home when the ring was placed on the husband's finger.

She had not thought so far ahead.

It was not until they were once more outside that she looked at him. He was studying her, not with confusion or malice, just staring in that oddly studious manner that only he seemed to employ. It was like she was an enigma that he could not fully understand, and perhaps if he could stare long enough a hidden door would open into her thoughts finally allowing him access.

She cleared her throat to dislodge the uncomfortable feeling he gave her when he did so, and she fingered the small bag which held the significant item that so desperately needed to be placed on Erik's finger. And suddenly, she wanted to return home. As the sun rose higher, more people emerged from their homes to take care of their daily shopping, and she felt quite crowded and bothered by the noises of bustling life about her.

And she simply wanted to give Erik his ring in the privacy of his home. *Their* home.

"May we return home now?"

He was still eying her, but seemed to understand the shift in her mood so for the final time that day placed her hand in the crook of his arm and led her through the twisting allies and streets that led to the entrance at the Rue Scribe.

As it was so bright in the morning light, she was able to focus on the approaching doorway and missed the small creature huddled on the side of the alley entirely—tripping quite ungracefully and was quite grateful for Erik's gentlemanly behaviour. His arm was steady so she did not fall, and she even shivered at the other arm which quickly had encircled her waist to hold her upright. That did not however keep her from twisting around to glare at the offending object which had almost caused her demise.

It was not a box or a piece of refuse as she had supposed, but there, the epitome of all things pitiful, was a kitten. Still quite young—though not so young as to be entirely dependent on the mother— the small creature was rather filthy and undernourished due to the realities of living in the Paris streets in winter.

She wanted it. The same childish impulse to save the poor creature starving on the street as she had felt so many times in girlhood stirred within her, and she tried desperately to quell the impulse. The underground was no place for such a kitten—and surely Erik would not allow it. Not on his fine Persian rug and especially not where tiny claws could scratch his furniture. So she steeled herself to walk away, forever to wonder the fate of the tiny creature on the cold street.

But suddenly, her heart melted. Not just for the kitten with its blue eyes which seemed far too large for its triangular face, but for her husband who leaned down to scoop the creature into one hand. He did not step over it to continue his journey home as so many men would have done. He did not even pause to rationalise its ability to survive until spring. He simply saw a small insignificant creature abandoned and acted. "Come along, Christine. I believe you wished to return home."

Just like that? No hesitance in his decision to add another member to their little family, nor did he consult her thoughts in the matter. But she could not truly fault him as they continued walking toward the darkened hole which led to their home. Not when the kitten mewed pitifully in Erik's encompassing hand, and especially not when he pulled her into his side as they traversed the blackened passages, never distracted from his supreme goal in keeping her safe from all dangers—including ones she could never hope to see.

And that was when she knew she was entirely in love with her husband.

XVII

Erik had never felt quite as warm as he did on his walk home. Perhaps he had come close when buried within his Christine, but there was something especially appealing about having his wife pressed in his side as well as having a warm body encapsulated in his hand.

He had always adored animals. They were God's creatures born without the malice so ingrained in the very fibres of humanity, and therefore they could accept him for the creature that *he* was as well. He had seen many such pitiful animals needing care, but he had not taken such pains as to deem himself worthy of pet ownership. But he was different now. Christine had seen to that and in the most awe inspiring ways.

When he had begun his surprise for her it was not with the intention of locking her away in her bedroom for days at a time, it was simply to fulfil a wish she had so desired and that was within his capability to provide. And so he did.

He would have to blindfold her before allowing her entrance into the room of course. Surprises were about the proper unveiling; it certainly would not do to have it spoiled on poor execution.

They had been growing steadily closer the past few trips to and from the above world. He remembered how cruelly aloof she had remained in their early days. The barest touch of her fingers as she kept her body fully unattached from him was all he could hope for, until in desperate straits for her further affection he had refused to even carry a lantern to guide her. He had no need of it. The traps all bowed at his whim, and he was accustomed to the darkness.

Too adjusted in fact. The bright morning light had been nearly painful on his vision, and he was certain to have need of a remedy once Christine had been gifted her surprise. Nothing too strong—he had no need for the more enticing treatments when Christine was near to alleviate the terrible aches of his heart.

But such things were in the past. His arm was fully around her waist, and she neither recoiled nor trembled in that dreadful way that pierced him so utterly. She would shiver sometimes, and it would cause him to look to her eyes for guidance as to how she was feeling—to see if perhaps she had not managed to stop the fear she felt toward him. But like the good girl she was, there was not a trace.

She was too good to him—so very trusting. Even as he now had released her waist to reposition the blindfold across her pretty face, and worked diligently to keep each curl away from the noose which threatened them. He would have to deposit her in her bedroom again in order to prepare the sitting room for the unveiling. Perhaps she could bathe the kitten while she waited...

She did not protest much to his happiness. He could not bear to force her, yet it should so spoil his toils of the past few days if she were to be unhappy with humouring him for a few moments longer.

He carefully steered her through the slightly untidy sitting room, and he could not help but smile at the sigh she gave to be once more in her room. He adored her lip when she pouted. It was plump and pink, and he no longer had to wholly restrain himself from touching it. And so he did. Though not with his lips as he so wished—he would not press his advantage with her when she was so blinded. She must always have the option to reject him—even though it pained him to allow it.

He removed her blindfold and feeling rather ungentlemanly discerned the gender of the tiny kitten. A female. Such a pretty girl she was too...

He passed her cautiously to the woman who was studying his interaction with the animal with interest. Was he truly so curious? Surely many men enjoyed the companionship of pets. "Perhaps you would be so good as to wash her while I prepare a few things."

"It is a girl?" Had it not been obvious? She should have quite plainly seen the lack of testes which belayed her sex. But Christine was such an innocent girl—perhaps she had truly been unable to distinguish the difference. His darling girl.

"Yes, she is a girl. And it would be detrimental to allow her to wash all of the grime for herself." He paused, suddenly wondering if such a thing would be distasteful to her. But she had looked so forlorn when she had seen the living thing which had caused her to nearly fall, and he knew then that there was no possibility of allowing the kitten to remain in such conditions. And surely one so small would not be too difficult to manage. "I could do it if you are uncomfortable."

She grasped the kitten a little closer to her chest, eyeing it rather adoringly. He would *not* feel jealous. "No no, I can do it. Will you be very

131

long?" It was far easier to refrain from envious feelings when she turned her eyes to him in that imploring way and begged his company.

But it would not do to allow her to think she affected him as much as she did with her pretty eyes and pink lips. "If Christine insists I could perhaps be persuaded to hurry my task."

She *smirked* at him. His Christine was certainly becoming cheeky the longer she remained his wife. And it made his heart grow warm. But when her lips found the corner of his mouth, all complaint as to her impudence fled his mind. "Yes *please* husband, do hurry. I should very much like my surprise soon."

His eyes narrowed of their own accord at her mention of the surprise. How did she know that was what he was going to tend to? "And you shall not peek?"

She looked at him rather peevishly for his insinuation. "Have I not behaved thus far?" And when she tilted her head in that challenging manner, he was helpless to resist the urge to kiss her temple. She was always so very soft.

And just like the impertinent girl she was, she smiled at him cheekily— almost as though his kiss was her aim from the beginning—and told him to *shoo*. He, the very man who instilled the fear of death into all manner of men, was being told to *shoo* by a tiny slip of a girl—his *wife*. And the warmth in his heart grew all the more, even as he obeyed her command.

He had yet to take off his newly created mask. Though by far the one which provided the most normality, he rapidly was discovering it was not something conducive for daily use. The fine leather offered very little ability for his skin to ventilate, and although it was of the highest quality, the horrendous skin of his face was prone to sensitivity. But he had no time to change it as it certainly would not take Christine so very long to see to the kitten's cleanliness.

But before he could fully prepare the room for Christine's perusal, he quickly fetched a small dish of cream—the very cream his wife so insisted swirl against the blackness of her tea—and deposited it on the night table of Christine's bed for her to feed the small creature when she had finished its bath.

Such trivialities complete, he began the tedious process of reassembling the sitting room. He hoped he had not soiled his suit as he checked the final preparation of her gift—thankfully finding it sufficiently dry for a proper reveal. A bit of kindling, a piece of rubbish known as newsprint, a generous amount of logs, and finally a match were all that was required to complete the affect.

He painstakingly removed the last of his tools and set the furniture to rights. And as he eyed the room, now with its cheerful blaze and subtle warmth, he found it to be quite *seductive*.

It became startlingly clear why he had put off the necessary task of seeing to the damaged fireplace when he imagined how Christine's skin would look tickled by its glow. She was tempting enough in the warmth of candlelight—for that matter she could torment him into madness in the utter darkness of one of his unlit rooms.

Perhaps he had been selfish in locking her away the past few days. But she needed time to heal, and when he thoroughly exhausted himself with the labour intensive masonry, it allowed him the exhaustion necessary to remain by her side as she slept and refrain from the carnal urges to further damage her delicate places. But surely enough time had passed that it would not be cruel to instigate such relations once more.

And so with such thoughts he went to collect his wife from her bedroom. She had completed the task of washing their tiny new addition to their underground home, and he was relieved to see she had managed quite well judging from the pure white skin of her hands—unmarred by the potential weapons of a small cat's claws. Ivory fur was now visible—belaying the Siamese origin of its ancestry. She was curled up in the middle of Christine's pillows, and was obviously content to remain there for quite some time, now that her small belly was distended with cream.

Would it be brutish to enjoy making love to his wife outside of her bed?

Christine had a look in her eye he had not seen before. It seemed almost—maternal? And when she tore her eyes away from the sleeping creature, she looked at him with so much affection he could easily mistake it for love—though he tried desperately to remind himself that he should not make assumptions of his wife's feelings lest he be left vulnerable to disappointment. But he did know it was impossible for him to put a blindfold on such eyes when they could look at him in such a way.

So he took her hand—her lovely, lovely hand—and led his delicate angel into the rapidly warming sitting room. She gasped in that way which always told him she was pleased, and suddenly it was *she* who tugged on his hand as she rushed to sit before the flames.

"Oh, Erik, it is *warm!*" And that look was once more in her eyes as she pulled on his hand for him to join her on the floor. He did not know why she had such a penchant for sitting on his rug, but he could deny her nothing—even if it meant spending the next hour cushioned only by the finest Persia had to offer. And if her eyes continued to look at him with such affection, he truly would be in danger of being entirely ensnared by her charms.

"Does it please my wife?" He knew it did, and perhaps it was wrong of him to ask, but he very much wished for her to shower him with her praises. He only wanted to be a good husband after all.

Her lips were on his, suddenly and fiercely, and he was rather startled at her exuberance. When she pulled away her eyes were shimmering, and she brought his hand and deposited an object he had not dared considered.

A wedding band.

His wedding band.

"Erik, I have something I must tell you, but I fear if I say it when you wear your mask you will not fully believe me." She looked at him with those beseeching eyes but it did little to quell the feeling of dread which welled within him. He prayed she would not speak it—it was impossible for her to look at him in that wonderful way when he was not wearing his mask—but her lips moved and he shut his eyes to the sight.

"Please Erik. *Please.* I promise you will not regret it." How could he trust her? She had so brutally exposed him not but a few months ago, and closer still she had recoiled in abject horror at his visage. He had removed his mask only in the darkness of her bedroom—when he *knew* she could not see—where he could pretend for a moment they were normal. Oh but her curls had felt so good against the sensitive skin of his face! Her lips were the softest silk as they kissed his withered flesh, but why would she do so if he removed his mask?

But refusing her went against every fibre in his being—for pleasing one's wife was the most basic of husbandly duties. So with every expectation that his desire to love her on the very rug they sat upon fled as quickly as it had entered his mind, he slowly pulled the tightly fitted leather from his face and neck.

And he could not look at her. He never wished to see the warmth melt from her eyes only to be replaced with the utter revulsion that he had seen so many times from her. He very nearly fled the room, but she must have sensed it as her hands were suddenly on his face—so very gentle, yet binding as they held him. Her lips were so very close to his, yet she did not touch him. Her breath was sweet as it washed over him, and he very well could have died in that moment and been the happiest of men.

Until she spoke.

For when she did, the warmth that had steadily built in his heart for his wife overflowed into the cold caverns of his soul, until he could hardly remember their existence.

"I love you, Erik."

He must have misheard her. But when she whispered it like a prayer, kissing every inch of withered flesh she could reach in between her promises of love, he felt the slightest trickling of belief enter his body. She loved him? *Loved* him?

His Christine. The angel who had had watched and adored, nearly lost to a fop, and whom he nearly committed mass murder to ensnare, *loved* him.

And she was tugging at his hand once more and he feared she was asking him to rise—and he was sure his legs would not support him as the magnitude of her words was washing over him with the ecstasy of more delight than he had ever known.

But she was not asking him to move, but pulled his left hand into hers and slipped a warm circlet of gold around the third finger. *His wedding ring.*

"With this Ring I thee wed," she was repeating the very words he had spoken before the very priest who had pronounced them man and wife. "With my body I thee worship," how could she worship *him* when she was the goddess meant to be adored? "And with all my worldly goods I thee endow." She blushed then—that delicious pink blush that matched her lips and made his fingers ache with the need to caress every expanse of pink flesh. "But I am afraid I do not have any worldly goods to offer you."

What did he care for meaningless items when she offered up her very soul to him? And she looked almost nervous, and her hands had released him as she twiddled them anxiously. Why was she distressed?

"Erik, are you not pleased?" And it was *her* eyes that shimmered with tears, and he did not know how to answer her.

So instead of speaking the words that refused to come from his dry lips, he kissed her—utterly and thoroughly. He did not concern himself with the thoughts that swirled in his head that he had no right to kiss her in such a manner—for she was his *wife* and she *loved* him—so his tongue moved to truly *taste* her. And he moaned.

He had tasted the finest delicacies the world had to offer, yet nothing compared to the taste of his wife's pretty pink mouth. He had kissed her the night she had given him the gift of her innocence, but he could not help the feeling that he was intruding on her enough that she should not also have to suffer the plundering of her mouth to this extent. But he would not hold back this night.

But his darling girl still required breath, so he reluctantly pulled away and listened to her gasp for oxygen—and quite morbidly he thought of all his victims who were fortunate enough to be released from his Punjab lasso. They had made similar sounds. But his Christine was never to know the horror of true deprivation—she would simply suffer the consequence of too much passion from her adoring husband.

She was wearing far too many clothes. He did not care if in the light of the fire she could see the corpse-like figure of her Erik. Not when she loved him! But he could not seem to discard their clothes fast enough and she took pity on his desires and hastily divested herself from the troublesome corset and her dress.

He felt as though he might die in the time it took for him to strip himself of his own clothes, and when he was finally free he found the pantaloons still encasing her lower body to be the most wretched articles he had ever known. He should be ashamed, but even when he heard the ripping sound he could not still his hands as they found the smoothness of her skin, and the sound paled in comparison to the gasps and whimpers his wife was making.

He thought there no greater sound than that of Christine's singing voice, and he nearly sobbed at the realisation that such was not the case. She was not lost in the wild abandon that threatened to consume him, and he wondered if he would ever learn to play the contours of her body with as much skill as he learned the instruments at his disposal. But as she tugged gently on the ragged strings of his hair, all thoughts flew from his mind other than imbedding himself in the welcoming warmth of the only woman—only *human being*—who could bring themselves to love such a man as him.

His fingers skimmed the lines of her torso, and he found that when he dared to touch the plush mounds of her breasts—the very ones which tormented him as he was forced to heal them—his Christine made the loveliest sounds of encouragement for his attentions. But he was afraid of hurting her—did not know what could instil such passions that would mimic his own—so he left only the barest trail of contact as he skimmed her flushed skin.

He should have wondered if the silk threads of the rug burned her skin as he thrust into her. He should have prepared her more for his intrusion—but he did not know *how!*—for she winced slightly at his entry. He had not readied himself for such an action. He had told himself the first night that her discomfort was only to be born the one night—any night beyond that was due to his failing as a husband.

And with dismay he was about to withdraw—to apologise for his thoughtlessness, but Christine was gripping his shoulders, and when she tensed the inner muscles of her womanhood she gripped him so very tightly, and all thoughts of leaving her flew from his mind. "I am alright, Erik."

And he had to trust her.

For in all the books, novels, and every scrap of literature he had read there was a common theme. Without trust, there was no love. And he would prove to her that he trusted her—now that he possessed the love he had craved for so many years. She could have whatever life she wished. He would be her willing slave now that she had given him the most precious of gifts—one that he would covet jealously.

And when he pressed all the more into her yielding flesh, Christine gave no more evidence of pain, or discomfort. Her eyes were soft as she looked at him—her hands stroking the strands of hair which fell over his unmasked face as he hovered above her. "I love you so, my Christine."

And so with hands clutching the curls he adored, his own lips coaxing her pink one into his mouth, he felt the coiled tension of release as he filled his Christine with his essence—the very thing he so feared would cause her body to succumb to the dead quality of his own. So though his eyes had closed when the ecstasy of her love had fuelled him to fruition, he warily opened them to check the health of his beloved wife.

She smiled.

Even though he had bedded her on the soft floor of his sitting room, even though he had not spoken the practiced words of the lovers of old, she was smiling, and was still caressing his skin with her soft touch. He was loath to remove his flesh from hers, but his now utterly spent body begged for the luxuriating comfort of rest, but only if Christine would remain with him.

Now that his mind was no longer clouded with the frenzied thoughts of love and ardour, he became aware that he was lying naked before a fire—painfully exposed to his wife's perusal. And never wishing for her to gaze too long at his form lest she come to her senses regarding his person, he made to find more suitable attire in his wardrobe.

But Christine had other ideas as she nearly pressed her entire body upon his when he made the slightest move to rise. "Stay with me, just like this. Just for a while longer." And when he looked at her, the supple lids were covering her eyes as she used him for her pillow and simply enjoyed the warmth of the fire as well as being encased by her husband's embrace.

"Will you say it again?"

Her eyes fluttered open at his request, and she looked at him so softly—so *lovingly,* he could not bear the thought of looking away, even if it was to shy his face away from her eyes.

"I love you, Erik. So very much."

And as she fell asleep on his shoulder and he felt the seductive prowess of its siren call as well, he wondered if perhaps he should have repaired the hearth earlier.

XVIII

Her intent had not been to make them spend the entire night on the floor. And when her eyes had shut and she drifted into the blissful dream world after Erik's love making, she had only meant for a short rest before adjourning to the comforts of their bed. But instead she had felt so content, and the fire was even warmer than the many blankets she used to sleep each night, and she feared Erik might hide himself away in the morning, so she simply closed her eyes and embraced the everlasting relief of sleep.

But she surely had not meant Erik to remain as well. She knew he would be uncomfortable without the reassurance of his mask and—she blushed at the thought—*clothes,* but he seemed content as well to remain by her side as she slept. Until now at least.

The fire had died down during the many hours of her rest, and it was the cold which awoke her. Erik seemed unwilling to move, and he eyed her warily from his position nearly entirely beneath her. When she slept alone either at the home of Mamma Valérius or in the dormitories, it had not occurred to her that she moved very much in sleep, but now as she slept near Erik it was becoming evident she did so. No matter how modest her position as she fell asleep, she was always closer to him when she awoke.

Her body slightly ached—not the ache of newly exercised muscles she was rapidly becoming used to with such new activities as marital joining—but instead it was her body's protest to spending such a long period on the unforgiving stone floor with nothing but a rug for cushioning. She was sure Erik had not fared much better, unless years spent in the hard wooden confines of a coffin had built up his immunity to such unpleasantness.

"Good morning, Erik." She moved to roll off him—and find her own clothing now that she considered it—but her husband seemed to be of a different mind as his arms constricted around her for a moment longer.

Though he kept her trapped within his embrace, he still managed to seem shy as she looked at him in the dying light of the fire. But there was more to it than that. He seemed almost—pleading?—but yet did not vocalise what it was he desired. And when she considered, it seemed so very obvious.

She kissed above his heart— it fluttered so beneath her lips!—and she met his gaze once more. "I love you, Erik."

He relaxed immediately at her words and she felt terribly sorry that he should have lain awake for however short a time once more questioning that her love would have diminished over the course of a few hours. "You are so beautiful, Christine." His fingers were in her hair, and he touched her face with his immeasurable tenderness that made her heart ache for him.

She could certainly not answer in kind, but her smile seemed answer enough, and to her surprise, he returned it. She had never seen him smile without his mask. For that matter, she was not positive she had ever witnessed a true smile from him at all. Smirks, sardonic laughter, and the occasional rapture had twisted his lips into semblances of happiness, but this was entirely different.

And she wished to see it again.

"Erik would like to invite his wife to an evening at the theatre. Would you be agreeable?" An opera? *With* Erik? The notion filled her with delight. To not be hounded for her own performance, but yet to enjoy the insight of her Maestro to the fullest was both intriguing and thrilling in its prospect.

She could not help the smile that broke out on *her* face as she answered him. "You mean upstairs?"

He graced her with one of his eye rolls as he tapped her gently on the nose. "Yes of course upstairs. Unless there was another production house you know of?" He was teasing her, as obviously, it was impossible for her to possess such knowledge if he did not. But she did not feel embarrassed as she might have before—well—before she loved him.

"No, I am sure the Opera House shall suffice." His lips quirked once more, and the shimmering in his eyes showed his happiness.

"I am glad you can deem to grace them with your presence, Christine." His voice lowered as he pulled her face closer to his. "Though an angel such as you surely deserves far greater than they could provide." *Now* she was embarrassed. But instead of shying away from his praise, she simply kissed him soundly on the lips.

They were interrupted then as a soft mewing was heard and was steadily coming nearer. "Ah, *félin* Christine has finally emerged." Christine looked at Erik as though he had suddenly sprouted a second head.

"*Félin* Christine? You cannot possibly name the kitten *félin* Christine." He had the audacity to look confused.

"Why ever not?" And now it was her turn to be pressed underneath *his* weight as he had so endured the entire night through. She shivered as his eyes bore into hers, and she felt the stirrings of his loins against her thigh. "Why should Erik not wish for such a creature to love him as his wife does?" His breath was caressing her—teasing her flesh even as his fingers did not. "And if *Christine* loves him," he paused, almost waiting for her affirmation that he was right in saying so. Her tongue felt numb, so she quickly nodded her assent. "Then perhaps naming our new familiar *félin Christine* would only aid the process."

How he could manage to appear so seductive, yet so utterly bashful at the same time was beyond her comprehension. And perhaps even more strangely, his rather odd logic as to the kitten's name seemed quite rational. She was the only one to ever have loved him—much to her own heartache—and he simply wished for their new family member to love him as well.

But that did not mean she particularly liked the name. So with lower lip extended, she pouted prettily even as his lips tantalisingly did not quite brush her flesh. "But will it not be horribly confusing having two Christines in the house?" His lips were at her ear, tickling her mercilessly with his shallow breathing.

"No."

And then he was away from her, quickly and dexterously replacing clothing with such speed and agility she seemed to only blink and he was almost entirely dressed. He brought her own dress closer, but it seemed rather wasteful to put it on when she meant to immediately remove it for her bath. "I am afraid we do not have much time to prepare before the performance begins."

How could that be? Surely it was morning aboveground... But no, it would not be. Such a curious thing, how days and nights were switched due to their unnatural dwelling.

Erik held out a hand to help her from the floor, and she grasped it gratefully.

"Are we going to sit in Box Five?" She was not sure how she felt about such a public display. It was not that she was ashamed of being seen with Erik—certainly not!—but she wondered at their continued anonymity should someone recognise her—the missing diva!—and a masked man settled in the ghost's box.

Erik chuckled at her question. "And risk my pretty wife? I think not." He brought her hand to his lips and he kissed it softly. "But perhaps you would still like to dress for the occasion? Even if only your Erik shall see you." He looked rather dejected that she could not wish to dress in all her finery unless it was *other's* eyes which were upon her. Christine thought that notion ridiculous.

"Erik, we are attending the opera and one must dress accordingly. And besides," her expression turned rather coy, and she would have thought she looked quite silly except for Erik's inability to look away. "I think I am becoming quite spoiled with the attention *you* give me, and I would hate for you to stop now."

His eyes shimmered and he squeezed her hand tightly before releasing her completely. He did not retire to his room but instead picked up the kitten and made for the kitchen. "Come along *félin* Christine, let us see to your breakfast."

And Christine was terribly suspicious she was not the only one who could soon be entirely spoiled by Erik's attentiveness.

She could not help but giggle as she made to ready herself for her date with her husband.

Freshly washed, with curls becomingly pinned in an elegant fashion high upon her head—befitting a married woman or so Christine told herself—she nodded at her reflection approvingly. When she had chosen how her hair was styled, she had not completely ignored Erik's preferences. As such, she had left a few tendrils down for him to play with as he so seemed to enjoy. When it came to her gowns however, she was not quite so certain as to his tastes. And she did so very much wish to please him...

Then she saw the champagne velvet gown hanging in the as of yet untouched section of her wardrobe. Erik liked to *feel* and wearing such a supremely soft gown would surely inspire such affections. The straps were thin and revealed much of her shoulders—obviously only appropriate for evening attire.

So taking great pains to ensure her undergarments were befitting such a graceful gown, she finally slipped it on. She was delighted by how sophisticated she felt with its slightly sweeping train and revealing nature. Christine hurried to study her reflection in the small mirror in the powder room. The neckline was low—much lower than she had previously worn—and the colour against her skin gave her a sort of glow she thought Erik would appreciate.

Then her eyes settled on her scars. In the slightly dim light of the room they were not so prominent, but they were still quite visible. Perhaps she should find something more concealing...

No. For she was dressing for a night with her husband, and when she thought of how adoring his lips had been as he teased the skin of her décolletage, there was no room to doubt his love for her—and her scarred flesh.

And so, determined to make her entrance as grand as possible, she fumbled with the laces until finally the dress was cinched to properly accent her curves, and as she took one last look, she found herself to be quite pleased with the result.

As was Erik, if his sharp intake of breath was any indication of his pleasure at her appearance. Feeling quite lovely, she turned slowly to give him the full affect. "What do you think?"

Erik's fingers were trembling as they came close enough to touch her, and as she hoped, they played with her loose tendrils before descending to ghost over her exposed collarbones. "Erik thinks you are perfection itself." And then his lips were brushing her scars, and perhaps she did not mind them so very much if it meant he would kiss her like that whenever he saw them…

He pulled away far too soon, and sighed as he looked at her. "I am beginning to think you purposefully intend to leave the house without a wrap just to see if I notice."

She stood a little straighter in her indignation at his accusation. "I wanted you to be able to see the dress, you foolish man."

His lip quirked in that roguish way—and she stifled her laugh at the thought of Erik ever being compared to a *rogue*—but in that moment he truly resembled one. He was no longer wearing the mask that made him appear so very average, but was once more in his death's head. When she thought back to the night before—blushing slightly while doing so—she supposed there was something not quite comfortable about it. His skin had looked a little too red, a little too inflamed, and she would not wish him to be in pain.

So when he returned and looked rather sheepish when he caught her taking in his appearance, he seemed to feel the need to apologise all the same. "It hurts you see. Apparently looking like everybody else will have to be a seldom occasion." And she stood on her tip toes and kissed his masked cheek all the same, perfectly content to simply have him willing to take her out in the evenings. *Just like everybody else,* even if he could not look like them.

A wrap firmly around her shoulders, Erik did not lead her to the entrance of the Rue Scribe as was his usual route when travelling with her. They had crossed the lake many times, but this time was different. For the first time in many, many crossings, Erik had brought a lantern. It made all the difference in the world for her enjoyment. Instead of the terrifying darkness that could house so many possible dangers, she watched the light twinkle against the surface of the lake—the very lake that seemed so treacherous not so long ago.

Once across, Erik continued to hold the lantern high, but that did not stop her from holding onto his arm. Partly for his benefit, partly for it was the ladylike thing to do, and most of all because she loved the feel of his cashmere evening suit beneath her fingers.

Eventually however the passage became much narrower and it became apparent they were travelling behind the walls of the Opera House. Tiny shafts of light passed through in some more decaying places, but that did not stop her from holding Erik's hand for fear of becoming lost. The passage ended, and her husband simply touched the darkened wood before them and a doorway was revealed. They appeared to be in an antechamber, with two doors on either end, and an iron stair in the middle of the room.

A staircase that Erik was currently pulling her towards. And when they were through the tiny door at the top, it became quite obvious what the chamber was. It was one of the many rooms surrounding the domed ceiling, used by maintenance men to tend the chandelier and ceiling. And along the entire dome was a balcony hardly visible from the seats below.

One more trick from her husband led to two seats appearing from the curve of the ceiling. She should be frightened—*terribly* frightened—but as she looked down at the stage, she found the experience to be entirely exhilarating.

That was until Erik lowered her to the seat and her eyes fully focused on the stage below. They were *very* high. Erik seemed to notice her distress and quickly occupied his seat beside her. She nearly screeched as he nudged her playfully on the shoulder, and would have truly been angry with him had his arm not been securely around her waist as he did so.

However, that did not save him from the look of severe agitation she sent him. "Relax *mon Ange*, you are in no danger." And with his hand stroking the velvet of her bodice, she was sufficiently distracted from being afraid.

The slight hum of the audience suddenly quieted and the blaring lights of the chandelier dimmed and left the lights surrounding the stage as the focus. The curtain drew back, and suddenly *Faust* was echoing through the hallowed halls of the Opera house. Even though she knew that Erik had prepared *her* to play the part—that it was his dream that she grace the stage as the lead soprano—she was entirely satisfied leaning against her husband as she watched the small figures dance down below.

Erik moved slightly in the beginning of the first act and handed her a pair of opera glasses, and she delighted in the critical look it gave her as she peered down on the unsuspecting performers. They were obviously created especially by Erik, as none other would have offered the clarity and distance that these small gold pair allowed.

At the intermission he produced a fresh pear—where on earth had he found such a thing in the middle of winter?—as well as a muffin. She tried very hard to keep both off of her gown, and giggled softly as some crumbs slipped beyond her grasp and sprinkled onto the innocent patrons below.

Erik did not eat, much to her chagrin, but he did eye her lips lustily when they glistened with the fresh juice when she bit into the scrumptious fruit. She licked her lips self consciously only to quickly find them entrapped by her husband's mouth. "Delicious." She blushed at his comment, but found herself to be rather delighted.

But then the lights once more dimmed, and it was time to turn her attention away from the still smouldering gaze of Erik and return them to the stage.

"Would you care to look?" She felt rather guilty as at nearly at the end of Act Two she finally thought that perhaps he would care to see as well.

His hand had not stopped its ministrations upon her velvet gown, and a few times it had driven her to distraction. She was certain he would wear through the fibres soon with all his petting—though she had no intention of telling him to stop.

"I am perfectly content watching my lovely wife enjoy herself." She smiled at him, happy that he was happy, and turned to watch the finale.

It was apparent the production was chosen as a haphazard attempt to reinstate the accreditation of the Opera after Erik's rather shocking debut all those weeks ago. She was not positive, but she strongly suspected there had been a stall in rehearsals following the drama of her disappearance, as there were some rather noticeable mistakes in the staging and cue. But she thoroughly enjoyed it all the same, and found she did not miss the act of performing nearly as much as she would have thought. Not if it meant giving up her little bedroom with her husband—and now *félin Christine* she begrudgingly added—and Erik's constant presence.

And when the applause rang out in an almost deafening roar due to the acoustics of the room, Erik helped her rise and held her hand as he led her to the doorway leading back to the passage to his home.

But when he slowly opened the door, it was not to the empty antechamber they had passed through. For there, pressed up against the far wall in a most shocking display, were two *fornicators*.

Christine's mind was entirely blank as she stared at the two impassioned individuals. The man was thrusting forcefully into the woman who clutched desperately at his shoulders. What was most shocking was the indecent placement of his busy *hands* underneath the woman's skirts, and the consensual rhythm from the woman that seemed to be a key source of her sinful enjoyment. And the *sounds* she was emitting!

And suddenly Erik was pulling her backward through the door, clearly planning to leave the two lovers blissfully unaware of their audience. He was leading her to a different door—one hopefully unoccupied—but Christine could not focus fully on the journey home.

She could not seem to shake the images of the man and woman as they were lost in their passions. She quite enjoyed Erik's love making. He was slow and tender, and made her feel as though she was the most treasured woman to have ever been blessed by the attentions of a man. But was her lack of participation somehow forcing Erik to be satisfied with only a sort of half-wife?

The thought sickened her. Erik had been so long without the physical affections due any living creature—let alone a *man*—and for him to be forced to endure a life shielded by her ignorance was a distressing thought. But what if in her exploration of his person he became uncomfortable? She had tried so very hard not to be caught looking at his body, and so even though they had consummated twice now she had yet to fully indulge in looking at his true form.

And if they were to ever have a true marriage—one built on the love and trust as all should—she could not fear such things. Were not their bodies given to each other at the altar? And though she was loath to admit it, she *was* terribly curious to explore the part of Erik's anatomy that filled her so entirely.

Soon they were upon the shores of Erik's home, and he was leading her once more through the doorway into the sitting room. *Félin* Christine was curled upon the settee, and as she entered, she could not help but wonder if it was wrong to proposition her husband into allowing such explorations to begin now.

And when she turned to the very husband who had been so very quiet the entire journey home, she could tell by the intensity of his gaze—he shared the same thought as she.

XIX

Erik came toward her slowly, and she had the distinct impression he was *stalking* her. Dressed in his black finery he greatly resembled a panther she had seen once in one of Erik's more extensive Encyclopaedias. Though she had tried to read them, she found the picture infinitely more fascinating.

But he did not pounce on her; he simply took her hand and led her to the bedroom. "You remain here *félin* Christine." The kitten neither protested nor acknowledged the command as she continued to snuffle quietly on the settee.

Christine was reminded of their wedding night—well, their wedding night in every way that mattered—as they were fully clothed as they approached the bed. They had not been awake nearly enough for this to be considered proper time for sleep, but as she looked further at Erik's expression, he had no intention of allowing them to sleep for quite some time.

Did she have the courage for this? Her thoughts drifted back to the outrageous display of sexual relations she had witnessed on their date, and if some—*strumpet*—could muster the courage to arouse a man who was most certainly not her husband, than was it not Christine's duty as a *wife* to at least attempt the same?

She had heard talk that some husbands chose to visit houses of ill repute when their wives were inadequate—and the idea of Erik finding comfort in anyone else's arms than her own made her feel physically unwell.

She scolded herself for such thoughts. Erik *loved* her. And she loved him as well, and now was not the time for such insecure thinking. Not when Erik was unlacing the shining leather of his shoes as he climbed onto his side of the bed. And when he gazed at her with such a look of question that clearly asked if she planned to join him soon, she quickly acquiesced.

He seemed so distracted when she left her undressing to *him,* so she hurriedly undid her velvet gown, divested her shoes and corset, but deliberately left the chemise and pantaloons. She was determined that *he* would soon submit to her explorations, and by no means would she allow him to be driven to distraction by her nudity.

When she joined him on the bed, he had removed his cravat and jacket, and was currently undoing the buttons of cuffs. And the present was certainly a fine enough time to begin her ministrations. She would not be a pliant wife—suffering the attentions of her husband through obligation only. Surely he would appreciate her efforts!

So with slightly unsure fingers, she leaned over him and began to undo each tiny white button that so entirely hid his deathly pale flesh from the outside world. His breath was shallow as she began, and when she managed to undo each one until she reached his waist—and she blushed as she began to unbutton his trousers—his hands found her wrists and pulled them to rest against his chest. "Do not molest Erik in his bed."

What?

Did he truly think her so ill meaning that she would hurt him in some unimaginable way? But when she looked at him in horror, he was looking at *her* with a smile caught upon his lips.

And before she could pull away completely—retire to the sitting room with the small kitten who surely would never tease her in such a way!—Erik had rolled over her until she was entirely pressed into the softness of the mattress.

"My Christine...." He was breathing on her again—that delicious air that skimmed her skin and made her shiver from both the cold and delight. "What did you see when you saw those two?"

She blanched. Surely he was not going to *discuss* this with her? Proper individuals would never have admitted to having witnessed such erroneous acts of immorality, and yet he was asking her to *describe* the tryst?

She would refuse. After all, that was the only decent thing to do. But then Erik was lifting his mask ever so slightly, and his lips were nibbling at her ear..."Tell your husband what you saw."

And the words were coming out before she even had time to contemplate stopping them. "They were so *forward,* and she was so... *active,* and Erik," she was blinking them, trying to tell her eyes that crying would accomplish nothing but upset Erik—and that was something she certainly did not want. "I am sorry I have not been more like her!" She started to push at his chest, trying to get him to turn over so she could make *him* feel how much she wanted him to experience the rapture she saw between the two lovers.

But Erik would not move, and simply brought his lips to her throat before rising slightly to look at her as he spoke. "No Christine, you should never be sorry. It is *my* fault for not being a proper husband to you." Not a

147

proper husband? He had consummated their union—what else was there for him to accomplish? She had simply to be the willing vessel.

Seeing her confusion, he turned his attention back to her neck and ever so slowly caressing downward to tease her collarbones with his lips. "Erik has been so very negligent in his *wife's* pleasure." Her breathing hitched as he nibbled lightly on her flesh. She would have thought that any such action would make her cringe in remembrance of too hard bites, but when *Erik's* lips were the ones tormenting her, entirely different reactions were at the forefront of her mind.

And when he rose again to look at her, his eyes had turned pleading. "But Erik *swears,* it is because he was too afraid to try!" He looked suddenly nervous and almost frightened as he contemplated his inadequacies. "What if he *cannot* please his wife?"

Please her *how?*

He was a constant source of her pleasure—when he played music for her, or gave her pretty things, or simply did something so uncomplicated as washing their shared dinner dishes. There was obviously something she was unaware of, but he *could not* think that she could ever be displeased with his efforts to shower her with his adoration.

"Erik, you are continually pleasing me! I could not ask for a better, more attentive husband." The sigh he released was one of frustration, but she honestly could not fathom what she was missing that had him so distressed. "I love you."

He kissed her soundly at her words, and though he still was not satisfied with her lack of knowledge and reassurance of what he was truly asking, he seemed content to know she still loved him.

"Erik will simply have to *show* you." And she was certain he was going to make love to her again, but she could not—*would* not— do so when he still was wearing his mask.

She cautiously raised a hand to remove it, eyeing his reaction carefully. He grimaced slightly but seemed to expect the gesture and made no protest to its removal. And when she was about to object to his amount of clothing, he silenced her with his lips, and she found the true feel of his face against her palm as he caressed it to be infinitely more pleasurable than that of his mask.

She did not understand his intention, as he had surely showed her such attentions during their other unions. But somehow this seemed—different. Perhaps it was because he was resolutely keeping on his clothing even as she continued to try to remove them, or perhaps it was because his fingers were beginning to explore more than they had dared.

He was pulling at the ties of her chemise, and each movement was with the utmost care. But she was supposed to be pleasing *him!* But at every reciprocating gesture, he would gently place her hands back at her sides and

DESTRUCTION OF OBSESSION

away from the fastenings of his clothing. "My loveliest Christine, be a good girl and have patience with your Erik."

She shivered as he drew the chemise down her shoulders and uncovered her breasts. He had done such delightful things to them—things that made her feel as though the scars were not so very terrible after all—and as his lips descended to pay them favour once more she arched reflexively as she anticipated his adoration. And he did not disappoint.

His breath was a cool breeze against her suddenly heated flesh, and when his tongue found the planes of her skin a most delightful treat and he began to *lick* her, she gasped at the contact. And then his breath followed and sent the most delicious shocks of absolute *cold* that she whimpered when his lips smoothed the puckered skin of her flesh.

"Pleasure is not just for the husband, Christine." And she thought of the utter bliss that twisted his features as he found release through her body, but how could she possibly mimic such things when she had no seed?

And he was pulling her chemise down around her hips, and his head was lowering to taste the underside of her breast, and it tickled, but in the most *delicious* ways, and she wanted him to stop, but then his hands were at her pantaloons and she could only lie still as he tortured her.

He had prepared her that first night—his fingers had entered her and he had coaxed some sort of feeling from her, but this felt so very different. It was as though her blood had turned into champagne—tiny bubbles burst over her at every touch of her husband's long fingers. And suddenly, he was no longer testing the readiness of her womanhood, but instead seemed to look for something—something she could not fathom until he was *pressing* her, and the bubbles all seemed to explode at once and she whimpered at the feeling.

But the tingling did not abate, but only seemed to be fuelled by the ministrations of Erik upon her body—almost as though he were learning her reactions as well as she was learning to feel them. And he could not possibly feel this way when he was within her, could he?

"My beautiful Christine, you feel it do you not? *This* is what a husband should do for his wife—when he loves her so very much!" His breathing was hard as his head nearly lay upon her bosom as his hands never stopped their exploration. He would press, he would circle, and every so often he would simply hold her as he studied her reaction.

But she was not an insect to be considered by the scientist with a curiosity for the macabre, and she could *feel* the readiness of Erik's own body as he lay against her, yet he made no move to complete the act as it was meant to be. And was this not so very wanton of her if it did not bring her husband completion as well?

But when his lips were suddenly suckling at her breasts, all thoughts flew from her mind as her muscles tensed in preparation for… *something.*

149

His fingers were once more filling her, yet his thumb seemed insistent on brining her pleasure from a place she had not known existed, and the bubbles were popping so very quickly, and his lips felt so very good...

And she nearly sobbed when finally her muscles clenched one final time and her vision clouded until her eyes were shut so tightly as the unfamiliar feelings washed over her. And when she thought she might die from the sensations, Erik was kissing her cheeks and whispering how much he loved her and how very, very wonderful she was.

Trembling, quivering, and feeling so very strange, she opened her eyes to see Erik petting her hair away from her overheated face, even as he brushed tears from her eyes. "Do you see now?"

And she *did*. While she had thought the moral of the encounter with the young lovers was that she should be a more active participant in engaging his affections, Erik had clearly gleaned a far different meaning. God had most obviously designed the female body—*her* body—to feel the most exquisite form of torture by the hands of her husband. When that husband loved her enough to discover them.

And her poor, poor Erik, who was as inexperienced as she, who *still* feared her rejection in these most intimate of acts had been too afraid of her misunderstanding to try to extract such feelings from her.

But now it was different. Now as the idea of making those delightful bubbles return to her skin, and to also get the infinite satisfaction of seeing *Erik* so enraptured by her entered her mind, she pushed Erik over slightly so that *he* lay upon his back.

"I see, Erik." And she was kissing him, and her hands that had wanted to divest him of his trousers were now even more determined to see to their removal.

Erik's eyes which had once been reproachful—though still filled with longing for her continuation—were now filled with love as she carefully undid the fastening of his trousers and pulled them carefully down his legs.

It felt odd undressing him. But she found that she was fascinated by each inch of yellowed skin that was revealed, and her fingers could not help but skim the length of his leg. Erik nearly kicked her and she smiled at his ticklishness. "I am sorry." But apparently she was not convincing as he huffed.

"I highly doubt that, my Christine." And she responded by returning her hands to the edge of his drawers. But before she pulled them down, she looked to him to make sure he was fully comfortable with her action. And by the intensity of his gaze, nothing would please him more.

Her fingers were trembling as she tugged at his underclothes, and she gasped slightly at the sight of her husband's virility. She had no way of comparing him to any other men, but she could not help but be surprised that he had managed to fit such a... fascinating... piece of anatomy within her.

And suddenly, with a most uncharacteristic outpouring of brazen behaviour, she wanted to *touch* it. For she knew his reaction to being *within* her, but she wished to know if such tumults of emotion could be persuaded to ensue from simply touching—as so were obvious of being done with *her*.

And when she did, her husband's hands clenched swiftly to the bedclothes, and she felt such overwhelming glow of *pride* as her delicate hand encircled the only truly warm part of Erik's body.

But she was inexperienced, and she was not sure how much pressure to apply for fear of hurting him—and she *never* wished to hurt him!—and unexpectedly it became quite clear how her poor Erik must have felt when faced with pleasing *her* in such a manner. How was one to understand how best to pleasure their most beloved when one was so very inexperienced?

Except her Erik had learned. Her Erik had brought her safely over the precipice of unearthly delights, and she so very much wished to do the same.

And she could learn.

But perhaps... perhaps she did not need to yet grant his pleasure with her hand. Perhaps he would be satisfied with *her* feeble attempts at bringing forth the conjugal bliss of full union.

So carefully—so *very* carefully—she brought her torso to align with Erik's and kissed his thin lips. Her breasts pressed deliciously against his chest, and she revelled in the feel of his slightly raspy skin against her still sensitive flesh.

And she told herself they had done this before—that it would not hurt her to impale herself upon his hardened manhood—but still she felt nervous as she slid slowly onto him.

Erik hissed.

She moaned.

And suddenly she understood.

Pleasure could be felt by *both* at their unions, and if they would only look beyond their own doubts and fears, they could truly feel the outpouring of physical satisfaction sanctioned by God in his creation of their humanity.

Erik was panting as she leaned heavily on him, not yet daring to move for fear of chasing away the feeling of completeness as her husband filled her. But then his fingers were in her hair, and he was pulling her to look at him, and she could see he was nearly in tears. "Please Christine, *please*. Do not torture your poor Erik!"

But he did not shift them so that he may partake of her—and he did not seem distressed as though she was truly causing him pain. But obviously her lack of movement was driving him to make such pleas, and how could she refuse him?

So still leaning upon his chest, entirely unsure as to how she should proceed, she simply—*shifted.* And she found that being pressed so completely against her husband pushed achingly into the unknown places Erik had discovered not so long ago, and when she moved again, Erik's moan was mirrored by her own.

Erik seemed determined to allow her this time to fully understand this new part of their relationship—as so far their love making had been wholly sanctioned by his own knowledge. And Christine would not be a child. She was a woman now, and she was entirely enthralled with this new aspect of love, and as she felt an overwhelming satisfaction at Erik's abandonment of his formality, she wished for nothing more than to make such relations a habitual part of their marital bed.

And though he had wished for her to lead the pace, when she found how his lips twisted in such a sure sign of delicious agony when she quickened her movements, he could not resist and helped her slightly in the forthcoming of their bliss. His hands found her breasts, and those hands— oh his hands!—which were once the tools of nightmarish extractions were now one of her most favourite attributes of his physicality. How she could ever watch him pluck at the violin strings without thinking of his ministrations upon her bosom, she could not fathom.

But with each touch brought her further toward the glorious clenching of sinew and muscles, and as her own pleasure overcame her, Erik's breathing came in shorter pants as he was so entirely affected by her own body's connection with his.

She whimpered.

He gasped.

And then they both were utterly exhausted.

And she wished to sleep like that forever. She did not care that he was horribly bony, and his body was not at all a comfortable replacement for the softness of the mattress. If she could remain within the glow of love, cherishment, and adoration she had felt when they had lain together this night, she would be the happiest of wives.

But surely she was too heavy for him, and though reluctantly, after a few moments in which they both regained the normalcy of steady breathing, she moved to find her own place on the bed. By his side of course.

Erik did not seem to find her action pleasant. "Stay." His voice was raspy and slightly choked, and she wondered if he was crying. His eyes were dry as she looked at him, but his thumb was moving gently over *her* cheek, and she realised that it was her own eyes that leaked salty tears.

"Why do you cry, Christine?" He looked concerned, but not the frantic fear he so often displayed when confused with her emotions. She felt as if they had truly bonded this night. As if maybe—just maybe—they had finally begun to trust each other like truly wedded couples should.

So when she looked at him, and pressed a kiss into the thumb which had paused over her lips, she felt no great panic that he would misunderstand. "Because I love you so."

And he smiled at her—and she nearly wept at the tenderness as he stroked her hair and held her to his chest. "You are a silly girl, Christine."

And she sniffled, trying to stop the ridiculous tears that refused to quiet. "But you love me regardless."

Erik's grip tightened around her shoulders, and she felt him place a kiss on her forehead. "I love every part of you, my wife."

And Christine felt so very foolish and naïve that she had ever doubted this man—ever doubted that her *husband* could ever have been a monster unworthy of her love. She hated the thought of being aboveground, away from him and their new familiar—the pretty kitchen that held so many happy memories, and their settee which had witnessed so many milestones of their love.

So still intimately connected to the man who had captured her heart so entirely, she felt her eyelids droop even as Erik hummed her lullaby and continued to brush her hair with his fingers.

And suddenly she wondered if perhaps their kitten was not the only new member of their family.

XX

Christine was nervous. She could not remember the last time she had felt such a sense of unhindered *dread* settled in the pit of her stomach, but as she looked at the small calendar Erik had purchased for her, she again counted the days from their wedding to their consummation, until she was fairly certain of the exact date.

Far too long.

She shook her head determinedly. No, not *far* too long. Reasonably late. It was as if every terrible costuming mishap had taken place, and though only a few seconds late for the cue, the Maestro would still chastise thoroughly for such tardiness.

Just as Erik would surely do when she told him of her late menses only to find that a few days later it would appear, ordinary as ever, and she would have caused such a fuss for nothing.

But that did not seem enough to ease her anxiety. And unfortunately the way she twiddled her thumbs and avoided Erik's gaze at all costs was beginning to be noticed by her husband.

"What troubles you, Christine?" She should lie. She should tell him she had a headache and retire to her room to wait for her flow to begin and then this whole business would be behind them.

But she did not want to lie—especially not when she was so very dreadful at it and Erik so very perceptive. He would surely discover her dishonesty and the glorious past days they had shared would be swiftly discontinued.

And she wished those days would never end. According to her calculations, it had been ten days since Erik had showed her the true delight of wifely duties—and both of them had been quite active in requesting the performance of their spouse.

That was not to say they did nothing but explore the newest facet of their relationship. *Félin* Christine had certainly seen to that. She was in much better health due to Erik's methodical care, and her coat now had a healthy sheen to it. While Christine loved the cat dearly, it was Erik who seemed truly attached.

And she had been proven correct that the kitten would be spoiled past any normal means of familiar affection.

When Erik was not preoccupied with pleasuring or simply being in the company of his wife, he had taken to adding new additions to their family home. Small tunnels now ran throughout the rooms—including to the exterior—so that the *félin* Christine could pass unencumbered. The pathways to the outdoors were in keeping with Erik's genius, as he had ensured that it was impossible for anything *but* the small creature to pass through. Much to his wife's relief.

And they had been so very happy. Meals were shared, music was begotten, and many nights were spent on the floor before the fire as Erik alternated between stroking their kitten and petting his wife.

But now she was to jeopardise it all with telling him of her betrayal.

Surely she should have known of some way to prevent pregnancy—for was that not the responsibility of a wife? But most wives were charged with providing their husband an heir, so such things would not have been a part of her education! But perhaps it should have been, and she had now trapped Erik in something he would never accept.

For while he now believed *she* loved him, how could he ever be persuaded to believe that a growing child blossoming in her womb could ever love him as well?

And he had asked her a question and she had not responded. In fact, her thoughts had turned even more unhappy the longer she pondered the issue, and the frown which marred her features did not go unnoticed. "Christine!"

His sharp tone finally caused her to look at him. "Stop thinking, wife, and tell your Erik what is wrong!"

Christine knew then she would have to be truthful. It did not matter if he would pull away from her—if he would ignore her for a time—for perhaps the responsibility of creating a child lay on *both* their shoulders. And surely her menses would come and this entire matter would be resolved without such dramatics on his part.

But she still had to tell him. "I am simply concerned." She bit her lip nervously. This was not a proper subject to be discussing with *anyone* let alone one's husband! She looked at him quickly to gauge his reaction. He did not look annoyed but did give her a nod to signal she should continue. "My menses is late." There. She had said it, and in a much more direct manner than she would have thought she had courage for.

Erik froze, and she chanced a further look at him. His hands were fisted tightly at his side, and his mouth was pressed into a firm line. But his eyes were wide and she could see the slightest trembling of his looming frame.

"Are you certain?"

Christine huffed in slight irritation. Even though she knew such a topic would be surprising for him, she more assuredly was not silly enough to have brought it up unless she was certain she was in fact beyond the day or two which was her normal fluctuation. "I am certain I am *late,*" she was about to continue in a more scathing tone, but Erik's eyes had turned so absolutely terrified she softened. Rising from the settee where she had been settled with her beloved primer, she went to her husband and gripped his fist tightly. "But Erik, I am not at all certain of what it *means.*"

Erik let out a shuddering breath—one perhaps of relief, though it was not definite. "Of course. There are many reasons why Christine's cycle might be delayed." His voice was calm, but his eyes were frantically searching hers—desperately seeking some explanation that she could miraculously provide him.

Would having a child truly be so terrible?

That thought troubled her more than she would like to admit.

But her role as a mother was not one she had yet to be called to perform, and now her husband was seeking comfort—*her* comfort—and how could she possibly deny him?

So searching for any possible explanation she had ever heard in regard to such delays from other girls in her dormitory, she scrambled for one that could fit her circumstances now. And more importantly, one Erik would possibly believe.

It had happened to little Jammes once when their ballet mistress had been particularly strict on her, and subsequently the stress had caused her to dry up for a time. But she was unmarried, and though fanciful, was a good girl so not much had come of it.

And so clinging to the only plausible explanation she could think of, she told him. "Stress might delay it for awhile."

She thought Erik had been distressed *before.* "Erik has not been taking proper care of his Christine?"

He was pulling away from her—both physically and mentally—and oh how she wished she had remained silent! But she had not, and she could not—*would* not—let Erik abandon her now. Not when they had finally, *finally,* been happy!

But how could she assure him she was not with child when her bosom was beginning to swell? She was not so naïve as to think she was beginning to produce her child's nourishment, but when she looked into the mirror that morning and fastened her corset, they were undeniably tender.

It seemed the more she tried to assure Erik of her non-pregnancy, the more she managed to convince herself she was indeed with child.

"No, Erik, no! You have been perfect." And she felt so tremendously frustrated that she should be forced to deny the possibility of her—*their*—child, but Erik continued to look so very frightened, and she *could not* comfort him by denying something that could be the truth.

She felt like her skin was too tight. She felt as though everything she and Erik had built over the entirety of their marriage was slipping away, and all she could do was helplessly stand back and watch it take place. For there was nothing, not one thing she could say that could make Erik's fears disappear.

And the room began to spin, and with the surprised gasp from Erik echoing in her ears, she fainted.

When she awoke she was lying on her bed, with its crisp clean sheets freshly put on that morning as they had mussed the previous ones terribly that very morning. If only she had not been tempted to look at her little calendar! Erik was not beside her, but she could make out his figure standing partly in the shadows on the far side of the room.

She detested the space.

He was staring at her—watching for what she was not certain. Just to see if she awoke promptly? But his perusal was too intense, and she had the distinct feeling he was looking for any evidence of change. And by his expression, some seemed to have been found.

She was crying. There was a time when she would try to stop her tears for she cried so very often, but not now. Now she welcomed them as her tongue felt uncooperative and she lacked the words that her tears confessed so readily.

She was sorry—so very sorry.

Sorry she could not tell him what he wished to hear, but even sorrier that he could not be happy with their new experience. Did he hate her now?

But he was coming to her, and his thumbs were wiping at her tears, and she grasped his wrists tightly—desperate that he not pull away so soon. She had grown spoiled with their touches, and the idea that he would refuse to do so now was unbearable. "I am sorry, Erik."

His ministrations stopped at her words, and then his head was pressing into her shoulder as his hands removed themselves from her grasp only to clutch her body to his. "Christine should not be sorry! It is all *Erik's* fault."

His fault? What on earth could be *his* fault? And taking a deep breath, she resolved that her childishness would end. *Now*. No more tears, no more fainting spells. She was Erik's wife and possible mother of his child, and she *would* understand her husband's thoughts on the matter.

And though she could not comfort him with denial, she could comfort him with soothing touches. So her hands found the strings of his hair and smoothed them gently, and she kissed his head as she ever so slightly moved them both in a calming rhythm.

"What are you afraid of?" He was trembling in her arms, and she tried urgently to maintain her own composure.

"Erik is afraid that Christine shall be hurt. She has already fainted!" He tightened his hold on her, almost to the point of pain, but she did not dare protest. "Erik is afraid that Christine shall grow to despise her poor Erik for what he has done to her." He pulled away slightly so he could look at her fully. "He is afraid that any child will be tainted by Christine's poor Erik."

Tainted? How on earth should something born of their love be *tainted* by anything? And then she felt utterly ridiculous. He feared a baby would be tainted by Erik's own deformity. As if that should matter to her! She loved Erik unconditionally—whether by product of necessity or by the grace of God it did not matter. And any child she birthed would be loved the same.

And Erik should know this! But yet it seemed he did not. Not when he looked as though he was waiting for her to bolt from him at any moment. And though she was dumbfounded by his articulation of fears, she knew that each needed to be addressed before it had time to fester. "Erik, if you and I are ever blessed with a child, I shall love it with every fibre of my being. For that child shall be an extension of *you.*" That did not seem to encourage him if the shudder he gave was any indication. "Even if our baby were to look like you, that would not change how I would feel."

He suddenly looked angry. "You cannot know that. Erik's mother hated him, yet when she was pregnant with him she thought she loved him! You cannot possibly know!"

She would *not* be angry with him. Even though she felt the welling of indignation and *hurt* that he would still doubt her ability to love, she knew he was simply extending his past experiences onto the future. And now was not the time to chastise him. "Erik, I am not going to argue with you. We are not even sure I *am* with child. I should not have mentioned it."

His eyes flashed dangerously. "So you would keep it a secret? You would choose to suffer on your own to keep Erik from knowing the full measure of his monstrosity?"

She could not help the welling of tears that threatened to spill. How could she not cry when the man she so adored still thought himself so incapable of love?

"Erik." Her voice was choked as she desperately tried to hold back her sobs. "You are *not* a monster, and it pains me to hear you say so."

His face was nuzzling her neck, almost as though he hoped to be absorbed by her, and she could feel his shuddering breaths as they permeated her skin. "I do not wish to see my Christine hurt."

She kissed the top of his withered head—what more could she do? "I know." And so she held him as he clung to her, and she thought of the many times he had held her this way before—not from terror but from passion—but she thought it would be terribly wrong to distract him in such a way. Not that she should regret their union, but that she wanted him to know he could seek comfort from her in whatever way he wished, not simply to be diverted by her feminine wiles.

And it was not until the insistent mewling of *félin* Christine at her place on the floor, obviously voicing her displeasure at being unable to join her keepers in their embrace. It was her presence that finally seemed to snap Erik from his spiralling thoughts.

Erik pulled abruptly away—nearly frantic to see to the kitten's whim. "There now, *félin* Christine, there is no reason to cry so." And when he picked up the creature, all traces of his distress were gone. Though nothing had been resolved, Christine found herself rather grateful for the distraction. Perhaps if Erik simply had time to absorb the mere *possibility* of a child, he would not be so terribly afraid. She had certainly considered it before. But then she had mostly thought of children before she knew how they were procured—which was quite silly now that she thought of it.

Erik had joined her once more on the bed, though his eyes darted every so often to the door, revealing his desire to leave with her feline counterpart. But though he had not spoken to her about it, she could not allow him to fully leave her side. So while he petted their cat with one hand, she firmly grasped his unoccupied palm with her own.

And she spoke of other things.

"Do you think your Persian friend will ever return?" She had no idea why the man had suddenly entered her mind. Perhaps it was because she could not help but feel he was the only one who could possibly enter their humble abode, or perhaps it was merely an errant thought that seemed relatively innocuous to discuss with Erik.

If Erik was surprised by her change in topic he did little to express it— though perhaps his hand tightened ever so slightly around hers. "The Daroga has made himself a nuisance for many, many years. I should highly doubt he would cease now."

She nibbled her lip thoughtfully. "But I asked him to leave." Certainly the lady of the house making a specific entreaty for a person to depart would be sufficient to ensure he *remained* departed. She almost scoffed at her foolishness. Here in the underground it was not as though the laws of civility remained in high standing!

There was no mistaking the sardonic look he cast her. "If I had a franc for every instance I requested his absence, there would have been no need to embezzle funds from our dear managers."

Christine had never heard him speak so plainly of his dealings with the Opera house. The idea of his being the elusive Opera Ghost seemed almost laughable now. Not when his child might even now be growing within her—

No.

She would not think of it now. She would ignore it until it could not possibly be denied. Or until her menses came—whichever came first.

She looked at Erik's lap where *félin* Christine was currently kneading his thighs quite efficiently. Why the small animal found anything resembling of its mother from Erik's bony limbs, she could not imagine. But it was purring loudly, and between Christine's soothing pressure on Erik's hand as well as the comforting ministrations of his beloved cat, Erik seemed to be relaxing quite steadily.

He even allowed her head to rest upon his shoulder.

Christine played absently with the gold circling his ring ringer. "Do you think me a faithful wife?"

Erik sighed. "My wife is full of questions this evening." She smiled. Her Erik was returning. This Erik was the one who teased her—who made every small token of devotion seem as though it came from the longsuffering of his very soul instead of his deep routed desire to please her.

And she could not help but think perhaps their marriage could last the turmoils of the continued madness of her darling husband.

She tugged at his sleeve insistently, relaying her desire to still hear his answer. "You have given Erik no reason to think you anything but faithful." But suddenly his hand clamped down on hers in a vice grip, and she could not help her startled gasp. "Does Christine have something she wishes to confess?"

He was giving her a calculating glare, and she wondered at her own thoughts—and inability to censor which questions would possibly be misconstrued. But she had grown spoiled in Erik's emerging normalcy, and she was ill prepared now for the reminder of his lack of control when faced with self doubt. "I love you, Erik."

For that was all she could think to say.

And truly, was that not all that mattered?

Erik seemed to think so as his grip loosened until he released her entirely, only to then encompass her in his arm as he pulled her into his side. "Erik is sorry."

She kissed her forgiveness over his heart, and she knew he was apologising for more than his latest outburst. He was sorry for hurting her hand it was true, but also he was sorry for not being able to accept the normalcy of a *child* like everybody else, and he was sorry for not pleasing her.

And though it pained her—made her curse those who abandoned him—she was rather glad for his insecurities. Oh she wished to heal him, certainly, but if it had not been for his past experiences, he would not now be twirling her curls in his fingers as he began to hum the lullaby he so often used when she found herself unable to sleep on her own.

Her eyes were drooping as he sang, and she was powerless to resist his desire for her to succumb to the wonderful feel of sleep surrounding her. But just before she allowed the final remnants of consciousness to disappear, she whispered her final thoughts aloud—more for her own benefit than to Erik. "I want to have your child."

And she forgot to fear his rage, or that she would frighten him with her request. But how could she when his lullaby continued to swirl around her like the most comforting of caresses? It did not waiver at her words, and for a moment she wondered if they were even breathed into the stillness of the room.

But then his arm was slightly tighter around her back as he held her so securely against him, and his hands were whispering over her flesh as he willed her to sleep. And for the tiniest moment the song abated, only long enough for the melodic voice of her husband to whisper his answer to her entreaty.

"I know."

XXI

Christine awoke some time later. Instead of the harsh treatment she expected as her corset constricted tightly upon her ribs and bosom while she slept, she found that Erik had somehow managed to undress her and exchange the day dress with her soft nightgown.

Even when terribly upset with her, he still considered her needs.

Erik was not in her room, though *félin* Christine remained curled peacefully on Erik's pillow. Christine eyed the kitten irritably, though still with begrudging affection. *Erik* should be the one inhabiting that pillow. But still, before she rose to seek out her husband she let her lips linger on the downy softness of the kitten's fur.

She thought perhaps she should dress before going on her search of Erik, but quickly thought better of it. They had not exactly resolved their almost dispute last night and she was anxious to know how he felt this morning. And *true* irritation surfaced when she realised she had no knowledge if it was in fact morning.

Though she had asked time and again for a clock to be put in her room, Erik would tsk at her that such things were not necessary in their humble abode. Should she even be up at this hour?

And Erik was not beside her so she had no interest in the loveliness of her bed. So wrapping a shawl around her shoulders, she left the Louis Philippe room and padded out to the sitting room.

When she saw Erik at his organ, she felt a tremendous knot of dread settle in her stomach. She could not bear if he took to ignoring her again!

She approached him rather timidly, hoping that any anger he may have felt at their situation—or *lack* of situation as the case may be—would have evaporated while they slept. And when he turned to her before she could reach out and place her hand on his shoulder, his eyes did not *look* angry.

"Good morning, Christine." She tried to cease the look of wariness she was sure was quite obvious in her expression.

"What are you working on?" He was not playing, though she knew that meant little. Erik did not seem to have to play the notes to create masterpieces. He had told her once that she should have been able to do the same if she were truly proficient in knowing her scales. And to a point she was, but she could not imagine composing without *feeling* the music as it was absorbed through actual sound.

Erik however did not seem to appreciate her question as he quickly thrust the sheet music placed before him under a nearby pile of similar parchment. "Nothing of consequence."

She highly doubted that, if he felt he must hide it from her. But she chose not to press the matter, as he seemed cordial enough, and she could be patient and allow him to show her when he was ready.

And there was certainly an added benefit to him putting it away as soon as she entered. He now had no excuse to avoid breakfasting with her as he could not claim his work was overly pressing. And she was hungry— terribly hungry if she thought of it.

"Are you joining me for breakfast?" Erik was quick to respond, and there was something in his lack of enthusiasm that seemed to prepare her for his rejection. Perhaps it was that he had not kissed her in greeting as had become his custom—at least it was before the dreadful events of yesterday. Curse her foolishness!

But he seemed to sense her distress—or perhaps he simply chose not to ignore the pleading look she gave him—and sighed before standing. "Of course, if that is Christine's wish."

Normally he would have taken her hand as he escorted her to the kitchen, but he passed her without so much as a brush of his fingertips, and she *hated* the lack of contact. He was already halfway across the room before she hurried after him and tugged at his sleeve.

"Erik," the tears were already forming in her eyes, and though she despised how manipulative they made her seem as they gushed whenever she did not have her way, she did not care so long as he did not continue this aloofness. "Are you terribly angry with me?"

He seemed offended at her question. "Whatever made Erik's wife think he was mad at her?"

"You have not touched me." She sniffled, even as she told herself to stop being silly. Erik surely had better things to do than shower her with affections every moment of the day.

But he seemed to soften at her statement, and his hand carefully captured hers. "Such a needy wife." His tone was bordering reproachful, but he had made such comments before and she found them rather endearing.

She leaned her head against his arm as they walked into the kitchen. "I know."

Those were the very words he had spoken before she fell asleep the night before. He had not told her she was a stupid girl, or that she was cruel and heartless to ask such a thing of him. But he had not been pleased either.

Why was she thinking of such things? She had resolved not to wonder over such trivialities which were so entirely beyond her control. Right now she was going to make breakfast with Erik, and that was what mattered.

"Did you feed the kitten?" She knew it was rather pointless to ask. Erik was far more mindful of the tiny animal's needs than she, and Erik was well aware.

"Christine, she does have a name." Yes of course she knew that, but it seemed so very odd to actually call the kitten by her own name. Simply tacking *félin* before it did not make it any less strange.

She glared at him indignantly. "I believe I was there when you bestowed her with the name." His hand released her as he made to pull ingredients out of the cupboards.

"Where else would you have been?" Where else indeed. Now that she thought of it, she had not been without Erik for over a month now and the idea seemed quite—unpleasant.

Erik was cracking eggs into a bowl and was quite obviously intent on turning them into the fluffy delights of his omelettes. Though she tried many times, she never could seem to bring them to the perfect amount of completion without sacrificing the texture—and if she were honest with herself she was quite content to allow Erik to do most of the cooking.

But as she watched him expertly pour them into the pan, she could not help the feeling of disgust as she watched the eggs begin to congeal—an odd reaction from her to be sure, but not one worth mentioning. Especially not when she knew with absolute certainty the delicious quality of Erik's omelettes.

So she busied herself with preparing the tea service, and soon the plates of steaming eggs were deposited on the dining room table—*two* plates much to her happiness—and the tea was poured and awaiting their consumption.

And the most curious thing happened when she poured her customary dash of cream. The smell of the salted ham wafting from the eggs mixed with the ever so slightly sour smell of cream reached her nose, and she immediately lost all semblance of appetite. She did not fear actually becoming ill, but the very idea of eating anything before her seemed entirely unappealing.

Erik did not seem pleased. But instead of being offended at her obvious distaste to the meal, he appeared genuinely concerned. "Christine? What is wrong?"

But she had no answer. Not when she had no explanation for her sudden queasiness other than one she was certain he did not want to hear. Erik sighed and abandoned his breakfast entirely as he rose from the table.

"Go find a dress to wear, Christine."

She was alarmed at his command. Even though she did not relish the thought of eating, she would if he demanded it of her. "No Erik, I shall eat!" She grabbed her fork and put a small amount of egg on her tongue, but found the idea of swallowing quite revolting.

Erik was tugging at her hand as he tried to make her release her fork. "You look rather green, and Erik is not so cruel as to make you eat what he serves simply to please him." She stopped fighting him and relented with a sigh. "Now, please go prepare yourself. We are going out."

Perhaps some fresh air would do her good. Though she adored the warmth her gifted fireplace produced, the crisp winter air would be quite refreshing and would hopefully settle her stomach quickly—though she did not find the idea of the boat ride across the lake to be entirely appealing.

She dressed swiftly, and even remembered to procure her cloak without Erik's reminder. She gave the kitten still resting upon the bed a quick kiss goodbye before returning to the sitting room in search of Erik.

He was dressed entirely in black—including his mask. It was a harsh exterior and she suddenly wondered where he was taking her. There was nothing conspicuous about his attire, and it was obviously intended for blending into shadows rather than into the general populous.

And though she regularly saw him in his masks, this one she despised the most. It was hard and cold, and covered far more of his expression than she could bear.

But she scolded herself thoroughly for her thoughts. This was still her Erik, and no matter how he chose to cover his face it would make no difference as to how she treated him.

So she crossed the room and grasped his hand as he led her through the darkened doorway. She was correct about the unfortunate necessity of crossing the lake. The damp air did little to settle her stomach and she wished desperately to reach the other side.

Erik did all he could to keep the ride as smooth as humanly possible, and he carefully lifted her from the craft when they reached the farthest shore. "Are you well?"

She hugged his arm to her chest and felt quite childish her in sickness. "No." Was it terribly wrong that she wished he would carry her?

While Erik did not seem frantic at her response, he did seem concerned. And then he sighed, and *gloriously* lifted her into his arms. "My poor, poor Christine."

She nuzzled into his suit and found being encased in his arms as he wove them through the labyrinth of his tunnels to be very pleasant indeed—especially when the higher they travelled the fresher the air. And even though Erik himself radiated the coolness of one not entirely human, the finery of his clothing welcomed her warmth and returned it tenfold.

Christine was not surprised when they emerged into the darkness of Paris. The sun she had seen on their last visit was no more, and not a soul was in sight as Erik carried her with purposed steps through the vacated city. She had no idea where they were headed, and for a moment she was frightened as Erik began to take them farther away from familiarity.

Soon he was knocking on a heavy wooden door, and she was not entirely sure she was comfortable entering such an establishment. The night air had done wonders for her nausea, and she very nearly told Erik wherever he was taking her was unnecessary. But before she could do so the door opened, and an elderly woman dressed fully for bed was in the doorway.

"Do you have no concept of time?" Christine found it quite startling that such would be her response when a cloaked figure came bearing a young girl huddled in his arms. And her desire *not* to enter this house was steadily increasing.

"I can assure you Madame, my ability to tell time is not in question. The status of my wife's health however *is*."

She could very nearly feel the perusal of this woman as she regarded Christine with an assessing gaze. "I am not a doctor."

Christine could feel through the stiff quality of Erik's muscles that he was rapidly losing patience with her lack of cooperation. "I am fully aware of your accreditation, and can assure you that you are qualified to answer the question at hand."

The woman finally sighed and motioned for them to enter the dimly lit room of her small abode. She led them to an even smaller room in the back which was occupied by a lone bed which Erik was quite obviously about to lay her upon. "Erik, why are we here?"

She whispered the question in his ear as she did not wish to seem as though she were being mistreated by her husband—though it was impossible for this woman to think that Erik *was* her husband solely based on his dress. He seemed far more likely to have snatched her off the streets and was taking her to this woman for some sort of late night ritualistic murder.

Perhaps what she *truly* needed was more sleep.

But Erik simply squeezed her all the more to his chest before releasing her to the confines of the cotton bedclothes as he laid her softly down. And for the most fleeting of moments she wished they were back in their little home and was about to ravish her with kisses.

But they were not at home, much to her dismay, and this grey haired woman was currently bathing her hands in some sort of concoction. "Now what makes you think you're pregnant, young lady?"

Erik had brought her to some sort of *midwife?*

Not that she was ungrateful for his caring, but certainly he could have consulted her on the matter first! And there were certain means of decorum that should be followed with one's doctor, not a stranger who seemed ready to manhandle her.

Her suspicions were confirmed when she was asked to untie her pantaloons.

"Why is this necessary? I most certainly am not going to disrobe!" The woman was looking between Erik and Christine, obviously trying to judge their relationship that she would be brought here without any sense as to *why*.

But Christine was soon distracted as Erik grasped her hand tightly in his. "Christine," his breath was tickling her ear, and his voice had taken on the lilting quality that seemed to erase all thoughts from her mind. "My wife, we need to *know*. So please cooperate. Erik hates the thought as much as you."

She highly doubted that. *He* was not the one who was being asked to remove his undergarments! And for exactly what purpose she still did not know.

She could not deny Erik though, especially not when he had purposefully brought her here to determine if she was with child. She desperately wished to know, and for him to have been the one to instigate such knowledge was quite unexpected—and one for which she was tremendously grateful.

So with slightly shaking hands she shimmied her pantaloons down her legs, carefully manoeuvring them around her shoes as she did so—though she resolutely kept her dress covering her legs. She then maintained the position requested, and found that she was not quite so nervous if she was able to stare at Erik through the procedure.

Christine flinched when the cool hands of the midwife touched her, and she tensed involuntarily as these unknown fingers pushed gently at her womanly place. She scolded herself fully at her nonsense. While a stranger, these were the practiced hands of a professional, and Erik would *never* have allowed anyone but the most qualified to make such an important diagnosis.

The midwife's other hand began to massage gently over Christine's abdomen, but Christine resolutely looked into the darkened face of her husband. His hand was in hers and she would squeeze tightly whenever she felt any pang of fear or apprehension. He was humming to her softly, and perhaps this was not so very bad—not if Erik was near.

And soon it was over.

The fingers withdrew, and the midwife was asking her questions about her eating habits and temperament—which Erik answered with more remembrance than even Christine could have acknowledged.

"My congratulations then to you both."

And even though Erik was the one to have brought her here—that *he* was the one who had in fact carried her to this very place to determine the validity of Christine's suspicions, it was still him who seemed the most shocked to have them confirmed. "You are *certain?*"

The elderly woman looked rather offended. "You may feel free to check for yourself if you feel you know better than all my years of experience."

This woman was not blind like the priest who had married them, yet she did not seem surprised or intimidated by Erik's manner or attire. Did she often see men in such strange garb?

Erik on the other hand was gripping Christine's hand so hard her fingers nearly became numb. "Erik, please." His grasp loosed immediately.

"My apologies, Christine." His gaze had been fixed on her after he learned the news of his impending fatherhood, but it swivelled almost reluctantly to the midwife. "I thank you for your services, Madame." And he released his wife entirely and pulled out a small pouch of coins which he handed to the woman's outstretched hand.

And Christine barely had time to resituate her undergarments before Erik was tugging at her so they could depart.

She had held her tongue on the journey to this strange little house, and even had done so inside the invasive room, but there was no possible way she would remain uninformed once they had returned home.

Her mind swirled with questions beyond the nature of Erik's midwifery selection, and she almost wished he had allowed her to stay and make such inquiries as to what she might expect in the coming months. Would her bosom remain so very sore? Would she be able to eat once more? What about the lovely nights spent in Erik's more intimate embrace?

But Erik was ushering her quite swiftly through the still darkened night, almost to the point of discomfort as she struggled to match his long strides.

"Erik please, you move too quickly!"

She had meant for him to slow to accommodate her, but instead she found herself once more wrapped in his arms as he made his way toward their home. She had so many questions to ask him, but there was a tightness to his mouth that belied his distress, and if there was to be an argument with him she would much prefer the comfort of their rooms than the harsh night air.

And there was a niggling worry that if he should become truly angry with her, he might leave her to find her own way home—and that was not something she could abide.

So she remained quiet the entire journey home, even as Erik seemed more and more unhappy for every step he took. She barely had time to think the words herself let alone be able to defend what should be a most joyous occurrence for her husband!

Soon enough Erik was depositing her on the settee, with *félin* Christine ambling toward her in greeting. Perhaps she should have let Erik hold the kitten as a means to soothe his rapidly fraying nerves, but she selfishly settled the kitten on her lap. "Where did you find such a midwife?"

That was obviously not the question Erik had been prepared for her to ask, as he stood blinking at her for a moment before responding. "Erik does not always sleep when you do. There are many things he must prepare for. Like his wife's *baby.*"

She felt as though he had struck her. *Her* baby? Did he possibly think that it was not *his* baby as well? And for a moment she forgot his confession of fear at fathering a child, and all she saw was Erik tormenting himself with visions of her clasped in Raoul's embrace, and she could not help the shudder as such thoughts pervaded her own mind.

"Erik please, you *must* know it is yours as well!" And he must have seen her terror, but that did not stop the glare he gave her even as he stood across the room. It was far more intimidating when from behind the black mask—how she wished he would remove it!

"Of *course* it is Erik's child—it had *better* be his child!—but that is precisely the problem!" She should have been more concerned with Erik's fear, but all she felt was an overwhelming surge that he was acknowledging her faithfulness—and that was something she had not been entirely sure she would ever achieve.

And then, with startling clarity it settled upon her for the very first time. She was *pregnant.*

While it sent her a shiver of delight to think the word, Erik very clearly had a differing opinion. He had taken such great care in keeping his voice low and tempered around her, but now—in his panic and fury—it rose to such great heights she felt it in her very soul.

"If the child *is* like Christine than she shall come to loathe her Erik, for she shall have something whole and perfect to love her. If the child is like *Erik,* Christine shall still come to loathe her husband, for it shall be a monster's child!" He was pacing and looked so very tormented she forgot any feelings of fear she might have harboured from his tone.

But she did feel horror that through it all he would resent this child. And it became startlingly clear exactly *why* he would do so when his body slumped and his voice became defeated as he sank into his leather reading chair. "Erik does not want to share."

And she went to him. She was angry, and hurt, and frightened that he would not find it within *himself* to love their child, but when she sank down on to the floor and rested her head upon his knee, she could only whisper, "I know."

XXII

"Erik *please.*"

Her husband sighed exasperatingly from his leather reading chair as he gave her a condescending look. "I believe your husband told you *no.*"

They had been having this rather heated conversation for the past few hours. Christine was quite certain he was being absolutely ridiculous while Erik maintained the perspective of one whose pregnant wife had completely lost her sense of decency by continuing to harp upon the issue.

She could not remember the last time she was so angry with him, and it only further enraged her when he looked up at her calmly from his book without any hint of regret for his unreasonableness. "Why may I not know how to do the laundry?"

Christine knew she was pushing him. But as the past two weeks since she found out the reality of her pregnancy progressed, she often awoke feeling dreadfully nauseous—and most humiliatingly, at times she was not able to even rise from bed fast enough before dispersing with the contents of her stomach. That had led to the arguments with Erik regarding washing her own linens.

She was grateful for his patience through her symptoms, but she found it absolutely ridiculous that he would not allow her to tend to normal household tasks. Though she was now in the process of creating a child did not mean she was willing to shirk her wifely duties!

But that was another matter entirely—Erik had refused to touch her intimately as well.

She had tried to tell him she was certain that husbands and wives were not disallowed from expressing their love throughout the full term, but he had looked at her as though she had gone completely daft. "And what would you say if Erik somehow injured your baby?"

And Christine sorely wished she could return to the midwife and ask her to explain such things to Erik, even as she firmly told herself that *she* was correct in her assumptions.

Even as she now stared at Erik as he seemed so very relaxed in his arm chair, she wished she could return to the pleasant love making they had engaged in. Was that so terribly wicked?

Erik had returned to his book, and she found in a moment of sheer defiance, she ignored any attempts he had made to rebuff physical contact and tugged at his arm and promptly sat upon his lap.

He did not immediately remove her as she feared, but instead eyed her warily as his hands held her waist in rather a restraining manner—not to hold her steady but to keep her from pressing herself wholly against him. "Christine, what are you doing?"

She bit her lip for she did not fully have an answer. She was angry with him—not truly for the laundry. Did it matter *how* the sheets became clean just so long as they did? No, she was angry that though he had been sleeping with her every night, not once had he made efforts to touch her. Any efforts on her part were gently but firmly stopped with a kiss upon her forehead even as he said goodnight.

One night he even threatened to leave the room.

And she was angriest of all that through his withdrawal she was beginning to resent her *child*.

So she acted.

Ignoring the hands at her waist, she pulled his mask away from his face, not caring if he became incensed. She had avoided removing it through the course of this marriage—more from fear of his reaction than avoidance of his face. And she was angry at the mask as well as Erik had taken to wearing it more and more even when she begged him to remove it.

He was hiding from her.

But no more.

He was surprised at first, and she could quickly see it melting into fury. But before he could rage at her—before those restraining hands could lift her from him—she pressed her lips to his in desperation.

She knew he was afraid of this baby, and if she admitted it to herself so was she. She knew nothing of children, only that she knew that this child—if Erik could bring himself to allow himself the happiness it could bring—would bless their little family.

Erik was moaning, and she could tell by the way he pushed at her that he was struggling more with himself than with her. For his lips were moving steadily against hers, and though his hands were still at her waist, they were steadily moving higher, and she could nearly feel his desire for them to touch her free flowing hair.

She pulled away for air, hating the necessity as she did so. Erik had ceased his efforts in removing her and instead had pulled her closer until she was quite undignified across his lap. "Oh my Christine."

Her anger was abating as quickly as it had come, and she snuggled pleasantly into him. "Do not push me away, Erik, I cannot bear it." He was kissing her curls, and she did not know if he was consciously doing so, but his hand had settled across her womb. There was no evidence of her condition of course, but she could not help the sensation of protection she felt at his movement.

Erik was quiet for a moment longer, and she worried he would not engage in conversation. His arms constricted suddenly, "Do you still love your Erik?"

She should be exasperated. She should be hurt that no matter how much love she showed him through action and word he would continue to doubt her affections. But no matter how many times he asked it of her, she continually wished to weep whenever the words would escape him. "Very much so, which is why it hurts so very much when you will not truly *be* with me."

Erik had buried his face into her neck and curls, and she could feel feather light kisses being pressed into her throat. "I have been reading." Yes, she could see that, but she had not taken the time to enquire as to the nature of his literature. "According to the text, if I am sensitive to my wife's needs, there is no harm in engaging in," she wondered if he would actually *say* the word. "Intimacies."

He looked up at her suddenly, and it was quite plain how fearful he was. "But Erik is always so, is he not?" Christine cupped his cheek tenderly, and he shuddered at the contact.

"You are always very attentive to my needs."

And when he looked at her again, his eyes were smouldering. "I have missed you, Christine."

She did not know if she had the strength to take him to their bed for the want of him was so tremendous. "Erik, you have to promise me you will not hide from me again." Christine softened her entreaty by gently pressing kisses into the sunken cheekbones of his face, and as his fingers tightened around her, she knew he was not wholly unaffected.

"I promise to try." She should refuse. She should remove herself from his lap until he *did* promise, but such methods would not truly be effective—not until he meant it in acknowledgement of how much it pained them both.

Her hands drifted from his face to his throat, where she timidly began to unbutton the tiny buttons of his collar. When he reciprocated by undoing the top of her own dress she finally felt as though he was in fact accepting the changed nature of their marriage. That even though she now was the mother of his child, she was still perfectly accepting of his husbandly pursuits.

She nibbled at the exposed flesh she uncovered of his torso, and paid particular attention to whatever scars and marks she could find. They were both tainted by the hateful actions of the world above, but down here—in their own little world—they could relish in their survival.

"I want this child, Erik." Her hands drifted downward even as Erik pulled each sleeve delicately from her arms.

"Christine should always have the things she wants." He had pushed her gently away so as to better gain access to her throat, and she could not help the soft sigh that escaped her at his attentions.

"But what it is that you want?" Erik deftly released the front bindings of her corset, and lips tugged at the neck of her chemise.

"I want for my wife to be happy." Before he could drive her mad with his caresses of her breasts, she finished unbuttoning his shirt, only to move to the fastenings of his trousers.

They had yet to make love with so many clothes, as each time had led her to remember other such contact with the forceful confinement of cloth, but now, as she thought of how much effort it would be to fully undress them both, and how she despised the length of time it would take, she quickly removed Erik from his confines.

"But do *you* want this child, Erik?" She was always still timid when first beginning to lathe Erik with womanly affections, but she could feel how pleased he was by her actions.

"I want a healthy child, Christine." His hands had drifted underneath her skirt, and she nearly whimpered as they skimmed her inner thigh—terribly exposed by her pantaloons. "I want you to not hate your poor husband if the baby should not be healthy."

And then his fingers were mimicking the actions she performed upon his own flesh, and soon there was not breath left for speech.

She did not think it was possible to forget the *feel* of him after so short a time of abstinence, but when he joined them fully with a lifting of her waist, she nearly sobbed as they were finally *complete*. The wool of his trousers scratched deliciously at the skin of her thighs, and his hands had found her hair and brought her to his mouth.

His kiss was forceful even as his penetration was soft—but she felt utterly ravished by both. Not in the violent way women often feared, but by the fulfilment of love which had been denied for far too long. And even as Erik allowed one hand to leave her hair and begin to stroke her intimate place, she could not help but whisper her love into his lips before he continued to plunder her mouth.

And he returned her declarations through both his intensity and the words breathed into her flesh.

He was mindful of her stomach, holding her neither too firmly nor harshly—and for a moment she almost missed the nearly painful pressure of his need, but was reminded of his caring for this child—even if he could not yet admit it to himself.

And she would be patient. Most days he would surely ignore her pregnancy altogether, but never for a moment would she doubt the caring nature of her husband, and surely that would extend to their baby as well.

But soon Erik seemed to lose himself from the restrained passion of his position beneath her, and she willingly joined him in the embrace of pleasure only sanctioned through their heavenly ordained bonds of matrimony.

And after, when they were still breathing harshly, and Erik had enfolded her tightly against his chest in a blatant refusal of releasing her from his confinement, she wondered that she had been angry with him only a few minutes prior.

"Do you think it shall be a boy or a girl?" Erik stiffened, and the hands which had been stroking her hair and back stilled momentarily. She prayed he would not be angry—but was it not the duty of parents to discuss the possibilities of their future child? And she adored the thought of sitting before the fire arguing over names.

Certainly she had heard the question before amongst the Opera occupants. Traditionally the parent would respond declaring their happiness should the child simply be healthy, and Erik had already done so. But she hoped that by her embracement of the normalcy of their baby, perhaps some of it would convince Erik as well.

"I would like a girl." He spoke resolutely, and so entirely without the hesitation she had expected, she was quite startled. She raised her head slightly to look at him, but he was staring beyond at the very fire she fantasised about not a moment before.

She stroked his cheek lightly in hopes of him meeting her eyes, and he obliged after a moment's pause. "Why is that?"

Christine was becoming quite familiar with the look he was currently giving her. A mixture of utter disbelief at her stupidity and sardonic elegance, it bespoke volumes of his temperament. "I have been blessed with two girls who seem to," he took a breath before continuing, "*love* me very much. Perhaps God would see fit to provide a third."

How she loved him! And to hear him *acknowledge* her love was nearly overwhelming. The second was of course *félin* Christine who was rarely away from her master for any duration of time.

She kissed his lips briefly. "Then I would like a girl as well." His eyes shimmered as she spoke, and she hoped he could find it within himself to be pleased. And she prayed the voices that tormented him with nonsense regarding his worthiness would remain silent.

"Perhaps we should exchange my coffin for a bassinet." Erik was teasing her, she knew, but she froze at his words. Raise a child? Here? Of course he would never consider leaving his beloved home unless there was a definite reason, but to Christine the birth of their child seemed like reason enough. And it certainly had never occurred to her that she should have to *ask* him to fulfil her dream of a home aboveground for their little family.

Not that it would be impossible to raise a child in the darkened rooms of their home—she simply did not consider it worth the risks to development. Children needed green grass and sunshine to grow! Poor Erik had surely been deprived of such things as a child, so he must be able to commiserate with her desire to provide such things for their baby.

"Do you... do you think perhaps it would be unwise to raise a child here?"

The teasing glint in Erik's eyes quickly faded. "Where would you suggest you do such a thing?"

Now it was *her* turn to forget her trepidation in favour of slight irritation. "Not *me*, Erik. *We*. We shall raise this baby."

He tugged at the ends of her hair, and his smile was indulgent as he nudged her playfully. "Of course, Christine." And though he professed his agreement, she knew from the slightly guarded expression of his eyes he was far from concurrent.

"Erik, I know we are happy here, but do you not think our child should be given the opportunity to live amongst others?"

If the fierce scowl was any indication, Erik certainly did not find such an opportunity agreeable. "And what could *others* offer the child that we could not?"

Was it terribly wrong that for a moment she could not remember what it was like to know anyone besides Erik? She had always travelled with her father, and he had been her only true companion for many years—until he was gone. And she was devastated, and alone, and it left her vulnerable to the preying of her Angel of Music. Though she loved her husband dearly, she would not wish such experiences on her poor child. And especially she never wished for them to feel the tremendous ache of despair when the only one to have loved them departed from the world.

And if something were to happen to Erik or her, such would surely be the case.

"Did you not have a lonely childhood? I know I would have liked a few playmates when I was young." She wished she could take the words back. Erik knew that *Raoul* had been her playmate, and if they did indeed have a daughter, Erik would most certainly be set against such relationships being formed.

But Erik did not rage at her. He did not throw her from his lap to hurl accusations of infidelity and continued unfaithfulness, but he did bring her mouth to his for reassurance. They had both taken their fill from their earlier love making, but she could already feel the fluttering in her stomach at his attentions, though she could not yet feel the same evidence coming from Erik.

Soon he pulled away, and though he was not overly forceful she could see he was angered by her question. "Of course Erik was lonely! But children are cruel, Christine, and your baby shall not have parents like everybody else, so *why* would you want to subject it to their torment?"

His hands were tugging at the still closed ties of her chemise, and soon he had exposed the entirety of her bosom to the slightly chilled air. Obviously the fire had suffered from their inattentiveness. And when his mouth closed over the tender flesh of her breast, being careful not to add undue pressure which would have surely caused her pain, Erik placed his mouth reverently against her creamy expanse of skin. "What is so terrible about the child remaining down here?" His voice was barely a whisper. "With *Christine* remaining down here…"

Soon his fingers were pushing down her dress completely, and with an expert manoeuvre shifted her so as to remove the garment fully. Her pantaloons followed closely, until finally she was left only in the flimsy covering of her chemise that puddle around her thighs and gaped terribly by his previous attentions to her bosom. "Why can I not have a happy wife and child in *this* home?"

And she had no answer. Not when he seemed so saddened by her rejection of his masterly crafted home where they shared so many sweet moments. And truly, was she so very prepared to reemerge in the world above? She had yet to even attempt so without Erik's guardianship and the very idea of him being beyond the reach of her hand was terrifying.

If they ever intended to embrace the world above as a *family* as she so hoped, it would take a great deal of practice on Erik's part as well as her own.

But certainly the well being of their child was worth such discomfort.

Christine was soon distracted by the roaming of her husband's hands as one gently rubbed the still smooth flesh of her abdomen, and the other teased the soft flesh of her thigh. She felt very wanton indeed so unclothed upon the nearly entirely dressed figure of Erik.

"Erik, we shall be happy wherever we can be together. I did not mean to say that we could not." The fire in his eyes dimmed at her words, and soon his lips were caressing the column of her throat as she tried to remove his arms from his coat. But he was unwilling to relinquish his hold upon her form, and instead rose so abruptly she gasped.

He walked swiftly from the sitting room to their bed, and she was all too happy to reacquaint their bed with the soft sighs and grasping fingers that so enjoyed the comfort of its embrace.

Erik lay her down gently before obliging her with the removal of his own clothing. She ogled him shamelessly, though she did try to scold herself for doing so. Erik was her *husband*, not a trinket to be gawked at in a shop window!

He was far from perfect, and even would be considered macabre in some unfeeling circles, but to her he was the instrument by which they both found infinite pleasures, and his body was the very thing which kept her safe from the atrocities above—atrocities which she now was determined she should no longer fear.

He peppered her skin with kisses as he joined her, paying special attention to the ticklish flesh behind her knee, and ghosting over her thighs before laying his head upon her womb. "If it is a girl, perhaps then she will look like you."

And she cursed her lack of memory. He had *told* her of his fear—that their child would look like him, and she confessed her desire to take that child to the naivety of others. But she could not believe—*would* not believe that a child born of their love could be anything but perfect.

So she tugged him up to kiss her lips—the pretty pink lips he found the most delight in nibbling—and sighed as he filled her once more.

"Erik, if we had a son and he looked just like *you*, I could love him no less."

And for the tiniest slip of a moment, when Erik looked into her eyes, she saw that he believed her.

XXIII

Erik had lost his mind.

Most assuredly he had moments of derangement before, but never ones that so entirely went against any sort of propriety such as *this*.

Christine had told him how she despised how fearful she was of being alone, and while at first he had seemed to take the position that such feelings were not wholly negative, she had managed to convince him of the detriment to her health when each time he disappeared she felt physically ill.

But she did realise the tremendous trust such an exercise would demand of him. He would have to believe she would not abandon him in favour of returning to certain acquaintances. And while she knew with absolute certainty that she would *never* betray him in such way, her actual faithfulness had never been tested.

But the issue at hand was that she simply could *not* prove herself to him while he currently held her corsets hostage.

"Erik, I *need* those if I am to go out!"

While it was true, she had taken to wearing more fitted camisoles in lieu of a corset while she tended to household chores, there was no possible way she could do so out of doors!

"Christine, while you are carrying this child you do not need to do it damage by squeezing it into one of these contraptions!"

She took a steadying breath so she could explain to her unreasonable husband the sheer necessity of those *contraptions*. "Most of my dresses will not fit if I do not wear one!"

He tucked them neatly under his arm and turned to leave the room. "Then it is a good thing you are shopping today."

She wanted to hit him.

And it certainly was a good thing, for the first stop she made would be to the seamstress to outfit yet another corset.

Selecting a suitable dress was rather a difficult task given her lack of foundation garments, but she settled on a skirt that was only slightly snug around her waist and a high collared blouse and jacket that did not show her slightly unsupported bosom.

But simply because she had managed to assemble an outfit did not mean she was any less irritated at her husband's lack of understanding toward a woman's grooming.

She nearly turned her cheek away from his lips when he bent to kiss her, but found she was not so terribly angry to hurt him in such a way. That did not however mean she returned the gesture. "You look beautiful, my wife."

It was rather difficult to assume she was properly attired when she was not sure of the time, but Erik made no mention of her being underdressed when he led her to the world above. It was light outside, and she supposed it was about mid afternoon—a lovely time to shop.

Erik was not wearing his special mask that would have made it possible for him to join her in such strolling, but then the purpose of this exercise was to prove to him—and *herself*—that she was capable of being on her own.

A sudden feeling of trepidation overcame her as she looked out from the alley that safely sheltered them. Erik was handing her something, but her breathing was becoming laboured as she wondered how much begging would be necessary to keep him from leaving her. "Here is money for your excursion." It was a coin purse that would hang delicately from her arm—if she could keep it from shaking of course.

"You are certain you can find your way home?" He had taken special care in pointing out landmarks on the walk to the street, and under normal circumstances she would have had no trouble finding her way back to the Opera house. She had after all frequented these same shops before her marriage.

But this was different. This was a new Paris, one full of ill content and frightening men who would harm her in ways she dared not imagine.

She chastised herself greatly for such thoughts. She refused to raise a child with such fear clouding her mind. It was best to accept such realities, of course, but by no means did that indicate she had to remain locked away for the remainder of her days. And most assuredly her baby would not be caged either—though perhaps on such occasions it would be best to have Erik present. Simply as a precaution.

"Yes, I am sure."

He eyed her warily for a moment, obviously judging her certainty. "Very well then, I shall await you at home." Then he kissed her once upon the forehead and melted into the afternoon shadows.

She had never felt so alone.

But she refused to call out for him to return, and instead straightened her shoulders before joining the afternoon customers.

True to her previous decision, she went first to the seamstress. There were premade gowns, lingerie, chemises, and above all, corsetry.

"May I help you, Madame?" Christine nearly laughed as she finally tore her eyes away from the clothing samples and saw the shop full of women. She could not remember the last time she was without the company of a man!

And seeing the smiling faces of the tailor, seamstress, and other patrons, she felt herself relaxing. "My husband seems to have mislaid all my corsets and I am in need of more."

Her attendant giggled. "You would be surprised how many cases of *mislaying* we hear of. Especially with newlyweds!" Christine blushed at her insinuation, but did not bother to correct her.

The little sales girl showed her to the samples and she picked the fabric and styles which would suit her other gowns best. But then her eye caught a sample book on another small table.

Robes de maternité.

And suddenly she did not care so much over the vanity of corsetry, not when she thought of the gowns she would wear confined in the delightful rooms of their little home in the final days of her pregnancy. It would be wearing those gowns that she would decide on the name of their baby, she would make tiny baby clothes, and even scold *félin* Christine from sleeping in the basinet as it waited the coming of their child.

The attendant saw her eyes stray from the scraps of jacquard and she giggled once more. "Congratulations, Madame! When are you due?"

The midwife had failed to give such a date, but she quickly determined the baby would be born mid November. Perhaps remaining in the insulated underground through the stifling heat of Paris summers would not be such a terrible notion after all.

"Late autumn."

"Ah, then you will not be needing these for quite some time! But one does love to dream." Christine nodded, and was pleasantly surprised in finding just how close to reality her imaginings were becoming.

She spent the next hour picking out other types of clothing, some of which she asked especially to be made without the need of a corset for the times when Erik would notice. She blushed when the attendant brought out a catalogue of pretty sleeping attire, and though she thought the entire process to be rather mortifying, did pick out a few risqué items simply so she could enjoy her husband's reaction.

Once she had placed her orders she found the little bakery Erik had taken her to—the very one where she had fed him little bits of baguette, and he had looked at her so enticingly. And suddenly all she wished was to return home. Not for fear of being hurt as she had presumed would be her response to being alone in the busy streets, but because she simply missed her husband.

But she could not return without some of the pastries that stared at her so delightfully.

She was not certain which would be Erik's favourite, so she ended up with five different flavours, though she was not at all concerned that they would be wasted. It was amazing how rejuvenating to a pastry a few minutes in the oven seemed to be.

So brown paper bag in hand, Christine began her walk home.

The shadows were growing long on the street as the sun steadily began its decent. People were beginning to return to their homes, and though she told herself she was perfectly safe, she could not help but feel slightly on edge by the foreboding nature of dusk. She would be home soon. She would have a cup of tea with Erik as they bit into her delectable pastries, and Erik might even tell her to eat two since she could hold down so little of her breakfast.

She quickened her pace at the thought.

When she was passing one of the darker alleys, she nearly screamed as a presence appeared beside her—and truly did cry out when that figure grasped her arm.

Her vision swam as her heart beat wildly in her chest, and suddenly the figure was bringing her closer and she was struggling so very hard…

"Hush my Christine, I did not mean to frighten you." And Erik was bringing her to his chest, and she should be so very angry with him for grabbing her, but instead all she felt was an outpouring of relief so she gratefully stepped fully into his embrace.

"Oh Erik, I thought you were someone else!" Erik pushed her gently away and cupped her face so he could better look at her.

"And who should be lying in wait for my wife?" She sniffled pitifully and kissed his palm before burrowing her face in his chest once more.

"I do not know." And suddenly it occurred to her that Erik should be waiting at *home*, not in some alleyway awaiting her passing. "How did you find me?"

Erik almost looked sheepish, but it was quickly doused be a look of pure indignation. "Do you honestly believe I would allow my wife and her child to traipse the streets of Paris unprotected?"

Her head rose sharply. "You followed me?" She went through this entire exercise for nothing? He was supposed to *trust* her, and yet now all she had proven was that she was capable of spending his *francs* without his presence by her side!

But Erik would not let her move away, and instead put an arm around her waist as he led them back toward home. "You need not sound so offended, Christine." They had just passed through the entrance of the Rue Scribe, but he had yet to take them so far into the tunnel that the darkness was overwhelming, and pressed Christine against the cool stone wall, pressing his lips to her neck before whispering in her ear. "You were such a good girl."

She shivered as he spoke, and though she should be angry that he had tricked her, she felt herself instead wishing he would stop so they might continue this escapade in the warmth of their home. But Erik did not seem to be quite finished as he continued to lull her with his voice. "I was going to let you go alone, but then I wondered if perhaps Christine would feel the need to meet with the *boy*, and I could not let you go!" His hand drifted from her throat to cover her womb. "Not when you are with Erik's child."

He was pressing his lips against hers, and she felt so very sorry he had worried. She knew that he was aware of her fidelity—had *told* her so—but she was not so naïve as to think the voices which told him constantly of the impending cruelty of humanity would silence merely at her word. And so she allowed him the comfort of her lips as she waited for him to release her.

And though he allowed their lips to part, he did not however remove his hand from her waist as he led them home.

He did not ravish her as soon as they entered the doorway, but instead seemed to find simply being in her presence to be quite necessary. He followed her to the kitchen as she prepared the tea, but would not allow her to endanger herself by warming the pastries, and instead did so himself.

He carried the tray for her as she moved into the sitting room, and nearly pulled her into his lap once he joined her. She would have thought that proving her fidelity would have made him more confident of her love, but he seemed to crave her affection now more than ever.

His face was nuzzling her neck as she looked at the array of pastry flavours. "Which one would you like?"

Erik's lips stilled for a moment. "You are not mad at your husband for accompanying you?" She turned slightly, but the grip Erik had around her waist nearly negated the movement.

"Does it sadden me that you still worry I would return to—"she caught herself before saying Raoul's name, mindful of his distaste for it. "Someone else, even though you *must* know that I love you? Since she could not caress his cheek as reassurance she settled for smoothing her fingers over his. "I am not mad at you."

He released a sigh, and it was not until that moment she realised that his chest had been still against her back. "It is a terrible thing to have an angry wife." His grip tightened slightly around her. "But better an angry wife than no wife at all."

It was not lost on her the meaning of his words. Though she had come to love him regardless of his actions, it was still quite clear that Erik did not regret his infamous abduction of her—and would still do whatever he must to keep her.

But it aided neither of them to dwell on such things. She had no intention of *asking* him to release her, so did it truly matter knowing he would refuse? It was not as though she would take well to *his* abandonment either.

So she simply leaned more fully into his arms before he finally seemed content enough to allow her to pour the tea. "Which pastry would you like?"

Erik eyed them all placidly, and it did not surprise her that he showed no great enthusiasm—not when he seemed to eat more for her benefit than for any true enjoyment. "Whichever one my wife does not desire shall be sufficient."

Christine replaced the teapot on the tray before turning back to him reproachfully. "Erik, that is ridiculous. You must have some sort of preference!" He looked at her rather oddly, but she would not yield. "Is it not the responsibility of a wife to know her husband's tastes?"

He nodded slowly, though he seemed rather doubtful. "Lemon, please."

Though Christine smiled at her Erik for his confession, she eyed the pastry rather differently. She only had chosen for fear she would fail to select the very pastry Erik would deem worthy, but she could not help but feel rather sickened at the offending item. It was not her usual morning sickness making a reappearance, but instead it was yet more glaring evidence of their differences.

While she cared for everything sweet, luscious and creamy, Erik cared for the tart. Things that were most assuredly more of an acquired taste. She was inclined to believe it evidence of her own childishness compared to Erik's refined palate.

So it was with some slight embarrassment that she reached for the chocolate pastry, and nibbled at it thoughtfully while Erik did the same. She had yet to lean against him, and though it made eating far easier, she could not help but feel she was refusing his touch more for insecurity of her sophistication than for lack of want of him.

But Erik seemed to find her stiff posture disagreeable, so with his tea artfully positioned on the arm of the settee, and pastry settled on its plate upon his knee, he tugged her to recline more fully against him.

And when he leaned to whisper in her ear, she wondered for not the first time if he possessed an inhuman ability to peer into her thoughts. "You are sweetness itself Christine, and I am simply the sour old creature you blessed with your hand." His lips hovered against the corner of her mouth, and she nearly gasped as his cool tongue reached out and *licked* her. "And chocolate has never tasted as delectable as when it has touched your flesh."

And though she should feel mortified that there was *further* proof of her immaturity, the look he gave her was far from innocent. "You are not a creature, Erik." She kissed him fully upon the mouth, not finding the flavour of the lemon curd to be as delightful as her chocolate. "You are my husband."

Erik *still* did not ravish her, but instead kissed her forehead softly before settling back to enjoy his tea. "So I am, my wife."

The calm of the moment was only disrupted by *félin* Christine's announcement as to her presence. She had grown considerably under Erik's care, and with her larger frame came even more impressive vocalisations. She regarded Christine as it was obvious her favourite position on her master's lap was already filled, but she settled herself rather reproachfully in Erik's reading chair—though not without first throwing a glare in Christine's direction.

Erik had finished his pastry and seemed content to sip his tea as his other hand occupied itself drawing circles over Christine's abdomen. She could not seem to help that whenever he did so it inevitably drew her thoughts to their child. "Have you given any thoughts as to names?"

Erik's hand stilled, and for a moment she feared he would extract himself from her so as to shut himself away again. But presently he began again, much to her delight. "Christine, you are hardly showing yet. Do you not think it early to *name* the child?"

She looked up at him indignantly. "I most certainly do not! This will be the same child in seven months as it is now." Christine plucked slightly at his sleeve. "And you must agree, names are very important for parents to give a child."

It was rather cruel of her, she knew. Erik's own parents had not even bothered to give their son the blessing of a name—and most assuredly not a *christening!*—but she hoped then Erik might be sympathetic to her desire to do things properly for their baby.

Erik's hands moved from her waist to her hair, and he began sliding them through her curls methodically. She was beginning to realise that this was both a means for soothing himself as well as her. "Then I suppose we must discuss names."

Her answering smile was nearly painful. "Very well, if you insist." Erik nearly growled at her, but she silenced him with a kiss before tucking her feet beneath her and settling herself quite firmly in his embrace. "We could name him after you."

"I think my wife is a tremendously silly girl."

She giggled at his response. It was wretched of her to test him, but every time he proved himself more caring and accepting of his expanding family she felt such warmth in her heart she could not help but do so again. "And you may not name a girl after *me*."

Erik tugged at her hair playfully. "Are you certain? I would be the happiest of men with my home full of Christines."

He was teasing her—she *knew* he was teasing her—but at that moment is sounded very nearly that he had imagined even more than *one* child. And she smiled all the more. "Yes, I am quite sure. Between me, and Mlle. *Félin,* I believe we have enough."

"Very well, if you insist." How Erik managed to make his voice resemble hers so exactly she could not fathom. But she laughed—not the simpering laugh of one politely acknowledging humour—but a warm, full laugh that seemed to melt into Erik's very soul. And he *smiled* at her.

And she never would tire of his smiles.

"Come now Erik, be serious. What if we are expecting a girl?"

"Then she shall be the spitting image of her mother, and shall be adored by all the world." She moved to reproach him, but Erik's thoughts no longer seemed to be on discussing anything resembling future children. "But now I think our thoughts could be put to much greater use." He lifted her in his arms, and his face was buried in her throat. "What say you, wife?"

And finally, *finally,* he was going to ravish her.

So instead of proving to himself that she was *his* as he seemed to want against the cold tunnel of the Rue Scribe, Erik took comfort in her tea and her smiles until at last he was able to love his wife to the fullest simply for the sake of hearing her whimper and moan as he pleasured her.

And Christine did not mind so very much that they still had no name for their child.

XXIV

Christine was crying.

Though not an uncommon occurrence when faced with the daily influx of hormones and irritants, these were the wracking sobs of one possessed by a malice far beyond her control.

Erik had promised to take her to the Opera once more, and when she had tried to find a dress befitting the opulence of such an excursion, she found that none could fit her blossoming waist—especially not without a corset.

She had not thought she had begun to show. Only slightly into her fifth month, there was only the slightest swelling of her womb to suggest her condition—but obvious it was enough to make her entire wardrobe unusable.

Her husband had taken to avoiding her at such times—and she truly could not blame him. He eyed her warily now, as if awaiting the change in mood that would have her either crying or abusing him with raised voice and sulky looks. He tried his best, certainly. When he had startled her by entering the bedroom in his silent manner she had dropped a tiny figurine she was admiring and had subsequently locked herself in her bedroom for the better part of an hour. Her eyes had hurt from crying, and when she finally emerged to apologise for her overreaction—and most importantly the hurtful things she had said to Erik about his natural grace—she found the figurine repaired and sitting upon the side table by the settee.

And now she regretted every time she had shouted at him, for that was what kept him now from rushing to her side to offer comfort.

But just as she was about to seek him out—sniffling and heaving breaths along the way—Erik cautiously entered the room. "Christine, what possibly could these gowns have done to offend you so?" It was true, before she had crumpled under the weight of depression she had removed most of them from her wardrobe and once deemed them defective, had flung them thoughtlessly around the room.

"Erik, why did you not *tell* me I was grotesque?"

She was being dramatic, she knew. She did not however anticipate Erik's reaction to her statement. "Be silent! You will *not* think such things when you are carrying Erik's child!" He had pulled her from the floor, and though his tone was harsh his touch was gentle as he sat her upon the bed. "Christine…" He touched her face reverently as he brushed away a few tears that had remained. "Why did you not come to me? I shall always provide what my wife needs."

And though she had looked at the styles for maternity gowns on her trip to town those months ago, she had placed them on order for *future*, and they had not been prepared. The rest had been prepared within a week, and while Erik greatly approved her new chemises, he absconded with the new corsets as well. She had taken to wearing her new gowns most of all, but they were *day* dresses, and tremendously inappropriate for the finery of a gala.

Erik left her for a moment and returned with a large white box tied with blue satin ribbon. Her breath caught in her throat as she carefully untied it and shook out the contents. Inside was a sapphire silk gown that shimmered pleasantly in the light of her bedroom. And while the waist was nipped flatteringly, it lacked the structure of those meant for women outside of her condition. "Oh Erik, it is beautiful!" She looked at him reproachfully. "Why did you not bring this in before?"

He touched her hair affectionately. "I must have time to prepare myself you know." And when she finally looked to *his* attire it became obvious why he was late in bringing in her present. He was in the blackest of evening suits, and while he would have normally chosen his Death's head mask for their trip into the Opera, he had forgone it for a more subtle selection. She found herself blushing as she eyed him, for he looked quite—*dashing*.

"Now, will you require assistance?" She had risen to look at the full length of the gown and noticed the full set of buttons down the back of the bodice.

"You did this on purpose, did you not?" She had a sneaking suspicion that whenever he purchased a gown for her, he specifically asked the seamstress to only fashion them with buttons—simply so he would have the pleasure of helping her.

And though it felt entirely foreign to be placing an evening gown on without the formality of a corset, she found that there were stays sewn expertly into the material so as to lend shape, but never constrict.

Erik was behind her, and she shivered whenever his cold fingers skimmed the nape of her neck. It was now summer, and she found the silk he had chosen to radiate coolness in the most delightful of ways. The neckline was low, and she happily noticed when she looked down that her scars were hardly noticeable.

Their home remained relatively cool even on the hottest of days, but when Erik opened the door to the lake the humidity still remained ever present. She was certain her hair would be showing the ill effects of such moisture, but she was positive Erik would not mind.

She was eternally grateful when her sickness had passed, and even the smooth rocking of the boat did little to upset her stomach. But Christine had begun to wonder if her moods were even a worse affliction than the ever present nausea. She did not mean to be so very hurtful to her poor Erik!

They both cautiously entered the antechamber of the domed ceiling, both wary of catching another interlude with young fornicators. Though now that she considered them, she supposed she should be rather grateful for their sin—if one could be so of course. If it had not been for their display she wondered if Erik would have ever had the courage to show her the benefits of the marriage bed—and perhaps then she would not currently be carrying his child.

But the chamber was empty, and though she felt some trepidation at sitting in their seats so high above the stage, she had confidence in Erik's ability to keep her safe. And perhaps the opportunity to sit gripping Erik's arm for the entirety of the night was not such an unpleasant activity.

"What are they performing?"

Erik did not disappoint as he held her tightly to him even as he manoeuvred them to sit. "I believe they are showing *Les Huguenots* this evening." The heat that had accumulated through the auditorium had risen to their places above, and Christine found them to be obnoxiously warm. Erik's natural coolness brought some relief, but she still wished for some furtherance of breeze.

From an unknown pocket in Erik's coat he drew a slim gold object, and for a moment she thought he was about to pass her the Opera glasses she had used before. But instead she was pleasantly surprised to find a delicate fan.

It was ridiculous, but she found her eyes welling once again at his thoughtfulness. Though she raged at him, mistreated him at every turn for things beyond his control, he still thought first of her comfort.

She kissed his lips in gratitude.

Christine found the breeze her new little fan created to be delightful, and when Erik occupied her other hand with the matching pair of Opera glasses, she found herself entirely prepared to enjoy a night of musical diversion.

She knew this particular Opera was popular, but she had never seen it for herself—and it was especially surprising when she discovered the male lead was named *Raoul.* Christine would have thought such a happening would have kept Erik from wanting to see such a performance, but she did not question him.

Throughout the presentation she tried to find some hidden meaning that Erik would have intended for her to glean, but though she appreciated the religious subtext and lovers torn from one another due to duty and love, she could not fathom what those had to do her own marriage.

However, it did not escape her notice how Erik's hand would tighten ever so slightly around her waist whenever Valentine proclaimed her love for Raoul.

But her ponderings did not keep her from the enthralling tale, and she gasped quietly as each character embraced the harshness of death.

And when it was over, Erik left her standing for a moment while he looked to the antechamber beyond, presumably to ascertain its emptiness. He returned promptly and was able to usher them unseen—and without any viewings of their own—back to their little home.

When she had settled against the cushions of the settee and Erik had divested himself of his cloak and gloves, Christine motioned for him to sit beside her—and he warily agreed.

They had never truly discussed Erik's opinion of their change in circumstance, and though she wanted to believe this evening out was simply an outpouring of affection, she wanted verbal confirmation of his intention. "Erik, I had a lovely time."

Erik's posture beside her was stiff, and she thought how rare it was that they were seated thusly and she was not in his arms in some way. "I am glad you enjoyed the performance, though I must say the part of *Nevers* was hardly executed adequately."

Christine had not noticed any flaw in the man's vocals, but she was not nearly as critical as her husband. "What inspired you for such an evening?"

Erik was picking non-existent lint from his trousers. "Does a husband need a reason to dote upon his wife?"

Christine slid her hand into his to put a stop to his avoidance. "No, but there is usually some thought behind it, and I am curious as to what it was."

Her intention of pausing his distraction was for naught when his instead took to fiddling with her fingers. "Perhaps I was simply wishing to spend some time with my wife," he took a large breath, "where there is music."

Such a thought had not occurred to her. Erik had played many times, and she had certainly been in the room…

But never singing. When he had learned of her pregnancy, never once had he requested her vocals, and she had not thought to question him. He had composed, but many times it was in his silent manner—very rarely had he actually *played.* And while their relationship had steadily flourished through both time and conversation, she now realised an integral part of her husband had not been tended to.

And though she was sorry she had not been able to see to each need, this only further proved his continued inability to *ask* of her what he needed. How was that a marriage?

"Oh Erik, you should have *said* something! I would have been more than happy to sing for you."

He was twisting her wedding ring and had yet to look at her. "But perhaps it is selfish of me to ask things of you when you suffer so very much from carrying Erik's child."

She gripped his hand tightly with one hand while with the other she tilted his face toward hers. "Then I have something else I must apologise for." His eyes looked torn as he regarded her, and she wondered if other women also had to deal with the childishness of the fathers-to-be. "Erik, I am sorry for how I have treated you. I do not *blame* you for my condition, nor am I *suffering.*" She caressed his masked cheek lightly. "I am *happy*, and I had rather hoped you would be as well."

Now it was her turn to feel abashed as she considered how demanding *she* was of Erik's time and emotions. It was not enough that he brought her to a midwife for confirmation, or that he brought her maternity gowns when she had not thought to retrieve them. No, she also wished for him to learn to *share* when such a thing was quite obviously a new concept for his underdeveloped emotions.

And though her husband possessed his genius, it was painfully noticeable how much he coveted her love and affections, and how difficult it must be to sacrifice his desires for her for the sake of someone else—even if that someone were born of his flesh.

Though she still desired to ask him of living aboveground, of names for their tiny baby, she knew now was not the time—although *soon* would be. She would make sure of it.

So instead she rose quickly and tugged at his hand, pushing him lightly down upon the bench of the organ. "Where would you like to begin?" Erik still looked unsure, though she could tell his façade was crumbling quickly when the excitement of having his favourite instrument at his disposal was overtaking him.

"We shall have to begin with scales," he looked at her reproachfully. "My wife is frightfully out of practice." But before his fingers met the keys of his organ, he gently touched her hand. "Such a good girl you are." And she saw his gratefulness, and she told her tears they were bothersome and unnecessary. "But you eat far too much sugar."

The tears were rapidly replaced with a giggle, and then his softness hardened into his strictest glare. "Your C scale, Madame."

And Christine obliged.

And found quite humiliatingly that Erik was correct in his description of her practice.

But Erik did not seem to mind how her voice strained on the high notes, and in fact the excitement in his eyes grew each time he gave her instruction, and it became startlingly clear how much he had missed his pupil.

So her cheeks cooled as the blush melted away and she simply took each direction as she was told. Erik did not push her too hard, and she was grateful that her abdomen was not yet so large as to press heavily on her lungs—and she dreaded the day it would be.

That was not to say that Erik was by any means *lenient*.

But he seemed to be aiming for something in particular as though he allowed for a few rests when she grew fatigued, he would look at her rather pleadingly for continuance.

And she could not say no.

But *finally* he was satisfied that though her voice was not nearly the perfection he had moulded before his opera, it was satisfactory for whatever piece he had in mind.

It was in his haste to uncover the particular piece that led to the unveiling of Erik's true diversion the past few months.

While Christine had caught him scribbling musical notes on the parchments, it had never occurred to her that he might have made use of the back as well—and now as papers littered the floor, she understood why he would hurriedly place them out of her sight.

It was obvious now that while she always went to sleep with Erik's presence beside her, he did not remain there for long. For there—scattered throughout their sitting room—were dozens of charcoal sketching of a slumbering Christine. And while that was not entirely unexpected, the shocking attribute was that Erik had lifted her nightgown to reveal her torso in nearly all of them.

She lifted one to examine it more fully even while Erik darted to and fro desperately trying to hide them from her perusal. But as he saw Christine looking dumbly at the drawing in her hand, he slowed, still kneeling at her feet. "Erik, what are these?"

Erik was trembling at her feet, and it struck her that he had not done this in so very long—and she wished he would not do it now. She was confused of course as to why such pictures were necessary, and she was even slightly embarrassed at such nudity, but never once did it occur to her that she should be angry with him. He was her husband, and had most certainly seen more of her than a simply her abdomen.

While one hand was clutching at her skirt, the other was reaching to snatch the drawing from her hands. "Christine should not look!"

She pulled away from him, as she flipped the page over revealing notes and scales. For the back of each drawing revealed a different piece of Erik's compositions, differing in both tone and range. And she wondered if perhaps each song would signify Erik's emotion as he watched her.

She should be horrified. She should tell him he had no business exposing her and then drawing her image without her consent, but as she moved to look at each one more closely she saw the slight changes in her body and felt as though Erik had given her a gift. Perhaps this was not how he meant it, but in her eyes he was giving her a keepsake for their first child, both with the tangibility of her growth as well as how Erik's emotions evolved through each term. If only he would play them...

But her silence was obviously distressing to her poor husband as he now nearly keened on the floor, and there was a steady stream of apologies flowing from his throat. "Erik is sorry! So very sorry! But Christine changes so very quickly now, and he does not wish to forget!"

She knelt before him in a position that mimicked so many of these episodes before. "Will you play them?" But her poor husband was too far gone in his anticipation of her horror, and paid no mind to her question. He nearly recoiled when her hands touched his face, as she tried to make him *see* that she was not upset with him.

Ever mindful of his distress, she carefully and quite plainly moved her hands to his mask and tugged gently in her removal. He seemed ashamed of himself and nearly entirely moved away from her, but she anticipated his withdrawal and held him fast before kissing his forehead softly. "Erik. My poor, poor Erik."

He shuddered and gasped as she continued to reassure him with words of her love and how she was not as very angry as he had feared. "Will you play?"

Erik had been clutching at her, so she felt not so much as saw his nod of consent.

When he rose Christine was left feeling quite small upon the floor—even with her slightly swollen womb. Erik carefully lifted her up and sat her beside him on the bench before he selected what appeared to be the first of the series—if the smoothness of her stomach were to be believed.

She thought he would place the side with the musical notes facing toward him, but instead the picture of her remained, and he stroked her form slightly with this finger before moving them to the keys.

Christine was correct in her assumption of his emotions. Some were horribly sad, others were livid nearly to the point of hatred, others belayed his absolute terror at her condition. And what she hated most was that while she *knew* he felt each of these emotions, it was not until he played for her that she felt as he did. Most certainly she was frightened of bringing a life into the world, but never had she felt the abject dread her child would bring.

And when she felt that Erik was incapable of feeling anything positive for their baby, and he placed another of his drawings before them and she began to plainly see the rounder quality of her body, the mood finally shifted. No longer was he angry. There was trepidation to be sure, but there was also a state of wonder and curiosity that could not be denied. And finally, when he reached the final drawing, he played the lightest, most beautiful melody.

It was a lullaby. Not the one he so often hummed when she complained of the damp quality of the air, or when she was restless and finicky. This one was more complex, and almost had a darkness that threatened to overshadow it, but never quite was able.

And it was the most beautiful things she had ever heard.

When Erik had finished, he was quiet—almost as if he were waiting for her word of approval that she had understood and still cared for him after she had witnessed just how much he had struggled these past months. "I am sorry, Christine."

She took his hand in hers, and turned his face so he might look at her. "I love you, Erik. You need not be ashamed of these." She smiled at him. "I am your wife after all."

Erik looked at her searchingly for a moment longer before his lips quirked ever so slightly in return. "I believe your maestro was not quite finished with you yet, wife."

And more than happy to allow him to escape once more into the diversion of her voice, she sang.

XXV

If there was any doubt as to the vitality of their child, all was gone by Christine's eighth month. Having an inverted schedule of time was proving non-existent to their baby, and so many nights when Christine desperately wished for sleep, the baby found such times perfect for exploring the cavern of the womb and its elasticity.

And that was how she found herself awakened on her birthday. Tiny hands pressing firmly into her lungs woke her with a gasp, and she would have cried had Erik's own hand not settled comfortingly on her abdomen. She was so very tired!

"Hush now, Christine."

She had not actually told Erik it was the day of her birth. Not for the childish reasons most wives withheld such reminders from their husbands to test their remembrance, but for the simple fact she felt rather guilty for not knowing *his* birthday. And how could she rightfully celebrate hers when she could not acknowledge his?

But Erik seemed to know regardless of her silence. "Now now, little *enfant*. It is your mother's birthday and I told you last night you must be kind to her."

It was true, Erik had begun to speak to their baby when he first began to feel the movement beneath his hands. At first he ignored this strange new ability, but when Christine revealed how heartbroken she was at his disinterest he began his nightly routine of pressing his face into her stomach as he murmured words she could not always understand.

Christine was also convinced their child was a girl. In one of Erik's medical books it had suggested that how the mother carried was evidence of its sex—and even now she was small. But Erik was not convinced, nor would he oblige by choosing names of either gender. "Would you not be insulted if your parents called you by another name?" He had given her a disparaging look. "I have many things on my conscience but that shall not be one of them."

So their little *enfant* was nameless, but that did not make it any less loved—though Erik still had his days of choosing to ignore the pregnancy entirely in favour of making Christine practice her vocals. But she did not begrudge him his moodier days, for he had to put up with far more dramatics from her—and with far more patience than she anticipated.

But now Erik was distracting her from such thoughts as he planted a kiss on her womb before granting her lips with one as well. "Would my wife care for some breakfast?" And though what she thought she wished for was another few hours of blessed unconscious, at the mention of food such notions were quickly forgotten.

"Yes please!" She began to sit up quickly, but Erik looked at her with pure confusion coming from his unmasked face.

"What are you doing?"

Now it was her turn to be perplexed. "I am going to dress for breakfast."

Erik busied himself with propping up pillows so as to ensure her comfort while reprimanding her gently. "You shall do no such thing. You shall rest while your loving husband brings you breakfast delights."

"To *share?*" He had taken to providing her double portions while refusing to eat himself—something she found truly vexing. Even his own medical books had stated such notions were to be disregarded! Though she did find when he bought her boxes of chocolate she did not argue so very much about how plump he—*and* his child— were making her.

She was seventeen today. It was an odd thing to consider. Not the age itself as it was a perfectly ordinary number. It was the comparison that was naturally drawn to that of her husband—and he seemed so very old! Not in a senile sort of way, but simply in his natural maturity—only rivalled by his inborn immaturity. Her lovely Erik.

And this very same Erik was now bringing his swollen wife a tray full of delicacies. Not necessarily the same as she might have consumed had she not been with child, but wonderful confections all the same.

She had abandoned eggs entirely as the remembered sickening feeling upon her last consumption so many months ago had remained fast, and Erik was hard pressed to find more edible ways to ply his wife full of essential proteins. Thin slices of ham were acceptable so long as there were amble muffins to accompany it.

And such was now before her—with a much smaller plate similarly prepared for Erik. A now fully grown *félin* Christine had settled into the place Erik had vacated, and though Christine was saddened to see the creature disturbed, her husband had no intention of forsaking his rightful place by his wife.

It was a lovely breakfast, and it was one they would cherish for many years to come. For when Erik was inquiring as to what activities Christine desired to partake in for her day of birth, a siren mangled the pleasant quiet of their little home.

Any trace of doting husband was quickly hidden as Erik whipped a mask from the pocket of his jacket, and he nearly ran from the room, though at Christine's frightened cry he slowed and returned to her. "Perhaps Christine would be so good as to dress." He looked into her rapidly pooling eyes and attempted to soothe her, though she could plainly see how anxious he was to dart from the room. "It is most likely nothing. Silly rats you know like to play in Erik's traps!"

She most certainly did not know of any such rats, but rose quickly—or as rapidly as her body would allow in its current state—and slipped on one of her most simple dresses over her nightgown. Christine worried terribly that it was the Persian. And though she had not intended to do so, it did irk her greatly that he would make his reappearance on her *birthday*.

And when the door in the sitting room opened revealing a scowling Erik and the rather drenched body of his acquaintance, her irritation grew tenfold.

"I tell you this Daroga, if you fall into the lake once more I shall not assist you out."

The soaked man was dripping quite inexcusably on the fine rug beneath him, and when he *purposefully* wrung out the hem of his cloak onto it, Christine felt no need to pretend at hospitality.

He had the audacity to practically glare at Erik—the very man who *had* just pulled him from the deathly waters of the lake. "I would not frequent bathing in your lake if you would allow me proper entrance into your home."

Before Christine could make it quite clear that the revocation of his welcome into their home was still very much in effect, the Persian's eyes slid from her husband over to her dishevelled person.

All was quiet for a moment, and still indignant with anger of his treatment of her husband and the fine articles of his home, she felt only slight embarrassment from her not quite appropriate appearance. Any such feelings quickly melted when he began coming near her with a nearly wild look in his eye. "You *impregnated* the child?"

Before he could reach her—*touch* her to see if her swollen womb was in fact because of a child, Erik had grasped his arm firmly. "You *will not* touch my wife."

The Daroga turned on him, eyes flashing dangerously. "Erik what have you *done?*"

Christine wanted him to leave. She wanted her day as it was meant to be, not have to suffer through watching Erik hastily disintegrate before her eyes. "Yes, what *has* Erik been up to?" Any other man would have run from Erik's fury, but this foolish, *stupid* man remained, staring steadily at her husband. "What has he done to his poor Christine where no one can save her? Do you think she cries when he takes her? Do you think she cries when the fruit of his demon seed moves within her?"

While still obviously angry, the Persian at least was not unfeeling to the foul words spewing from her poor husband's mouth. And though Christine wanted to go to him, to soothe the voices that shouted in Erik's mind in confirmation of that horrible man's insinuation, she had their little *enfant* to consider, and she would never put Erik in the position of possibly harming their child in his anger.

But that did not keep her from crying out to him from her place near the bedroom door. "Erik, *please*, stop saying such things!"

"Erik, my friend, you go too far. I am sure you did not mean to harm her. We all lose ourselves in our passions..."

She could take no more. Though she feared Erik's anger, she could not allow this *man* to say such things to her husband when he simply could not understand how happy they had been in their marriage! So she cautiously approached her husband, and gently placed her hand on his sleeve. "Erik, please do not listen to him, you *know* I love you."

And though she hoped he would take comfort from her, he instead looked at her with as much anger as he had for the Persian. "What pretty words my wife speaks."

It was too much. She should have been able to ignore his words and solely focus on calming him, but she felt inexplicably hurt and angered— both at Erik and this horrible man who brought strife whenever he appeared—and so she looked at Erik with all the dismay he had caused, and shot one last hate filled glare at the Daroga. Who *dared* look at her with pity.

And when she escaped to the sanctuary of her bedroom, she clutched their cat to her bosom as her tears fell. She had shut the door firmly behind her, but she could still hear voices echoing through the solid wood. Erik still had not calmed, but within a few minutes she could plainly hear the slam of the outer door.

There was a resounding ache in her heart as she cried, and she waited for Erik to return and apologise—or simply to return. One of his books had said it was important for her to remain unstressed, and as her little *enfant* roiled in her womb, there was an unfamiliar ache that mimicked what she felt in her heart.

While one pain originated emotionally, one was most definitely of a physiological basis. Any anger she felt toward Erik was rapidly being replaced with a desperate need for him to come assure her that their child was remaining safely in place and that this ever increasing pain in her side was only the cause of some unrelated muscle strain.

But when she felt liquid trickle slightly down her leg, and she rushed to the powder room and saw it was not incontinence as she had—rather oddly—hoped, but instead was red with blood, she let out a frightened cry that whatever madness possessed Erik would quickly fade so he could see to her—and their *child!*

And the pain was increasing, and it was not the pulsing, fading nature she had come to expect of labour pains, but instead was of as if a knife was pulling at her womb—and she was desperately afraid.

When she was certain that Erik had left with that *stupid* man, she felt cold hands reaching for her as she lay upon the floor beside the bath, and she was quite sure that the sobs ripping from her own throat were not the only ones being produced.

"Erik is so very sorry, Christine!" But she could not find the breath to comfort him, not when her sole attention was on keeping from crying out in anguish.

And she wished he would stop staring at her and simply begin the journey to the midwife.

Between her sobs and whimpers she must have communicated the great necessity of such haste, and though Erik was entirely unprepared for the reality of his child's birth, he quickly wrapped Christine in his cloak and more swiftly than in any of their previous outings had brought her to the outdoors. He did not bother with a carriage, nor did he ask her to walk on her own, but simply carried her through the cool night air until they reached the seedy alley of their trusted midwife.

The pain was still ever present, but Christine had tried to muffle her cries as best she could so as not to rouse any potential witnesses. She was not at all ready for this! She was still arguing with Erik over his presence in delivery, him entirely against the notion, while she knew somehow it was only by the lending of her husband's strength that she would be able to endure.

But her husband was in tears, and though he had managed to subdue his cries as well, she knew that he was possibly even more terrified than she. She had faith in the process of birth and the holy sanctioning of this child through the blessings of above. Erik did not.

And now he did not even wait for the old midwife to awaken but with a simple flick of his heavily burdened wrist did he open the blockading door and deposit Christine in the bed she had previously encountered.

He disappeared then, and though her mind knew it was simply to awaken the midwife and call her to the bedside, in Christine's heart she doubted his return—and it was confirmed that she was far too afraid to do this alone. Especially not when blood was present and potentially threatened the very nature of the delivery.

But he returned, a sleep bedraggled elderly woman in tow. She alerted quickly upon seeing the crimson stain upon Christine's dress, and hastily set about preparing her tools.

Christine knew she was far from ready to deliver the child—her little *enfant*. Her canal had not had time to prepare, and if their baby was distressed, by the time it was fully opened would be too late to save the child.

Erik was by her side, desperately asking her to breathe fully and deeply, but as each morbid thought passed through her mind, she could not stop the choking gasps as her sobs were confined within her throat. "Christine, *please,* you must breathe! Erik cannot do it for you!"

The midwife returned and directed Erik to remove his wife's gown. At his slight hesitation she practically barked at him to act. "Now is not the time for propriety, Monsieur. *Move!*"

And quite hysterically, Christine wished to laugh.

And when her gown was removed and her chemise pulled up to reveal the entirety of her rounded stomach, the midwife probed lightly against her canal and emerged with bloodied fingers. "Well my dear, it would appear you shall be having this child this evening."

Her calmness was not appreciated by either party, and especially not by Erik. "Why does she bleed?"

The midwife eyed Erik sternly. "Quiet yourself, you are putting undo strain on the mother. There is not as much blood as you would think. Her waters have released and there is slight bleeding which has mixed with the fluid. While startling and concerning, it is not so uncommon when one gives birth this early."

The pain in her womb was settling somewhat, and as it receded Christine was able to think slightly more clearly. "Am I going to lose the baby?"

She had grasped Erik's hand, both to restrain him from throttling the patient midwife, but also for her own comfort. "Not if you remain calm." The midwife replaced her fingers in Christine's channel. "You appear to be moving quite rapidly which would explain your levels of pain. Have you been stressed?"

She looked at Erik suspiciously, and Christine wanted to defend him but knew in truth that the scene with the Daroga was partially to blame for her anxiety. But her poor husband was so very distressed, and he blamed himself entirely for her condition—both for implantation of their tiny baby as well as its imminent arrival—at least if his pacings were to be believed.

But due to the midwife's sharp tongue and threatening of expulsion was she able to calm both Erik and Christine as they waited through each contraction. Time ceased to have meaning, and though their arrival was met with such urgency, Christine's body was steadfastly retaining their child for as long as humanly possible—and far too long for either of their tastes.

The sun was peeking over the skyline when she began to push. Tears were steadily streaming down her cheeks as she held tightly to Erik's hand, and she was certain he was causing him pain. And though there was some small satisfaction in such a notion, she did feel rather sorry for being the cause of any of his distress. But the temporary abuse of his appendage was mild in comparison to his reaction to *her* pain. And there was certainly nothing she could do about that other than endure, push, and breathe.

"Christine, you must *relax*. You're putting undue strain on the baby!"

But how was she to be still when it hurt so very much? Black spots began to cloud her vision, and she could faintly hear both Erik and the midwife telling her that she must *not* close her eyes, but she was too tired to continue! Her little *enfant* had not let her rest the past few nights, and though her body was desperately trying to expel her little child into the world, her mind wanted nothing more than to slip into oblivion. Surely this woman could allow her just a little time to rest…

"*Christine!*" But it was not Erik's voice that she heard in her delirium, it was the Voice—her *Angel*. And when the Voice spoke, she was bound to obey. "Christine, your child needs you. *Our* child needs you! You are so very strong, Christine. Stronger than your poor, unhappy Erik!" Yes, her poor husband—who she made stay with her even when he had requested the one seemly part of societal customs which required his removal from the delivery room.

But now she heard the humming of the Voice as he breathed into her ear, and it was not the lullaby he had made for her, but instead the one Erik had created for their child.

And it seemed that when she was lost in the timbre of his voice, her body consented to the wishes of the midwife while Christine's mind floated blessedly in the realm of the heavenly cadence.

Thus she continued until the Voice dissolved into a sob and above the gasping of Christine as her body finally released the tiny creature so encased there for the past eight months, all that was heard was the faintest mewling of a newborn.

Freshly delivered, and still attached to the vital connection to her body, her little *enfant* was deposited on her breast as the midwife coaxed the remaining tissues be eliminated.

And though she was tired, and wanted nothing more than to slip into slumber, Christine's eyes overflowed at the sheer rush of love and adoration for this tiny new member of their little family.

It was a *girl.*

She had not released Erik's hand, and when she raised her hand to touch the still mewling infant, she brought his hand in addition to her own. The baby was covered in blood and a sticky white paste, but she was whole, and *perfect,* and so very, very beautiful. And for one startling moment,

Christine thought she looked exactly like Erik.

"Cat."

Christine blinked away from her newborn to look at Erik as he reverently stroked the back of the still whimpering baby.

There was nothing deformed about her. She was simply so delicate and thin, with a slightly wrinkled appearance that seemed so very like her father. But she was pink, and alive, and she knew that as Erik looked at her any feelings of resentment he had toward her presence was being swiftly swept away as his heart melted at the sight of his wife and child.

"What was that?"

Erik looked at her with shimmering eyes, and she thought *she* would begin sobbing as he saw the look of rapture coming from him. "She is perfect. She is *pure*. I did not taint her!" He looked once more at his *daughter*. "And her name is Catherine."

She should be offended that all the times she wished to spend selecting names he had quite expertly forgone the subject, but now that he had spent only a few moments with his daughter he was proclaiming her name without even consulting her. But she knew he must have his reasons for the name, though she knew little of the origin.

The only thing that concerned her was that his mumbling of *cat*, sounded suspiciously like *chat*. And so help her, if he named their daughter after a cat...

The midwife gently interrupted as she asked Erik if he would be so kind as to incise the cord, and with trembling hands he obliged. She took Catherine for a few moments to bathe her in warm water, and for a moment Christine thought Erik looked as though he was about to follow— possibly to ensure the safety of his daughter—but instead he knelt by her side and rested his head upon her breast.

He was crying—she could feel the shuddering sobs as he released them, and she knew he was truly overcome if he allowed himself this moment of emotion in the home of a practical stranger, but when she felt his lips brushing over her heated skin and heard the whispered words, she knew his state transcended the physical.

"Thank you, God."

And she found that her own thoughts mimicked quite the same.

XXVI

Erik was not a religious man.

It had been well established that matters of an omnipotent God who purposefully cursed and shunned him since birth was best to simply follow the path seemingly chosen by such a being. He murdered, he stole, he lied, he *coveted.*

But when he married his Christine—when she had bathed him in the blood of her purity, and they had conceived a *child,* it was the final test of such sanctification. And when his daughter emerged, crying and perfect, it truly was evidence that *something* from his cursed flesh could be of an innocent nature.

And though he knew that as the child's mother Christine had all the right to name their daughter, he could not help christening her *Catherine,* as he beheld her for the first time.

Pure.

But as she slipped from Christine's exhausted form, she sounded more of a tiny kitten than a human child, and he knew intrinsically that such an attribute was fated. His little Cat.

It was a foreign feeling, this desire to follow the midwife as she bathed *his* child, for he never thought it possible that something would make him wish to leave his wife's side. But she had been through so very much—the sheer trauma of the past hours on her poor body was more than he could bear to witness, let alone fathom.

And it was upon this altar of his living wife that he professed his newfound faith to this living God.

It was not long before the midwife returned—a tiny bundle securely in her arms. But Erik did not want their little *enfant* in that woman's arms. Forever she should be enshrouded in either the embrace of her mother or himself.

But before he could growl at the woman who had so proficiently cared for his wife through the delivery—quite aptly informing her that such services were no longer required—she was placing the bundle once more on Christine's chest. "I know you are exhausted, but you need to learn to feed the little one."

Perhaps she could stay a moment longer.

He wanted to rip her hands off for touching his wife's bosom. He wanted to gouge her eyes out for having *seen* so much of his wife at all. He might very well have been tempted to except for one very important issue. As she showed Christine the proper way to massage and entice the nourishment from her very breast, the midwife had gently placed his *daughter* in his unsuspecting arms.

And *never* would he allow any harm to be witnessed by this tiny creature.

Erik had never held a child. In truth, Christine was the first person he had embraced that did not immediately result in their demise. But while his wife was all womanly curves that roused such feelings of adoration and carnal appetite, an unexpected feeling of pure *protectiveness* of his newest angel was nearly overwhelming.

And he very much did not wish to cry in front of the midwife.

So he simply gazed at the delicate features of his daughter, and tried to look at her critically. She was too small for a healthy child. She lacked the chubby arms and legs that many privileged children who remained in their mothers the proper amount of time were born with. Her hair was nearly non-existent, but from what clung to her tiny scalp was of a soft brown. His Cat possessed the plump pink lips of her mother, and they puckered in just the same manner when he placed his finger upon them. And possibly to his most supreme delight, she had a *nose*.

And she took his breath away.

But soon the midwife was asking him to place her by Christine so she could begin to nurse, and quite reluctantly he did so. It certainly would not be seemly if within the first hour of his birth he was already putting his own needs above hers.

So he watched with some level of morbid fascination as his two angels bonded, and chose to ignore the midwife as she busied with tidying the mess of the delivery.

Christine was looking between her baby and her husband with tears glistening in her eyes. "She is so perfect, Erik."

And though he had been shocked himself at her absolute flawlessness, he still managed to look imperious as he looked at his wife. "Of course she is, how could you think differently?"

As he supposed, Christine simply looked at him indulgently before turning back to stare in amazement at their newest addition. "I do not know your name, *mon ange.*"

Well that was certainly ridiculous. She had bequeathed her name upon her entry from the room, and most assuredly Christine had heard him utter it. He was about to correct her when she looked to him. "I do not even know *my* name."

And for one terrifying moment, he was certain a blood clot had gone to her brain and at any moment just as he had watched the birth of his daughter, he would watch the death of his wife.

But Christine must have seen the look of abject terror as he warred with himself on how fast he could reach an *actual* physician, for she quickly amended her statement. "Our last name, Erik." She stroked the cheek of their still suckling baby. "I never asked for it did not seem to matter, but now…"

He had no answer for her. At first there was the rush of relief as the adrenaline from anticipating her end faded, but then he was left with a feeling of hollow inadequacy. His wife was asking for his *name—her* name— and he had no response. For in truth, he had none.

Oh most certainly his mother had been born of a house with a name. As had his father. But to take their name would be to acknowledge that he was a part of their blood line, and that was something he was not prepared to do.

But this was *his* family. One born of the love between himself and his wife, and as such, should it be so very odd for him to simply claim a name for his own?

And though that seemed the most logical, it was also the most deceitful. To tie his newest family to a name not their own would be keeping them enthralled in the underhanded tactics born of necessity in his lifetime.

He could only pray his Christine would understand.

"Then I am afraid I do not know either." He did not know *how* to explain to her! But he did know there was far too much space between them, so he went to kneel beside her bed—being quite careful not to jostle the now sleeping infant. "I cannot take the name of those who birthed me. I *cannot* . Nor do I wish to give you a name that is not lawful." He had been looking at their daughter as he spoke, dreading the disappointment in her eyes.

"Then Erik, Christine, and Catherine we shall be." Erik was startled by her acceptance, but when he looked at her—his worn, dishevelled wife who had never looked so very beautiful—she showed nothing more than contentment. "I love you, Erik."

And he kissed her hand as he fought the urge to cry once more. "I love you so very much, Christine."

He felt her hands stroking his head as he gazed at her. "I am so tired." And then it was his turn to pet *her* hair as her eyes began to droop.

"Then you shall sleep."

Her eyes fluttered open determinedly. "But I wish to go home!"

He had not expected her adamant request, and in truth he was unprepared for it. Home was a relative term now.

When she had first brought up the subject of moving outside of their current abode, it seemed entirely beyond his capability to consider. But as her pregnancy progressed, the niggling thought that perhaps they could be *normal* in a secluded cottage away from the prying eyes of the world, but still affording his wife and child the sun and fresh air so important for their happiness, he had begun consulting with a realtor.

Through correspondence of course.

He had planned on surprising Christine once the baby had arrived. In the outskirts of the same village that had bound her to him in the sanctity of marriage, there was a tiny yellow cottage completely surrounded by a gate and trees.

The property had once been owned by a man with considerable wealth, but when the manor house had burned to the ground—taking the entirety of the family with it—only a cottage had been erected in its place. But when the owners of said cottage had perished in suspicious circumstances, any thoughts of the neighbouring occupants of subletting the land for furthering their small village disappeared, leaving the cursed cottage to remain vacant.

And though the realtor had only mentioned it with the most dubious of tones, Erik knew that such a place filled with ghost stories and horror would be the only one to welcome him with fervour. But his wife was exhausted, there was no possible way he was going to allow her to spend the next few hours sequestered in a carriage—though in truth he did not know if he even *could* get her into such a contraption given her previous experience in one. Especially since her entreaty for her own bed was obviously meant to be the one in the Fifth Cellar of the Opera house.

He could not carry both her and his little Cat.

So perhaps the short jaunt to his underground home would be a test of his wife's ability to handle the enclosed space. He could not offer her an open carriage, nor could they remain in the midwife's home for the duration of her recovery—even if he did compensate her handsomely.

"Then return home you shall, my wife." She smiled at him weakly, and he could tell she was about to succumb to sleep despite her desire for the cool embrace of their dwelling. "Sleep for now, and I shall awake you when it is time to depart."

She nodded sleepily, and before leaving himself to find proper means of transport, he carefully settled his daughter so she would not slip off her mother's body in sleep.

He informed the midwife of his preparations, and exhausted herself, she readily accepted her payment and made to her own bed. "You know where to find me for the next one."

Erik froze momentarily, before choosing to ignore her statement altogether.

Another, indeed.

It felt like the darkest of blasphemy when he walked away from his Christine and baby. His place was beside them where he could protect them from all evils, but in his daughter's rush to enter her parent's world of music and love she had left him unprepared.

And so going against every instinct in his body, he trailed the shadowy streets for a carriage.

The reason he had chosen this particular part of Paris for the birth of his child had more to do with the reasonability of discretion afforded by the common goings on—fornication and illegitimate births being the most predominant. But the convenience of these streets was that only a few alleys over one could find far more reasonable living—and awaiting transportation.

He would not risk a driver—*never* again. And though he wished to allow his Christine to rest her head on his lap as they were driven home, he would not risk contact with such professionals ever again.

It was early still, and it was far too easy to render a sleep deprived cabby unconscious than would have been called sportsmanly. In his younger days the man would have been killed. And in truth, though Erik would make every attempt to live a more refined life since the embracement of his new family, he did not count out the possibility that such actions could potentially remain in his future.

But this man was quite simple to disarm, and the lasso had only remained around his neck for as long as strictly necessary.

The carriage was small, but more than adequate, and Erik wasted no time in returning to the front door of the midwife.

Christine was asleep when he returned, as was their daughter. He was loath to wake them, and wondered at the necessity, but determined it would be best if they returned swiftly to their home should any of the elderly woman's other customers need her assistance.

He took Christine first, gently cradling her in his arms, as he lay her down in the seat. Though he knew it constituted as theft, he still took one of the blankets from the bed in which to wrap her as she had no clothing or cloak to shield her from the early morning air. Erik was grateful for her slumber, for the last thing he desired was her fear at being there alone. But because she slept, it was impossible for him to leave their daughter in her care, so instead he swiftly retrieved the sleepy infant and managed the reins with only the use of one hand.

The sun was steadily rising, and he was grateful for the cool morning of autumn that seemed to be keeping many indoors. His hood covered him almost entirely, and he was careful to situate it around the bundle of his daughter so she might not become too cold.

For unlike his Christine, she could not inform him in that impetuous way of her discomfort.

He was not however certain how to go about leading mother and daughter down the many steps to their home. Christine could not be asked to walk, and he felt resigned that he should have to wake her.

But it could not be helped, so descending from the carriage mount— being careful not to jostle his tiny burden—he entered the carriage to rouse his wife.

He nearly cursed the location of their home when he saw how beautiful she looked when sleeping. Erik had not ceased his nighttime ritual of outlining her body in pencil as she slept, and he longed for his tools now.

But those were selfish desires when tempered with the necessity of his family's rest, so with soft lips he kissed her temple. "Christine, you must awaken."

She grumbled, but her eyes fluttered open all the same. "Where are we?" Her eyes widened as she beheld the black interior. "Erik?"

Quickly distracting her by placing Catherine in her arms, he explained their descent homeward. "I am afraid you shall have to hold her as I carry you." He took her face gently in one hand, though his eyes were firm. "So *no* sleeping, Christine."

At any other time she would have at least looked offended at his insinuation as to the mistreatment of their daughter, but Christine was so very tired she merely nodded solemnly at her charge. "Then you shall have to keep me awake."

Erik detested small talk.

But if it meant the safe transport of his littlest angel, then so be it. He did reconsider his decision of taking her to *this* home however, but when he thought of abandoning *félin* Christine for the many days required to get his wife settled, he thought better of it.

And so carefully keeping Christine's blanket around her—and seeing that she had a firm hold on their daughter—he lifted her into his arms.

It was an odd feeling indeed as he carried them into the black abyss of his tunnels. He felt no remorse leaving the horse and cart where it was as there was an emblem on the side of the buggy ensuring it would eventually make its way back to the original owner. No, it was the overwhelming feeling of having the most important women in his arms for the very first time.

And they *loved* him.

Of course there that was assumption on his part that his daughter loved him—it was not as though she could tell him otherwise if it were not the case. But time and again Christine had assured him that when she soothed her acrobatics in the womb whenever he was near, or when he hummed her lullaby and she settled, those were all indications that she loved her father.

And so preoccupied with handling his burdens with the utmost care, he did not notice startled eyes looking on from the street, watching the figures disappear.

Erik could tell by the lolling of Christine's head that she was having great difficulty keeping her promise to remain alert. So steeling himself for her reaction, he made the conscious decision to forego the element of surprise, and simply enlighten her as to the preparations *he* had made for the arrival of their child. "I have acquired a cottage."

"For what?"

He chuckled at her question. Obviously Christine was more exhausted than he realised. "For *you*, Christine. You wished to live aboveground did you not?"

She was quiet for a long moment, and he almost thought he had done the wrong thing in offering her such living quarters. But before he could assure her that they did not *have* to move—that the lovely yellow cottage that he had so vividly pictured his Christine living in would remain vacant—she answered in a small, quivering voice. "Truly?"

Erik nodded though he knew it would be impossible for her to see the gesture. "My wife can be very persuasive." Catherine made a tiny whimpering noise, and for a moment they were both preoccupied with ensuring the contentment of the baby. "We would have returned there after her birth if she had not come so very early."

Christine sniffled against his coat. "You are so good to me, Erik. To *us.*" He pressed a kiss into her curls before settling her into the boat. "Where is it?"

"Not far from the chapel." Erik did not find it tremendously important to elaborate on *which* chapel. As if there was more than one which would hold any significance for him.

Christine placed a kiss on the forehead of the sleeping infant. "Good, then the priest may perform the christening."

Erik froze and allowed the boat to drift momentarily unaided. "Christening?" Though he had reaffirmed his faith in a merciful God, the ritual of christening a child was still foreign.

His wife gave him a look that clearly showed the stupidity of his question. "Of course a christening! Receiving a blessing from a priest is important, as well as our commitment to raise her in a godly fashion."

Well that was foolishness itself. They had reached the other side of the lake and Erik pulled Christine once more into his arms as he answered. "And why, my wife, should we require a *vow* to properly raise our daughter?"

He passed through the sitting room quickly and placed Christine down on their bed—Catherine finally finding the jostling too much to rest through as she blinked perplexedly. Before Christine could consider tending to their daughter instead of resting herself, Erik picked her up and rocked her slightly.

Christine was looking tremendously worn, but while Erik busied himself with bringing her a fresh nightgown and pantaloons, she still managed to tell him of his nonsensical lack of knowledge in regards to religious upbringing. "Erik, it is not that we will not *love* her less, it is just to confirm our commitment before God!" She was *pouting* at him. "We were *married* before a priest, why should the love for our daughter not also be blessed?"

Erik sighed, knowing full well that no matter his opinion he would relent to Christine's desires. "Very well, you may have your service."

She beamed at him as she pulled her new nightgown over her head and fastened the ribbon of the pantaloons around her waist. "I am going to sleep now." Christine looked at Erik carefully for a moment. "Will you be alright with her?"

Would he? He had no idea what he was doing. Half the time he lacked the knowledge of how to be a *husband,* let alone a father. But this was his Cat, and though he had feared he would be unable to touch her in case of tainting her with his sins, he was relieved to find that such panic did not come. He was afraid of her breakability of course. She was so very small...

"Sleep, Christine."

She smiled at him tiredly, but did as she was told, and Erik slipped from the room in favour of the sitting room. *Félin* Christine was there waiting for him, and she eyed the new bundle suspiciously, but soon found it to be rather uninteresting compared to depositing silky white hairs along Erik's black dress pants.

Catherine was blinking up at him, and he could tell she was fighting to keep her eyes open, though why she should wish to deny sleep at this age, he did not know.

But suddenly a thought came upon him. One startling, horrific thought that he knew would never settle unless he acted. He should not do it. It was madness to consider it on the day of his daughter's birth, but he *had* to know.

And so with his daughter's blinking eyes still fixated on his mask, with trembling fingers he removed it.

Whatever reaction he expected did not come. There was no wailing, no horror, nothing that belayed the torment she should have felt as her father revealed his face to her for the first time. Instead she merely yawned in the tiniest of ways, shut her eyes, and fell asleep.

Leaving Erik to think perhaps she did love him after all.

XXVII

When Christine awoke it was to a rather frantic Erik holding an unhappy Catherine. Though her daughter's lungs should have rightfully had another month or two of development, she still had no trouble voicing her distress in her mewling cries.

Though quite honestly, *félin* Christine cried louder when she was in want of attention.

"I believe she is…" He made a vague gesture over her bosom. And though she knew it was rather wicked, she blinked at him innocently as she waited for him to *say* what he thought his daughter required.

"Yes, Erik?"

He huffed, seemingly understanding her intent. "I believe our daughter would like nourishment."

She had though her hormonal outbursts would have ended upon delivery, but if the tears welling in her eyes were any indication, such was not the case. "You said she was *ours.*"

And if any man could look imperious holding a crying infant, it was her Erik. "That is ridiculous. Christine. Of *course* she is ours." With that he was handing their little *enfant* to her and looking at her expectantly. "She is too much like her mother."

His tone was reproachful, and almost—pained? "How do you mean?"

There was no mistaking his sadness as he looked at his little family. "Her tears hurt poor Erik as much as yours do."

And abandoning any semblance of composure, it was with teary eyes that she unbuttoned her nightgown and placed Catherine at her breast. The baby quieted almost immediately, though it took a bit of whimpering and suckling before any sustenance was produced.

But she knew the longer she cried the more it would hurt her poor Erik, so she tried to distract herself with the menial. "How long was I asleep?"

Erik let out a sigh and obliged when she motioned for him to join her on the bed. "A few hours." He looked at her quite imploringly. "I would have allowed my wife to sleep longer, but my Cat seemed to have other ideas."

Keeping an arm securely supporting the baby, Christine held Erik's hand in hers. "It is alright. I feel much better now." Her *mind* felt much better at least. Her body however felt more sore and abused than ever before—but Erik did not need to be informed of such unpleasantness just yet.

"And Erik, she is not a cat."

Her husband looked at her quite oddly. "She certainly sounds like one."

That quite begrudgingly was true, but by no means did it indicate she should be *called* one—though quite plainly, Erik did not seem to agree.

"How has she been?"

"For all her anxiousness to enter this world she has not spent much time observing it." Though he was wearing his mask, she could still make out the distaste in the set of his mouth. "She became soiled."

Christine looked at him in surprise. "You changed her?" It should not have surprised her given Erik's impeccable care he gave to those he loved. But most husbands would never have dreamed of doing it *themselves*. Either he would have woken her to do so herself, or he would have hired a nurse to perform the less pleasant duties.

But not her Erik.

And she adored him for it.

But for some inexplicable reason, she knew if she thanked him, he would be insulted. And such was not her intention. So instead she squeezed his hand tightly, and he graced with a small smile in return, and she knew he accepted her gratitude all the same.

"When do we move?" Erik chuckled at her, though there was nothing malicious in the sound.

"Restless are you?" He brought her hand to his mouth and kissed it. "When you are feeling up to it, I will be happy to transport you to your new abode." The teasing glint in his eye faded. "But you must know it will require a carriage."

She had not thought of that. Though she had been in one yesterday—or was it still today?—it had hardly counted seeing as she had remained unconscious for the duration of the trip.

Erik looked at her worriedly. "It could be similar to yesterday. I would drive with Catherine and you and *félin* Christine may be in the cab."

And though the idea of having an entire carriage to themselves—without danger of *drivers* or their intentions—a terrifying stillness overcame her as she considered what might have happened to the previous driver. Had Erik killed a man on the day of their daughter's birth?

She desperately needed to know if such had been the case, but how

211

could she ask such a thing? If he had not, he would be terribly hurt by her doubt of his goodness, and if it were true…

It had not occurred to her that their marriage had not reformed him. He was far more stable to be sure, but she had assumed that when he finally had a family who loved him, his murdering and seedy dealings would cease. And she simply *had to* know. "Erik…"

He must have seen the fear and trepidation in her eyes and understood the cause, for he sighed heavily and pressed his lips to her temple. "The man was merely unconscious, Christine."

And a wave of pure relief swept over her, and she desperately tried to quell the sob that threatened to escape. She should have *known*. She trusted Erik implicitly, and she cursed her wretchedness for thinking him so capable of senseless murder. "I am sorry."

"Hush. It is a valid thing to question. And perhaps your husband should be very sorry for that." It did not escape her that he was *not* sorry for such a thing—simply that he *should* have been. Perhaps.

But she did not want a quarrel, and though it was not for the safekeeping of a cabby, but for entirely selfish reasons, Christine did not want Erik to perform the act of a driver. "I would much prefer if you were with me."

That was obviously not something he had considered, as he pulled back from where his head had been resting in her curls. "Why?"

"Because I am only afraid when you are not with me." Catherine had fallen asleep during her meal, and Christine took the opportunity to move her so she was lying entirely on her chest, while she was able to then cuddle further into Erik. "And I would much rather you ride *with* me."

Erik sighed and kissed her hair, but seemed to relent. "Very well. Then as soon as you are well."

It was unreasonable, and far too much to ask of him, but Christine was a silly girl, and though she had celebrated her birthday—did this mean she now shared it with her daughter?—she was still a young woman of seventeen, and Erik had offered her a *home*. And she wanted to begin living there as soon as possible.

She nibbled on her lip, before cautiously entreating her husband. "Would it truly prove very strenuous?"

Erik began petting her curls, and the sleepiness was swiftly returning. "Are you growing impatient, my wife?" He kissed her again. "Here you had your husband believing you *liked* surprises."

"Oh I do!" She just liked them especially when they were no longer a secret.

He chuckled again, and it was becoming quite apparent that his ministrations were entirely for the purpose of causing her to sleep. "Alright then, wife, you rest with our young and leave the preparations to your

Erik."

And entirely trusting him to see to everything they might need, she did just that.

When she awoke a second time, it was to the unhappy sounds of her daughter—either from inattention or from hunger, and she lacked the experience to immediately tell. Catherine was not where she had last placed her, so it was apparent that Erik had seen to her before, and most likely tended to her diaper.

He was going to thoroughly spoil her by caring for their daughter so completely.

She was in the midst of once more feeding her when her husband entered. "Ah, you are awake." Christine moved to sit up more fully, and winced as she did so. "My poor, Christine. I would give you something for the pain, but I fear it would also go into my Cat."

It was also rapidly becoming clear that Erik *did* in fact name Catherine after *félin* Christine, and not by some other more pertinent reasoning. But it was too late to do much about it now, though she refused to call her little *enfant* such a name herself.

She supposed she might ask the priest to give her a different Christian name, but she could not imagine crossing Erik in such a blatant way—and she was already quite attached to the name now.

"I am feeling alright, Erik." She nibbled her lip thoughtfully, hoping he was feeling well bodied enough for her request. "Will you help me to the..." She made a vague gesture toward the powder room.

If he felt any discomfort at her request, he hid it well. Catherine having finished her small meal was placed carefully on Erik's side of the bed, while her husband offered to carry her. And though it was a very tempting offer—she did so love to be carried by him!—she knew there were many other women who could not afford to spend many days in recovery and she would do little damage by trying to move on her own. Well, not fully on her own as she leaned heavily on Erik as she made the short trek to the adjoining room.

Though she truly only needed to use the facilities, Erik quickly began filling the bath and putting the same healing salts in that had aided her last time. "Have your bath, and then we must be going."

Christine felt a tremendous amount of sadness for leaving their little home, but when she had relieved herself and settled in the warm, soothing water, she found that she was anxious to begin the journey. Erik would be with her in the carriage—holding her hand and petting her curls—and she knew with absolute certainty that *nothing* would harm her when he was near.

And they were going *home*. While she had come to think of this underground abode as her home, there was still the niggling thought that it truly would always be Erik's. There were many memories—both horrific and magnificent—but she longed for a lovely house of their own.

Which Erik was so lovingly providing.

Walking was still a highly tedious and painful process, even with Erik's healing bath, but she managed to do so without calling for Erik's aid—though by the time she reached her wardrobe she very nearly wished she had.

Her womb had certainly shrunken now devoid of its precious bundle, but that by no means meant it was back to its previous size. She supposed she could return to wearing corsetry, but she had grown used to the comfort of her especially fashioned clothing. And it was not as though her non-maternity gowns would fit in any case.

Erik had not taken any of the gowns from the wardrobe, and she was left to assume he had supplied the new cottage with the necessities—otherwise he had planned to confine her based solely on her lack of clothing. So with that mind, she selected her favourite of her maternity gowns, and slipped it over her chemise quickly, quite certain that Erik would enter at any moment to enquire as to her readiness.

She did not wait long, as he appeared just as she could no longer reach the buttons necessary to hold the gown closed. "Why must gowns be so difficult to fasten?"

Erik's chilly fingers skimmed over the back of her neck. "I believe it is to wheedle out doting husbands from those ingrates who merely supply a lady's maid."

She let out a quiet giggle, ever mindful that the action sent a particularly unhappy spasm through her ribs from the abused muscles.

Erik made a noise of sympathy, for which she was grateful. Even though it was perhaps mildly wretched on her part, it was rather satisfying to know that her pain did not go unnoticed. "Are you ready?"

She nodded, and Erik scooped her gently into his arms. "I hope you were not overly rushed. It is only necessary that we hasten for there is a rather perturbed *félin* Christine in the carriage above."

He paused for a moment in the sitting room in order to obtain their daughter and situate mother and baby comfortably in his arms. Christine watched as he flicked the door open one last time in his mysterious way, and felt a moment of longing to remain. "Will you miss it?"

Erik flexed his arms around her in a gesture of comfort as he closed the door for a final time. "I have been the most miserable and the happiest of my entire life in this house." He kissed her curls thoughtfully before lowering her to the boat. "I am taking what is important."

And it was true. The material items now locked away in the cavernous darkness of his home were not nearly so important as the living creatures gliding quietly through the tunnels of the Rue Scribe entrance. And it did not escape Christine that perhaps the managers of the Opera House might be able to breathe a touch easier now that their resident Ghost was vacating the premises.

Erik must have sensed her despondency as he whispered encouragingly into her ear. "We may come back, Christine, if it so pleases you." And it was such a promise that made her feel lighter, and far more excited for their journey above.

As promised, the carriage was waiting, with a small trunk attached to the back, though she did not know what Erik had selected to take with them. She could hear the lonely cries of their cat even before Erik placed her on the cushioned bench seat, and Christine was anxious for when she could be let out. Though that was not the typical means by which animals were transported, surely she would enjoy the freedom of moving around the carriage more than being contained.

Erik did not leave her side, but simply gave a loud smack to the roof of the carriage and pulled her head into his lap. She was not tired, but found being reclined to be the most pleasant of positions, and Erik was even so kind to produce a small pillow to cushion her head.

She kept Catherine tucked into the back of the bench, and Christine found this to be a very pleasant means of transportation. Though she wondered how it would have been to not have the joy of Erik's fingers running through her freshly washed hair, she would not have traded this moment for any sort of reassurance of her ability to remain independent.

After a quarter an hour—or at least what she *thought* to have been—Erik shifted slightly in order that *félin* Christine might be free—and subsequently stop wailing. She sent both her owners a hurtful glare as she leapt onto the opposite seat, and continued to do so as she washed and preened.

Perhaps there really was too much female blood in this family.

She could not help smiling that such was even a possibility.

The trip was far longer than she remembered on the night of their wedding—but then perhaps her ability to differentiate time had long since been disrupted. Still, Erik pulled out a small bag filled with fruits and sandwiches for her to sample, and even a flask—which he assured her was water. "Do not be ridiculous, Christine."

And even though the journey was long and tedious, and filled with frequent stops for her to relieve herself as she was still overcome with unpleasantness after the delivery, Erik was patient, and Christine found herself enjoying the journey far more than she would have anticipated.

Erik directed her to look out the small window when they reached a large stone gate, and for a moment she worried that she would feel trapped in whatever property he had purchased. But when the gate was opened, and they drove for some time yet she realised the expansive nature of the land surrounding whatever house he had acquired.

He had said it was a cottage—but what if it was some vast manor? How tedious to clean!

But soon, bathed in the light of a waning sun, a small cheerful cottage appeared, entirely surrounded by greenery, even if the blossoms had already succumbed to autumn's chill.

And though she told herself that she was being silly, she still felt tears welling in her eyes. "Oh Erik, it is beautiful!"

He was holding her arm as he helped her descend the steps of the carriage—her hands still occupied with Catherine—and she was momentarily startled out of her reverie at her new *home* when *félin* Christine bounded out to begin her exploration.

"Please wait a moment, Christine." She was not certain why Erik wished for her to wait before beginning her own wanderings throughout the house. But she managed to wait relatively patiently as Erik emptied their possessions from the carriage, paid the driver, and even followed to ensure that he had vacated the premises before firmly locking the gate behind him.

He walked quickly back to her, and though she was nearly trembling with excitement at being able to have her very own home, she was grateful for his thoughtfulness. They were really and truly alone now, and he could point out the wonderful qualities of their new home at his leisure.

It was obvious the door had been replaced. There was no traditional key hole by which Erik could simply slip an iron key and allow them entrance. Instead it was entirely smooth but for the raised panels giving a rather expensive quality to the door. It did however cause Christine to sigh. Was he at least going to inform her how to open *this* creation?

And much to her delight, he did.

It was quite simple really, if one knew precisely where to touch. He took Catherine in one of his arms so he could direct Christine's hand with the other, and soon she realised how convenient never having to think of keys or their ability to be picked—she truly loved her husband.

Her excitement outweighed any thoughts of discomfort from walking, and though slow, she was still the one tugging at Erik's hand as she became enthralled with her new abode. Everything was light and open, with soft wall coverings, and comfortable furniture. There was a parlour, a dining room, and a kitchen she could envision making biscuits with both Erik and Catherine. There were even *stairs!*

She had always wanted a house with a staircase. At Christmas time she would wrap garland around it, and perhaps even place some candles to make it truly glow. There was only a bedroom upstairs, which judging from the size of the bed would be for Erik and her to christen when the time came. There was even a tiny bassinet situated to the side—and her heart swelled at the care Erik had taken in preparing their bedroom.

Further investigation downstairs proved to hold three more rooms—a study which was completely surrounded in books and held a desk and two comfortable leather reading chairs. And a *hearth*.

Though she knew there would be no possible way for her to participate in any marital joining for some time, it did not escape her notice how these rooms were especially accommodating for such ventures.

The other two rooms were entirely bare, but it was quite obvious to her for what they would be used. The one with the small bay window would have a window seat installed and would become Catherine's room, while the other—which now she and Erik were standing in—would have to become Erik's music room.

"Why has this room not yet been completed?"

Erik made a noise of noncommittal as he drifted to look at the nearly dark yard. "I was not sure if a music room was entirely appropriate."

Christine could not imagine anything more absurd. Erik without his music?

Before she would enquire further, he continued. "For so long music was the only thing for Erik to love—to love *Erik*." He looked down at his daughter and touched her cheek gently. "Such is not the case now." His eyes swivelled to hers, and his desire for her to confirm his words was nearly palpable.

"I love you so very much, Erik."

He smiled softly, and returned his gaze outdoors. "I do not wish to be so occupied with my music then."

Christine loathed how slowly she had to move in order to place her hand on his shoulder, but she knew the trek was necessary when Erik gave a soft sigh at the contact. "That does not mean you cannot still utilise something you enjoy." She nibbled her lip thoughtfully. "But perhaps then it may become a diversion instead of an obsession."

She hoped he would not be angry at her assessment, but instead of anger, his eyes held only a begrudging agreement. "You think it is not healthy to be so consumed?"

Christine placed her hand upon his cheek, and gently removed his mask. She could tell he had not expected the gesture, and she was nearly surprised that he did not snap at her for doing so in front of their daughter, but he seemed to relish the feel of her fingers ghosting over his flesh too much to be truly irritated. "I think I would not wish to lose you to your hobbies." She tilted her face so that Erik would realise her intention, and he obliged by stooping down to place a kiss upon her lips.

"But I think this should still be a music room." She dropped her gaze to Catherine and touched the little fingers that had fallen out of her cocoon. "Besides, you shall need to teach her to play."

And Erik's answering kiss communicated his gratitude far more than any semblance of speech could possibly relate.

XXVIII

If Christine had thought their bed in Erik's underground home was one born for her complete comfort, she was dreadfully mistaken. She supposed it would take time to become once more familiar with the rising and setting of the sun, but when the drapes were closed, and she was sufficiently huddled beneath the bedding, the bed seemed to welcome her. And she in turn *adored* it.

It was a little larger than their previous bed, but by no means did that mean Erik slept farther away. She knew Erik had worked hard the past few days—both with the pregnancy, and allowing *her* to rest. But it was most curious when on their first night in their little cottage, *he* slept first.

She dared not touch him lest he waken, but she could not help remaining awake a little longer in order to gaze upon him as he did to her so very often. Christine could not bear to allow Catherine to sleep in the bassinet just yet, and she was cuddled carefully between husband and wife. And she could so strikingly see the resemblance between father and daughter.

There was a certain roundness that Christine thought all babies possessed—and perhaps if her little *enfant* had remained in the womb for as long as she should have she might have been plumped sufficiently. But as it was, she could see the emerging cheekbones that would lead to a striking young woman in years to come.

Christine had to admit she would certainly envy them.

There was a delicateness to her skin that was quite obviously inherited from her father. Pale, though perhaps with a flush of pink instead of Erik's yellow, but it still appeared rather thin. She wondered if she would also harbour the hidden strength that Erik so possessed.

And she loved them both so dearly.

It was too early yet to see which eye colour she would receive. As of now they were a light blue—a bit lighter than she had seen from the few newborns she had come into contact with, but surely even Erik had been born with such eyes as well.

Secretly she rather hoped she would inherit his striking colour, yet she supposed she should wish her daughter to have the benefit of normalcy as much as possible.

But she found that the longer she knew Erik, the more beauty she found in certain aspects of his physical appearance. While horrific as a whole, there were things she found to be quite appealing, and could not help but wish her daughter could enjoy the same.

Not that she would ever tell Erik so.

Eventually however, her eyes closed of their own accord, and for the first time in a long while, she slept when the rest of the people of France were also basking in the bliss of slumber.

Catherine awoke her sometime later, not quite willing to accept that nighttime was for sleeping. Though Christine supposed she could not blame her, as she had been quiet and compliant for nearly the entire carriage ride to their new home. Erik promised to tend to her as much as need be after Christine fed her, and in her sleepy state she readily agreed.

She promised herself however that come the morning, it would be *Erik* who was allowed to see to his own needs, while she cared for their baby.

When she awoke the second time, it was to the delicious feel of *sunshine* caressing her skin. Erik had opened the draperies, and the entire room shone with the light of early morning sun. She could not remember the last time such had been the cause of her awakening!

She was still rather sore, but not enough to confine her to bed, and she found she could move much more freely than the restricted steps she had taken yesterday. Much to her chagrin, she was still expelling much of the fluids from her pregnancy, and she hoped dearly such would pass quickly.

Having freshened up in the adjoining powder room—an equally cheerful and delightful space as the bedroom—she went in search of Erik and their daughter.

It did not take long to find them. Even from the stairs she could hear Erik's voice wafting from the direction of what would become Catherine's nursery, and sure enough she found him describing elaborate plans as to décor and toys he would make her. "But we must be sure your mother approves, of course." His tone turned rather stern. "You must always listen to your mother."

The firm voice was gone as quickly as it had come, and he settled instead for humming to her softly. Loath to intrude, but not wanting to be alone in the hallway, Christine quietly entered. "You are so good with her."

Erik looked at her rather chagrined. "Apparently she is not the only one who is fascinated with my voice." He tapped the baby's cheek lightly. "And she would not be quiet unless I was speaking, but she must learn to let her mother rest!"

Mother.

She had heard Erik use the word three times now, and still it sent her shivers to hear it spoken. It was only some short time ago that she thought herself a child—that *Erik* thought her a child—and now they had made a perfectly wonderful specimen of their very own.

And she was a *mother.*

Who now wanted to prepare breakfast for her husband.

She was not certain if Erik would have stocked the kitchen before their arrival judging from the unexpected date of their move, but true to his mysterious ability to take care of things before she could even think to ask it, she found fresh foods and baking ingredients all stored neatly in the cheery kitchen.

Erik followed dutifully behind—obviously intent to make sure she did not destroy *this* kitchen as she so aptly did the last—but he allowed her to familiarise herself with it without encumbrance. Feeling rather adventurous, and quite delightedly, she found an *English* cookbook that she requested Erik select something simple.

And with his guidance, she made scones.

She had tasted them before of course, but never by her own hand. Erik particularly enjoyed them, as they were not overly sweet, and he ate them without the addition of preserves—though Christine lathered them quite thoroughly.

They ate in their new dining room, and Christine found that though she had come to love their little underground home quite thoroughly, there was something positively thrilling about building only sweet memories in this new room.

Once she had completely filled herself with the warm morsels, and finished the entirety of the teapot, she considered how best to spend the rest of their day. Visions of going to tiny village shops to select nursery décor seemed quite obviously of importance, but as she considered their daughter, she remembered what must happen first—before any such frivolity of room enhancement.

Their daughter needed to be christened.

And she dearly hoped Erik would not fight her on its necessity.

She had purchased a tiny baptismal gown when she was in her sixth month of pregnancy, as the long white arraignment hardly was gender specific. But such was most likely still buried beneath the Opera House, and it saddened her considerably to know that the garment she had selected with such care would never grace her tiny child.

"Why are you frowning?"

She smiled regardless of her darkening mood. Her husband certainly lacked tact sometimes. "Erik, please be open minded."

He eyed her suspiciously across the table. "Erik's mind is always open."

She pursed her lips at his tone. "You certainly do not *seem* very open."

He sighed, and rearranged his masked expression to one of intent listening. "Why are you frowning?"

Christine could not help but giggle at his foolishness. "I would like to have Catherine christened today, and I was simply remembering that I left her gown behind."

Erik looked rather offended, and sat back in his chair. "*You* might have abandoned it, but I can assure you, *I* did not."

He did not leave it behind? So that meant...

"You will allow her to be baptised?"

Now he looked *truly* insulted. "You made it quite clear that it was important to you. You think me so cruel as to deny you something of such great importance?"

Completely disregarding any remaining tenderness to her abdomen, Christine abandoned her place at the table in favour of bestowing her husband with a kiss. "Thank you."

"You have gratitude for very ridiculous things, wife." But he had snuck his arm around her waist and stood so he could embrace her properly. "Are you well enough for such an event?"

Christine nodded emphatically, and Erik let out a low chuckle. "Then I suggest you prepare yourself. Would you like to see to Catherine or shall I?"

Remembering her earlier promise to herself that *she* would be the one to care for their daughter today and relieve such a burden from Erik who also had to secure transport for them, she quickly alleviated him of such notions. "I would like to do it, if that is alright." She looked at him thoughtfully. "But I do not know where her gown is."

Erik tugged at her curl playfully. "It is in the trunk, you silly girl." Seeing how even the mention of the trunk provided no sense of comprehension on her part, he elaborated. "In our bedroom."

She fully acknowledged that she was indeed an incredibly silly girl, but it did not stop the slight thrill that passed through her at his use of the word *our*.

Christine placed a kiss once more upon his lips before taking Catherine from the little bassinet Erik had arranged in the corner of the dining room for ease of eating. "Come along then, my little *enfant*. You are going to be blessed today."

She purposefully ignored Erik's incredulous shaking of his head.

It was upon arriving at the bedroom that Catherine awoke and determined a meal for herself was also necessary. Christine supposed it would take some time to become used to thinking of another person's schedule before her own.

Erik had thoroughly spoiled her that way. Other than the time he had purposefully locked himself away in the throes of his music, he was always glad to abandon his own desires in want of pleasing her. And little Catherine had no knowledge of priests or baptisms, and the only thing important to her at the moment was the discomfort of her empty belly.

So with a resigned sigh, Christine abandoned rifling through the trunk in search of whatever treasures Erik had thought to bring, and sat in the little arm chair which so becomingly faced the window.

Now that the land was bathed in sunlight, she could properly see how vast the property truly was. She knew nothing of this houses' history, and she was terribly curious why such a small cottage resided amongst so much emptiness.

Not that there was a lack of foliage to be sure. There was a small yard in front and back nicely manicured to lend a welcoming appearance, but there were a great many trees beyond. It made it seem quite—cosy.

Catherine apparently satisfied with her mother's offerings, promptly returned to her state of blissful sleep. Perhaps such a thing should not be allowed to better promote *nighttime* sleeping. But for the moment Christine was grateful for it meant she could begin her preparations with little distraction.

Settling her baby carefully in the middle of the bed, she knelt before the steamer trunk Erik had so meticulously packed, quite curious to see which items Erik had chosen were of most importance.

At the top was the white bonnet and gown she was in search of, and though her quest was technically complete, that did not quell the curiosity of what else might be hidden inside. She did not have time to search through everything, but she did pick up the large leather book directly beneath the christening gown.

It was Erik's drawings.

One by one he had painstaking bound each one in progression of her growth, and had even made additional ones she had never seen.

She started to cry.

She supposed to anyone else it might seem strange that a husband would take such liberties as to draw partially nude charcoals of his wife, but to her she saw his intensity of caring—how much he truly *treasured* her and each change her body made to accommodate their little *enfant*.

Oh how she loved him!

So it was a sniffling Christine who searched through her new wardrobe trying to find something that appeared to remotely fit her still distended torso. It had receded some due to her rest and simply time, but it was nowhere near how her figure had appeared before her pregnancy.

She eyed each waistline of every gown with a critical eye, and found that most were fashioned by Erik's mysterious tailor so as to accommodate the body she currently possessed. *Without* a corset. Her bosom was heavy, and for a moment she quite wished she still had one of the accursed contraptions simply for the support.

But instead she selected one of the most modest gowns that allowed for the most coverage—she *was* attending church after all—and was quite pleased to find that this particular gown utilised *front* closures so she did not have to call upon Erik's services.

It was a pretty dress of green muslin, and she found it perfectly suited for a morning service—especially when autumn had yet to truly give into the encumbrance of winter.

The only difficulty she found was that Catherine required changing in an additional nature—something she had not yet encountered. And for a terrible moment, she felt as though she was the most neglectful mother imaginable. Her daughter was now two days old and her mother had yet to change her diaper!

But before she could truly become distressed, her husband appeared, supplies in hand. He moved to take the infant to perform the task in another room while Christine finished changing, but she quickly scooped Catherine into her arms. "You must show me how to do it."

Erik looked rather baffled by her emphatic statement. "I am perfectly capable of taking care of the child, Christine."

She was being irrational. It *truly* did not matter who cared for her as long as she was safe and happy, but in this moment, Christine found it entirely necessary for her to learn to do it for herself. "That is not in question! But I do not even know *how* to take care of her!"

Erik still looked at her with eyes searching for whatever madness had taken hold of his wife, but acquiesced all the same. It was most certainly an uncomplicated process, and it struck her as quite odd that she was taking lessons from the Opera Ghost on how to properly change an infant.

But she did not allow her thoughts to stray too terribly far as she watched Erik's practiced hands make quick work of both the diaper and donning Catherine in her white arraignment.

She retired to the powder room to see to her hair, and determined that it would be quite appropriate to wear her hair entirely up this morning. It was not as though she wished to encourage Erik's pettings in a church!

Satisfied with her look of maturity and proper demureness befitting the solemnity of the occasion, she returned to the bedroom only to find Erik looking thoughtfully through the leather book.

"I see have found your birthday gift."

Christine had entirely forgotten about her birthday—and for a moment she felt an acute pang of regret that she had not experienced whatever lovely happenings Erik had planned.

"It was not quite finished of course." There were a few blank pages at the back which evidenced the lack of completion. "She was not to have come so early." The tone of his voice worried her, and she wondered if he was truly prepared for the birth of their daughter.

Neither of them had been, most certainly, and it had been a terrifying experience for both of them. "She could still have medical issues you know." He was finally looking at her, and she could see the sadness in her eyes. "They may simply not have presented as of yet."

Was he purposefully trying to frighten her? She did not know much about premature births—only that if the baby were so very small, death often came swiftly.

"Why are you saying this?"

He touched the book once more before coming to stand before her. Erik stroked her cheek tenderly before placing a kiss on her brow. "Forgive me, I am simply a man with too many thoughts."

While she did not doubt this to be true, she was also quite certain that such worries were not born of nothingness. "Did you notice something?"

He sighed heavily, and she could plainly see the worried lines that formed around his eyes. "I have reason to believe she has difficulty with her lungs."

Panic. Blind, unadulterated fear that radiated from Christine's heart and pervaded her entire body.

Christine tore away from Erik in order to ascertain exactly what *reason* he would have to believe her perfect, tiny little Catherine could possibly give her father to cause him such concern.

He bade her press her ear to the infant's chest, and the slightest wheezing could be heard. Faint, but present.

And Christine wanted to cry—*did* cry.

"Will she be alright?"

She could tell Erik was warring with himself. In past, *he* would have been the one to moan and curse God in his despair for allowing their little *enfant* to be so endangered.

But not now.

His fingers trembled as they stroked his wife's and daughter's cheeks, but his voice was sure as he made his declaration. "She will be fine."

And she believed him. *Had* to believe him.

Her husband had changed so very much since their marriage. And in that moment, when she felt his assurance take hold in her panicky body, she revelled in his strength.

Now more than ever, she wanted Catherine to be christened. She would have faith that God did not bless them with their little *ange* simply to remove her as quickly as she had arrived.

But she wanted the same priest who had blessed their marriage to then pass on such heavenly ordinance to their daughter. All had not been well when Erik and she had taken their vows before, and why should things now be any different?

She was not so ridiculous as to presume there was something mystical about the priest's ability to pronounce happiness upon those he blessed, but it could not worsen things by doing so.

Erik left Christine holding Catherine as he once more fetched her cloak and led her downstairs to the small awaiting carriage. There was no driver, and it was quite obvious that Erik would be the one who directed the lone horse, but with her experience the day before, she did not worry for her peace of mind.

But then, there was no particular reason she should have to sit in the carriage alone as it was. She would very much like to distract herself with the lovely views of their new surroundings, and surely sitting by Erik's side would be much more conducive for such things.

And quite happily, Erik was in agreement.

It was quite an odd experience riding openly with one's husband—when one's husband was Erik at least. He was in his mask that made him so very uncomfortable, but made him look like everybody else. He had not worn it since she had purchased his wedding ring, and truthfully, she had not missed it.

Yes, her life was one of seclusion, but that was not the same oppressive quality of solitude. She had quite pleasant company indeed.

They paused only long enough for Erik to release them from the gate, and then it was merely pleasant country lanes enshrouded by lush greenery that arched overhead. It was some time before other houses could be seen, each being small but no less quaint for their simplicity.

Christine loved each one.

And soon, with not a fifteen minute ride later, they were at the little stone chapel that she had once gazed upon in such dread.

It was not until that moment, when Erik had swept down from the carriage seat to cross quickly to help her down, that Christine fully appreciated how very much her life had changed. Erik no longer suffered from his fits of madness as he once did—at least when unprovoked by foolish pandering from Persian gentleman—and she in turn had found herself to be blissfully happy with their little family.

Their daughter might not be of supreme health, but she had two parents who adored her and would take every precaution necessary to ensure her continued development.

And so it was that Erik led her by the arm into the chapel, and this time a smile was her companion instead of her tears.

XXIX

The church was entirely empty when they made their way through the large wooden door, and for a moment Christine feared that perhaps they had missed their opportunity.

She had no knowledge of how one made appointments with priests, or if in fact they simply lived within the hallowed halls of their sanctuary awaiting those in need of counsel and prayer. In this particular occasion she hoped for such to be the case.

Upon entering, a slight shuffling could be heard and soon the priest appeared, looking rather confused but good natured nonetheless.

"Who goes there?"

"Father Martin, I believe you agreed to baptise our daughter." Christine was rather surprised that Erik would speak so casually to the man, but she supposed the priest having no knowledge of his abnormality would have given him comfort. She did not however believe that such a statement would be met with recognition—surely many people came to christen their daughters.

But perhaps the man's blindness provided some sort of increased capacity for remembrance and recognition simply by voice, for he seemed to know exactly who they were. "A bit early are you not?" His pale eyes narrowed as he considered how many months had passed. "Here I believed you to be a gentleman when I married you two."

He came forward with sure, but measured steps, and held his arms out for the infant. Christine felt a moment of apprehension at his insistence, but knew such was necessary for the ceremony. "Ah, well that explains it." His tone softened considerably as he felt the small figure in the bundle. "Such a tiny thing you are. Probably scared your mother silly being born so early!"

It struck Christine that he had *expected* them to be here with a baby. Either he had made a general assumption as to the productivity of their intercourse, or perhaps Erik had in fact planned this ceremony for quite some time. The latter thought made her heart swell.

"Shall we begin? I take it you have no witnesses." When Erik and Christine both remained quiet—Witnesses? Were those necessary?—Father Martin only nodded pleasantly. "No matter, God is witness enough as it is."

He led them to the altar, still speaking softly to Catherine as he went. Erik took Christine's hand, and it was such contrast from nearly a year ago, she squeezed his hand in comfort. "We have changed, have we not?"

Erik looked at her thoughtfully, before nodding slowly. "I believe we have grown up."

It was such a silly thing to say. *She* was the only one who could possibly have had any maturing left to do given her short years, and Erik was probably well into his forties—or fifties for that matter. She could not bring herself to ask him.

But he was right. Erik had viewed her as a child would view a favourite toy—something to be coveted and never to be shared. But now—now he freely provided for Catherine not merely for the sake of pleasing *her,* but because he truly loved her as well.

They had grown up. *Together.*

"Do not dawdle, you two. You are setting a terrible example for the young one."

Perhaps they had not quite reached their *full* potential for maturity.

She smiled at the thought.

Christine had never been to a christening before, and she had a sneaking suspicion that Father Martin had his own special way of performing the ceremony that was not entirely in keeping with the formality usually enacted.

While the vows themselves for Erik and Christine to bring up their child under God's holy ordinances were clear enough, each line was punctuated with thoughts of the priest. Either tips for colic, or how best to facilitate ease in teething, and even so far as to express the necessity of ensuring the continuance of marital relations.

Christine was blushing thoroughly by the end.

When it was time for the actual baptismal, Christine was horrified when the priest turned to Erik and looked at him expectantly. Was there some part of the ceremony that Erik was required to recite?

But such was not the case.

For Erik *left.*

She had made the mistake of believing Erik had fully planned this event—that it was all with his consent and that he had the ability to see it through. She was uncertain as to what exactly had provoked his departure, but she felt the welling of disappointment, for their daughter *could not* be baptised without Erik's approval!

Before she could begin to make her tearful apologies to the priest, the door of the chapel opened once more, and Erik appeared holding the black case of his violin.

And Christine felt more wretched than she would have thought possible.

It was certainly not traditional, but it seemed quite appropriate in their own little way that Erik would wish to give an offering of his talent on the day of his daughter's christening.

And she had doubted him.

Would she ever learn to fully trust that he was a good man with only her best interest at heart?

She swore to herself she would not make such a mistake again, and would stop any traitorous thoughts before they could take hold.

Thoughts of any kind fled her mind as soon as Erik began to play.

The piece was not overly long, nor embellished with Erik's expertise. It was a simple melody, but full of joy, happiness, and praise for the precious creation still being held in the priest's arms.

Catherine must have been so very used to her father's playing, she hardly stirred through its entirety.

Christine however was continually awed by her husband's abilities to so convey the feelings that they so often shared. Father Martin was no less impressed, but given the solemnity of the occasion—for which he must have forgotten with his previous comments—he recognised the piece as a private showing of Erik's thankfulness to God, and did not mention its beauty.

Instead he waited for Erik to replace the violin in its case and rejoin Christine before him, before he commenced with actual baptismal. "And do you, Erik and Christine, profess such faith as to which this child may be baptised into the sanctity of God's holy covenant?"

She had not been expecting such a question. She knew of her own simple faith, and she prayed it would be enough to please God, but Erik's was an entirely different matter. He had thanked the Lord when Catherine was born, but Christine was not so naïve as to think a lifetime of pain could be undone simply by the birth of their daughter. Especially not when the health of her tiny lungs was now in question.

But Erik's voice was sure as he spoke the essential words, and entirely unequivocally, she believed him. "We do."

And Christine was entirely ashamed for the outpouring of relief she felt at his assurance.

The priest was efficient in his ability to remove Catherine's bonnet one handed, and Christine was struck at his ability to function from both age and without sight. "Then I baptise thee in the name of the Father," Catherine let out a terrible wail—the loudest by far of what she had hence accomplished—when the cool water touched her precious head. "And of the Son," Erik tightened his hold on Christine's hand, either to keep her from comforting their daughter, or to keep *himself* from doing so. Christine could not tell which. "And of the Holy Ghost. Amen."

He turned his unseeing eyes back to the awaiting parents, and they were twisted into a glare. "If you had given me proper notice I would have heated the water for her."

Erik reached for his daughter, much to the reluctance of the elderly priest. "I apologise for my oversight."

Father Martin nodded once more, and made his way to the same registry that housed Erik and Christine's signature indicating the validity of their marriage. "Come put her name down."

Christine had been so dazed and saddened when she had last seen the book, she had hardly noticed its contents. While she perused the names and dates and attempted to find where their names were located, Erik spoke from his residual place before the altar.

"I believe Catherine would like to go outside." That might entirely have been the case as she was still giving out pitiful wails, but Christine suspected that Erik was the one who truly wished to see to her without witnesses.

Silly man. As if it was a crime to be an excellent father in view *of* a Father.

Christine gave her consent to allow him to leave her to fill out the registry alone, and for a fleeting moment it felt quite odd to be alone in another man's presence. Not that she considered anything against propriety to be alone with a priest, but it had been so very long since such was the case.

"You were not a happy bride as I recall."

Christine stiffened, and thought frantically that she would have to *lie* in order to protect the happiness of her little family. Surely he would not understand. "I was nervous."

His laugh was loud and boisterous, and entirely unbecoming to the hallowed halls of the chapel. "My dear, there have been nervous brides since the beginning of time, but you were weeping—and not of joy." His withered hand came to rest upon her arm, and all humour left his face. "Was I wrong to have married you to him?"

She half expected the indignant anger to rise in her as it did whenever the Persian questioned their marriage, but when she thought of how she must have seemed to this man—this man who had married a girl entirely against her will to a stranger—it became more her duty to comfort him than to assume he could understand the dynamics of her relationship with Erik.

"My husband is a wonderful man." She smiled softly though she knew he could not see it. "I may not have thought so at the time, but I can assure you, ours is a happy marriage."

He seemed to take heart at her words, and patted her arm comfortingly. "I am glad then."

Christine made quick work of the registry, though she did take a moment to touch Erik's name as it lay scrawled beside hers. She still could not make out exactly what he had written as a last name. Even though he had told her he did not wish to give her a false name, she still was quite curious which name he had taken for his business affairs.

The book signed, the priest pulled her into an embrace as he wished her continued happiness. "And to see you on Sundays!"

She smiled bemusedly, wondering how she could possibly convince Erik that a religious upbringing was important to Catherine's development as well, but promised to come when she could.

Christine was grateful for his understanding.

When she emerged from the chapel, Erik was holding a sleeping Catherine who had determined her father's smallest finger made a rather soothing replacement to her mother's breast. "Are you finished?"

Christine sighed. Would she ever be able to comfort Catherine as aptly as Erik? She felt awkward and unsure when she cried—the urge to provide a soothing embrace apparent, but she lacked the confidence that such actions would prove effective.

Her husband must have seen her distress for he made to pass their daughter to her. "Are you very tired?"

She blinked, wondering how on earth he had come to such a conclusion, but then remembered she had never answered his query. "Yes, we are finished, and I am not tired." She stroked Catherine's cheek softly as she still suckled on Erik's finger. "You are so very good with her."

Feeling despondent that Erik might feel put out without any contact for himself, Christine placed her hand on his fully covered cheek. Though only the second time had worn this particular mask, she was steadily growing to despise it for the lack of *actual* contact it afforded. "You played beautifully, Erik. Thank you for doing this."

He did not reproach her this time for her vocal gratitude, but leaned further into her palm and kissed it lightly. "I believe we have two additional rooms to furnish."

She had come to the previous conclusion that she had reached a new height of maturity these past months, but at the mention of shopping, she still felt the childish thrill well within her. And she was even further grateful for the distraction.

"I am not tired!"

Erik chuckled softly at her enthusiasm. "So you have stated."

"Are there shops nearby?" Though she would not freely admit it to him, she was quite excited to begin familiarising herself with her neighbours and fellow townspeople. That was not to say of course she was loath to return to their little cottage, she simply wished for them to truly *belong* here.

But Erik needed his music room!

And most assuredly, Catherine required a nursery.

Erik stated that there were in fact quite a few shops in what she thought was a tiny village. She was slightly surprised, but such thoughts quickly evaporated when she realised *Erik's* idea of nearby and hers varied slightly.

Not that she minded the fresh air. Erik's hat was pulled low over his face, and from his profile he looked perfectly ordinary, so she did not worry for their safety. It was more the anticipation of picking out the rocking chair she would use to nurse Catherine, and possibly even seeing which instruments Erik would decide were necessary for his music room.

Would they have another organ?

Or perhaps a *pianoforte*. Such would be entirely more appropriate for the size of the house, but somehow it did not seem... grand enough for Erik's particular tastes.

But perhaps his taste in music had evolved as well given their current circumstances.

His lullaby for Catherine was certainly what some might consider morose, but if the exuberant song he had played in the church was any indication, perhaps the simplicity of the percussion instrument would be far more accommodating.

Whatever Erik wished was enough for her. She wondered if he would still like for her to sing, or if perhaps her duties as a mother were more pressing in his mind than her voice. But she would leave such decisions entirely in his hands.

For in truth, it was his reaction to her singing that pleased her more than the act itself.

Erik had given her the baby so he could freely manoeuvre the reins as he skilfully led them through the winding country roads. They had yet to see any passing buggies, and Christine wondered just how far from civilisation they truly were.

After over a half an hour's ride, other individuals finally came into view.

Not many to be sure, but enough to give her hope that they were not so wholly removed from the world. At this rate, it was an hour's ride from their home to the nearest shop!

And to think she had hoped Erik would allow her to frequent the grocers instead of mysteriously allowing food to grace their cupboards without warning.

She would not complain however, not when he stopped before a shop whose windows led her to believe she would find the perfect items for her daughter's room.

Any ire she felt melted away, and she kissed Erik's cheek soundly before practically hopping from the carriage in her haste to begin her activities.

When she entered the store, she was suddenly very grateful for her love of sitting beside her husband in the carriage, for otherwise there would be no possibility of taking all of her desired items home.

Home.

Not to an underground lair, that while she had grown to love it was also the evidence of years of torment and loneliness for her husband. Instead she would return to her little cheery house that did not at all resemble the depressing nature of the windowless structure they previously resided.

She was being absolutely ridiculous, but when she selected the colours and items so necessary for the nursery—the chair, the changing station to ensure betterment and efficiency for the more unpleasant tasks, and even the linens for her daughters bassinet—she kept in mind the possibility of further use in case of more children in future.

Christine would not be greedy. She would never mention such thoughts to Erik, seeing how difficult he had taken news of her previous pregnancy, but it seemed a mite ridiculous to think such consequences would not arise due to their love making.

Something she had no desire to forego—and she hoped Erik was in agreement.

With such thoughts in mind, she selected her items in pale greens and creamy yellows—both of which would nicely compliment the wall coverings already hanging in the small room.

The shopkeeper was quite impressed with her amount of purchases, and she was told that her business would always be well received.

She had no doubt of it.

Erik had entered behind her as she flitted from shelf to shelf, though he had remained quiet and allowed her to make her own choices in so far as décor—though he had added a few things himself that he deemed an oversight on her part.

Mainly little baubles of entertainment.

Their next stop was a seamstress in search of more diapers and more tiny infant clothing. They had packed some—at least she *thought* Erik would have, though she had seen none for herself.

Erik had more preference in this regard than he had with room trimmings. "She will look like a doll." The scowl on his face showed no evidence of humour, as though such a notion personally offended his sensibilities.

"Erik, she is a *baby,* that is perfectly acceptable!"

"And how, pray tell, will she be able to *move?*" Truthfully, there were not so very many frills that such thing would be of concern, especially given the fact that their daughter could do little more than suckle and grip Erik's fingers. Considering crawling and walking did not seem to be of great significance at the moment.

But they were already placing their orders for suiting the needs of a growing infant—she would *not* consider that her little *enfant* was truly sick enough for such dreams to be unrealistic—and so with such things in mind, she chose simplistic items that while still feminine, were more practical in nature. She also purchased small woollen items for when the weather turned cold.

That at least gained a look of approval from her husband who tapped Catherine's nose. "Your mother does appear to have *some* sense at least."

Christine only huffed.

She only purchased an additional dress for herself that would work in interim as her body slowly began to accept the removal of the baby— though Christine *was* quite shocked by the measurement of her bust size.

Erik however merely looked greedy.

If the seamstress gave any indication that having one's husband present when picking out such mundane items was any rare occurrence she did not make such thoughts known. She had only given Erik a cursory glance when he arrived, but when Christine began to prattle and make her exorbitant list of necessities, any attention she paid Erik was quickly forgotten.

His mask truly was something entirely unmemorable—it was only a pity it pained him.

With that in mind, Christine finished her personal shopping—with one final request for more pantaloons and camisoles—and she settled her hand into Erik's free arm as he continued to hold his Catherine.

"Do they have a musical store?"

She would feel dreadfully guilty if Erik was unable to furnish *his* room as well, and happily he began to lead her down two more streets before entering a tiny shop which housed a small selection of instruments as well as a few tables of hand written music.

Erik was not impressed by the instruments, and he made his displeasure quite known to the owner of the establishment. "It amazes me that you are able to maintain business!"

When the small bell cheerfully announced their arrival, a middle aged man had appeared. He seemed quite flustered by the obvious knowledge of his customer. "Well we mainly sell to small parlours, for children to learn for their education. Things of that nature."

That only seemed to offend Erik more. "Even children deserve instruments of a high calibre. Anything less pollutes their sensitive hearing and musicality."

It was to her very great surprise then that Erik ordered a *piano*. Not the small delicate instrument in the corner of the shop, but one specially requested for its prominence. "And do not bother stringing the instrument, I highly doubt your competency."

The shopkeeper was insulted, but at the price of the order wisely remained silent as to the rudeness of his customer.

It would not arrive at their home for another week or two, and Christine quite looked forward to their little home having its first delivery—though she supposed that was not entirely true as the house was quite furnished as it was.

But all the same, she was rather excited.

Erik was still mumbling as he led them back to the awaiting carriage—entirely filled with packages—and aided Christine into her seat and allowed Catherine to settle in her mother's arms. He soon followed.

It was about halfway home that Catherine awoke reminding Christine quite assuredly that she had not eaten since before her christening.

Propriety dictated that Christine only feed her child in the privacy of her own home—or truly she give the baby to a wet nurse for nourishment—but such was not an option. Erik would surely never allow his child to remain hungry, and Christine was not comfortable with such a notion either.

But the carriage was full of purchases, and the idea of asking Erik to allow her to step into the woods to nurse was laughable.

Erik stopped the carriage of his own accord, and removed the long cloak he was wearing and laid it over Christine's shoulders—quite effectively shielding her bosom as well as Catherine.

She steadfastly ignored the lasso peeking out from the folds.

And it was in such a way—entirely embracing the country attitude—Christine nursed her child in the sunshine while Erik drove them *home*.

XXX

Their journey home was not as quiet as the trip to the little chapel had been. Erik still complained mightily over the state of the instruments— "But Christine, they shall think that is *music!*"—while Christine wondered over which one Erik would teach Catherine first. Though she supposed the child could be more skilled in voice, she secretly wished her daughter would utilise her father and grandfather's proficiency—if only so she could enjoy sugar and cream like a normal child.

The other difference was the presence of others on the road. When they were nearing their own cottage, they were waylaid by a neighbour pruning the garden. Christine was left pondering whether now was the time for such things. Perhaps Erik had a book on it...

Her thoughts on gardening only distracted from the immediate plans of what to fix for their late luncheon—for that matter she contemplated skipping to tea time—when the voice of the woman called out to them. "Hello neighbours!"

Erik grumbled slightly but slowed the carriage at Christine's insistence. The woman was older than Christine by at least ten years, but she was still quite pretty despite her more weathered appearance. It was quite apparent that the outdoors had been her companion for some time now.

She was simply attired and had smudges of dirt on both hands and apron. Christine thought her quite delightful.

"Good afternoon." For reasons she did not know, Christine felt rather nervous. Her social graces had certainly suffered with only Erik for company, and she was tremendously grateful her impromptu feeding of Catherine had already been completed. Such would have been mortifying!

The woman took pity on the silent couple and stepped forward good naturedly to being introductions. "I'm Marie. Did you take the house three down?"

Christine looked to Erik for an answer as truthfully she had no concept of how many houses they had yet to pass until they reached their little home. She held his hand encouragingly, gently reminding him that while he certainly *looked* normal, he still needed to *act* the part. And neighbourly friendliness was certainly part of the act. "I am Erik, and this is my wife Christine. We are four down."

While Christine was contemplating the shortness and rather cold nature of Erik's introduction, Marie's eyes went wide, and she cast Christine a horrified look. "*Four* down? You poor thing!"

Christine narrowed her eyes at the woman, wondering how she could possibly pity her for anything in their mere minute of acquaintance. Erik was being friendly—well, friendly *enough*—and she was quite positive there was no sign of how their marriage had begun.

Their neighbour saw her confusion and quickly explained. "That house is haunted. Has been for as long as I've lived here at least." She looked to Erik. "Perhaps you should enquire about moving next door. Smaller property to be sure, but it would be such a pity for a ghost to take your little one!"

Christine held Catherine a little more firmly to her chest. Haunted? Their perfect little yellow cottage?

Erik's hand tightened on her—in reassurance she supposed—and answered for her. "Thank you for your concern, but I am certain we shall be fine."

It was obvious she was about to argue, but a dark, curly head suddenly popped through the front doorway. "Mamma! May I have a biscuit *now?*"

When the dark eyes found the carriage stopped outside the fence, the rest of the body followed the shaggy head. A boy of about seven appeared—all signs of perfectly curious boyhood now visible. He eyed the carriage inquisitively for a moment, before bolting from the yard and standing next to the carriage while his mother cried out her protests.

"Armand, you naughty thing! I have told you to stay inside the fence!"

The boy paid his mother no heed, but stood to the side staring up at Erik with fascination. "You're a man, aren't you, Monsieur?"

Christine could not remember a time Erik had looked so startled. It was one thing to *look* like everybody else, it was another thing entirely to be mistaken for one by a child. Notoriously the age group who spout honesty without prompt, it was quite meaningful that he would consider Erik a *man*.

And though his mother had pitied them for their choice of house—for which she would most assuredly be enquiring of Erik—she was immediately fond of this little boy.

The boy—*Armand*—did not wait for Erik's confirmation, but simply prattled on all the same. "You're tall like my papa. He's gone now, but

Mamma keeps his clothes so that one day I can wear them!" He thrust out his short legs proudly, as if Erik could somehow picture them at their adult length.

Erik tore his eyes from the little boy and turned them to his mother. "Your husband is deceased?" Christine was horrified at his bluntness, but Marie simply rolled her eyes.

"No, my husband was in the military, but has since retired. He is currently away on business, but I'm afraid Armand has a rather skewed sense of time." She walked to the side of the carriage and held the boy's hand. "He is referring to his father's old uniform."

Erik was frowning as he observed the mother and son, but when Christine's stomach let out a low sound of dismay at its emptiness, he quickly made to leave, offering a rather formal goodbye.

"You'll come for tea soon won't you, Christine? I should very much like to know my neighbours better."

Christine nibbled her lip thoughtfully, and she looked to Erik for guidance as to her answer. It was simply a call of hospitality, and there was truly no danger in it, but she was loath to make an engagement without first consulting Erik as to his feelings. She was surprised then when a soft voice whispered in her ear. "Of course you may have a friend, Christine."

When she turned to him once more, he was leaning nowhere near her ear, but she had plainly heard the words in her husband's timbre. "Thank you for the invitation, I would be quite happy to join you."

Marie practically beamed at her, and Christine was left with the distinct impression that the older woman rarely had company. She could not imagine Erik leaving her and Catherine for a business arrangement!

Erik was quiet on the way home, and it was not until Christine had placed Catherine in his arms and began making a quick meal of sandwiches that he spoke. "Why would a man leave his family unprotected?"

If anything was bothering him, she thought for certain it would be the little boy's reaction to his presence, not whether or not there was an adult male capable of protecting the home. "I am sure this is a very safe village, Erik, I doubt there was any chance of harm." She carefully sliced each baguette in half. "Besides, surely they were in need of money, and that is why he went away."

She cast him a reproachful look. "Some men have to do such things for funds, you know."

Erik looked at her quite innocently as he lightly brushed the sparse amount of hair on Catherine's head. "I can assure you, I worked very hard for our *francs*, wife."

Christine hummed a noise of noncommittal. Worked hard indeed.

Erik was suddenly behind her, and she could feel his cool breath on her neck. "Do you doubt your husband, Madame?"

Christine shivered at his tone and quickly distracted him with handing him a plate full of sandwich. "Do not be silly, Erik. Now eat."

Holding Catherine in one arm and his plate in the other, Erik moved into the dining room while Christine busied herself with preparing tall glasses of water.

She truly did need to learn to cook. But such things were dependent upon being able to attend the grocers, and that was entirely based on Erik's allowance of her into his mysterious confidence.

Now seemed as good a time as any for such questions.

Erik was of a differing opinion.

"I have taken care of you *before* have I not? Why should now be any different?" Christine sighed. She had a feeling he was still thinking of Marie's lack of husband, and not on the question of who prepared meals.

"Because I am your *wife*, Erik! Preparing meals should be something I should excel in, not simply provide minimums!"

Erik picked small pieces of baguette apart with his fingers as he expertly avoided her gaze. "What would Christine do if she did not need her Erik?"

She told him the ridiculousness of such a statement, but for her efforts for the first time in months she saw a flash of anger directed at *her*.

"Marie did not need *her* husband! Marie would let her husband leave his wife and child, and she did not seem so very unhappy!" Perhaps this was the true reason it was better for them not to be in the presence of others.

Erik began to doubt her.

She thought the experiences with the Daroga were isolated instances— the horrible events caused by a man who simply *could not* understand her husband for all his protestations of friendship.

Christine sighed and taking her plate in hand, moved it to the side of Erik's and patiently waited for him to move slightly so she could sit upon his lap.

It did not take long for him to relent.

He was most certainly not the most comfortable thing to lean against, but in comparison to the pain *he* felt upon contemplating her lack of need for him, such things were inconsequential.

"Erik, whether or not you deliver the groceries will not make me love you any less. I do not think anything could accomplish that."

He sounded entirely petulant, but his hand had found her curls and he knew he was not too terribly upset as he stroked them. "There is a difference between love and *want*, Christine."

She nodded slowly, contemplating the statement. It was true of course. It was quite possible to love something but not want its presence for very long—to grow tired of it. She felt that way sometimes about flavours of biscuits.

But Erik was not a biscuit! And she *did* want him!

It was the first time in a long while that she thought about the purpose of marital intercourse. Whenever Erik was with her in such ways, she felt such a culmination of love, need, and want so acutely there was never a doubt in her mind as to how he valued her—*treasured* her.

Perhaps he felt the same.

When her womb had grown, their conjugations had most certainly become less frequent—almost to the point of non existence but for a few attempts. Erik was afraid of hurting her, and Christine was terribly uncomfortable though she should still have endured another few weeks of pregnancy.

But now Christine entirely wished she had lain with him one last time before their forced separation. Erik's book had clearly stated that intercourse would have to be denied for at least six weeks to allow healing of the mother, and any pressure from the father was evidence of his brutality and impatience.

While Christine knew that such was not the case with her poor Erik, she did know her body was nowhere near prepared to receive him.

And truly, he did not feel aroused as she sat against him, though she blushed thoroughly from the thought. Perhaps what he needed was more of an emotional connection than a physical.

"Erik, I *love* you, and I want you. Very much." She looked into his eyes, tugging at the horrible mask that so hid him from her. She understood its purpose, truly she did, but she still hated it.

Erik seemed to understand her desire, and peeled it from his yellowed skin, and sighed when her hand cupped his cheek gently. "You do not need to doubt me, Erik. I shall not tire of you. If ever you have to leave, for business or some venture we have yet to face, I shall always want you to return home to me."

He looked at her for a long while, and even though his mask was not removed, she had difficulty understanding his expression. "What are you thinking?"

The corners of his mouth lifted slightly, and he kissed her lips softly. "That you are too good to your Erik."

She smiled at him, but rolled her eyes all the same. "You speak nonsense, husband." Satisfied that Erik was sufficiently comforted, Christine returned to her sandwich and bade her husband do the same.

She remembered then what Marie had said about their house being haunted. Visions of Erik ghosting through the Opera House floated through her mind, and she wondered if he had done something similar to this house in preparation for their arrival. "Why did she think our home is haunted?"

Erik stiffened, and swallowed his bite before resting his head on her shoulder. "I can assure you, wife, your husband is entirely blameless. There was a fire some time ago, and this little house was built in the manor's stead." His lips tickled her ear as he whispered. "It seems there have been some *accidents* since, and no one has wished to test Fate."

Christine turned sharply, nearly hitting Erik in the process. "You mean it could really be haunted? I thought it was you playing one of your games!"

Erik looked rather offended and sat back in his chair with an imperious look directed at Christine. "I can assure you, I do not play *games*. And do not be ridiculous, Christine. As if there were really such things as phantoms."

She supposed that was meant to be comforting, and while she firmly believed Erik would protect her, she was always slightly prone to believe in things that transcended the physical world. Erik had preyed on her belief of angels, and why should a wronged spirit be any different?

Erik sighed and pulled her back to him before she could run off and search the cottage for any signs of distress. "You are fretting unnecessarily, which is precisely why I did not tell you of the town's superstitions." His hand crept around her throat and she shivered as his voice took on the lulling timbre that left her entirely powerless. "You have nothing to fear, Christine."

And though she still considered asking the priest to come give a blessing of the ground, she did believe him.

Their lunch finished, and dishes quickly washed and dried—with Erik utterly distracting her by throwing his voice into odd corners of the room in eerie tones, quite cruelly making her jump as she thought a ghost was upon her. He even had the audacity to look innocent when she snapped at him that he was being horribly unfair, and finally she threw a towel at his head and told him to dry.

The afternoon was far more pleasant. Erik apologised for frightening her in the kitchen, and as such allowed her to utilise his person as she saw fit while he unloaded the carriage and arranged Catherine's nursery.

His only complaint was when she directed him to place her basinet under the window—at least until the window seat could be completed. "Do you have any idea how simple it would be for someone to slide open the casing and snatch her away? That is madness!"

Christine on the other hand had visions of sunlight bathing the baby as she slept, and how her daughter would never look more angelic. And why should she be worrying over Catherine's ability to be *snatched*? Erik was certainly a protective father, but it seemed ridiculous to allow such thoughts to determine the placement of furniture in one's own home.

It was only when her fingers skimmed Erik's cheek and she looked piteously into his eyes and mumbled a quiet, "Please?" that he finally relented—though in the subsequent days the bassinet steadily moved inch by inch closer to the middle of the room, much to Christine's chagrin.

But for now she was satisfied, and Erik only rolled his eyes and grumbled about impossible wives. She smiled at him coyly.

Seeing as they had no music room as of yet to reinstate her lessons—and in truth, Christine's muscles did not agree that she was prepared for such a thing to begin once more anyway—they instead retired to the study. The setup was mostly the same as their previous sitting room, and with the drapes closed and a slight fire flickering, it felt quite homey and familiar.

Félin Christine had apparently claimed this room as some sort of home, for silky white hairs could be seen on quite a bit of the rugs and sides of the furniture, and the cat herself was sitting atop Erik's desk with a quizzical look. She was quite plainly curious as to why her human counterparts had entered her domain.

But Erik simply pet her head affectionately, and she seemed to allow them entrance, so Christine settled on the small sofa—a much more plush version of their settee that she quickly learned to adore—and waited for her husband to pick out which novel he would like to first read to his wife in their little home. And their daughter.

Christine would be quite happy to have Erik as the only school teacher her daughter would ever know. She would not grow up with the lack of ability that Christine suffered through inattentiveness and boredom, and surely being related to Erik such things would come far more easily than to her mother.

Erik had chosen the same book of fairytales as when he had first begun to instruct Christine on her words, and when she enquired as to his choice, Erik looked at her as though she had said something entirely foolish. "There is a child in the room, Christine."

Of course.

Though Christine enjoyed thoroughly when Erik read to her—to *them*—she could not help but feel slightly despondent. Would she ever be as mindful as her husband seemed to be in regards to their child? She had given birth, yes, but it truly felt as though she were more of a nurse than the child's mother.

What was it to be a mother?

She had no recollection of her own, and Mamma Valérius was most certainly the closest she had. But the woman was elderly, so it was more similar to living with a doting grandmother than a true mother.

She had thought of this before—the issue of motherhood—and it had only filled her with delight at such a prospect.

Was she growing less naïve, or more aware of her inadequacies?

Christine was so deep in thought that it took Erik's hand skimming her neck to draw her attention. "What are you thinking of, wife? Your brow is puckered, and I wish to smooth it."

The wife in question let out a very unladylike sound at Erik's comment, followed by a slight giggle. She was married to such a silly man!

Erik smiled slightly at his apparent success at the removal of the offensive line, but still prompted her to speak her mind.

She was being ridiculous. Surely motherhood was something learned, just as being a singer worthy of Erik's attentions, or even reading. But as she thought of how little she had done for her daughter since her birth— she did not even know how to *dress* her until Erik showed her!—she could not help but feel grossly inadequate.

And she told Erik so.

She had experienced doubts before of her own competence, most importantly as a wife. But Erik seemed happy enough, and perhaps what plagued her was Catherine's inability to vocalise how she felt about her parents. Other than tiny whimpers and wails, there was no way of ascertaining what distressed her. Everything was so open to interpretation!

Erik was quiet as she told him of her thoughts, and finally when she had expressed all of her concerns, he softly laid Catherine down so he could better attend his wife. "Christine…"

There was nothing condescending in his tone, nothing that would offer useless platitudes, and in fact, if she were not so certain he was to respect the six weeks of healing, she would almost say it was *seductive*. She very nearly trembled.

His fingers found her hair, and his breath was ghosting over her skin, and any trepidation as she thought of the daunting nature of motherhood seemed to melt under his attentions. "Do you love her?"

Such was not the question she was expecting. Perhaps some form of inquisition as to her capabilities, but not something so terribly simple—and absolutely evident.

"Of course I do! She is my daughter." She looked at him rather tragically, wondering if perhaps there *was* no evidence of her supreme love for her child. Perhaps she loved *him* too much—that somehow she did not have enough to give her daughter as well as her husband. "Do you not think I do?"

His lips skimmed her cheek, and she closed her eyes at the feeling. "Nothing is more clear than how much you love our Cat." Erik leaned back slightly and gently stroked her cheek so she would look at him. "And you forget something very important, my Christine." He was looking at her so very tenderly, and she cursed her still unbalanced hormones that made the tears tinge her eyes so easily. "She loves you as well."

She was an infant. She was a tiny defenceless creature that surely had no preference as to who cared for her as long as her belly was full and her diaper dry.

But when Erik began to speak of how she had cared for her—*loved* Catherine before any other person—she quite unexpectedly began to think of Erik's own childhood. At least, what she supposed of it. His mother might have cared for him first—when he was still within her womb and she knew not who she carried. But the test was from birth.

And she was quite certain Erik would have loved his mother until she had turned him away. Even then, a young child would desperately seek what everybody else had. And though her own mother had perished, she still loved her dearly.

She would learn. And perhaps Catherine would prove to be a patient recipient of her faults and ineptitude, just as her father proved to be time and again.

And surely Erik had such concerns as well—they were both so inexperienced with children—and perhaps *together* they would raise their child through the grace of God just as they had sworn to the priest they would.

And when Erik finally, *finally* kissed her, she entirely believed that though frightened of the prospect, she and her husband would make very fine parents indeed.

XXXI

Christine's worries were proven unnecessary over the next few weeks. While patience was never an attribute she would use to describe her daughter—if her persistent whimpers were anything to judge by—it was evident when sometimes she would only quiet when it was her mother who held her as opposed to Erik's arms.

He tried not to show his disappointment, and to a point Christine was sure he understood—it was just as important that Catherine learn to take comfort from Christine as it was from her father. He did however protest one day when she would not even quiet for her lullaby—something entirely unheard of in her short life—and it was not until he reluctantly placed her in Christine's arms that her mewls turned to quiet protestations.

"You carried her for months, Christine, why may I not do it now?" She smiled at him indulgently, for in truth, how does one answer such a question? She did not determine Catherine's whims, she merely indulged them as readily as Erik.

So she instead told him that he could sit with her on the sofa—their favourite room in the house, much to Christine's surprise—and could hold *her* instead of their daughter.

Erik did not seem to mind the arrangement.

Catherine was growing steadily, and her grip when she tugged at Erik's finger was becoming stronger. The slight wheeze in her lungs was still present, but had done little in the way of worsening, and Christine tried not to worry. She would find Erik at times leaning over her bassinet, simply listening to her breathe, and he would murmur soft words that she could not hear.

But she highly suspected they were prayers.

The bleeding she had suffered after the delivery slowly lessened, and she was entirely grateful to no longer have to prepare her pantaloons as though

244

she were experiencing her menses.

Erik had finally relented, but instead of telling her how their laundry had been done in his underground home, he had shown her how it was to be done in their home. In a move of entirely ridiculous notions, he told her that Catherine's diapers should be *disposed* of instead of washed.

Christine had never heard something more ridiculous.

She had obliged at first, but it seemed entirely wasteful to have to make such frequent trips to the shops in order to acquire more—so finally she learned for herself how to do so, while Erik simply told Catherine how disobedient her mother was.

Christine merely rolled her eyes.

One morning, about three weeks after they had arrived in their little home, Christine was quite startled to see a man wandering the grounds. She had practically screeched for Erik to come, and he did so looking quite frightened at her outburst.

"What is wrong?"

She pointed out the window, clutching at his arm, though she knew her reaction was rather extreme given the circumstances. Many people had visitors!

Erik seemed *relieved* when he saw the man coming up the front path, and tapped Christine's hand with his own. "We have lived here for this long, and you had yet to see the groundskeeper?"

His tone was incredulous, and Christine found herself blushing at her inobservance. "I am generally in the kitchen in the morning, I had not..." Her rather stuttering reply ceased when she remembered she could be angry at Erik for not having *told* her there was an unknown man wandering their property. "You should have informed me of his presence!"

Erik chuckled, and pulled her fully into his arms. "And why should I have done so? It is very common to have a groundskeeper, and I am slightly surprised it had not occurred to you that someone was caring for the horse."

Christine huffed, but pressed her head into Erik's shoulder. "But it is a *man.*"

She had expected Erik to act sympathetically to her—she could admit it, her rather irrational wariness toward the opposite gender—but instead she felt him chuckle *again.* "He is over seventy five winters, Christine. I doubt very much you are in any danger."

But that was not the point. She still felt as though her privacy had been breached, and Erik was doing little to comfort her. She tried not to sniffle, honestly she did, but Erik still managed to hear, and his hold tightened as he began whispering the soft words she so longed to hear. "I would never allow you to be in danger, my wife. Surely you know this by now."

He kissed her, and she was very grateful that he had yet to return his mask to his face since they had awoken that morning—though now she was rather surprised he would risk such a thing when there was a *groundskeeper* wandering around the property.

Though she had thought that was all the comfort she would receive, Erik had pulled her to sit on the settee in the parlour, and his lips had yet to fully leave her skin. How she wished there was to be no more waiting!

"Do you not think it will be nice to awaken each morning, not to your husband leaving your side to tend to the grounds, but instead providing you so much pleasure?" Erik had never spoken to her in such a way. He had spoken words of love to be sure, but mostly when they were committing such acts with one another, and never when he knew they could not indulge.

His hands were skimming her breast, and having only had the touch of her daughter for so long, she had almost forgotten how different it felt when *he* touched her.

He was not being fair.

Erik smirked at her devilishly when he pulled away. "Do you understand his necessity?"

She could only nod dumbly, and Erik's smirk only grew more to see how overcome she was by his attentions.

The rogue.

He must have seen the gleam in her eye which gave away her intent to make *him* feel as she did, but before she could begin, he made a rather unexpected suggestion. "Perhaps you should meet with your neighbour friend for tea."

Erik had taken her on a several walks the past few weeks, and each time they had seen Marie out in her garden—sometimes with her son, and other times not. The last time they had seen her, she had made it abundantly clear that if ever Christine was available, she should feel free to stop in for tea, no matter the time or warning.

Though grateful for the invitation, Christine still did not feel entirely comfortable allowing Erik to be at the house by himself, though whether that was her own misgivings or actual concern for her husband, she was not certain.

Slightly suspicious that he was simply looking to get rid of her, he was quick to assure her. "I am sure she is lonesome, Christine."

"And will *you* not be lonesome without me?"

He sighed, and pulled one of her curls between his cool fingers and twisted it lightly. "Of course I shall be, but I believe there is a task I must see to that I would not subject you to."

Well, if she had not been suspicious *before*, she certainly was now. "What are you going to do, Erik?" She hated to ask, but he was being quite evasive, and not in the way that would lead her to believe he was in the midst of constructing a surprise. "Is it legal?"

"Such a nosey wife I have." Erik rolled his eyes, and she was grateful he was not angry for her question. "I am going to the music store."

Ah. That would explain his reticence in allowing her to come.

The man had promised the specially ordered piano would be delivered within two weeks, and it had already been three without word as to its location.

Christine had never seen Erik so agitated.

When they had lived in their previous home, Erik had gone many weeks without playing, but perhaps it was that composing was in fact an option.

And to make matters worse, Catherine had begun a tedious routine of wailing whenever he played the violin.

They had never heard her cry so loud as she had when Erik had given into the impulse to play at least some form of instrument. Erik had ceased immediately, and had refused to touch it since.

He had spent the next few days sulking and feeling quite nervous about doing anything with his daughter, but when Christine had finally huffed and pulled out his child development book, it had stated clearly the sensitivity of an infant's hearing, and how the high pitched wail of the violin would be quite traumatising.

Erik had then apologised profusely to the sleeping baby, who had forgotten the incident days ago.

So it was with that in mind, Christine agreed to make her first social visit as a married woman. And inexplicably, she was rather nervous.

Erik was going to ride the horse into town, and quite seriously offered to hold both Christine and the baby in his lap while he took them four houses down the lane to Marie's dwelling.

And though she trusted Erik implicitly, she was in no way prepared to allow for him to take such liberties when Catherine was still so very young.

So she explained to Erik that such ventures could not be attempted yet—silently she added *if ever*—and Erik took it rather well, only teasing her gently that she was a distrustful, silly wife.

She would gladly accept the title if it meant keeping Catherine safe—not that she doubted Erik's dedication to her health.

But so it was that Erik walked the horse down the road, once more in the horrible mask that so hid his skin from her perusal as it had become his customary mask when taking Christine on short walks or to the market.

It was true, there were closer shops than the ones he had chosen on Catherine's christening day, but it was obvious the reason they had driven so far was to be able to find a music store. Christine was simply grateful she was able to learn to go to market on her own. Though Erik was with her of course, she still felt as though she was contributing more to her family than just her presence and ability to change diapers.

But today was different, as instead of a quick jaunt down the lane to the market, they were in fact parting ways—and that felt entirely foreign and disturbing in its own right.

Erik paused before they reached the gate leading to Marie's yard, and she was glad for the moment of privacy. She could not remember the last time he had left her in such a way—where they *truly* would be parted.

He had given her the idea of solitude of course, with either shopping or simply a walk, but she had become used to a following shadow that both comforted and irritated her.

But now—now she knew she would miss him. Hopefully Marie's company would prove riveting enough distraction that she would not dwell *too* much on his absence.

He held the reigns in one hand, and one of her hands in the other. She was being foolish, but for one irrational moment, she wished to beg him not to leave her.

Erik must have seen the tears beginning to well in her eyes, for he pulled her into his arms—ever mindful of the bundle wrapped carefully in her own—and kissed her temple. "You will be safe, Christine. You shall drink tea, and eat far too much sugar, and you shall not even miss your poor husband."

Christine very much wondered how long she would be influenced by her pregnancy, but hearing those words filled her with such dismay, she worried the grip she had on his bony frame might hurt him. "Of *course* I shall miss you!" She sniffled pathetically. "I miss you already."

Erik brushed a stray tear away with his thumb, and gave her another kiss. "Is it wrong that I feel grateful you would do so?"

Christine shook her head emphatically, thankful that he at least he accepted how much she appreciated his presence, even if it meant showing him through his absence.

She still hated the feel of the smooth, artificial material against her lips as she kissed him, but it was simply too important to have such a parting expression of love she dismissed the thought as quickly as it had come. This was still her Erik.

Drawing away regretfully, he brushed her cheek one final time before allowing them to take the last few steps. Erik did not enter the gate, but watched from the road to ensure Christine was safely inside before departing.

His concern made her feel so very cared for.

Marie was surprised by her company, but nonetheless excited for a friend. Though they had spoken a few times now, Christine wished for further acquaintance if only so that their exchanges may be more comfortable.

The house was similar to Christine's—what a funny thought to have a home of one's own!—but more worn and disarrayed.

Christine was certain her own home would begin to resemble this when Catherine began to grow.

She was directed to the sitting room, and Marie bade her sit while she prepared the tea and some sort of confection. Christine thought she would be spending the next few moments alone, but instead the same shaggy head she was now becoming accustomed to seeing pop around corners was running into the room. "Company!"

Marie was calling out for him to hush even as she could be heard making her preparations in the kitchen, but Christine could not help but smile at his enthusiasm.

It was apparent by his lack of manners that he had little in the way of socialisation, for instead of the polite decorum expected of most children, Armand simply scurried to sit by Christine on the settee.

"You were with the man!" Christine laughed, and confirmed that she was indeed such a person. Armand did not seem to require it as he was already prattling about what objects he had found in the garden that morning. "There were *two* worms, but they looked like *one* with two heads!"

Christine blushed, and was entirely grateful when he caught site of Catherine still settled in her arms. "What's that?"

The baby in question was awoken when Armand's finger found her cheek and poked at the pink softness. "Gently, Armand, she is quite fragile."

Armand crinkled his nose, and looked at her speculatively. "But what *is* she?"

"This is my baby daughter, Catherine." Had he truly never seen a baby before today? Catherine had been with them when they first met, but the small boy had been standing on the ground and was much shorter than the carriage had been. But no one else in the village had children?

"Mamma! The pretty lady has a *baby!*" Catherine was not pleased with the sudden cry of excitement, and she began to whimper.

Though there was no relation between her husband and this boy, the horror seen in his eyes could only be rivalled when Erik had learned he had hurt Christine in the early days of their marriage. "I'm sorry, baby! Don't cry!"

He looked at her as if he had just committed some great sin and looked about to cry himself, and Christine was quick to offer comfort. "It is alright, she was just startled."

Marie came in with a tray of tea and a plate of *palmiers*, which Christine eyed greedily. Perhaps Erik was right after all…

"Armand! Were you behaving for Madame…?" She looked to Christine, obviously waiting for the addition of her last name.

How could she possibly explain that she had no last name to offer?

"Madame Christine is fine." She smiled at the boy who still looked to his mother almost fearfully. "I would like to be his friend as well."

"I was being good, Mamma! She was startled, that's all."

Marie was quite apologetic for any upset he might have caused, but taking in the boy's tragic countenance allowed him to remain in the room, and even settled him with a cup of milk of his own. "Only *one* biscuit, and do not try to sneak more or I shall know!"

Christine wondered at the mother and son relationship. Having spent so little time with them, perhaps she was making a rapid judgment, but Marie did not seem overly affectionate with the boy.

They spent the next half hour discussing the regular pleasantries and generic conversation expected of a first time tea.

For a moment Christine wondered if such was what she would have experienced if she had ever engaged in a normal courtship.

And for a fleeting wisp of a thought, Christine entirely understood why Erik took such drastic measures to avoid it.

Armand remained quiet and alternated between staring at Christine and Catherine. When conversation dwindled between the two ladies, he cautiously reached out one small hand lightly brushed the Catherine's visible arm. "She's so *soft…*"

Marie smiled at her son in an indulgent manner, and Christine was glad she could still see the adorable qualities of Armand. "Darling, why don't you go play?" Though she asked it as a question, her tone directed him toward obedience.

He reluctantly hopped off the settee, and made to exit the room, but not before looking back to Christine with big dark eyes. "You won't leave without saying goodbye, will you?"

The tragic look was back, and it was impossible to deny him. "I will not, I promise."

He gave her a dazzling smile, and Christine was very aware of just how handsome he would be when he reached adulthood.

She wondered if Catherine would ever notice.

When the little boy had left, Marie let out a long sight. "I love my son, you know."

Christine blinked at her for the unexpected turn of conversation. "I did not doubt it."

Marie rose from her seat across from Christine to join her on the other side of the settee. In truth, Christine missed Armand's presence on the same cushion.

"His father's absence has been difficult on both of us. As you can see, he does not get many chances to interact."

"Does he not go to school?" Though she did not know his exact age, surely there would be some sort of village school he could attend for stimulation. Children prone to boredom were certainly more troublesome, so perhaps a quest for knowledge would be an improvement.

But Marie shook her head sadly. "Many of the residents of this town have lived here for years and their children have grown and moved away. Most to *Paris.*" She practically spat the name. "I'm sure it is a beautiful place, but I can't help but wish more would choose to stay. Armand needs friends, and goodness knows, so do I."

Her hand had reached for Christine's arm, and she looked at her pleadingly. "I know you're uncomfortable, that is rather obvious, but you have to understand, it can be a lonely life when one's husband is away."

It was a lonely life when Erik was gone for a few *hours* let alone days.

And though she did not feel near the amount of affection as she felt for the woman's son, she resolved to at least try to remain as friendly as possible.

Perhaps more genuine feelings would arise in time.

They had with her marriage, had they not?

"When do you expect him home?" She felt dreadful, knowing that if Armand had been enthralled with Erik's presence simply for him being a man, his father must have left some time ago, but that still did not help her from feeling the pang of loneliness that her own sweet husband was not due for some time yet.

"Another month. He has been gone for five. It was always his dream to be an author, but when they kept rejecting him in Paris he began to travel." She sighed, and looked began fiddling with her hands. "I told him he could have six months—that was all—and if nothing came of it he would return home and find some respectable work here." Marie placed another *palmier* on Christine's plate, and she was grateful for the distraction, for she could see the tears prickling the woman's eyes.

"How do you make these?" Always looking to improve her baking skills, she marvelled at the thin delicate pastry that melted on her tongue.

Marie smiled, and nibbled on her own. "With much patience. I'm afraid I've had a bit too much time on my hands of late, and baking seems to be the only thing Armand will allow me to do in peace." She laughed humourlessly. "I think he just likes the results."

"Do you tire of his company?" That seemed to be the material point, as perhaps Marie could simply not fill the void of her absent husband with only her son for companionship.

"He exhausts me, and I know he would like for his father to be home. I fear letting him roam outside. What if I could not find him? My neighbours are elderly, and they could do little to help. So I keep him in with me."

Christine did not know of such things, but the idea of allowing Catherine—even when she was much older—to be alone for any length of time out of doors seemed impossible.

Though it had only been little over an hour since Erik had departed, a knock upon the door interrupted their visit, and a peek outside revealed the brown mare that had so efficiently pulled their carriage.

Erik had returned!

Marie seemed disappointed they could not speak longer, but quickly went to the door and ushered Erik into the sitting room and offered him tea.

Christine could see the set of his jaw and tightened eyes even through the full mask, and rose from her seat and went to his side. "I thank you for your offer, Madame, but it is time for us to return home."

She nodded in understanding, but before Erik had successfully removed Christine from the house, small feet came bounding through the hall. "Wait!"

Armand ran to Christine's side, and reached a tiny hand up to pat Catherine in salutation. "Goodbye, baby. Do not cry anymore. Goodbye, Mme. Christine!"

Erik looked rather horrified that he had admitted to witnessing his daughter's tears, and Christine knew she would have to make quick work of explanation once they were alone.

She kissed Armand's cheek in parting, and assured both he and Marie she would return so to continue her visit.

Erik requested Catherine's presence in his arms, and Christine rather gratefully obliged. Though a tiny thing, having any sort of weight for an extended period proved taxing. "So where is your piano?"

Her husband practically growled, and gripped the reins a little tighter as he led the horse down the path. "*Three* more weeks, Christine. *Three.* I can assure you, I made it quite clear that I did not approve that man's competency."

She should have wondered if he had killed the man, and perhaps at another time she might have. She had in fact questioned what happened to the carriage driver when he had driven Catherine home from the midwife's, but now she did not consider it.

Instead she leaned into his side, and though he could not hold her as his hands were occupied with other important tasks, she was simply happy to have him back at her side.

"My poor, Erik."

He merely sniffed his agreement.

XXXII

Life settled into a perfectly mundane routine, and though Christine was quite sure at some point in future she would find it dull and uninteresting, for now it was the epitome of bliss that she could provide such normalcy for her husband and daughter.

If only Erik agreed.

To a point he did, and he thanked her often for the love she gave, as well as for whatever biscuit she baked—though once she had seen the physical recipe for a *palmier* with its many layers of dough rolled paper thin, she had dismissed them as things to be eaten only from a bakery.

No, the issue was his music. He was terrified of playing his violin, and though Christine suggested he attempt it in order to see if his daughter's sensitive ears had matured slightly in the past weeks, he resolutely refused.

So she began taking walks.

Not long ones, and though she would have liked the company of her husband, she quite cheerfully took Catherine through the many paths of her property while Erik had free reign of the house and could release his passions through music.

And Christine highly suspected that was the true reason for his ire.

Any other time he might have contented himself with the emotional outbursts of an instrument should he be unable to physically love his wife, but with Catherine demanding the quiet of an unused violin, and Christine still not fully healed, he was left without an outlet.

She was grateful that he did not resent their daughter, for he still doted on her ceaselessly, and hummed her to sleep when she was fussy after a feeding or simply was unhappy for some indeterminate reason. Christine was grateful for how little sleep he actually required, as he took it upon himself to tend to whatever nighttime necessities Catherine required—other than nourishment of course—so his wife could rest.

She had no idea how she could have done this without him.

It was six weeks to the day since Catherine had been born. While still far too small for a girl her age, she had grown steadily, and her lungs had yet to prove any great hindrance—and in fact they sounded better each week she grew, much to the relief of her parents.

Christine only worried for when she began walking. Would such excursions exacerbate the delicate tissues of her lungs?

But now was not the time for worrying about such things.

Erik had taken to allowing her to walk the relatively short distance from their little cottage to Marie's unaccompanied, as he had spent one night surveying the adjoining houses and found one vacant, one belonging to the groundskeeper and his wife, and the other to an equally elderly couple.

Satisfied that there was no immediate danger from one house to the next, Christine made her walks with only Catherine for company. She knew he would have still joined her, but the mask required of him hurt terribly if worn too often, and by no means did she wish for him to be in pain, so she simply kissed him goodbye, told him she would be careful and safe, and made her journey.

In truth, this was the first time she was truly glad she had Marie for a friend, as in general she would have been forced to be satisfied with almost no knowledge on the subject and simply hope for the best.

But now she had someone with experience who she could *ask*.

And though she blushed, and stuttered her way through the question, and assured Marie that any such questions did not need to be answered if she deemed them improper, she enquired as to how one felt upon joining with one's husband for the first time after delivery.

Marie was surprisingly helpful. She did not laugh, nor did she blush, but instead *smiled*. "Oh Christine, I'm so glad you feel comfortable talking about such things!" She most certainly was not *comfortable,* but she supposed the sentiment was more directed toward her trust in Marie as a true friend with which such things could be discussed.

Christine's blush did not quiet the entirety of the conversation. She was asked if she still bled, if she still experienced any pain with movement or when she was seated, and then most important of all...

"Is your husband a gentle man?"

Erik would be furious if he ever found out she had discussed such things. But when faced with the opportunity to express to another living being—*not* someone like the Daroga who was intent on believing his own whims as to Erik's character—she could not stop herself from speaking. "He is *very* gentle and loving. But it hurts him to see me in pain, and I at least wished to be able to give him warning."

Marie nodded her understanding, and patted Christine's hand gently.

"I'm glad you found a good man. He seems to love you very much. And Catherine." Her eyes travelled to the baby who was sleeping on her stomach upon the rug. Such had been discovered to be her favourite manner of slumber. "That can be a rarity sometimes, but I am happy for you."

It was only a pity that such a thing could be true.

Having determined that Erik would be sensitive to Christine's comfort, Marie felt no reticence in encouraging their resumed unions. "It is true, you will most likely hurt, but if he is gentle and *slow*, it will still be pleasant."

Christine was greatly comforted with such advice, as she dearly wished to rejoin her husband in such a manner, and was glad that she would be able to tell him of the possibility for discomfort. But he had been so very kind when she had lain with him the first time, so she was not overly concerned that he would be unable to maintain his tenderness.

She was also glad to see that her frequent visits seemed to put Marie in a better mood in general, and she seemed far more affectionate with Armand, and even allowed the little boy to play more out of doors. "At least until the frosts come."

That seemed perfectly reasonable.

But Christine was antsy to return to Erik, so she took her leave, and settled a bleary eyed Catherine in her arms. "Thank you, Marie. I very much appreciate your candour."

Marie laughed, and hugged Christine in parting. "Enjoy yourself, Christine. I'm sure your husband will be quite happy to have you back."

Christine was very much in agreement.

The only thing she was left to wonder was timing. She doubted that Erik would have counted exactly how many days it had been since Catherine's birth as Christine had been doing with her little calendar—the very one that had fuelled her consideration of pregnancy to begin with—and as such he would not be waiting to pounce on her as soon as she returned.

If he *had* been conscious of the date, he most likely would have given her a much different greeting when he awoke her.

For some inexplicable reason, such a notion made her sad.

She opened the door in the special way he showed her, and with her arms full of Catherine she was quite grateful for her husband's genius, and upon entering the house went in search of him.

She found him in the bare music room, his violin in the exact spot in the corner it had been when she left, while Erik sat unseeingly against the wall.

Before she went to him, she hurried to the adjoining room and placed Catherine in the bassinet—now a full two feet away from the window—and kissed her once in blessing of her rest, and went to join her husband.

"Erik? What troubles you?" And though she was rather glad this was not the day the piano was delivered—she very much wished he would not be driven to distraction on this date!—she was heartbroken by the desolation she saw upon his unmasked features, and cursed her selfishness.

She slid carefully down the wall and rested her head upon his shoulder, and his hand moved slowly to cover her own. "Erik does not wish to be a brute."

Christine would have laughed if his tone was not so deadly serious, and her body stilled at his words. He *did* know.

"It has been six weeks, Erik. That does not constitute brutality, your book said so!"

He shook his head fervently, and how she wished he would not have such thoughts that would plague him with ideas of his needs being too much for his wife to fulfil!

"I wanted to ravage you this morning. I wanted to play for you so your passion might awaken even before your mind, and then perhaps you might consent." He sighed. "But Catherine was hungry."

It was true, the only reason he had woken her that morning was to place a whimpering infant at her breast. He had left the room quickly after.

Christine turned so she could look at him fully, but he was resolutely staring away from her, and refused to move his head even when her hands gently pressed. "You think I do not think of you also? *Need* you also?" She pressed kisses onto the cheek which faced her, and it was only so his lips could cover hers that he finally relented in facing her.

"Do you know why I went to visit Marie?" She had not intended on telling him the nature of her conversation, but perhaps if he saw that she had truly considered this—*planned* it—he would realise how important their relations were to her as well.

Erik shook his head. "To give me time to compose, I assume." But his eyes were flashing as he looked at her, and she knew he was to reveal something that had been plaguing him the past few weeks—since she had begun her walks. "But you seem to be under the impression that I can compose when you are *not* here. And perhaps I could have before, but not now. *Never* now!"

She had never considered that. For years she supposed she had held the place of muse, but it had never been because of her physical presence. "But you cannot play when Catherine is here. At least not yet. She *will* get better, Erik, she just needs time."

He practically rolled his eyes at her. "Of course she will. She is a child, and children require time to grow. I am not an imbecile, Christine."

If Christine considered him anything, an imbecile was never what she thought.

"Would you rather I not go? I was only trying to help you."

His look was so very serious, and so very intense she very nearly began to tremble. "I need you to help me in other ways, Christine. *Never* by you leaving."

Even though he was making such statements of her never leaving his side, she knew he did not mean they should never be parted. He simply did not wish for her to leave to give him time *alone*. Perhaps when they had been married longer—surely husbands required their privacy as well!—but for now he still craved her company.

And who was she to deny him?

If in fact having herself and Catherine in their home was more important than his music, then she would cease her walks unless Erik was also able to meander the grounds and learn each expanse of foliage and trees.

That would certainly make them more pleasurable for her as well.

"Yes, that was the reason on most days, but not today."

He raised one thin eyebrow in question.

The blush that was so prevalent in Marie's parlour reemerged, but she resolutely looked into her husband's eyes as she told him of their conversation. "I wanted to ask her what it was like the first time after a baby was born."

Erik's mouth nearly fell open at her disclosure. "Why would you discuss such things?"

Christine could not help but grow indignant for him questioning her motives. "Because I did not wish to be unprepared! I knew when we were together the *first* time that it would be uncomfortable, but I did not know about *this* time." She softened as he saw the rather pained look he bore at her mention of her discomfort on their belated wedding night. "I regret *nothing* we have done, husband. Nor should you. I simply wanted to be able to give us some warning."

"What did she," Erik swallowed, and was quite plainly uncomfortable, but still allowed his question to be given voice. "What did she tell you?"

Christine took his hand, and made soothing circles on it as she spoke. "That it may be uncomfortable, and that you should be gentle and slow." She was still blushing, but did not regret her decision to ask such questions. If she still had a mother—or even Mamma Valérius—she would have asked them.

But she did not.

Though she did think perhaps she should attempt to contact her surrogate mother in the near future, if only to assure her of her safety and happiness.

Such was to be thought on another day.

"Are you frightened?" She knew that it filled her with a slight sense of apprehension—she had grown to be accustomed to nothing but pleasant feelings from their conjugations, even in the later stages of her pregnancy— and she was loath to revert back to the slight grimaces at his entry.

Erik nodded, and for a moment she worried he would insist they wait even longer to resume their intimacies, and she knew that the only thing keeping them from being truly happy in their little home was the discord from lack of physical expression.

The priest had told them so.

"I am not." She pressed her lips softly to his throat, and leaned slightly so she could whisper in *his* ear. "Erik, you have proved your thoughtfulness and gentility time and again, and I know now will be no different. I *miss* you." She pulled back slightly and could not help but look slightly impish. "And it is not for a husband to deny his wife."

It felt odd reverting back to their titles in order to convince him, as such things had become unnecessary in their little cottage—so unlike their time underground. But change did not happen overnight, and for every step of progress there was most certainly a period of adjustment and regression, and it was ridiculous to feel discouraged.

And it was *impossible* to feel thusly when Erik moaned and placed both hands in her hair and kissed her lips hungrily.

Any thought of Erik's unwillingness to resume their activities in the light of day were gone when his lips coaxed the slumbering passions that so desperately wished to be expressed.

She was fully prepared to simply begin their love making on the soft carpet of the music room—truthfully the only thing Erik had placed in this room since they had entered the home—but Erik pulled away, eyes still burning with his desire for her, and told her to check on Catherine. "Erik does not want to share his wife for a good hour. Perhaps she will be happy to allow such a thing if she has a moment with you."

Of course it would be quite impossible to anticipate how she was fare for an entire hour, but Christine quite reluctantly relented, even when her blood pulsed madly in her veins and she simply wished for Erik to have carried her to bed.

When she listened hard enough she could hear his footfalls—nearly silent when one was not truly listening for them—and she was grateful he was not fleeing from her.

Catherine had been fed before they departed for Marie's, and their established schedule leant to the notion she would not be hungry for at least another two. She was dry, she was sleeping, and her expression was entirely peaceful as she used two of her fingers as a means for slumbering comfort.

Christine was very grateful for her daughter's cooperation.

So stealing quietly from the room—leaving the door only partially open as her daughter's cries would most likely be unable to pierce a fully closed obstacle—Christine went in search of her husband.

Erik was fully dressed, and was simply staring out the window when she entered the room. She desperately hoped he had not changed his mind in the short time it had taken for her to ensure Catherine was content.

But when he turned to her, it was quite apparent he had not.

He did not draw the curtains, and did nothing to stop the bright autumn sun from illuminating the room, and Christine realised this was the very first time they were going to show their love in the daylight.

Even in Erik's underground home, when surely sometimes it was day, there were still shadows and firelight to give an eerie glow to the room and in truth, to their bodies.

And for a moment, she felt rather self conscious.

Though Erik had no difficulty seeing in the dark, this was the first time he would be looking at her so intimately with her body so very changed from pregnancy. She had yet to regain the flat quality of her stomach and even though Catherine was small, she still bore some rather purple marks that evidenced just how round she had become, and her breasts were surely changed due to their ability to now function as modes of nourishment.

And though she had felt beautiful and motherly when pregnant, now she heard all the times Erik had teased her for liking too much sugar, and felt simply *plump*.

Perhaps they should be waiting after all.

Her walks had helped her regain some of her figure, as well had her husband's gentle massage upon her womb in the beginning weeks since delivery so as to help facilitate its return to a more reasonable size. But now...

Erik had remained silent as she let her thoughts show plainly on her face, and Christine knew it was quite obvious she was feeling embarrassed and unsure.

He came toward her slowly, not stalking her like he was about to ravage her as he had stated, but instead tenderly began to undo each clasp, button, and tie that fastened her dress together.

Slowly, methodically, he unveiled new expanses of skin, and much to Christine's chagrin, surely he would notice how much *more* skin there was to behold.

But Erik did not seem at all repulsed by any of her changes, and if his eyes were any indication, he was in fact quite pleased when he was finally able to shimmy off her gown and watch it pool in a useless pile at her feet.

He helped her step out of it and she was left in only her chemise and pantaloons, finding the corsets nearly impossible to wear while nursing as Catherine was quite unable—or possibly simply unwilling—to allow her mother time to undo the numerous clasps.

Erik had not minded.

His hands reached underneath the long cotton garment, and he tugged at the strings of her pantaloons, allowing them to drop unceremoniously onto the floor as well. She expected him to immediately divest her of her last remaining clothing, but instead, still looking into her eyes, he removed his own jacket.

Christine did not think she would ever be used to the sensuous way Erik undressed. Even when hurried in the heat of passion, his fingers were experienced and never stumbled as he deftly unbuttoned and tugged at the fine materials that made up his clothing.

And when he took of the *entirety* of his clothes, she could plainly see what he was doing.

Yes, the ultimate purpose was to allow them the expanses of flesh in order to feel as connected to one another as humanly possible, but by so exposing himself to her, he was laying himself vulnerable to her ultimate perusal—in the *daylight*.

He was not perfect. No part of his skin was the angelic white it should have been had years of abuse not been heaped upon him, and it was a startling sight when seen in sunlight. She had felt the crisscrossing texture beneath her fingers many times, but never had she so clearly seen how his skin was knit back together when it had so cruelly been torn asunder.

And she felt *incredibly* foolish. This was her husband, and she loved him so very much.

Any changes to her body had been the result of bringing *his* child into the world, and she would never regret any mark or extra bit of plumpness clinging to her hip if it meant not having their daughter.

And if Erik was half the man she knew him to be, he would be in agreement.

But it was still with trembling hands that she slowly raised her chemise over her head, and she could not quite meet his eyes as she felt his gaze on her unfamiliar body.

It was not until his hand gently cupped her chin that she looked at him fully. "You are *so* beautiful, Christine. You should never doubt my thoughts on the subject." He held her hand as he took her to the bed, and though she supposed it might be considered slightly discomfited without the overwhelming passion for joining that makes being entirely exposed agreeable, Christine still felt as though this was *right*.

Had the priest not said so?

Erik was barely touching her, yet she felt in every nerve the devotion he poured through his touch. He did not even begin to touch her most womanly places until she was nearly whimpering for him to simply allow her to *feel* him, when finally, *finally* he placed a hand where she most desired his attention.

There was nothing hurried in his movements, each calculated to best allow her comfort and gentility, but somehow it felt... wrong. Erik had been denied pleasures as well these past months, and though she acknowledged his supreme desire was to see to her comfort, it seemed so very wrong that he should have to be so analytical—watching every catch of breath for sign of pain or discomfort.

So leaning up to capture his lips in hers, she ever so lightly—yet firmly—pushed him so he was lying on his back while she rested above him. He was always so careful not to put his full weight on her, but she did not think he would mind it coming from her.

He looked at her with wide eyes as she ever so slowly manoeuvred herself onto him. It felt different. She hated that it felt different, that there was pain when he was fully within her, but when she leaned to kiss him, brushing her breasts against the plane of his too thin chest, she became distracted once more with the feeling of simply *him*.

So positioned, she did not feel him so very deeply, and the space that had opened so fully for Catherine was hardly pressed upon. "Is this alright?"

Erik had never laughed before when they were so intimately connected, but he did—loud robust laughter like she had never heard before. But the way his hands flexed on her hips, and the look in his eyes never once led her to believe he was laughing at *her*, so she fully enjoyed the sound.

"Anything you do, wife, is alright with your husband." She smiled, and ever so slightly began to move.

Erik helped her, teasing her skin, and aiding to keep her distracted from any twinges of pain, and in truth, when he had pulled her back to himself and began to whisper how much he adored the roundness of her flesh, how it felt in his hands, how she made him feel like a *man* and not some unworthy creature, she did not find it so very difficult at all to lose herself in this rejoining of bodies and souls.

There was nothing hurried about their venture. It was a relearning of what had once been familiar, and for which they both longed to have established again.

If only they knew such would not be the case.

XXXIII

"Erik, you are being unreasonable."

"And *you* are being unreasonable for trying to tear Erik away when he *finally* has his piano!"

He did not in fact have his piano, but instead had what fully *looked* like a piano but lacked the ability to make *sounds* like a piano.

And they were out of food.

Of course Erik was not intentionally being cruel by denying the mother of his child sustenance, but he had waited relatively patiently the past five weeks for his instrument to arrive, and when he had promised to take her to the market that morning, it had been before the delivery boy had shown up at their gate just as they were leaving.

He would not let her go alone.

"You allow me to go to Marie's unaccompanied!" Which was true, though her company was becoming rather tedious now that her husband was due to return at any moment. She could hardly keep still long enough for conversation and her eyes constantly flickered to the window. Though Christine could hardly blame her not having seen the man in nearly six months, it did not make for ease in discussion.

Armand was tense and fidgety, and truthfully, Christine spent most of her time speaking to him while sipping cups of tea and eating pastries.

So on the whole, her visits were not entirely without entertainment.

But the fact remained, they were in dire need of groceries, and Erik was unwilling to take her to the market. And she would *not* go hungry for an instrument!

"Erik, husband, I love you, you know I do, but I am going to buy food. Catherine and I shall walk, and you may stay and fiddle with your new toy." Perhaps her tone was rather biting, and Erik did scowl at her quite forcefully, and while her original plan had been that he would acknowledge his foolishness in not putting the needs of his family above the needs of an inanimate object, she was quite put out when he instead waved his hand at her.

"Very well then, enjoy yourself with your *food*." He nearly spat the word as though it was something entirely worthless and without merit.

And she had to admit, she was angry.

So bundling up Catherine and herself as the autumn days were swiftly becoming filled with the more biting winds of an incoming winter, Christine made the rather long walk to the grocers.

She told herself it was the chill of the breeze that made her nose begin to run and her eyes to water, and she quite determinedly told Catherine such was the case. The infant had no protest to the cold, as she was afforded warm blankets and an even warmer chest to rest upon as her mother walked.

Perhaps it was silly to lie to oneself, but Christine did not wish to acknowledge that the sweetness of yesterday afternoon, as they had experienced the rapture of rejoining with one another could be spoiled by one simple delivery.

Christine had never felt such a feeling of spite toward music as she did in that moment.

The walk was truly not *that* long, though she did wonder how she would manage to bring very many things back home without the use of the carriage. She would have taken it, but that would also have required Erik's assistance—which quite obviously was not being offered.

So she would stick to simple things that could be kept in the pockets of her cloak and the rather small canvas bag that she carried on her arm—not being entirely thoughtless when she departed the house.

Apparently many others decided today was not the sort of day pleasant for shopping, for the market was mostly quiet except for the vendors, and Christine only picked out the essentials—and perhaps a small glass jug of cream for her tea that truthfully was the main reason she *needed* to go to the grocers on this of all days. Though they really were out of edible foods other than baked goods.

And those were not proper nutrients for Catherine, even though it was rather a roundabout way of thinking of it, but her daughter deserved better sustenance than her mother's milk full of sugary items.

That went horribly with tea without cream.

It was when she was picking out apples that she had her first dilemma. She truly required two hands to bag her fruit as well as see to payment for the woman offering her wares, and she looked rather flustered for a moment as she tried to handle so many responsibilities at once.

The keeper must have pitied Christine's distress, for she offered to hold Catherine while Christine situated herself. "Come here, pretty baby, let your mummy get her coins."

Christine was digging through her purse in want of the proper *francs* when a man's voice enquired if he could hold the child. "May I?" But he did not ask Christine, he asked the shop keep, and before she could protest the exchange, Catherine was passed into the man's awaiting arms.

The Persian's arms.

She was not certain why, but she felt more fear at that moment than she had even when being molested by the horrible carriage driver all those months ago. For that was her *child*, and though this man had never done any direct harm in way of physical violence, she did not at all trust his motivation when it came to the protection of her family.

"Please give her back, Monsieur." Her voice should not have quivered. She should have held onto the angry feelings he had so instilled in her whenever he spoke to Erik in his condescending tone, but as he had not yet given her back her child, her little *enfant*, she did not wish to upset him.

"Come now Christine, I am simply going to take you home. Take you *both* home. There is no need to be frightened." Her fingers were trembling, and they ached with need to hold once more her baby in her arms, but he was beginning to walk away, and she *had* to follow him.

"We are quite capable of walking home, but I thank you for your offer." He smiled at her pleasantly, but he was already beginning to enter the awaiting carriage. "It is no trouble, Mme. Christine. I would be reticent in my duty as a gentleman to allow you to walk in this weather."

She would not have gone. If she had Catherine safely in her arms, she would have simply turned around and begun the half hour walk home.

But she did not.

This *vile* man who ignored a mother's request to be given her daughter was coaxing her into a carriage with a promise of home. And though it went against every fibre of her being to follow him—to allow him the satisfaction of her presence upon his command—she could not leave Catherine.

She wanted to believe he was taking her home, but such hopes were short lived when the turn was missed, and it became quite apparent they were heading in the opposite direction—more toward the direction of Paris than of *home*.

But even then, she wished desperately to believe he had made some mistake, and still thought they lived in their little underground home. "We have moved, Monsieur, your driver is going in the wrong direction."

Catherine had woken and had begun to cry, and the Persian was jostling her slightly in what appeared to be some sort of method of comfort—that was quite obviously not effective. "*Please* give her to me."

The man sighed, and looked at her with pity. "Christine, I am not doing this to harm either of you. I am only interested in saving my friend's *soul.*

This was very wrong of him to do, and he has you so enthralled you believe everything he has told you. Perhaps if you were away for him for a while you would come back to yourself."

Catherine was letting out a full on wail and blatantly ignored the shushing of the man holding her. "Give me my daughter!"

He seemed surprised by the forcefulness of her tone, and the rage she had so dearly needed when in the presence of witnesses—near people who could *help* her—was finally flowing through her fingertips.

She suddenly knew exactly how Erik had felt when he killed the carriage driver. They had never spoken of it, but as she looked at this man, she wanted nothing more than to see him lying lifeless upon the ground for keeping her from comforting her little *enfant*.

Christine would have hurt him—fought him—if only her precious bundle was not in the way. Tears of rage were welling in her eyes, and finally the Daroga sighed, and passed her the mewling infant. And though she wanted nothing more than to continue unleashing her temper on this man, her baby needed her and her needs must come first—had not Erik told her so?

Oh God.

"You *have* to take us back to him. *Please,* he is my husband!" Catherine would not be soothed, and she continued to cry and wail, and she nearly sounded choked by the forcefulness of her cries.

Christine was quite certain she had never cried so hard, for either of her parents was quick to tend to whatever ailed her. But she must have sensed her mother's distress, and being in the arms of an unknown man had given her no comfort.

And Christine was never so frightened for her daughter's poor lungs than at that moment.

When the Daroga opened his mouth to argue further his point as to *why* he was brutally kidnapping them from their very source of happiness, Christine cast him a dangerous look. "*Silence* you stupid man, I must calm her."

She sounded like her husband, even to her own ears.

And she felt a rush of giddiness that she was becoming like him.

Not the part where madness once consumed him, but that she could possess some of the regality that surrounded him—that people *listened* when he spoke.

For far too long her own thoughts and desires were turned asunder by the will of others, and even if she could not change their course of action, by no means would she silently allow them to think they had her consent.

Her decision was confirmed when the Persian thankfully closed his mouth and allowed Christine to do her best to calm the still crying baby.

The only thing that seemed to give her the slightest bit of comfort was the lullaby Erik had given her. She would not quiet completely as Christine's own voice was *nothing* compared to her father's, but only tiny whimpers continued to be emitted, that only slightly rasped when she inhaled.

Something was wrong with her, surely this *foolish* man could hear that.

"She needs to see a doctor."

The Persian looked at mother and child sympathetically, but made no move to signal a change in direction to the driver. "I am sure a doctor would be more than happy to see to her once we get you both home. But we really cannot delay, Madame."

Any good will she may have harboured—no matter how small—was entirely erased when he ignored her pleas. If and *when* Erik found them, she would do nothing to stay his hand.

After all, he was simply defending his family from outside forces who intended harm.

"Where is my home to you, Monsieur? Because I can assure you, we are thinking of two very different places."

The Persian blinked, almost in surprise, and then it was hidden behind his sympathy once more. "My dear, home is with the man you love. With *Raoul.* Surely you must be concerned for the poor boy. He has suffered greatly since you left."

Suffered? She had tried desperately in the beginning to put all thoughts of him from her mind lest Erik somehow notice her infidelity—even if it was merely through thought—and it somehow had become habit that she not think of him.

And though she no longer harboured romantic feelings for him, she could not deny that she still loved him. He had been her dearest friend and companion, and he reminded her of happier times with her father that not even Erik could bring forth.

Because he *shared* those memories—he *knew* her father, and though she would gladly forsake ever seeing him again if it meant this man would turn around and allow her to return to her Erik, she did feel a tinge of concern that he had suffered on her account.

"What is wrong with Raoul?" It felt odd even speaking his name aloud—even wrong. As if muttering his name alone was enough to send Erik a note of betrayal. He would believe she had left without her consent would he not?

He had the horse, and surely when he realised she had been gone too long, he would come for her. For *them.* Even if he was still angry with her, he would not allow Catherine to be out of doors so late at night. She had left after lunch, and soon it would be time for tea, and therefore unheard of for her not to make him a cup.

Surely his piano would not occupy him so completely.

"He has suffered both the loss of his fiancée as well as his brother, and it was only from the pleading of his sisters did he give up wandering the tunnels. I am afraid he has taken to the bottle a little too hastily."

Her sweet boyish Raoul a drunkard? She supposed that was how many men coped with the loss of those they loved, but it was difficult to reconcile the warmth of her friend to someone who could possibly be intoxicated and cruel—though certainly not *all* men were so greatly affected by drink.

Erik rarely indulged, and when he did it was always when he prepared dinner for her and it complemented the meal. She supposed he was slightly more talkative, or wanted to pet her more than was customary, but she never minded his attentions.

But she would mind them from Raoul.

"Is that where we are going? To Raoul?"

The Daroga looked at her for a long moment, obviously trying to ascertain the consequences of revealing their ultimate location. But finally he nodded, even as the carriage slowed.

It was impossible they were already in Paris.

"I am afraid this is where I leave you." The man opened the carriage door and slipped out, and greeted another, much younger man who exited a carriage coming from the opposite direction. "Greetings, Pierre. I trust you shall see Christine to her fiancé safely."

He was leaving her with another man? She had been doing so very well in her last few trips with this mode of transport, and she had no desire for that to change due to another male encounter. Even when Erik had not been inside, she still had Catherine, but the idea of being with a complete stranger was terrifying. She trusted the Persian not to harm her in the physical sense, but she did *not* trust his judgment when it came to males.

After all, he was taking her from the man who could with absolute certainty protect her person. "Wait! Why are you not taking me?" Even his horrid company would be better than a strange man's!

"There there, Christine, you have nothing to fear. This man is a good friend of Raoul's and will see you where you need to go. I am afraid I must return to Erik before he realises you are missing."

With one last entreaty she begged for him to return her home.

An unwanted hand was on her arm, but she let it remain in the hopes that some contact would convince him she was being reasonable—that she *was* of sound mind.

"Madame Christine, I am positive that once you see your fiancé you shall change your mind. You will be perfectly safe with Pierre, and do not fret, I shall explain your absence to your," he paused, obviously not favouring the word. "Husband."

But there should not *be* an absence to explain! The hands which had attempted comfort were now replaced with other, more boyish renditions, and they were steadily pushing her back into the carriage, and Christine momentarily choked on her tears.

Too many memories, too many terrifying moments were triggered by such an action, and she silently remained frozen in the corner of the carriage, desperately clutching at Catherine for some semblance of calm.

How she wanted Erik!

The carriage lurched, and she was once more being driven farther away from her husband, and the tears could no longer be contained as they poured steadily down her cheeks.

Cheeks that Erik liked to caress.

She tried to quiet her sobs so Catherine would not be distressed, but it was nearly impossible.

"There there, Madame, no need to cry! You'll be home soon. Raoul has missed you very much."

She looked at this man, *Pierre,* with wide eyes, trying to assess his character. He seemed aloof, yet concerned, and it was entirely obvious he bought the outrageous lie that she was merely upset with gratitude for being away from her abusive husband.

And any protestations she gave would simply be dismissed as the posturing of a woe begotten wife desperate to return to her captor.

So she remained crying softly, humming slightly to her little *enfant* in hopes of reminding both herself and Catherine that the moments they had with Erik were to be cherished, and *nothing* these brutal men would say against him were true in the slightest.

She *loved* him.

And more than anything, she wished to go home so she could tell him once more, and apologise for leaving without him. Yes, he was being unreasonable, but she should have known that the world he lived in was now a part of hers, and she could not simply happily traipse through it unscathed.

Pierre attempted to make conversation, either to soothe her or only because he was bored of watching a woman cry in front of him, but she did not want to talk. Not when anything she said could be twisted into further proof of Erik's unfit husbandry.

"Succulent…" Christine had been focusing solely on Catherine, but when the seemingly unrelated word slipped from the strange man's lips, she looked up. He had an apple in his hands, and he had taken a small bite of the red fruit. "Would you care for some?"

She shook her head fervently. Too many times had Erik read the fairytale of the poisoned apples, and this seemed a little too in keeping with the horror of the tale.

Pierre sighed and bade her look at him. "You do not need to be frightened anymore, Christine. Everything will be fine soon."

This was precisely why she wished he would simply *stop* talking. Everything that passed his lips as a means for comfort was utterly ridiculous and false, and therefore purposeless.

He seemed to realise this, as he returned his attention to the apple and allowed her to cry in peace.

Every moment the carriage continued seemed to make the hole that was steadily being ripped in Christine's soul to tear slightly more. And when she thought she could bear it no more, that the demonic munching of an apple could not possibly further irritate her, the carriage suddenly lurched and stopped.

Pierre muttered a quiet, "Finally," and opened the door, turning only to assist Christine from the carriage. But he seemed to be under the misinformation that Christine would *willingly* be removed from her confines.

The only thing worse than being inside her prison was to be removed, and the truth of her capture proven without doubt. If she could only remain, she could perhaps convince the driver to return her whence she came.

But Pierre was tugging at her, and she wanted to hit him—*hard*—but could not do so when she had a still unhappy Catherine in her arms.

"Oh do cooperate, Christine. I would hate to force you!" Comforting words indeed. But he tugged her a little too hard, and she almost fell from the seat if he had not steadied her. "See? Wouldn't this be easier if you helped me?"

Perhaps she would be safer, but there was something horrid about even remotely giving consent for *any* of this.

But Erik would *want* her to be safe.

And it was not simply about her. Catherine had to remain safe, no matter how Christine felt.

So only clinging to that thought did she descend the carriage, and come face to face with Raoul's home.

She had been here before of course, but each of the previous times had been accompanied with joyous laughter and warm smiles as she joined her young love for luncheons and walks through the park.

It looked so very different at night.

Looming and ominous, the house was surrounded by a rod iron gate that seemed to protest its opening as loudly as Christine wished she could at her entrance.

Pierre held her arm, not tightly enough to drag her, but enough so as she could understand he would keep her from running if that was her whim. She hated the contact, but did little to remove it.

Complacency.

Speak to Raoul.

Surely he could be reasoned with, unlike these two fools.

CATHERINE MILLER

Pierre did not even knock before entering, and did not allow her to linger in the foyer but took her directly up the stairs into the library.

Before a blazing fire sat a man who only in the vaguest sense resembled her oldest friend.

"Raoul?"

Christine never had such an urge to run as she did when he turned to face her.

XXXIV

Erik was not certain what came over him that allowed him to let Christine *leave,* but it was only when he heard the front door firmly close that he realised she was truly angry with him.

He sighed. Wives could be so very troublesome at times.

But now that he was once more able to play his Christine as his husbandly rights allowed, it seemed almost dire he be able to shower her in his music once more as well. The bed in their little home had been christened with the physical, but it had yet to experience the ethereal.

And he so wished for her to *sing!*

He was being utterly petulant, but he did not mind sharing his wife's lovely breasts with their daughter nearly so much as Christine's voice.

And that was the material point.

She had awoken before him, possibly her mothering instinct driving her to see to his Cat before he could even hear the quiet whimpers signalling her hunger. Therefore it was to an empty bed he awoke, and when he slunk downstairs to the nursery, it was to find a singing Christine nursing the baby.

While his heart swelled at the care she took at tending to *their* daughter, he still felt as though an integral part of their relationship had been neglected.

And she seemed not to *care.*

So when the piano—the *parts* at least—had miraculously appeared that morning as if in answer to his silent plea, he wanted nothing more than to complete it.

He should have gone after her, but the parts lying before him seemed to call out, and he was helpless to refuse. It was a small village, and he had made certain to keep careful watch their previous trips to market and make judgment of the surrounding populous. He had yet to see any nefarious characters in the idyllic town.

It was almost nauseating.

But Christine would be fine—*grateful* even for her independence she was finally allowed.

Alright, perhaps not, but he would apologise and pamper her—*play* for her—as soon as she returned, and all would be well.

Stringing a piano was a tedious process, and before long Erik was entirely distracted by properly tightening, tuning, and overall ensuring the instrument was worthy of the music it would soon be graced with.

It took him a little by surprise when the distinct sounds of someone incorrectly attempting to open the front door could be heard even from the music room.

Sirens were not strictly for the water.

He was further surprised to see how long the afternoon shadows had grown. Silly Christine had surely remained longer simply out of childish spite. And she must have her arms too burdened with food to be able to manage the door correctly. He felt a pang of guilt at the thought of her struggling with packages when rightfully he should have been the one bearing *her* burdens.

It was time to begin his grovelling, and he determinedly pushed away the slight pain at leaving the piano that was not *quite* finished.

Christine was far more important—and the niggling guilt at his rejection of her this morning weighed all the more heavily.

The serenity of country living was proving to be the downfall of his senses. He should have known the hands clumsily fiddling with the door were not the delicate appendages of his wife. He should have heard the heavy footfalls that could not possibly have equalled Christine, even burdened with the heaviest of groceries.

So he was entirely unprepared that instead of his angelic wife handing him his daughter, he was met with the dark eyes of the Daroga.

"Your doors are proving more difficult to open."

Erik scowled and crossed his arms—suddenly grateful he had donned his mask that morning, though he had seen Christine look at it warily when she had first eyed it. "I can assure you, Daroga, they are quite simplistic to those who are *invited.*" The last word was stressed for he had not forgiven his acquaintance the distress of his wife at their previous encounters.

"You wound me, my friend." The Persian eyed the foyer, but Erik had yet to move from his guard in the doorway. "Won't you invite me in?"

Though hidden, it was still quite apparent that Erik's expression had turned incredulous. "I believe my wife made it quite clear you were no longer welcome in our home."

The Persian shifted slightly—guiltily?—before standing straighter. "Is the Madame at home?" There was something in the set of his mouth that belied a *lack* of tension.

This impertinent man *knew* she was absent.

A distinct feeling of fear began grasping at his heart.

But fear was not conducive for gathering information. *Anger* was far more useful. So with a dangerous gleam in his eye, he stepped back and bade the Persian enter.

In truth, he did not want this man in his home. While grateful for the companionship at one time, now he was merely a painful reminder of the darkest moments in his life.

It seemed sacrilege to invite him in.

But there was something he seemed to know—and anything this man found valuable in way of knowledge was imperative to also know.

He ushered him into the study, as the music room was too close to his daughter's—he felt a terrible pang that it was now empty.

Where was Christine?

Erik quickly sat on the sofa, not because he normally would have sat in the presence of another, but because he could not bear the thought of the place he had spent so many sweet moments with his wife and daughter being defiled by another. "Why are you here, Daroga?"

The Persian settled in the reading chair across from him, his pose the epitome of relaxation.

Erik wanted to hit him.

"Let me begin by saying Christine is safe." Stupider words were never spoken. If the Persian had wanted Erik to remain calm, assuring him of *his* wife's safety when she was *not* in his vicinity only assured his panic.

The man was very fortunate Erik was seated on the sofa instead of the desk. The desk housed the lasso.

"Daroga," the word was low and dangerous in its fluidity, and any other man would have realised his impending demise. "What have you done?"

But the Persian was not any other man, and quite wrongly assumed his safety was assured simply because of supposed familiarity.

He was gravely mistaken.

"Nothing that the girl did not specifically request." His voice was calm and almost condescending. "Shortly after you moved here I received word through a chorus friend of Christine's, Meg I believe she called herself, that your wife was seeking my immediate assistance."

His expression was neutral, and in all accounts looked perfectly truthful. And though Erik wanted to deny it, a distinct feeling of betrayal was beginning to settle in his stomach that Christine should secretly be in contact with someone from the Opera house.

Erik told himself he would not have minded. She was allowed to have friends, all wives had their ladies to titter about inconsequential things that husbands did not wish to hear, and he was not so cruel as to deny her. But to keep it from him?

"She had a change of heart, but did not know how to tell you she wished to return home. No, do not give me such a look. She wished to return back to her fiancé. I told you I would not interfere after I learned of your marriage, but Erik, there was a child to think of now! So of course I helped her."

Christine wanted to… leave?

They had quarrelled. He had said she was unreasonable, but they had fought before and she gave no indication she was going to *leave* him. He realised now that he was the one at fault, that the needs of his wife and daughter were more important than anything he could wish for—music or no. But to *leave* him?

But the Daroga had said she contacted Meg upon coming to live at their little cottage—that she had been unhappy for so long that she should wish to leave so quickly.

But that would mean every utterance of love had been a lie.

That every loving look, touch, whispered word had been a falsehood, that the love they had shared last night was nothing more than a cruel way of saying goodbye to her husband before she disappeared into the night with the help of this man sitting before him.

And that meant she took *his* daughter.

To raise with another.

Erik rose slowly. The Persian eyed him warily but with the sickening compassion that made Erik want nothing more than his eyes to be permanently removed from his head. He walked equally surely, his decision already made.

He went to the desk—the lovely, mahogany structure that *félin* Christine so liked to bathe upon.

His fingers wrapped around the coiled rope within the drawer and he caressed it softly.

It should have been his wife's skin beneath his fingers. It should have been the downy hair of his Cat's tiny head.

Erik sighed. "Did she say why?"

The anger simmered as the Daroga looked at him with *compassion,* as if he was offering condolences to the man who just accepted the loss of his wife and daughter. "She did care for you, Erik. But that was not enough once she had her daughter—a daughter who deserves to grow up in a normal, happy home! You should not deny a mother the opportunity to nurture her child to the fullest."

Erik's eyes flashed, and his hand gripped the catgut firmly. "You think I would deny *my* child anything she required?"

"I do not believe you are capable of knowing what a normal child requires." And was that not the problem with this man? He did not view Erik as husband and a father. He assumed him to be the same man who utilised his genius for the pleasure of the Shah—never for how to best please those he loved.

And he had helped Christine leave him.

But if that was truly what she wished—that she thought him unable or unwilling to raise their daughter as she deserved... he would let her go.

It would kill him.

He would spiral into the depths of his despair and it would be impossible to ever revive. There would be no happiness. Now that he had tasted how life could be when one experienced love and acceptance, to have it ripped away so cruelly would leave him desperate and dying.

"You have to let her go, Erik. She loves the boy."

And Erik *smiled.*

The Persian for the first time looked frightened, and became even more so when Erik began to *laugh.* He knew how Christine felt when he laughed with happiness of spirit, and she would look at him with such adoring eyes.

And quite strangely, that was how he laughed now—perhaps that is why the Persian looked so very frightened!

"Daroga, it no longer amazes me that you are unmarried." His fingers were once more soft upon the lasso, but he no longer hated the feel. "*Trust* is such an integral part of the foundation. As is *love.* And *faithfulness.*" His voice was calm without the foolish wavering of one as distressed as he was. "And do you know what else? Christine's *God.* For she would never betray me, for that would be a betrayal of *him.*"

Too many things had happened. Too many perfectly wonderful things that time and again showed how much she loved him. And for all the times he had accused her of unfaithfulness, it would be a betrayal of *her* if he should allow the foolish pandering of the frightened man before him to influence his opinion of her fidelity.

Which meant Christine was indeed gone, but not of her own volition.

This man had orchestrated the kidnap of his wife and daughter.

And were men not allowed to defend their families?

The lasso released a satisfying song as it made its journey across the short space and around the Persian's neck. He took no joy in the killing, but the rapture of knowing—without a shadow of doubt or apprehension— that he was *lying* about his wife overruled any feeling of remorse.

Perhaps he should have.

Perhaps at the last moment he should have loosened his hold—let their little cottage remain undefiled of murder and death. But this did not feel as other murders had, and after all, should he not be the judge? He did not kill this man out of malice, or hatred, but for the simple reason that he was the ultimate threat to his wife—had *acted* out his harmful purposes against his wife and daughter, and therefore as a husband he had the right to defend.

Therefore his only regret as he eyed the now lifeless corpse—he shook his head ruefully that it *still* did not look like him, even though this man was most assuredly deceased—was that he did not know the immediate location of his family.

But the man was determined to see them lost to Erik, and it was unlikely he would have divulged their location without precious moments being lost with the mundane of torture and pain finally leading to his ultimate demise—still without the imperative knowledge.

And though he wanted nothing more than to rush to his wife's side, wherever it may be—save her from whatever torment she was facing because of this man's stupidity and lack of compassion, he *would not* bring his family back to a home that had a decomposing carcass slumped in the study.

He had been a friend at one time, and in memory of his companionship, he would be given a grave—shallow though it would be since he *was* sincerely pressed for time.

And even as he lifted the monumental dead weight and pulled it from the house, Erik was well aware he would be spending a good deal of time in the little chapel, confessing the sin he had just committed.

Such an odd thing.

Even as his fingers trembled that the deed was not yet finished—that nothing was as important as the immediate retrieval of his Christine—the foresight that at some point he would seek forgiveness was an oddity.

But something he was sure his wife would be proud of—and after all, did that not make it worth it?

He was rather ashamed of how easy it was to remember the proper way to dispose of a body, though he did make slight attempts to ensure the sanctity of the site, though not by much. Erik did mutter a quiet, "May God have mercy on your soul," before nearly running to the stable.

Too much time had passed already.

His hands nearly shook as he saddled their horse—a horse he was amazed had not even been named as of yet. Though he supposed *he* was the one who took to naming things in their marriage, Christine always seemed to be the type to find it necessary to name every living thing, and he found it odd that in this case she would not have proposed anything.

Perhaps he had something else for which to apologise.

He did not know from where the thought came, perhaps God revealing some existential plan beyond their tenuous relationship, but he vowed that should they be blessed with another child, Christine should be the one to name him.

So long as she named him decently.

He refused to wonder if they should even be given the opportunity for such an occurrence, or if his wife was lost in the maze of the blasted Persian's games.

And he did not want to think. The thought of pondering how many places she could be—at whose hands she might be at the mercy of—filled him with such rage he could barely mange to place the bit in the horse's not quite willing mouth. Soft. Gentle. How he had been to Christine last night before their argument over nothing.

Oh God, it *hurt*.

Then the bit was in, the saddle tightened, and he was urging the mare more accustomed to the steady pace of carriage pulling than the thunderous speed Erik wished to go.

Slow. Gentle.

He would find her. He would pull her into his arms and *beg* her forgiveness for ever allowing her to go alone. He should have followed her, should have kept her safe no matter what his own insignificant wishes were. For she was more important. Without her, he *had* no needs.

Erik had not taken time to don his hat, nor his gloves, and not even his cloak before he escaped into the evening air. It was too light, and people could see, and the only small comfort he afforded was that the lasso was tied firmly to the saddle.

But he was not afraid.

Not when the feel of the leather reins against his skin made him think only of the small suckling mouth that contented herself with his littlest finger when her mother was otherwise busied.

Any manner of force could attempt to stop him from regaining what was lost, and he did not fear them.

What God hath joined together, let no man put asunder.

Their union was blessed by *God*.

It had meant nothing to him at the time. In truth, he had forced the ordained marriage simply to spite Christine—to make *her* believe they were truly married. He thought them married the moment her trembling fingers had touched the Scorpion.

But now he realised his error.

So many things in his sad, pathetic existence had been about survival. Thieving, murdering, even his own talents had been used to simply continue living—though at the time he was not certain why. But perhaps all of that was the means to an end.

He saved a young girl from the despair of being alone—the same despair he knew so deeply in his very soul. And even though he treated her cruelly in the beginning—the desperate lashing of a man so badly hurt by her continued ignorance—she had come to love him. And they had begot a *child*.

A child christened in a church, by a priest who had blessed her with holy water. *His* child. And how could he have proclaimed the rightness of her birth if he had not married her mother in the same structure?

Only *that* would have tainted her.

Marriage was in fact ordained by God. And it amazed him how clearly his faith was built upon such a blessing.

He had been riding down the familiar lanes, urging the mare that haste was imperative, when it became necessary to select a definitive location.

Erik refused to consider his wife and his daughter would be in differing places—surely the newly deceased Persian would not have been so cruel. He made a noise of disbelief. Yes, he *had* proven himself to be so cruel. And he certainly had paid for it.

Perhaps he had taken her back to the Opera house, to her little friends who would titter over her experiences with the Opera Ghost, and gasp in horror at all the right places when she regaled her more *intimate* experiences.

But he did not believe that.

At one time he might have, that she was simply toying with him and at any moment would abandon him and be greeted with sympathy wherever she went.

But not now. *Never* now.

He had mentioned the *boy*—that she had requested being returned to him. Could it truly be that simple?

Christine had gone there many times during her secret *courtship* with the whelp, and he had followed her once. He would not pretend that his intentions were wholly honourable as he had gone to determine how *physical* their relationship had progressed.

His concerns had been unfounded.

While the amount of smiles she bestowed upon the boy still made him nauseous, the extent of their contact was relegated to a brushing of hands when Christine poured their tea, or harmlessly brushed stray crumbs from his jacket.

Not that his blood did not boil at the sight.

But as he looked back on those times, the level of anger was simply not the same. He had the love of his wife, and to be resentful of her for those childish moments with her friend seemed almost beneath him. For in the end, was it not *him* who had enjoyed Christine to the fullest?

But the Daroga would not have seen that. He would have noticed his wife's smiles at the boy and determined that to be love, and so erringly, he would have returned her to him.

Someplace she did *not* belong.

She belonged in a yellow cottage, where roses would grow and flowers would open at her approach, and soon little pattering feet would grace the hallways. She belonged in the home *he* had given her.

And he would be damned if she were kept from it.

So guiding the horse that *finally* was understanding its master's urgency, he pressed on to the home of the *Vicomte de Chagny*...

Except...

On the same day Christine had sacrificed her maiden name for that of her nameless husband, the boy was also given a new title.

Upon the death of his brother.

What a pity.

XXXV

This was not the well kempt man she knew nearly a year ago.

Had it truly been so long?

His eyes were glassy, and he seemed almost as though he could not focus on her—which in truth suited her just fine. He had the sad makings of a beard which belayed his continued youth as it was patchy and not at all becoming.

But it was Raoul.

"Leave us, Pierre."

Christine wanted to turn and refute the order, but before she could even move the door was once more shut and she was entirely alone with this unknown man.

How much could drink truly change a person?

She supposed she would quickly find out.

"Is that really you, Christine? Why are you so far away?" Her back was nearly pressed against the door, and by no means did she wish to come any closer. Though the fire was tempting after her long exposure to the cold, that would also mean getting closer to *him*, and she could not help feeling quite wary at the prospect.

"I thought he took you for your voice, but now it seems he stolen it away from you, Little Lotte." He chuckled, and it was not at all the carefree sound she remembered. "Come here Christine, I know he has hurt you, but I promise I shall not."

She could feel the indignant anger at his assumption trying to overcome the feelings of fear and trepidation, and it almost succeeded—that is until he nearly staggered out of his chair and approached her.

Christine did not know what she expected. A slap for her supposed infidelity? A rough handling against the door?

But neither came as he softly touched her arm and his eyes turned pleading. "Come sit with me, Lotte. That is all I ask."

If she moved of her own volition he would cease touching her. If she remained, he would further try to coax her toward the fire, and she desperately wanted his hands off her skin.

Curse her decision not to wear long sleeves!

She nodded slowly, and he seemed satisfied when she moved to the chair next to the one he had just vacated. Catherine chose that moment to protest her mother's clutching, and one of her more normal cries resounded through the room.

Catherine would very soon be hungry, and Christine prayed she would not have to resort to feeding her in front of Raoul.

The man in question had not reseated himself, but instead was looming above her—though she was happy to note he was not at all as imposing as her husband could be—staring down at the whimpering, mewling bundle in her arms. "Is that her?"

His tone was soft, and though her first instinct was to make a biting retort that *yes*, this was in fact Erik's child, he did not seem to begrudge her parentage, but was simply inquiring.

Perhaps he was not so very changed.

"This is Catherine." For the first time her eyes met his, for she was determined he would not misunderstand. "She is my daughter."

Perhaps it was not necessary to point out, but for one terrifying moment she wondered if they would dispose of her little *enfant* simply because they so misjudged her father. To them he was a monster of legend, preying on the innocent and murdering as he pleased.

And this was *his* child.

But if they could understand that little Catherine was just as much *hers*, perhaps they would be content to allow her to remain in her charge—until Erik came for them.

How she wished he would hurry!

If Raoul was offended by her statement he did not let on, but simply nodded in acknowledgement before once more turning his gaze to the infant. "May I hold her?"

The idea of anyone holding her little *enfant* other than herself or Erik seemed repugnant. But she did not want to offend him, not for some misplaced sense of civility, but simply for the fact she was not certain of just how he would react.

What if he became angry?

So she held Catherine a little tighter against her chest, trying to stay mindful of her daughter's protest from earlier at such contact, and looked at Raoul rather pleadingly. "Please, he would not let me hold her very long on the way here."

Not quite true, but true enough for the feelings to surface as she remembered how he had refused her entreaties in the market.

His eyes lost some of their glazed quality and she could see sparks of anger. "He would not let you hold your baby?"

Though still furious that he would be in any way involved in her abduction, she still relaxed slightly that he should be upset at such a notion. And he acknowledged Catherine was *hers*, which was something was it not?

Raoul sighed then and sank back into his chair, reaching for his crystal tumbler as he did so. "God, I have missed you, Christine."

It would have been appropriate to respond in kind—to assure him that she was in as much want of his company as he was of hers, but such would have been a lie, and most assuredly would have given him the wrong impression.

So instead she forced herself to settle back as well, and pretend at least she was at ease. "How have you been, Raoul?"

It still felt so very odd to speak his name aloud.

His turned to her sharply. "Should I not be asking you that question? You were the one who disappeared. You are the one with the..." He stopped himself from finishing the statement, but it was obvious from his gaze he was looking once more at Catherine.

She dearly hoped he was not imagining her conception.

But by the wrinkle in his nose, and the way his hands pulled roughly at his untrimmed hair, he was doing just that. "Did he force you?"

"*No.*" There was no thought of consequence as the word had flown out of her lips before she had chance to truly even think it. "It was not like that."

If possible, he seemed even more pained. "How *could* you Christine? He nearly killed me! He *killed* my brother!"

What?

For the first time since this whole wretched business had begun, her thoughts stumbled in Erik's defence. Philippe had been killed?

"What are you speaking of?"

Raoul snorted. "He did not tell you? Philippe drowned in the lake that day." He made a gesture over his person. "You are looking at the new Comte de Chagny."

His careless façade crumbled for a moment, and the sympathy for her friend came forth almost entirely without her consent. "I am sorry about your brother."

He looked at her sharply. "Are you? You seem to have forgotten all about me! The Persian told me as much." The last part was muttered in an angry breath, and Christine dearly wished she had the opportunity to have at least hit the man. She would have treasured such a prospect.

"I did not forget you, Raoul." There was no possible way this conversation could end well. If she admitted her love for Erik, it would serve as nothing more than confirmation of her inability to make up her mind. If she confirmed that she did still harbour feelings of affection—no matter how *slight* they were—toward her childhood friend, that would only make the sting of her intimacy with Erik more poignant.

"You slept with him." His tone was accusing, as were his eyes, and quite ridiculously, Christine heard Erik's voice in her head from so many weeks ago.

There is a child in the room.

She could have coddled him, twisted her marriage into the story of harrowing experiences he wished for it to have been. But that was dishonest, and though she knew Catherine was so very young, she *believed* Erik when he wished for them to be sensitive to what her infant mind should be exposed to.

And she would *never* say such things of her father.

"I was with my *husband*, Raoul. I did nothing wrong. There was a priest, there were vows, and whether or not I had been with Erik by choice, when it came time to speak my portion, I did so. And I did miss you, so very much! But I had to let you go."

He was shaking his head, almost as if he were trying to dislodge the words and their sincerity, before he turned to her. "Why did you not try to escape? I would still have taken care of you! I will *still* take care of you!"

"Is that what this is to be? You will deny me my rights to see my husband, for my daughter to see her *father* simply because you wish it? How is that so different from what Erik did?"

He rose swiftly from his chair. "Because I love you!"

Because he loved her. So simple, yet utterly meaningless when faced with the blinding reality of the things that matter most.

"And I loved you. But what would you have me do? Torture him with denying him my company? He deserves better than that!" Christine felt dreadful after her outburst as Catherine was once more equally upset, and her lungs had never fully settled from her last bout of hysterics. There was a distinct wheeze, and it sounded as if each breath was pulled painfully into her body, and Christine wanted nothing more than *Erik* to be here so he might tell her what to do.

Raoul just looked at her with a dumbfounded expression. "What's wrong with her?"

"I do not know! Erik thinks there may be something wrong with her lungs from being born so early, but it has never been this bad before!" Her anxiety was doing nothing to calm her little *enfant* and she took deep calming breaths to steady herself before choosing to resolutely ignore the man beside her and focus solely on her daughter.

Cuddling her close to her chest, but ensuring the baby's face was still within the proper space to receive plenty of air, Christine began to hum. But hearing the tune so often that was issued from Erik's own lips made her want to cry, but she *could not,* not when she was trying to remain calm enough so Catherine would follow suit.

It took quite some time before Catherine quieted and her breathing sounded relatively normal. Raoul remained blessedly silent as he watched mother and daughter—though Christine refused to thank him for it. "You love her."

Christine's eyes snapped to his, and she knew her expression was utterly furious though she willed her voice to remain low. "Of *course* I love her. As I love her *father.*" She stroked her daughter's downy hair for a moment and allowed the tears to well. "I do not want to be here, Raoul."

Raoul sighed and once more took his place beside her. "This was not how this was supposed to happen."

Christine looked to him, hoping he would simply continue explaining whatever idiotic plan the Persian had concocted, but after he remained silent it became obvious prompting was in order. "What *was* to happen? I am brought here and we simply restart our lives as they would have been?"

He tugged once more at his hair and then scratched the scraps of his beard in frustration. "I was not quite *that* naïve, Christine. He said you were confused, that you could not think straight while you were still living with him, and that you had a," he gulped and resolutely looked away from her and turned his gaze to the fire. "You had a child, but Erik was too unstable to care for it."

"*Her.* She is not an *it.*"

He nodded but remained quiet. "I was going to take care of you. *Heal* you from what he must have put you through for all these months." He chuckled humourlessly. "I was looking for you, you know. Every day I tried to go back into the lair, but finally my sister told me the estate deserved more attention than I was giving it. Philippe would have been insulted." His voice cracked at the mention of his brother, and that small stirring of compassion Christine had for her friend came forth once more.

"I am sorry you have been hurt, I never wished for that." When she looked at it him again she saw him truly for the first time. At first she had been startled by how changed he was, but now she saw he was simply a boy who had been forced to shoulder the burden of loss far too quickly. He had lost the brother who had raised him faithfully for years, as well as the woman he had loved.

But though she felt such compassion for him—wished to comfort him and ease his troubled mind—she knew with absolute certainty that was not her place.

Her place was at home, with her husband and daughter, comforting *Erik* when the cares of the world threatened to overwhelm him. And though she would do everything in her limited power to ensure she was returned, perhaps this was not such a very bad happening after all.

Perhaps now he could let her go.

"Do you see now that is not the case? Will you let me go home?" Her voice was soft and pleading and she hoped it would be more persuasive to him than a command.

He scrubbed furiously at his face and Christine was rather horrified to see tears had escaped his eyes. "We will not discuss that tonight."

Her stomach dropped. "You would hold me prisoner?"

He sighed once more, and Christine noted how his sighs did little to influence her when compared to the expressive ones produced by her husband.

"I need to think, Lotte, and you should rest. I'll have supper brought up to your room."

Tears of frustration began to fall and her words became choked in her throat. "*Please* just let me go home!" She did not want to sleep here. She had done it before, but only on the rarest of occasions when it had been so late at night it proved dangerous to return to her room in the dormitories.

But Raoul ignored her pleas and called for the footman to escort her to the same room she had occupied before.

She had not even fully left the room before this voice called out once more. "Christine, please try to be happy here for now. I know you are confused, but if you could try for your *Erik,* perhaps you can try for me."

No, she could not.

She followed the footman dazedly, ignoring the biting way Raoul spoke Erik's name and she thought of how her experiences were now so very similar.

But she could not go through this again—forcing herself to love a man when she had chosen to love another. It was impossible to duplicate.

Most assuredly the room was grand, with lush fabrics and an airy feel, but Christine hated it. She was reminded too much of her beginning days with Erik, when her will was stripped to nothingness and entirely disregarded.

Such days were supposed to have been over.

Would she never be allowed to simply be happy with the man of her choice?

She *chose* Erik!

Catherine was whimpering, and thankfully the wheeze seemed to have abated enough for the moment that Christine did not fear feeding her. Not in the sense of blocking her delicate airway, but she did not relish the thought of disrobing in this foreign place.

For it did feel strange and unfamiliar.

There were too many people milling about—servants and certainly that friend of his that had also refused her pleas to be returned home. She was used to the quiet of her little family and the occasional snipping of the gardener as he tended to their property.

So it was with quiet sobs she began to nurse her baby, but she chuckled despite herself when Catherine would give her a bewildered look when the nipple would fall from her mouth at a particularly shuddering cry. "I am sorry, little *enfant*."

She tried to think of anything else so Catherine could eat in peace, but she found it increasingly difficult as her thoughts constantly strayed to what Erik might be enduring in her absence. Did he know she was missing?

The Persian had said he was going to explain things to him, but she highly doubted he was going to do so in a manner that at all resembled the truth. Instead it was most likely a convoluted massacre of how she had begged to return to the drunken man a floor below.

Would Erik believe him?

Was he even coming for her?

Catherine had sufficiently tired herself with tears, and had fallen asleep soon after finishing her meal and Christine was anxious to see her settled so she could dissolve into tears herself.

Though she was still a captive in his home, she was at least grateful to see nursery items scattered throughout the room. The most pressing of which were the crisp white diapers situated on top of the dressing table— surely not a permanent home for them, but simply placed so she would know of their existence.

Her daughter barely moved or protested the manipulation of cloth, and soon was happily settled in the bassinet in the corner.

It was only because Catherine so desperately needed rest that Christine relinquished her hold, for the very last thing she desired was to be alone in this place. Catherine was her only feeling of *home*, and with her doubt that Erik would actually have faith in her enough to see through whatever stories the Persian told had her feeling desolate.

The bed was too cold, too hard, and there was none of the gauzy materials that she loved to burrow in with Erik. It was too formal and stringent, and she was rather surprised to note how very telling that was.

For all of Erik's pomp and formality of manner, the home he provided her was one of comfort and happiness—entirely lacking in gaudy trimmings and priceless artefacts.

There is a child in the room, Christine.

And as she sobbed, Erik's words echoing in her mind for the second time that night, she thought of why in their little underground home there had been such things. It had been warm and comfortable—at least when he had refurnished the fireplace for her—but their cottage was different.

For he bought it for Catherine.

For his *family*.

And little ones who would toddle around the house would never be able to play safely with such precarious items that were easily broken.

She had wanted such a family with Raoul at one time. They would have lived in this very house, and while their bedroom would have been different, the effect would still be the same.

Christine felt no love here.

She could leave. She had a few *francs* still in her purse that could pay the cab fare, and she could attempt to make her way home unaccompanied. But in doing so, would she face even greater dangers? Erik would want her to be safe. She had to keep *Catherine* safe, and a woman travelling such a distance on her own was dangerous.

She certainly had knowledge of that.

But if he would not come, what choice did she have? She would not stay here. She would not *ever* allow Raoul to play father to her baby when she had her *own* waiting at home.

The Opera house. She could go there. It was a safe enough distance from Raoul's home and she knew the streets well, so there was little chance of being accosted along the way. She was not certain she could brave the tunnels to actually remain *in* their other home, but at the very least she could send word to Erik that she was awaiting his coming.

So it was simply to wait until morning. She could do that. Her tears were already abating now that she had formulated a relatively well conceived plan that would put neither herself nor Catherine in unnecessary danger.

How she longed to argue with Erik over just some such thing!

She would have patience. Eat the food Raoul said he would provide for both her own sake and her little *enfant's*, then early in the morning she would slip out the front door and not look back.

Raoul would move on. He would grieve his brother's passing, and perhaps even the loss of his fiancée, but she would carry no great pity for him as she once more embraced the role of motherhood and wifedom. She did not belong in this world any longer.

She belonged with her husband.

Even though the baby made a quiet protest to the movement, Christine still carried her to the bed, not being able to stand the loneliness she felt as she tried to rest.

But her plan safely in her head, and her baby once more sleeping in her arms, she found she could do just that.

And she was entirely unprepared for the loud banging that proceeded downstairs.

Perhaps Erik had not remained home after all.

XXXVI

Erik had never felt such desperation as when the hour long ride to the *boy's* house seemed to take far longer than it should. While he was grateful when the sun began to sink for the protection it afforded his identity, it also indicated even more time had passed without his Christine.

And would that bastard have even thought to provide care items for Catherine?

But *finally* when he had seriously considered abandoning the horse in favour of running himself, simply for the benefit of feeling as though *he* was doing something productive, the district changed to the posh variety so favoured by the fop. His Christine did not belong here.

She belonged in a little yellow cottage where the sun glittered in her hair. And she would be there again. *Soon.*

He had no patience for stabling the horse, and he made a whispered promise that the mare would receive far better treatment in future—just as soon as her mistress was properly returned.

The horse merely nickered in response, and Erik took that as absolution of guilt for not watering the animal. Perhaps one of the fop's servants would see to it. Make themselves useful for a change.

But then his eyes fully settled on the house, and he no longer cared about anything besides the possibility that his poor wife might be frightened, or God forbid, *hurt.*

Erik supposed the front door was locked, but he never would know with the force he applied to his entry. It surprised even him the absolute rage he felt when faced with the obstacle, and unlike the nearly silent stealth that was his usual conduct, this robust display felt rather satisfying.

A man was coming toward him, rambling something inconsequential that he was not allowed an audience with such an entry. Stupid man. What about him made it seem as though Erik was *asking?*

"Where is your master?" Erik made his tone as stern as possible, and though the man shook slightly, he again stated he would not allow him to pass.

Erik rolled his eyes, and wondered if his extended time with Christine had softened him thereby making him less intimidating to his fellow man. His lip curled at the thought and he took a menacing step forward. "The location of your master, or I shall cease your ability to use your feet. That would make your ability to pitter and patter throughout a home which is not your own rather difficult, would you not agree?"

The man finally had the presence of mind to look properly terrified, and he lifted a trembling hand to point the direction. "He is in the study, sir. Up the stairs, second door on the left." Much better.

Time management was essential as it was quite probable the man would send for the gendarme as soon as Erik was out of sight. But for once *Erik* was in the right—contingent upon Christine actually being located here of course.

And as he approached the study door, he very nearly could *feel* that he had chosen correctly.

His wife had been here.

Perhaps it was years of treasuring whatever small doses of her he was allowed behind darkened corners, but he could swear he smelled the faintest trace of her scent lingering in the doorway. Subtlety once more became his method of choice as he quietly slipped into the room, shutting the door behind him.

"I said we would discuss it tomorrow, Christine!"

Erik's fists clenched at the harsh manner he intended to address *his* wife. He steadfastly refused to consider how *he* had spoken to her that morning. God, had it only been that morning?

"You confess your involvement quite readily, boy." The boy in question staggered from his chair to face the newcomer.

"You!"

Erik rolled his eyes for the second time since entering the house. "Yes yes, monster, murderer of your brother and tormenter of your fiancée. I can assure you, I am not interested in your posturing."

It was quite obvious the fop was intoxicated, which only furthered Erik's fury. How dare he appear so in front of Christine! And by God, if Catherine had seen...

"Give me my family, Comte, and I shall spare you for your idiocy."

Raoul scowled and returned to his seat though his hate filled gaze never wavered from Erik. "You do not *deserve* such a family."

Was that true? At one time he would have argued that he did—that it was his due for the torment heaped upon him since birth. But now that he had received it, he realised his folly. He was *blessed* with his family—they were not simply payment for his past wrongs.

Oh how he wanted his Christine!

And so even though his fists were still tightly clenched, he shrugged his shoulders in acknowledgement. "Regardless, they *are* mine. And they shall return with me." His eyes flashed. "Now."

The boy was sulking. How different one's life appeared when there was nothing to live for. He cared not if Erik hurt him if it meant losing that which did not belong to him, so he did not heed any of Erik's demands but simply remained flickering his gaze between the fire and Erik's own flaming eyes.

And he very nearly gave him his wish.

But just as his fingers drifted over the lasso, the door unlatched, and he quickly turned to assess the new threat.

The curls that came flying toward him most certainly belonged to no threat.

"Erik!" Whatever doubt he may have possess—no matter how small— as to Christine actually desiring him to come for her and their daughter melted away when she nearly leapt into his arms and refused to be parted from him. "You came for me! I was afraid you would not!"

Attempting to remain mindful of the unwanted witness to their reunion, Erik firmly stifled the tears of relief that threatened to fall. He swallowed inaudibly as he clutched Christine with equal fervour. "That is because you are a silly wife, my Christine." He kissed her pretty head. "Do you now relent that cream is highly unnecessary?"

Christine released a mixture of a sob and a giggle before raising her tear stained face to his. "Perhaps you will come with me next time." Her voice was small, and though she had laughed, he could still see the residual fear of her ordeal.

He touched her cheek gently as he subdued the guilt that threatened to overwhelm him. "Always."

As he felt her arms tighten around his torso, a feeling of dread settled in his stomach. "My love, where is Catherine?"

Her face was still buried in his chest so her answer was muffled. "Sleeping upstairs. I heard a noise and thought it might be you." She nuzzled his chest slightly, almost as though trying to burrow into his very skin. "I hoped it was you."

He kissed the tops of her curls once more and was fully intent on retrieving his daughter and never giving the fop a second thought. His lovely wife had other intentions.

"I am going *home* now Raoul, with my *husband.* I am very sorry for the loss of your brother, but please do not try to contact me in future." She had pulled her head from Erik's chest and stood tall and proud beside him.

How he adored her!

She took his hand and left a teary looking Raoul behind her without looking back.

The walk to her *prison* chamber—for no room in this house could ever truly be considered hers—was dark and formal, but he relished it, even with the niggling feeling that they must depart as quickly as possible.

He felt no great regret at leaving the boy alive as it was quite plain the Persian was the great schemer of their little plan. And though he was loath to admit it, he understood the pain of losing Christine to another and the desperate longing to regain her affections.

So he would live, but that did not mean *they* were safe in his presence. The threat of the gendarme was still very real and pressed heavily on his mind.

But for just a moment he pushed such thoughts away as Christine—still with tight hold of his hand—led him to the bassinet in the corner of the bed chamber.

It pleased him that the bedding was the exact shade of yellow that made his Cat appear sallow, simply further evidencing the incapability of the numb skulls who threatened to remove her from his care. And so though she must have been exhausted, he was anxious to remove her from the things that were not her own and held her gratefully in one arm as he held tightly to Christine with the other.

He was *home*.

It should have bothered him that he was embracing his little family with the same hands that had killed a man not two hours before, but it did not.

He simply felt as though he was capable of protecting those who depended on him most, and was not that the responsibility of every husband and father?

"Come along, my wife, it is time to depart."

She beamed at him as she donned the cloak she had worn that morning and tucked a few extra diapers in the pockets of the lining. "It is not as though they shall be missed," she muttered to herself to excuse her supposed theft.

Erik chuckled and held out a hand for her to take as they rapidly fled the house.

The brown mare awaited them and Erik had a great swelling of satisfaction when he saw patches of missing greenery in the otherwise pristine lawn. *Good girl.*

Christine was eying the horse with resignation, and he recalled her protestation of such travel when Catherine was involved. "We have little choice, Christine."

"Darling," her voice was sarcastic even as she used the unfamiliar expression of endearment. But Erik would accept any form of word from her just so her eyes would glitter with humour instead of tears. "I trust you, and I just would like to go home."

And he wanted nothing more.

Quite reluctantly he passed his Cat to Christine and hoisted her onto the mare's awaiting saddle before following himself. He held her tightly with one arm as his other was occupied with the reins, and the anxiousness to be away from this place settled once more upon him.

Catherine was crying, and no matter of shushing or humming from Christine could seem to quiet her, and it was becoming quite apparent that the longer she fussed the more agitated she became. "Erik, I think we should stay elsewhere tonight to let her rest."

There was something in her tone that worried him. There was something she had not yet told him, which should not surprise him since they had little time to truly speak since they were reunited. "Surely she will calm soon."

And then to his horror, Christine began to cry once more. "I was so frightened! She kept crying, and her lungs did not sound quite right, and the Persian would not allow me to take her to a physician."

Any thoughts of remorse for the death of the man flew from his mind.

Though he wanted nothing more than to get them all safely back to their sunshiny home where they belonged, the health of his daughter was of far more importance than his own desires.

If he had learned anything this day, it was certainly to put others first.

He had not expected to return there so soon, and it felt almost wrong to do so. This was from a different time that Catherine had no business bearing witness to.

But it was *for* her they were here, and he reminded himself of that fact many times as the looming presence of the Opera house came before them.

Grumbling all the while, Erik stopped almost to the Rue Scribe entrance, but he put a restraining hand on Christine when she made to slide off the saddle. "Not yet, my love." It seemed natural to refer to her as his dearest love, and he wondered why he never had before. Was he truly so secretive with his thoughts and feelings? It seemed to him as though Christine was the one difficult to read.

But this stop was necessary if he was to keep another vow he had made.

It was childish of him, but he always received a bit of a thrill that the managers passed some of their own *francs* whenever they passed this side of the Opera house. It was simply a loose stone where he had stashed a few, never with true intention of spending them.

Times like these made him sincerely glad for his dramatic inclinations.

Retrieving the funds was not complicated, and it was to a curious Christine he returned. "You shall see," he murmured softly in her ear, once more mounting the horse behind her.

And in truth, it became quite obvious why he needed the *francs* when he bribed a stable boy to tend to the horse. The boy was wide eyed as he took the money from the masked man, but held his tongue and simply nodded that she would be cared for.

Erik held tightly to Christine's waist as he helped her from the saddle, and she kissed his porcelain cheek in her decent. "You are very thoughtful, Erik."

Giving the stable boy one last glance, he once more took Catherine in his arms and slipped his hand into Christine's. "Hush wife, I have a reputation to uphold."

She merely cuddled into his side in response.

It surprised him how his eyes had changed in the weeks he had spent aboveground. While he had every nuisance of the darkness committed to memory, he relied more on such memories than his customary vision.

Life with Christine truly had softened him.

Perhaps it should trouble him more than it did.

Catherine had not stopped mewling since they had left the fop's house, and he was glad Christine had expressed her desire to remain in Paris for the night so he did not feel the sting of disappointing her when he made the conclusion himself.

And if they had waited, it would have been necessary to remain in an *inn*.

Perish the thought.

But Christine had such faith in him that he would lead them safely back into their little darkened home, and her confidence in him warmed his heart. And soon enough they were crossing the lake, listening to Cat's cries echo throughout the chamber.

Christine waited patiently holding the mewling baby as Erik fiddled with the door. It was not as easy to open as it was before, and he supposed if it became necessary they remain here any longer he should begin its maintenance.

He pushed such thoughts away.

They would return *home*.

Even though he was tempted to keep them here forever—where no one else could possibly dream of entering now that the Daroga was once more committed to the earth—he refused to allow them to hide. Discretion was important, but hiding away his love for Christine was not something he desired.

With a squeal the door relented to his ministrations, and he returned to the boat to aid Christine into the house. She still leaned heavily on his arm as the rooms were in total darkness, and he seated her in the settee before lighting one of the kerosene lamps.

Thankfully not everything had suffered without his presence.

Christine took in the sight of their previous home with wide eyes as Erik busied himself with building a fire to warm the freezing space.

Even to him it was cold.

He had no gloves, nor his cloak, and he was grateful Christine had her own to aid in keeping Catherine comfortable—though her cries certainly expressed her dissatisfaction in the arrangement.

Erik was rather glad they had left so many things behind, though his intention at the time was most assuredly not to keep this as an underground getaway should some peril befall them. But wood was still neatly stacked beside the fire, so with some kindling and coaxing, a cheerful blaze appeared and Erik was able to once more resume his position beside Christine who quickly passed a more quiet, but still discontent Catherine into his arms.

"Perhaps she will listen to her father, because she will not quiet for me."

He nodded solemnly, as it was upon many occasions his Cat was soothed more by his voice than that of her mother—though how anyone could be disillusioned to the angelic quality of Christine's voice he was not certain.

Perhaps it was the tremendous amount of sugar she consumed that tainted her vocal chords.

He sniffed at the thought, but began humming nonetheless.

But it was not until he had placed his littlest finger into her mouth and she began to suckle on it that she truly quieted and eventually fell asleep. Apparently his fingers held more sway over her moods than his voice.

Erik warmed at the thought.

Christine looked drowsy, but her stomach rumbled in protest, and Erik reminded himself that his own emotions could be felt by those closest to him, otherwise he would have made it known how very disgusted he was that she should have been denied nourishment.

And there was most certainly nothing edible remaining in the house.

He sighed, but accepted the unavoidable conclusion that he would be forced to make use of the Opera's kitchens in order to feed his poor wife before she could slip into unconsciousness.

It was not as though he could take her on his quest—not when Catherine was so very tired.

"I must go above, Christine, but you will be safe here until I return."

She shook her head furiously, and clutched at his arm. "You most certainly will *not* leave me!"

He had expected pleading, or possibly even tears though he did not relish the thought, but he did not expect her adamant statement as to his proposed action. Erik frowned at her. "You are hungry and I believe very much against the concept of starving, therefore I shall be required to fetch you some supper." His voice had been firm but he softened when the inevitable tears pooled, and if his hands were not occupied with Catherine he would have stroked her cheek in comfort.

But that did not mean that she could not be soothed through his voice, even if his Cat refused such placation. He leaned carefully down so as not to jostle the finally sleeping infant, and whispered gently in her ear. "Rest your tired eyes, my wife, and your husband shall be here when you awake." His lips caressed her flesh, and he relished the fluttering of her eyelids as she closed them. "With *food*."

Her stomach relayed her consent even though her lips did not, and he kissed her once more before standing.

Because he had not informed Christine of their relocation before Cat had graced them with her presence, his home was still prepared for the welcoming of an infant, including essentials such as clothing and bedding.

But it had been a trying day to put it mildly, and so ever so gently, instead of placing his precious daughter in the bassinet, he laid her upon their original marriage bed. Christine was already shuffling after them. "Must you go?"

She looked so like the child she once was. Gone was the pretence of strength she had adorned when the fate of herself and little Catherine were at stake, and she was once more looking at him with large blue eyes that pleaded for his attentions.

A sharp pain drove through his heart that he should be forced to refuse her.

"Yes." Erik could manage no more words than that or else he should beg her stomach to just forget the feeling of hunger so he might not have to leave her after all.

But Catherine would once more have to nurse before daybreak, and Christine's own body needed sustenance to be able to sustain such provisions.

And so he waited until she was properly situated beside his daughter before kissing her mouth soundly for the first time that day.

Then he found leaving her to be even more difficult.

She brushed his masked cheek tenderly for a moment before closing her eyes in resignation. "You are very good to me, Erik." Her eyes were already drooping, and he kissed her once more before forcing himself to leave the room.

Before he could make his way to the above, he needed to make one final stop to his—well—he supposed his bedroom, though he had long ago ceased to think of it as such.

He had told Christine he would evict his coffin from their little home when she had invited him to share her bed, but when he learned of her pregnancy, little had been done to go through with such a promise. In her mind the room should become a nursery, but he had larger plans of moving them entirely, and he was quite pleased with how his plan had come to fruition.

That did of course mean he was once more face to face with the location of his eternal resting place.

Erik realised now the sheer morbidity of the piece. While most certainly great lengths were taken before death to ensure the funeral and embalmment were to ones satisfaction, an everyday reminder of the nature of death was not something one needed on a daily basis.

But he refused to dwell on the room as it was of little consequence now. This was no longer their home, and it was trivial how the space was furnished.

He was taking his family *home*.

So donning his cloak, gloves, and hat whilst straightening his suit, he once more resumed his ascent into the Opera house complete in his garb as resident Ghost.

But his purpose was so very different this time.

Instead of seeking fortune or amusement, he was simply stealthily passing corridors in search of treats for his napping wife so she would be well rested for their journey.

It was the first time he had stolen with a smile.

XXXVII

True to his word, when Christine's eyes fluttered open it was to the smiling, unmasked face of her husband.

At one point such a sight would have startled her, but now she was only grateful that she would have such opportunities once more granted to her. Catherine was sleeping soundly, and now that Christine was awake she was fully aware of just how hungry she had become, and she was very grateful for Erik's care.

She had seen how much it pained him to leave her, but he put her needs above his own—even when his own denied the need of nourishment too frequently.

And now he was taking her hand to lead her into the dining room.

The door to the bedroom was kept ajar in case Catherine decided she did not care to be left alone, but when Christine saw the dining room spread with fruits and even a *ham* any thought of maternal instinct flew from her mind.

She was ravenous.

Erik let out a noise crossed between a groan and a chuckle as he watched her take multiples of each item and begin eating rather impolitely. She did not even wait for him to join her after pushing her chair. "That *boy* should have fed you."

Christine took a large swallow of food and forced herself to slow. "He said a tray would be brought up eventually."

Erik gave her a piercing look. "You defend him?"

She shook her head resolutely before taking a sip of water. "Never, Erik. What he did was wrong."

He seemed to accept her response and even took a few pieces of fruit, but he seemed far more intent on pushing them around his plate with flicks of his fingers than actually eating them.

Christine in turn slowed her consumption, suddenly feeling wary of his thoughts. "What is wrong?"

Erik sighed and ran his fingers through the sparse hairs on his head, and to her horror, Christine found herself comparing the gesture to Raoul's frustrated ministrations.

She *would not* compare them!

Perhaps such resolutions were unreasonable given the happenings of the past twenty four hours, but by no means did she wish to taint Erik's mannerisms with Raoul.

It had been quite customary that they would eat lengthwise on the table, and though it was not overly long, it still leant a formal quality to the otherwise sparse room. There were other chairs lining the long side of the dark wood, more for show than for any practical use.

Until now.

Erik stood abruptly from his seat across from her and carrying his plate, walked resolutely to the seat immediately to her left and settled there, brushing her hair with his fingers as he did so.

Seemingly satisfied with their seating arrangements, he took his first bite of food before turning to face her. "Tell Erik what happened, Christine."

Oh God, she did not want to.

She wanted to forget the whole business ever happened—that her childhood friend would remain in the rosiness of her memories and never be tainted with the harsh reality of adult consequence.

But such could never be—the Persian and his blindness had seen to that.

"Tell your Erik what happened," he repeated. And then the food did not seem so very appetising and her eyes filled with tears as the remembered fear and anger easily returned.

His hand had taken hers, and though he had moved nearer, she still found him much too far away. Allowing herself the comfort of her tears, she rapidly vacated her own chair in favour of Erik's lap—and he received her readily.

And maybe, just maybe, if the words were spoken aloud and he knew of each moment since their argument that morning, he would not be so very angry with her for having disappeared. For though he had remained happy to see her, not denying his touch or sweet words, she still very much was afraid he would somehow blame her for her disappearance.

After all, *she* was the one who had left the house that afternoon without his escort.

So she told him. Over and over she stated her unwillingness to go with the man—that she had *never* meant to leave him with such permanence, until finally he stopped her. "Do you know what the Daroga said when he arrived?"

The wary shake of her head confirmed she did not.

"The foolish man said you had been in contact with him and asked for his aid in leaving me." The last words were pained but lacked the desolation she would have expected.

"Were you terribly angry with me?" Visions of Erik storming to the Chagny home with every intention of punishing his stupid wife for her perceived infidelity filled her mind.

But he held her more tightly to him and she could feel a kiss pressed upon her head. "Only for a moment, and for that I must apologise."

She pulled her head from its resting place beneath Erik's chin so she could look at him in her astonishment. "Why should you apologise? At one time I might have done so, therefore it is reasonable for you to have come to such a conclusion." She looked down ashamedly.

Erik hissed at her words but his hands were gentle as they coaxed her to look at him once more. "But you would not now."

He spoke with such confidence and without the measure of demand sometimes present when he mentioned how she should act. "And Erik *knows* that and thus he must apologise for his doubt." His fingers slipped into her hair. "*I* must apologise."

He looked as though he meant to kiss her and she ached for him to do so, but his eyes grew sad and he leaned away from her. "I killed him, Christine."

She froze, and could plainly see the fear in Erik's eyes. "Who…" her throat felt tight as she tried to force the words from her uncooperative mouth. "Who did you kill?"

And for a moment, Erik looked angry. "The *Daroga* of course. He *took* you, Christine! He took my *Cat!* And I knew you would not have left me willingly. He came into our home and said you had pleaded to be free of me, and for a moment I believed him. And Erik feels so very guilty for that!"

What was one supposed to feel when one's husband confessed to murder? Betrayal, horror, and sickening dread surely, but she felt none of these.

Christine only felt relief.

The Persian could torment them no more. No misunderstandings or possibility of future separations by his overreaching arms.

They were *free*.

That did not however stop the guilt at her lack of compassion for a man who was now deceased. If only he had left them alone, allowed them their little cocoon of happiness that Erik so rightfully deserved, he would have lived.

And did that mean she should then be angry with Erik for killing the man?

Erik was quite obviously growing distressed from her lack of speech, and it pained her to see that *his* eyes were filling with tears. But how could she speak when she had yet to reconcile her own feelings?

He had not stated his remorse for having killed him, simply for having doubted her. She had witnessed his brutality before, and he had never seemed penitent for the murdering the carriage driver either.

And she had not asked it of him.

For she was grateful for that as well.

Erik was moving her, gently placing her down in his chair so he would kneel before her as he had done so many times in the early part of their marriage. He was grasping at her hands and whispering how sorry he was again and again, kissing her palms between laments. "I shall go to the priest, Christine, I shall confess what I have done. But you must believe I did it to protect you! To protect *Catherine!*"

And was that not something she could attest to? All he wanted was to care for those who loved him, and surely God could see such things.

She did not know fully what had transpired in their home while she was away, nor did she wish to. The details were unimportant, and would in fact deter her from fully rejoicing in the sanctity of their home.

So long as he repented...

Christine cleared her throat in an attempt to regain the faculty of her voice, and she tugged impatiently at Erik's hands—though to her dismay he took that as a sign she wished for him to remove his touch from her person, and nearly keened as he released her. "You are a stupid man, husband."

She sniffled loudly before firmly yet gently—*always* gently with the delicate skin of his face—pulled his lips to hers. His grasp was frantic as he embraced her, and she felt such sorrow that he would consider she would not forgive him for the steps he had taken in securing the return of his family.

But after a moment he pulled away and secured her in his arms before abandoning the dining room in favour of the little settee that had witnessed so many of their conversations.

"While I certainly acknowledge my stupidity, perhaps you would be so kind as to expound." He was still looking at her as though she would change her mind at any moment, and she knew it was up to her own foolish understanding of communication that he could be comforted.

Still nestled on his lap, with his arms tightly around her, Christine managed to twist slightly so she was nearly straddling him. How she wished they could utilise such a position to more pleasurable standards!

But now was not the time for such things.

Now was the time for *words*.

"I am not angry with you, Erik, but I would be more comfortable if you did go see Father Martin when we have returned home." She sighed, wondering if it was worry for Erik's conscience or her own that made her wish he would seek council of the priest. "And I do not think I wish to know how it occurred."

Perhaps it *would* be better to know the details—that her mind would no longer conjure gruesome images of how Erik felt and acted as he doused the life of a man who had so wronged them.

Erik must have seen her not quite resignation on the subject for he took her face gently in his hands. "I did not kill him out of anger, my Christine, nor did I derive more satisfaction than you and our daughter would be safe."

And whatever concern she felt flew from her mind.

After all, was it not hatred that fuelled murder? Erik *had* changed in their marriage, and she felt only a sense of peace that his subtle changes had not been undone by the interference of the Persian.

But there was one matter that still weighed upon her mind. "What happened to Philippe?"

Erik sighed and distracted himself with making small patterns upon her collarbones with his fingertip. "That was an unfortunate incident, but not one I could readily have rectified.

"What do you mean?"

She could not pretend that his touch did not distract *her* as well, but it was important that she fully understand the circumstances surrounding this event, and she was terribly curious as to what Raoul had been referring.

"I am, I suppose, fully responsible for his death, as I am for any other accident that befalls those who traverse my tunnels without invitation." His expression was guarded, and he had yet to look at her. "I believe he came in search of his brother, and he made it admirably far, but the lake appeared to be too much for him."

Since Raoul had been returned the same evening of her original kidnapping, that would mean Erik had discovered the body when releasing the Persian and her friend—her *previous* friend.

What a thing to find at one's doorstep.

Perhaps she should be troubled by how numb she felt at hearing of the death of others, especially when she had somewhat known the man personally. They had met of course, but he had not overly embraced her on such occasions.

"He... drowned?" It was such a foreign concept, this idea of drowning in Erik's lake. She supposed that was simply because it never had occurred to her that Erik should *allow* her to drown, therefore it stood to reason others would also be so blessed.

Apparently they were not.

Erik nodded in response. "His body was floating in the lake." His

301

fingers pinched a bit of the material of her dress, and he finally looked at her sheepishly. "The siren did not call, but I cannot guarantee I would have aided him should I have heard it."

She knew who she had married. In her mind he was guilty of murdering *Raoul* at that point, so did it honestly make so much of a difference now that she learned of the exchange?

Erik was different now. He had offered to go to a *priest* to seek forgiveness, and surely a man who would suggest such a thing was not the same as the man she had originally married.

And she felt that in her very soul.

"Then I am sorry for Raoul's loss, but I would not seek to punish you for it."

Erik let out a shaky breath and pulled her fully into his arms. "You are such a blessed girl, Christine. I do not deserve you."

She did not wish to think anymore. Not of the morality of the past day, nor of those days filled with anger and fear when they were first married.

Christine had returned to her husband, and all she wished was to be *fully* with him once more.

It was ridiculous really, how short a period it had been since they had last been together, yet it felt as though lifetimes had passed. When faced with the possibility of eternal separation, once more being given the chance to enjoy their union was not one to be shunned.

She was suddenly very grateful for the nap she had been allowed.

But before they could fully enjoy their reunion, it was of supreme importance that she ensure that *Erik* felt comfortable doing so. *He* was the one who had doubted her willingness to remain with him, and though he had apologised multiple times, it would not do to force him into such relations when he felt it necessary to deny himself in some manner of proving himself worthy of her affections.

So she asked.

And he moaned in response. "If ever you shall have want of me, it would be a greater sin to deny you than allow my foolish thoughts to refuse what you desire."

She wanted to return to bed—to remember every sweet moment of the eight months they had shared in its confines, but when her eyes flickered to the doorway, Erik took hold of her chin. "Not in front of my daughter, Christine."

Christine very nearly huffed her annoyance.

"She is merely an infant, Erik, I am certain it would not traumatise her."

A lone eyebrow raised in response. "And you should risk such a thing?" He stroked her cheek lightly with his thumb. "She has suffered enough this day."

He was right of course. Enough tears had been spilled on her part that she was loath to speak above a whisper in case she awoke.

But that did not mean she wanted her husband any less.

Beds were highly overused in any case.

The carpet before the fire had not been used for their intimate activities since that night so long ago. While they had christened many other furniture pieces before Christine's pregnancy made more traditional means of love making to become necessary, Erik had insisted that he was far too old to be lounging about the floor, and that Christine should always be cushioned.

Though he had never said, Christine took that to mean he was once more thinking of the baby.

But she was not pregnant now, and he was already lifting her and gently lowering her to the softness of the rug. The fire had dimmed some since Erik had left, and it was altogether a romantic feel, especially when the flames mimicked the expression of Erik's eyes.

They had been through so much this day, and though it had been imperative that they slow their movements the day before to be sensitive to her recovering body, such things were far from Christine's mind.

All she knew was that she had nearly lost her Erik.

And it was that thought alone which terrified her.

She should be telling Erik of Catherine's lungs, of how they should be even more careful of her moods and sensitivities. But it would cause her even more distress should they wake her now, and so perhaps it was not so very wrong of her to find more comfort in unbuttoning Erik's shirt buttons than urging him to fetch a doctor.

Tomorrow.

They could face the consequences of today's happenings then. But for now, she would simply savour the nearly frantic need of Erik's hands as he tugged on her dress and chemise.

"Perhaps I shall have to ban *all* of your clothing as I have your corsets." His tone was low and frustrated, and for a moment she fully believed she would wake one day and find her wardrobe vacant of gowns.

"Then that is also the day you shall find you have no more masks." It was an idle threat of course, as she had no way of knowing where all of his masks were kept, or would she subject him to the ridicule he was sure to feel if he did not wear it in public.

But his expression was reproachful before he leaned over her and nipped at her neck. "Touché, wife."

And he looked entirely too smug when with a loud rip, her dress was no longer an encumbrance.

Was it dreadfully wicked that it only excited her further?

It drove her nearly mad when he pulled away long enough to shrug out of his evening coat and shirt, and she wanted nothing more than to feel him pressed against her awaiting flesh.

Curse her chemise and its confines! She wriggled uselessly as she attempted to shimmy it from her body, and Erik chuckled at her attempt. "You are not a worm, Christine."

She huffed in frustration as she was made to wait *again* as he finished divesting himself of clothing all the while not moving from his place, keeping her entirely unable to free herself and finish disrobing.

"You are an infuriating man."

Erik grinned at her in response before torturously undoing *one* button. "Then you are forever bound to a stupid, infuriating man."

When his mouth found the small scrap of skin uncovered by the lone button, Christine felt as though she was about to burst.

And she wanted *more*.

Where her sense of wantonness came from, she was not certain, but it felt entirely fair that if he was able to make her suffer through the gentility of such attentions, he could feel the pain of want just as acutely.

It was a rare occasion that Erik allowed her to touch his manhood with her fingers. She had never asked what made him so uncomfortable about the venture, but his usual response was to grasp her hand and move it above her head while he simply lavished *her* with more attentions.

But not this time.

Being careful to keep her touch gentle, she grasped him softly and smiled triumphantly at Erik's startled gasp. "You are a minx, wife."

And she returned his look impishly, and let one finger trail ever so *slightly* over him. "Then you are forever bound to a silly minx of a wife."

Though their tones were light and teasing, it was so much more than simple affirmation of their bond. For it was that very bond that had been threatened, and when Erik kissed her, she knew he felt as she did.

Through the fires of lies and plots they had been tested, and both had become the stronger for it.

And it was with teasing touches upon his most sensitive flesh, and the coaxing of her tongue upon his that she *finally* impassioned him into tearing the chemise from her all too willing body.

His skin felt glorious, and so entirely of her husband.

Cooler than the warm air that encircled them, and with the scars that scraped slightly over the sensitive skin at Erik's hands, there was nothing of the tentative movements of the night before.

This was the deep satisfaction of an ache woken in them both, and it was through only hard thrusts and panting moans of love and commitment that it could possibly be soothed.

When Christine felt the precipice of nirvana, it was only through Erik's mouth being firmly affixed over hers that her near sob of relief was silenced so as not to awake the infant sleeping not so far away.

And when it was Erik following suit, it was her turn to catch his moans in kind.

Christine felt utterly languid and sleepy when they had finished, and was perfectly content to simply sleep on the plush rug in Erik's arms, but her husband seemed to find the idea unpleasant, for he once more carried her to their bedroom.

Ever so gently he placed her beside Catherine before taking the babe into his arms—which Christine watched with bated breath that she might awake—and depositing his daughter in her bassinet.

Other than a slight twitching of her mouth at the motion, Catherine gave no further protest.

Erik returned to bed once he had retrieved nightwear for the both of them, and would not settle until Christine had reluctantly placed the nightgown over her head. "Erik, I promise you she will not remember our nudity."

He kissed her head softly before pulling her into his arms. "And I promise *you*, I shall not risk it."

Christine huffed and relented, fully looking forward to a long nights rest with her husband by her side. She was nearly asleep when Erik's voice cut through the stillness.

"You said there was something wrong with her."

Perhaps their love making was not nearly as fulfilling for him as it was for her, for she was in no mind to discuss such things in her sated state. She almost told him so, but when she looked up to glare at him, there was a line between his eyebrows and a pained expression to his eyes that showed how truly concerned he was.

So she sighed, and snuggling further into his chest at the remembered terror at her daughter's choked cries, she relayed the entirety of the day's events.

Erik was quiet, and though the hand running through her hair would pause and his body would stiffen when she spoke of certain incidents, his only comment at the end was not of rage, but of fatherly determination. "We shall see a doctor before returning home."

And a pressure she had not realised was contracted upon her heart released.

They were going *home*.

XXXVIII

Christine was completely unsurprised when she awoke to an empty bed the next morning, but was entirely disconcerted as to where she was. There was no sunshine streaming through their bedroom window, and she felt too rested to have been awakened mid sleep to feed Catherine.

Oh God.

Where was Catherine?

Scrambling from the bedclothes which had deemed to hold her captive in their confines, Christine ran from the room only to find Erik putting out hot muffins onto the dining room table of their underground home. "Erik, where is Cat?"

Her husband raised an eyebrow at the shortened name which had slipped from her lips, but she was far too concerned to notice. "Our daughter is sleeping. You passed her in your scuffle with the sheets."

It was true, the sheets had continued to cling to her even as she drew into the sitting room, and Erik could plainly see the crisp cloth upon the floor. "Why did she not want her feeding?"

Had she so misjudged her daughter's condition?

Erik drew her into his arms and patted her back soothingly. "Hush Christine, she was simply exhausted. I am certain if you go to her now she would be more than happy to breakfast with us."

She took his calm to mean he had checked on her before beginning his preparations, and confirmed she was in fact *breathing*.

So firmly telling herself to regain composure, she returned to the bedroom, muttering curses at the bedclothes as she threw them back on the bed.

Catherine was in fact breathing, and was even blinking up at her mother when she leaned down to retrieve her from her cradle. "You worried your mummy, you naughty thing!"

Christine was quite certain she was being a ridiculous mother to scold her daughter for sleeping through the night for the first time since birth. Most likely it was about time she began doing so and their impromptu excursion the night before had merely prompted the milestone into taking place.

Perhaps not *only* bad things were to come of the event.

Catherine was apparently realising she had missed her midnight supper and was beginning to make her mewling whimpers that very clearly stated her discontent.

It seemed rather ridiculous that Erik would be so against exposing Catherine to any of their more risqué marital relations, yet the idea of nursing while consuming breakfast was not objectionable. She would have blatantly refused, but Catherine was quite hungry and was even going so far as to nuzzle Christine into complacency even as she walked to the table, and her achingly full breasts seemed quite ready to oblige.

And her own stomach felt far too empty as well.

Erik did not return to the chair across from her, but continued to use the one beside her, eyeing his wife and daughter with satisfaction—even more so when Christine moaned at the hot sugary muffin he had concocted.

She forced herself to crumble small bites with her fingers so as not to drop any on her suckling daughter, even as her mind nearly screamed she devour as many as possible as quickly as she could.

Erik simply chuckled at her enthusiasm.

The relief Christine felt at the release of steadily building pressure in her breasts was palpable, and she was very grateful Catherine's hunger was congruent with the amount of milk available.

And that Erik had provided enough muffins for a rather long stay at the dining room table.

They had much to do that day, and Erik was quick to remind her of their destinations—as if they could have slipped her mind. He had not forgotten his promise to visit the priest, though she could tell it troubled him that he could not go alone.

Since she had specifically asked for him to withhold details, it would become necessary for him and Father Martin to seek solitude instead of allowing Christine and Catherine to remain at home.

There was no possibility she would willingly be out of Erik's immediate hearing for at least a month—perhaps much longer.

It did however surprise her that he was more forthcoming about acknowledging his intent on seeking absolution than he was about discussing a doctor. He cleared his throat awkwardly and began pressing muffin crumbs into differing shapes.

"I do know of a physician who would be adequate." So his distress was not at taking his daughter to a man who was incompetent.

She continued to stare at him blankly, and he thankfully expounded when she offered no comment. "I do not have my mask, Christine."

He most certainly *did* have a mask—he had been wearing it when he rescued her from Raoul's home. It was the black one that gave him his most intimidating persona, and she had supposed out of deference to her quite blatant disapproval of it had ceased wearing it since they had arrived back in the underground.

Which meant he did not have his *normal* mask.

"If he is a worthy physician, it should not be a problem." She did not add that if he was a physician she would willingly take her daughter to, he had better accept the father.

Erik scowled at her. "What interest do you think he should take in *our* daughter should he know of her parentage? I can assure you, the status of her lungs would be the least of his concerns."

Christine frowned. "Then he does not sound like the sort of man I would like to see Catherine." Her expression turned pleading when it occurred to her what he was truly suggesting. "Please do not make me see him alone."

He sighed and finished destroying the remains of his muffin. "Do not look at me like that, Christine, it pains me so."

It was terribly wretched of her, but she would gladly continue to cause his discomfort if it meant he would not force her to see to such a vital appointment by herself. "The midwife did not care so very much."

Erik snorted—a very odd sound from one without a nose. "That woman has seen every derangement possible. She used to care for the brothel only a few streets down."

Christine paled. "Then why did you..." Perhaps she was being nonsensical, but for one terrible moment she felt dreadfully hurt. He had taken her to a midwife who only dealt with *whores*. He had entrusted the birth of his *daughter* to a woman who had most likely been of ill repute herself. And though she had no argument with the midwife herself as to her care, it still pained her greatly that Erik should think her worth such treatment.

But more than that, she was hurt that he did not protect her from such influence. As her husband he was responsible now for her safety and wellbeing, and for him to willingly take her to such a street—*leaving* her there even as he went to fetch a carriage when any number of things could have happened—it was too much to bear.

If Catherine had not still been suckling greedily, Christine would have stormed from the room. Perhaps returning to this home brought about the return of her more childish instincts, but Erik's choice in help left her feeling somehow sullied.

She could not look at him.

Erik was quiet, but when he brought a hand to touch her face, she turned from him quickly. "Christine, what has troubled you?"

He was so *blind*. A husband could not admit to taking his wife to be tended by a whore's midwife and then question her anguish. And he had left her...

But her refusal of his touch must have supported that something indeed was troubling her, for she could not remember a time when she had truly denied him contact.

Erik must have been surprised as well, and he gasped at her recoil. "Christine..."

His voice was pained but she held little pity for him. Turning to him angrily, the words nearly flew from her mouth without consent. "Why would you take me to such a place? Is that what I am worth to you that I could not have a proper midwife?"

Erik was taken aback by her outburst, and look genuinely hurt at her words. "What do you know of the doctors of today?" There was nothing accusing in his tone, and she was rather surprised by his question. Should he not be apologising for his choice?

"I only ever remember going to the physician here."

He nodded, and his hands grasped at each other in an effort to keep from touching her. "And he is trained in the issues of dancers and singers, and would well remember you, so how could I take you there?"

Erik was growing more agitated as he hurried to make his explanation. Apparently the simple fact that she did not *wish* for him to touch her was enough to make not touching her unbearable as his hands continued to fidget relentlessly. "To go to an outside source proved unwise. They are more interested in propriety and maintaining the modesty of the mother than for the safety of the child."

Christine felt a growing sense of guilt as she understood what he was saying. He had chosen a woman with experience, not for the clientele she was used to, but for the ease she had in the fundamentals of childbirth.

Her suspicions were confirmed when he continued. "The same woman who tended our laundry when we resided here suggested the midwife as hers had been a difficult birth and the woman proved most capable. And also conveniently, she did not ask questions."

She was startled of course that he should *finally* allow her into his confidence as to how their laundry was cared for, and she supposed it should trouble her that he would have been employing a woman who would also have been tended by the midwife. But she was not. She only felt ashamed of the conclusion she had drawn as to Erik's reasoning, when he had only further been providing the optimum care for the child who was then unborn.

And of course it was necessary she be used to clients who required discretion. While she had come to accept Erik, it was not as though others would be as forgiving in their opinion.

"Oh Erik, I am sorry." She reached out to him just as Catherine made a rather resounding pop as she released her mother's breast.

He was still avoiding her gaze as he reached for his daughter, and Christine relinquished her rather reluctantly—not because she wanted to keep her for herself, but because *she* wished to comfort Erik.

And just because his hands were occupied did not mean she could not.

She knelt beside his chair and rested her hand against his knee—grateful that the same plush carpets adorned this room as they did the sitting room. Erik was focused solely on Catherine as he patted her back and used his napkin to shield his black suit from any fluids.

Finally he sighed and looked down at her. "Do you think so little of me?"

She pressed her lips to his pant leg, hoping the gesture would do more than the actual contact. "No, *honestly* I do not. But I wish…"

He looked at her expectantly, and she realised the stupidity of adding a statement to the end of her emphatic encouragement. "I simply wish you would confide in me more, Erik. You know I am not nearly as informed as you in the ways of the world, and it is easy for me to draw my own conclusions." She gripped his pant leg tightly. "Though they prove wrongly."

Erik nodded slowly, obviously contemplating the notion of expressing more of his reasoning for certain behaviours and choices. He had led a solitary existence, and he had most likely excluded her not for the sake of doing so, but more for being entirely out of practice in the manner of consulting another before acting.

He had been a bachelor.

And most certainly, though they had been married almost ten months now, it was not until recently they had embraced the mannerisms of most couples in terms of house and home.

While they had resided underground, it had remained Erik's domain—in their little cottage, they were equals.

She wanted to go *home*.

Catherine being satisfied with her breakfast and the attentions of her father, settled comfortably on his lap but did not seem quite interested in napping. So much the better, as Christine was anxious to begin their journey, and the more she would sleep while on horseback the more comfortable the ride would be.

Her thoughts were interrupted when Erik's hand cautiously made its way to her cheek, and it pained her that he hesitated before lightly touching her. She kissed his palm in acceptance.

His eyes were utterly vulnerable as he stared at her, and she could plainly see that her rebuff of his affections had hurt him deeply. While not the first time she had denied his touch, this was the first instance in a long while that was accompanied by angry words—and it had taken its toll.

And she was to be the one who fixed it. No matter how he might have failed to communicate intentions, she was still the one who had overreacted to a comment made in haste.

She held his hand in hers and entreated him to be patient with her. That she loved him wholly and completely and no matter what should happen when they took their little Cat to the physician, they would be together, and such should lend him strength.

He nodded his affirmation, and helped her from the floor. "If you have finished breakfasting, I believe we should be on our way."

Erik was still acting rather cold and guarded as she readied herself and he tended to Catherine. The sheets were speedily replaced to the bed, and she did not bother to bathe, wishing only to do so when she was returned to her own pretty bath at home.

It troubled her greatly when Erik only loosely held her arm as he traversed the tunnels.

How she wished to change how this morning had begun!

The darkness below had once more proven disarming as it was not yet midmorning when they emerged. She had obviously fallen asleep much earlier than she had anticipated, for she felt fully rested when she had awoken.

Erik had donned a hat and heavy cloak, and truthfully little could be seen of his face. The voluminous folds even hid Catherine as she nestled in her father's elbow, and it was not until the brown mare was saddled and brought out of the stable that Christine once more held the child.

His fingers held her gingerly as he hoisted her into the saddle, and though his arms were securely upon her waist when he came up behind her, she could tell he was stiff and uncomfortable.

She felt like crying once more, but told herself to cease her foolishness.

It was a wife who had been cruel to her husband, and as such it was her duty *as* a wife to behave as a woman—not a simpering girl who would cry so her husband would forgive her.

The weather was nippy, and Christine thought it was an excellent thing so as to explain Erik's many layers, and she was grateful for the remaining clothes that still were housed in the wardrobe below. Her warm cloak was still nestled amongst the other items, and she was quite comfortable as Erik manoeuvred the horse at relatively high speeds through the streets of Paris.

The only negative to the speed of the horse, as well as the general position of being held face forward away from him, was the impossibility of conversation. He could have quite easily whispered in her ear, but she would have had to lean quite awkwardly around to be heard properly.

And she had always found that eye contact was important with Erik for true communication to take place.

So she waited, but every few minutes would wriggle further against him and after a few agonising times of him pushing her resolutely forward, he relented and allowed her to lean fully against his chest.

They had not been riding overly long before he stopped in a quite decent part of the city that was not overly expensive, nor run down. He kept his head lowered as he helped her from the mare, and continued to do so while he rang the bell for what she supposed was the doctor.

There was no immediate answer, and Christine took the opportunity to turn Erik to face her so she may recite the words she had been practicing for nearly the entirety of their ride.

"Erik, I truly am sorry. You expressed a fear and I did nothing to comfort—I only hurt you further. But I promise to do better! And if this doctor is at all unkind, we shall take our daughter home and look it up in one of your books." Her voice was teasing at the end but did not lack sincerity.

She had stepped quite close to him and implored, "Please forgive me, Erik. Allow me to support *you* as you do me."

He had been resolutely staring at the still closed door before them, but *finally* turned to her.

And held her hand.

She would have liked vocal encouragement that he had in fact forgiven her for her harshness, and perhaps he would have obliged had the door not chosen that moment to be opened.

Christine was surprised how young he was. The men Erik had intentionally exposed her to were at least middle aged, but the physician—if he in fact *was* the doctor—was in his late twenties if not a little younger.

The man blinked at the couple at his door, and if the crumbs clinging to his morning coat were any indication, they had interrupted his breakfast. "May I help you?"

He was eyeing Erik's mask speculatively, but did not comment for which they were both grateful. Perhaps this would not end so terribly after all.

Erik was remaining silent, and it was becoming quite apparent that while he would not abandon her, she was to be the one to have most contact with the man.

Catherine had been hidden in her cloak, properly lulled into oblivion by the canter of the horse. The doctor looked surprised by the unveiling, and his attention became fixated upon the infant. "Her lungs have been having difficulties, can you help?"

At the arrival of his patient, the man's gaze became entirely assessing as he looked at her. Finally he nodded and motioned for them to enter. "At the very least I can attempt to do so."

The apartment was rather small, and as she suspected there were the remains of a breakfast strewn across a table set only for one. He took them into a room in the back that was quite obviously for treatment and consultation—if the medical supplies neatly placed along the tables were any indication.

"My name is Dr. Phillips, and you are?" He was smiling at her pleasantly, but she could tell he held more interest in Catherine than in her or Erik.

As it should be.

"I am Christine and this is my husband Erik." If he found the informality strange he made no mention of it, and simply acknowledged them both before asking to be allowed to hold Catherine.

The last time she had willingly passed her child to a stranger, the unthinkable had happened, but she took comfort in Erik's hand that was still clasped in her own, and she allowed the physician to carefully take her into his arms.

"And who is this little lady?" She could tell the joviality was more for her benefit than actual doting, as his eyes were calculating as he looked at the baby. Scientific. Capable.

"Catherine."

"Well, Catherine, shall we listen to your lungs so you cease to worry your poor parents?"

The infant in question had woken while being passed to the doctor, and she was eying him warily. If a child her age was capable of doing so of course, though Christine took her frown to indicate such.

"How old is she?" He had pulled a stethoscope from a drawer and was gently undoing the small buttons of Catherine's smock so as to access her chest.

"She is six weeks of age." Christine was surprised that Erik should be the one to answer, and she gripped his hand a little tighter in encouragement. Perhaps he saw what she did in this man.

He could help them.

"Premature then." It was a statement and not a question. He was quiet then as he blew on the metal end of the instrument before placing in against Catherine's skin. Warming it, she realised, as Catherine would have wailed had it proved too cold.

He listened for a long moment and Christine and Erik could only remain holding each other as they awaited a diagnosis. They did not have to wait for long.

"Her lungs were not fully developed so they are vulnerable to irritation and distress." He spoke with such confidence and coolness that Christine fully believed him. And her heart broke.

Dr. Phillips must have seen the devastation on her face as he pressed on. "She shall grow out if in time, Madame, you must merely be cautious. Keep the house clear of dust and pollutants, and while all babies cry, do try to keep her pacified." He tapped the baby's nose lightly. "Without spoiling the child of course."

She could do that. Catherine rarely cried and when she did it was generally for a purpose. She could keep her house clean and tidy if it meant ensuring her daughter's episodes would not continue.

There was *hope*.

She only prayed Erik saw it as well.

And more importantly, she hoped he would understand that any defect Catherine may have was not a reflection of his influence—it was simply a challenge for her to overcome.

The rest of the visit was without any great happening. Catherine proved otherwise healthy, but eventually became tired of the doctor's prodding and manipulation of her limbs and began to fuss—and Erik was only too happy to steal her away and remind Christine they had another important appointment that day.

He paid the doctor with what she assumed was the remains of his secretly stashed coins, and the physician assured them they could return at any time for subsequent checkups.

Christine hoped they would not be necessary.

A weight seemed to be lifted from Erik as he held her tightly in the saddle without any extra wiggling from her to be close to him.

But it was not until he leaned against her and whispered in her ear that she fully relaxed.

"I forgive you, wife."

However, that did not mean she had forgiven herself.

XXXIX

The rest of the ride to the chapel was spent with Erik frequently placing tickling kisses to the back of her neck, and then looking entirely innocent when she would turn around to teasingly scold him.

She still felt as though she should do something to fully make up for her behaviour, and she resolved to do so when they had returned home—either by baking a special treat or perhaps something special in the bedroom...

Her blush was apparently quite evident to her husband, and it did not help when he whispered huskily in her ear. "And what are you thinking of, Christine?"

She should say nothing. It was improper to speak so, especially in public, and most certainly in front of Catherine—though Christine was positive she would never remember the first few years of her life.

But she was his wife, and perhaps it was acceptable as such.

So telling her blush to quiet, she leaned fully against his chest and he obliged by lowering his own ear so she could respond comfortably. "I was thinking of how much I have missed our bed at home, and how I would very much like to show you how I have missed *you.*"

His grip on her waist tightened, and she could quite assuredly feel the stirrings of his approval at the notion. "You minx, how you tease your poor husband as I am about to take us to see a *priest* of all beings."

"Then you should not have asked," she responded primly. Surely he must have known it was some such thing if it had been the cause of her embarrassment.

The naughty man.

Erik had slowed the mare to a walk, and Christine began to recognise they would soon be coming to the chapel, and she felt a distinct thrill of familiarity and sense of *home*—though they were still a short way from their little cottage.

They were once again coming to the chapel on a day without service, and Christine did wonder if they should ever be blessed by hearing Father Martin actually give a service. Perhaps someday Erik could be persuaded, though she was quite certain he would employ all sorts of methods of keeping her abed in the mornings if it suited him.

The chill morning air was giving way to the steady stream of sunlight, and it made for a very pleasant day indeed, almost to the point where Christine wished to abandon her cloak in favour of simply allowing the sun to warm her.

And thankfully they had finally stopped so she was able. Father Martin was sitting on the front steps, basking in the glow of sunlight, and his sightless eyes flickered in their direction as Erik helped Christine from the horse.

"Good morning, Father." The priest took a moment to process Erik's voice, and seemed to come to the proper conclusion as a large smile overtook his features.

"Erik and Christine! Did you bring the tiny newcomer with you?" He was struggling to rise from the stone steps, and at Christine's look, Erik rolled his eyes and went to assist the man.

Though it greatly went against his sensibilities to do so, this was a good man and he deserved Erik's courtesy.

Father Martin leaned heavily on his arm, and Erik wondered at his ability to have sat upon the steps in the first place if he proved so incapable of raising himself up. Perhaps he simply trusted one of his parishioners would aid him eventually.

He almost shuddered to think he was now about to be held under such a category.

Erik did not know how to do this. He had spoken to priests before, but always with the detached air of one who could not possibly be helped, but now—now he had specifically come to seek this man's aid and counsel.

They stood awkwardly on the front stoop until the priest finally released Erik's arm. "How may I help you both? A bit too soon for another christening, would you not agree?"

Erik did not want to do this. It was too personal, and this man was *not* his lovely Christine who would understand the qualifying measures of his actions.

And whether he wanted to admit it or not, this man would very much share God's opinion. It troubled him greatly that when he finally felt as though God was blessing him, he might have destroyed all possible hope of such continuances.

"My husband would like a word with you in private if that is alright." Christine had divested herself of her travelling cloak, and she looked truly radiant in the sunlight with his daughter who was once more awake and blinking at her surroundings.

"But of course! Come with me, young man, and let us have a talk." Erik nearly snorted at the elderly man's assessment of his age. He most certainly was *not* young and had not been for quite some time.

Suddenly he wondered how old Christine thought him to be.

Perhaps it was best she did not know.

Christine followed them into the sanctuary, but settled into one of the pews and held Catherine so she could look around to the stained glass windows and altar. She nodded to Erik to follow the priest, and though it went against his utmost desires to remain with her always, this was a chapel, and the threat to his family's safety had been dispatched.

But was not that the material problem?

He half expected to be taken to a dark line of confessionals, so he was surprised when instead the priest hobbled into a comfortable study and eased into a worn leather chair, gesturing for Erik to do the same. "Blindness seems to have afforded confessors all the privacy they require, and it is much more comfortable in here, would you not agree?"

Erik certainly did agree, and he allowed himself to relax slightly into the cushions. "I have never been to confession."

Father Martin laughed pleasantly. "And at the end of this, you still shall not. You asked for a word, not how I may absolve you from sin." His face grew serious. "*That* is between you and your maker."

Then what was the purpose of a priest to begin with?

He was about to ask that very question, and quite happily return home, when the priest continued. "But sometimes when we admit aloud our faults and sins it helps us to better understand what we have done wrong, and what God expects from us. So what have you done that you should finally seek counsel?"

Erik did not know where to begin. For the very first time since...

He did not know when. He had never felt the compulsion to confide. But Christine had only that morning said how very much she hated his lack of communication, and while surely she meant that he was to speak to *her* about his thoughts, there was still the niggling doubt that she would not understand.

But this wizened old man was not such a person. It was his duty to hear the needs of his congregation, and though they had never sat in his service, he had married them and baptised their child, and surely that would indicate he had some responsibility in the salvation of those in his church.

So he told him.

Erik would have thought it would take much longer to express the horrors of one's life in its entirety, but in truth it took no longer than three quarters of an hour. He did not feel so very bad as Catherine would have wished to be nursed once more in any case, and the pews were as safe a place as any for Christine to do so.

And much to his surprise, finally *stating* the abuses he had suffered was rather cathartic. He did not speak of his childhood, nor of his tales in the East, but only made it clear that he had killed readily and had not felt great remorse, though it had not been for entirely personal reasons so many had died.

He spoke mostly of Christine.

Given Father Martin's expression, you would think he had heard such harrowing tales on a daily basis, for he listened calmly and allowed Erik to speak on that which came to mind, only asking for slight clarifications when needed.

Erik had paused before actually speaking of the final incident with the Persian, and he was rather surprised to hear the tightened quality in the priest's voice when he finally spoke again. He almost sounded like Christine when she was about to cry.

But such was a ridiculous notion.

"So what made you seek me out this day?"

It was rather odd how different it felt telling this man of the Persian's demise than it had when he spoke to Christine about it. He had been so very afraid of her reaction—that she would not forgive him, or possibly even *leave* him for the incident, but he felt only a sense of relief to finally have confessed his acts.

And though Father Martin had told him this was not a confession, it certainly felt like one.

"Is your wife alright?" That had not been the question he had expected after stating the remainder of the tale. There was no condemnation, only genuine concern for the wellbeing of Christine.

"She was angry with me this morning, and I fear she is angry I allowed her to be taken in the first place—though she seems to be under the impression it was simply something I said."

"And Catherine shall be well?"

It seemed odd that a priest was asking over a mortal diagnosis, but Erik confirmed that according to the physician she would be alright with time.

Father Martin seemed quite relieved to hear it, and for a moment he was silent before clearing his throat once more. "I do not condone murder, nor does the Lord."

Erik felt his stomach drop.

"However, it is through our own conscience that we must seek forgiveness, and I cannot tell you how God sees these matters. He looks to the heart."

Until ten months ago, Erik did not believe he *had* a heart.

The priest began to whisper conspiratorially. "But between the two of us, I cannot say that I blame you for your actions. The lovely wife waiting so patiently out there has done you good, and I am happy to note has restored some of your faith in the good Lord, and you have been blessed for it. Now it is between the two of you how you shall atone for your past."

And that was it. There was no horror in the man's voice, only a deep routed compassion for the man seated across from him, and Erik felt almost...

Light.

Free from the burden of past wrongs, and fully able to embrace the future, Erik thanked the priest before hurrying back to his waiting wife and daughter.

Lilting laughter greeted him as Christine twirled Catherine around the sanctuary—acting nothing like a proper wife should in a house of God.

How he loved her.

She stopped when she caught sight of him, and hurried to him trying to calm her smile if faced with any anger on his part. "Are you alright?"

Hating that the radiant glow had faded from her lovely face, he tapped her lips lightly with this finger. "You should smile more, Christine, it suits you."

She blushed, and he was grateful to note a small smile once more graced her lips. "I was showing Catherine what the ballerinas do."

Erik eyed her incredulously. "I can assure you, none of the little ballet girls looked quite like your show."

She glared at him, but he could tell she was not truly angry.

Taking his daughter from her arms, he greeted her with an offering of his little finger, but instead of sucking on it pleasantly as was her usual mode of entertainment, she gripped it in her tiny palm, and *smiled*.

He felt his heart might burst.

Christine gasped softly as she witnessed the exchange, and he could see tears in her eyes which were in contrast to her beaming smile.

His beautiful girls.

Father Martin had said the state of his conscience was a direct indicator of his standing with God, and he felt that in his daughter's smile was further evidence that he was *forgiven*.

He was ready to return home.

The priest slowly reentered the room, to bid them goodbye, and Christine thanked him profusely for taking the time to meet with them, but it was quite obvious she was ready to finally be home as well.

"Anytime, my dear." His voice turned rather reproachful as he gave his parting sentiment to her. "But Christine, might I suggest you talk to your husband." He patted her arm—though there was some slight fumbling as he blindly reached for it—and bade them both have a pleasant day before retreating back to his study.

His wife was now looking at him with concern, but he could not bring himself to care. Not when Catherine had pulled his finger into her once smiling mouth and was sucking at it greedily.

"Come along, Christine, it is time we were home."

Thankfully she did not argue.

He was very reluctant to get back on the horse and thereby be forced to relinquish his hold on Cat, but he was anxious to be home and walking would certainly lengthen the prospective journey. So unenthusiastically he gave her to Christine and they rode steadily homeward.

Until the very wife he wanted nothing more than to embrace in his study was pulling at his arm. "Stop!"

With slight annoyance he did so.

It became clear what had initiated her demand, as in front of Marie's house sat a very sulky looking Armand holding none other than *félin* Christine.

It was quite obvious Erik had one more vow to make to an animal as to their treatment.

Christine insisted on being helped down, and with a sigh he obliged her, but not before sending a longing look down the lane.

They were so very close.

But suddenly the small boy was rushing toward them—much to *félin* Christine's dismay—and any hope of disappointing the child by their early departure was soon forgotten.

"Mme. Christine! Monsieur! You're wearing a mask today! Look at my kitty!" He held up his prize and Erik quickly walked over and rescued the poor cat from further endangerment.

He refused to think on the boy noticing his mask.

"And where did you find her, Armand?"

The boy shrugged and kicked aimlessly at the grass. "She showed up this morning, and Mamma said I could keep her if I let her and Papa stay alone in their room for a bit." The boy sighed pathetically. "But they've been in there for *ages,* and make such funny noises, and the kitty doesn't like to play fetch."

Christine walked over to give the boy a hug while Erik busied himself with assessing his cat for injury.

Thankfully he found none.

"Your father is home?"

Armand was on tip toe peeking at Catherine who eyed him sleepily. "Yes, he got home this morning. Mamma cried, but I did not for I am grown up." He nodded sagely at his pronouncement.

While Erik knew he would be just as enthusiastic at rejoining with his wife after such a long—and in his mind, unreasonable absence—it did not settle well with him that the boy should be left alone for such occasions.

Surely they should have waited until he was safely tucked in bed.

"I am afraid you have been caring for *our* cat while we were out of town." Erik had never been one to speak to Armand, and he was surprised how easily he found to do so. There was something horrifyingly similar in how lonely the boy seemed, and he wondered if he had been given the opportunity for schooling.

While Erik had excelled under self tutelage, surely others would require more advanced techniques in fostering intelligence.

He would have to ask Christine.

Erik did however feel quite sorry when Armand's face crumpled at the notion of no longer being allowed a pet. "What's her name then? I call her *Bleu.*"

Christine laughed merrily while Erik nearly choked. *Bleu?* True, her eyes were a lovely blue, but by no means was that reasoning for a name.

He was nearly as offended as he was sure *félin* Christine would be could she understand what she had been called all morning.

"You may come visit *félin* Christine whenever you wish, and perhaps I shall even have some biscuits for you. But I warn you, I highly doubt they will be as good as your mamma's."

Armand cheerfully nodded, and assured Christine that he would be perfectly happy with *any* biscuits she saw fit to give him.

Erik ignored that he felt entirely the same.

The promise of confections and the possibility of visiting someone else's home was enough to cheer the boy into some sort of fit.

Perhaps that was the wrong description, but the way he flitted around the garden, holding up objects for Christine to show the proper amount of enthusiasm for certainly seemed beyond what a normal child would find interesting.

And he wondered if Catherine would ever begin to do such things, if *he* could show as much interest as Christine did to the little boy.

With the glances Christine kept giving him, he believed she must have thought him capable.

They could not simply leave the boy alone—though Erik was sorely tempted to do so. He had been left to himself more times than he could remember, but he supposed that was not a proper example of a child's self sufficiency.

It did trouble him greatly that Armand seemed to only be quiet when he had his fingers somehow touching his daughter. There was a sort of rapt fascination whenever he did so, and Erik felt the stirrings of fatherly unease when Christine leaned down enough for the boy to place a *kiss* upon his daughter's slightly flailing hand.

His feeling was certainly not helped when Catherine smiled for the second time that day.

He would have to have a talk with this boy. *And* his daughter.

After nearly a half an hour, a very dishevelled Marie appeared, staring wide eyed at the visitors in her garden. "Oh I am so sorry! Has he kept you long?" She went to scold the boy but Christine was quick to inform her he had simply been helping her find ideas for their own lawn, and had indeed been truly helpful.

Marie looked rather sheepish and told Armand to come back into the house. Quite unenthusiastically he did so. "Did he tell you his father is home?"

Though it made him rather green to consider it, the woman must have been quite distracted by her morning interlude with her husband for she did not even take a second glance at the mask which covered her friend's husband. So much the better.

Christine was already slipping back to Erik's side and promised to return in a few days for a visit and to meet the elusive husband, and Marie was quick to agree, waving pleasantly as she followed her son back into the house.

"How could she leave him all alone?" The courteous smile that had graced Christine's face had slipped into a decisive frown, and though he never wished for her to be unhappy, he was grateful she felt as he did in regard to the importance of supervising children.

He did not answer, but took her hand and led her back to the mare who found much more interest in nibbling on tall grasses than paying attention to the conversation of her master.

Félin Christine had not fared much better.

With the addition of the cat, riding home was quite impossible, and Christine asked to walk when he offered to lead her home on horseback.

Would they ever reach home?

He prayed there were no more setbacks.

They should have been going to the market, as they still were out of the items Christine deemed so important that she left the day before, but he would beg her indulgence if she would only spend the rest of the day sequestered in the house with him.

He knew they needed to talk about what had instigated their argument to begin with. Erik was not certain he could ever look at the instrument without feeling the same pangs of worry and despair at his wife's disappearance, but he was so utterly selfish as to want to *try*.

And he needed to know if Christine's outburst that morning was fuelled by dissatisfaction in his ability to protect her.

He certainly could offer no argument on that point.

Christine's pace hastened as she saw the tall gates surrounding their property, and she nearly mimicked Armand's excitement as he slowly undid the heavy doors and ushered the lot of them through, placing the squirming feline safely within the bounds of the fence.

Foolish animal most likely escaped just to give him one more thing to worry about.

As it was not quite midday, the groundskeeper was still tending to his daily chores, and Erik was quite pleased to be able to leave the horse's care in his aged, yet capable hands. He also asked that some food be prepared and brought, so that his hope of not leaving their little cottage before tomorrow could in fact be fulfilled.

The groundskeeper promised his wife would be more than happy to oblige.

Christine had not bothered to wait for him to finish depositing the reins before scampering to the front door and hastily pressing the slots and grooves so it would open.

Her smile was radiant as she passed through the doorway.

And a weight he did not even know had settled on his chest finally lifted seeing his family once more in his home.

XL

Christine had never been so happy to enter a room as she was when Erik's study greeted her. Though she had only been gone for a few days, so many doubts of ever being able to reach their little home at all made it that much sweeter when she curled up on the rug, allowing Catherine to join her.

Félin Christine had also found the room to be highly welcoming, but was more in favour of waiting for Erik upon the desk than deeming to join her mistress upon the floor.

They did not wait long before Erik appeared, eyeing the display with incredulity. "Is there something lacking in the furniture?"

Christine had divested her feet of shoes and wiggled her toes comfortably. "Not at all, I just blame you for your impeccable taste in floor coverings."

Her tone had been entirely teasing, but Erik's expression grew solemn, and he sat down in his chair with a sigh, removing his mask as he did so.

She wondered if she would ever be used to witnessing the ease in which he stripped the object, but it made her smile nonetheless with the trust he had placed in her. "I think you blame your poor husband for much more than his taste in carpets."

Christine did not know that she wished to discuss this so soon. Could they never be allowed to simply be happy? They had indulged in the six exhausting but blessed weeks of normalcy that had been so cruelly pulled away, and it seemed unbearable to have to continue to dwell on the unpleasantness.

But she supposed they must.

There had been no answer given, so he continued with his supposition. "I think that is why you were so angry with me this morning. You *know* I do not think of you as some common trollop, yet you accused me of doing so. You blame me for allowing you to be," his face contorted in pain. "Taken."

She wanted to deny it. She wanted to assure him that by no means was it his fault, and in some ways she supposed it was not. But the niggling thought that if he had only come with her—had never allowed himself to be swept up in the inconsequential amusement of music—the Persian would never have had opportunity for her abduction to begin with.

And perhaps she had lashed out in some misplaced feeling of hurt and anger.

Catherine seeming to be quite content to maintain her position on the floor, idly waving her arms as the ceiling patiently watched, Christine rose in favour of sitting beside Erik—a tight fit to be sure, but perhaps their closeness would ease the pain of their conversation.

"I already apologised, do you not forgive me?"

Erik glared at her in response. "This is not about forgiveness! I am asking if you *blame* me for what happened. God knows I blame myself!" His tone was more firm than loud, and she was grateful he was not yelling at her.

She did not wish to fight with him!

Christine found it exceedingly difficult to fully look at him when she had to admit to both herself and to him that she did hold some modicum of resentment toward him. But with much stuttering and pause, she did so. "I know you did not... mean to allow it to happen." She remembered how angry she had been at his refusal to provide the essentials, and for a moment the same feeling flared once more. "But you should have been there! Why is your piano so much more important than you *wife?*"

Instead of looking hurt, or even surprised at her words, Erik looked quite patient as he took her face in his hands and made sure she was looking at him fully before he began to speak. "*Nothing* is more important to me than you, Christine. My love for you is equalled by no other, and it was selfish of me not to have gone out with you when you requested. But loveliest Christine," his thumb was tracing over her lips gently. "Do you not miss our music as much as I?"

Did she? In truth she highly doubted her love of music was in any way comparable to his, and she had so many other diversions that held her interest.

But she did. There was a closeness she felt when her voice comingled with his, and she relished the joy she brought him when his music that was specifically written for her matched his genius when she finally accomplished his goal.

"I do miss it, Erik. But there are just so many other things..." He looked hurt. More hurt than even when she had refused his gentlest affection. Now it was her turn to grasp his hands that pulled away from her face, desperate that he understand her fully before allowing his interpretation to take hold. "But I am happy with just you and Catherine! And I thought you were as well."

Erik sighed and squeezed her hand slightly. "How could I not be happy with my little wife and daughter?" His eyes strayed to the still wriggling Catherine. "You sing for *her*."

Christine blinked, trying to remember such occasions when she truly sang for Catherine. True, there had been mindless humming of all ballads remembered from childhood, but never had she given her soul as she did for Erik.

But apparently those simply melodies had been enough for him to feel left out.

Her silly husband.

For how far they had come in growing closer as husband and wife, they still struggled through the most basic of communications. They both tried to put the other first, but inevitably they denied the most fundamental of their own needs in the attempt, and unfortunately it led to the same measures of hurt they faced at this moment.

"My singing means so much to you? I had thought it was only a substitution for more physical acts of love." She surprised herself by not blushing at her implication.

Erik was not so fortunate, even as his eyes smouldered at the suggestion. "Never a substitute. An addition."

She kissed him then, not so much as to inspire his passions as they really did have to discuss the meaning of their respective pains, but enough to show that she was no longer truly angry and was willing to work through their difficulties.

The way he responded made her wish such discussions were not necessary.

But eventually his hands stopped their upward ascent to her full breasts, and he allowed her to regain the use of her mind as she groped into her thoughts for what they were meant to be solidifying.

"So you shall finish your piano, and we shall resume our lessons. Is that what you would like?"

The way his eyes glowed told her more of his excitement at the prospect than his placid, "If you are agreeable."

She would be if it meant pleasing him.

His hands returned to her cheeks, and the feel of his thumb tracing over her lips made her tremble. "And you shall forgive your poor, selfish husband for not accompanying you?"

Christine knew she would, and she resolutely pushed down the memories that were still entirely too fresh for comfort which threatened to make her respond with petulance.

So with that in mind, she nodded her head and he looked at her sadly in response. "I know you shall as you are a good wife, Christine, but I think you would still like for me to prove I can care for you as I should. I cannot fault your insinuation."

She felt rather wretched but turned to nestle herself in his arms. "You are too good to me, Erik."

He chuckled mirthlessly. "I highly doubt that, wife."

Her lips found the smooth skin beneath his ear, and she kissed it tenderly. "You came for me."

Erik's arms tightened around her, and he pressed a kiss to her temple. "I will *always* come for you, Christine. I just pray there will never again be a need."

She prayed the same.

Catherine found that moment to protest her ceiling friend as her only source of company, and quite reluctantly Christine left Erik's lap to tend to her—and *félin* Christine just as quickly found Erik's lap to be quite pleasing.

Christine scowled almost in seriousness and settled on the sofa across from him. "This, little *enfant*, is why he should not have given her my name. She thinks she has the same rights as me!"

Her feline counterpart meowed loudly in response, and Erik merely chuckled as he scratched behind her ear. "I must admit, she does tend to purr when I pet her just as you do."

Christine covered Catherine's ears in mock horror. "Watch your implication, sir! There are tiny ears in the room."

Erik merely sniffed in response.

Now that his tantalising lips and hands were fully removed from her person, she allowed her thoughts to drift back to her short meeting with the priest before Erik had whisked her toward home. "What did Father Martin wish for us to speak of?"

Her husband distracted himself with removing delicate white hairs form his suit when the cat decided she had enough doting for the moment and returned to Erik's desk. "I would imagine he was concerned for your wellbeing and hoped by my instigating conversation you should be comforted."

She was she supposed. There was something soothing about conversation with Erik, whether through their more playful bantering or by more honest discussion as to thoughts and experiences.

She was not however prepared for his next enquiry. "Do you ever wonder about your husband's upbringing? I am after all integral in the raising of our child."

Why did he wish to talk about this now? Had he revealed his past to Father Martin? She tried not to be hurt that he should confide in someone beside herself such intimate details that had not even been shared with her.

Playing idly with Catherine's fingers, Christine acknowledged her wonderings. "I have, but I did not think it was something you would wish to talk about, and you certainly have never given me reason to doubt your ability to care for our daughter." And really, did she truly wish to know?

It was one thing to have suspicions as to what Erik suffered—she felt the evidence scratch against her skin when they were entwined—but it was entirely different for him to actually express his abuses.

Her poor, poor husband.

She supposed when someone withstood the anguish of a childhood such as his, she should be concerned he might continue the cycle of wickedness, passing in onto any of their own sweet children they were blessed with.

But she was not.

It was true he had become violent with her when angered in the beginning, but not now—*never* now. They had argued numerous times, and never had she feared he would strike her.

So really, it did not matter if he revealed his past to her. Unless it was of importance to him—an unburdening of sorrows pressed upon his soul—she would simply continue loving him as the man he had become.

"Did you speak of it to Father Martin? Is that why you ask?"

Though his suit was divested of hairs, he was still resolutely looking for more. Finally she patted the seat beside her. "Come sit by us, Erik, you are too far away."

He seemed almost relieved by her entreaty, and she felt yet another pang of remorse for how she had treated him earlier, and she desperately hoped his reticence did not last too terribly long.

A plan was beginning to form how she might encourage him to drop his sense of boundaries.

Erik was gliding cool fingers through Catherine's downy hair, and she gurgled in response, much to her father's delight. "I do not wish for you to feel I do not confide in you—that I keep secrets. You expressed earlier your displeasure at such a notion."

She took the hand not occupied with Catherine's amusement, and gently held it. "It is true, I wish for you to be honest with me, but I do not want to cause you pain. Anything you choose to share with me of your past must only be for your own comfort, not because you feel a need to assuage my desire to be close to you."

He nodded at that, and was seemingly content to simply appreciate the reunion of their little family through silence, and Christine would have happily obliged had there not been a rap upon the door. "Do not fret, my wife. That must be the groundskeeper with lunch."

And though she felt a tinge of nervousness that it might in fact prove *not* to be the elderly man, she happily noted Erik's call to her that a lovely serving of soup and crusty bread was now available.

Perhaps having someone help around the place was not so terrible after all.

But before the man left, he turned back to Erik informing him that a man was waiting outside their gate, and had tried to bribe the gardener into allowing him entrance.

Erik gave him a tight lipped thank you that more resembled a growl than actual speech, and swept out the door, only stopping to bid Christine prepare their meal.

"This shall not take long."

Christine wanted to stamp her foot in annoyance. Could they never be left alone?

Though she feared what unknown man might be awaiting her husband, she did as she was asked and filled two bowls with soup and cut two large slices of bread for dipping.

And perhaps one more piece for her to nervously nibble as she awaited his return.

It occurred to her that it might be Raoul once more making himself a nuisance as yet another man refused to listen to her very precise words as to her desires and wellbeing.

If it was, she knew Erik would not hesitate to kill him.

There had been a reprieve for him as he had not truly been the mastermind of their little coup, but if he continued to interfere she did not doubt Erik would take swift action in ceasing any further meddling to their little family unit.

He returned rather quickly, and she had not been waiting long in the dining room before he took the seat prepared beside her and placed a small white envelope on the table. "A *Pierre* left this for you. It would appear the boy had not quite finished speaking."

Her eyes drifted to his hands, wondering if perhaps she could tell if he had just committed murder, but they looked perfectly ordinary—if anything about Erik's appearance could be described as such of course.

Erik sighed and rolled his eyes. "I can assure you, the man is currently riding back from whence he came."

Christine did not choose to acknowledge her thoughts by responding with her gratitude.

Instead, with slightly trembling fingers, she gripped the note, looking to him questioningly as to whether or not she should be the one to open it.

Erik simply began eating his soup.

"Should I not?" If it would trouble him—somehow cause him to doubt her sincerity that this was where she belonged, she would gladly throw it into the fire. But the part of her that longed for her childhood friend to have found peace with their situation begged her to open it and see if such could be the case.

Her husband shrugged and swallowed his bite of warm soup before eyeing the letter warily. "If you do not you shall always wonder as to its contents. I would prefer your mind not be so preoccupied with something of the fop's."

A fair argument.

However, it was upon opening the missive she discovered it might be entirely impossible for her to read the letter herself at all. While she had become quite fluent in the ways of reading books and type, it was only the rarest of occurrences when she was faced with something by hand—and it was quite apparent the dignified lettering of one of a high social standing had been greatly diminished due to drink.

The words were sloppy, and the cursive difficult to manage even under the best of circumstances. Though Erik tried to appear nonchalant about the message, his eyes flickered to her every few seconds as she struggled to interpret the words.

Finally he grew exasperated and abandoned the pretence of eating. "Well? What does he want?"

She did not want to disappoint him—to admit that while his excellent tutoring had so greatly improved her literacy there was still something she could not possibly understand on her own.

But she must.

"I do not think I can make it out." Before he could think she meant she could not make out the *meaning* of his declarations—and by the stormy expression he was indeed coming to such a conclusion—she hastened to clarify. "I have not read cursive before."

His expression softened. "Then perhaps I shall just have to begin writing you letters so you may practice." She doubted reading Erik's own scrawl would be much easier, but she would have far more incentive to toil over interpretation if it was from *him.*

She smiled at the thought.

"Would you like for me to read it to you?"

Christine nodded and handed over the parchment, wondering if in fact Erik could calmly read a letter from *the boy* as he put it. She did not think she would be overly upset if he could not—it was not wholly appropriate for a married woman to receive correspondence from a previous beau in any case.

"*Dear Madame,*" She was rather surprised at the formality, but perhaps it was his way of offering her the respect of her status instead of calling upon childhood familiarity—perhaps there was hope he was letting her go.

"*I hope this letter finds your daughter well as she seemed to be quite distressed when last we met.*" Erik grumbled something under his breath, and Christine was quite sure it was an unsavoury curse upon the Persian.

"While I am not certain you are in fact without danger in your current marriage, I do believe you to be happy in your circumstance, and that is not something I can look beyond. I am convinced you would have been satisfied as my wife, and I dearly long for such potential once more, but I cannot deny that conditions have made for such a venture to be impossible.

Do not think ill of me, Christine. I am but a lonely man who desperately wished for his lost love, but I also do not want you to live in fear of my continued interference. If ever you have need of me I shall always be at your disposal, but I shall not try to bring you further pain by separating you and your daughter from a man you seem to cherish.

Remember me with fondness, Little Lotte, and enjoy the life that has been provided you.

Yours respectfully, Raoul."

For a long while Erik and Christine were silent, and both returned to their meal with sombre attitudes. Christine did not know what to think. It was far easier to cast Raoul as the villain so that her heart might be saved from feelings of remorse over his loneliness.

Remorse, but not responsibility.

Erik was similarly lost in his thoughts, and though neither wished to discuss the matter, they still communed in the study after lunch so Erik might read to her and Catherine as they enjoyed on so many occasions.

Christine could not remember what literature he had selected.

Erik finally requested they move to the music room so he might fiddle with the piano, and Christine obliged without too much protest. She had agreed to further lessons, though she had no intention of singing on this day.

She felt grieved.

Erik worked until after supper—a simple meal that more resembled lunch than a proper wife would have allowed, but Christine did not have many options as they had yet to go to market.

But it was while preparing their evening meal she finally realised exactly what had upset her.

She missed him.

It was not such a longing that would induce her into betraying her husband's unspoken request for her to sever all ties with him, but she had loved him—still loved him in her own little way—and theirs was a friendship she had cherished.

And for the first time, she did not feel guilty for feeling so. It was not a betrayal of Erik as she had previously thought, but a simple emotion that did more damage when ignored than accepted.

But just as he was letting her go, she would also do the same.

So it was with new determination that when she prepared for bed, she pulled out one of the more transparent nightgowns she had not had the opportunity to wear when the fabric would have pulled mightily over her still rounded stomach. She did not feel self conscious, but instead felt a deep thrill as she prepared the intricate seduction of her husband.

A husband she had equally forgiven for not being there when she most needed him.

It was true, her middle was still more round than it had been, and her breasts were fuller even though Catherine had just completed her final meal of the evening—but she doubted Erik would complain on that point.

In fact, she doubted he would complain at all.

Her theory was proven correct when his eyes roamed over her in the dim light of the room. She had lit a few candles so the limpid quality of her shift was shown to its best advantage.

And for that matter, her body.

"I have been thinking that communication should be rewarded."

Erik still remained frozen in the doorway, but presently nodded jerkily. "Perhaps you are right."

Instead of going to him as she wished, she drifted to their bed—their wonderful bed she had missed the night before—and slid atop the bedclothes. "Will you not join me?"

She could plainly see the trembling quality of his fingers as he undressed. Perhaps when they were married for many years the anticipation would not be the same, that familiarity would begin to dampen the nervous feelings when they were about to be joined, but it was clear for both of them such was now not the case.

Christine had butterflies in her stomach as she watched him peel layer upon layer of clothing from his body, and she was not certain if it was from eagerness of what was to come or from the way his eyes never once flickered from her body.

He nearly threw his shoes across the room in his haste to be free of them.

In general he would leave his trousers till the last—allowing her to only see him fully undressed after their passions had taken them, but this time it was a fully nude husband that joined her on their marriage bed, and when his fingers began ghosting over the lines of her flesh she was entirely relieved they had as few impediments as possible.

She doubted she could ever be used to the feel of his hands on her inner thighs, or the tingling pressure that erupted when he touched her just *there*.

His lips were nibbling at the flesh exposed by the neckline of her nightgown, and she found the want of him to be more torment than she thought she could possibly bear.

Her fingers were tracing lines upon his back, and he was humming in response to her touches, but each of his own attentions were slow and deliberate as he teased her flesh into the aching, arching, *needing* entity he so desired. Each caress made her womb clench in anticipation of his filling her with his presence, and it was with a horse voice she made her plea.

"Please."

She could not contain the moan when he entered her.

Each stroke was deliberate, and every one made her wish he was not so very good at teasing her. But finally, *finally* when he began to feel the effects of pleasure hum through his own clammy flesh, he began to focus more on delivering them from the agony of denied bliss and with subsequent gasps and fevered clutches, they were spent.

She should have checked once more on Catherine. She should have made one final pass through the house to ensure doors and windows were locked and they were all safely secured inside the little yellow cottage Erik had provided.

But she did not.

For Erik was beside her, and never would she fear the outside world when her sly, deceptively strong husband was able to protect them.

It was some time later when he had taken her once more, and his hands were running through her untamed curls, and she was just about to drift into a fully sated oblivion when his words made her pause. "I feel pity for the boy."

Christine looked at him sharply, feeling quite sure she had misunderstood.

She had not.

"He is feeling how I did when you were obliging his courtship." He kissed her temple affectionately. "I would wish that on no man."

She felt pity for him as well, but lying in her husband's arms, knew she was where she belonged.

Theirs had not been a peaceful beginning, nor a happy one, but through prayer and determination—and patience from both parties—it was a marriage finally constructed through love and understanding.

They had their own perfect little daughter, a home aboveground where Erik could take them out on Sundays, and more happiness than she thought could possibly be afforded them.

Her husband had not been a kind man, and she highly doubted he had truly loved her in the beginning—not in the way one *should* love. Obsession had been his companion, and it was only through her own love he was able to curb such compulsions into the selfless love that provided so much for their little family.

Eventually they may be blessed with more children—more little Eriks and Christines running through their tiny cottage, possibly enough that renovations would have to be considered simply to hold them all.

But she firmly believed whatever God chose to give them, together they would bring forth beauty.

"I wish for Armand to come under my tutelage."

Christine smiled at his change in subject, and kissed the pale and withered chest she was using as a pillow, and murmured her quiet assent. "As you wish, husband."

So it was with a final kiss ghosted upon her lips, Christine fell into sleep with her husband.

Her Maestro.

Her Angel.

Her Erik.

Made in the USA
San Bernardino, CA
04 December 2013